THE YIELD

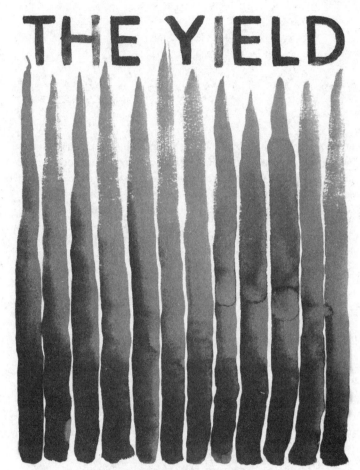

THE YIELD

a novel

TARA JUNE WINCH

HarperVia

An Imprint of HarperCollins*Publishers*

HarperCollins books may be purchased for educational, business, or sales promotional use. For information, please email the Special Markets Department at SPsales@harpercollins.com.

Originally published as *The Yield* in Australia in 2019 by Penguin Random House Australia.

FIRST EDITION

Designed by Terry McGrath
Map illustration by Tara June Winch

Library of Congress Cataloging-in-Publication Data

Names: Winch, Tara June, author.
Title: The yield / Tara June Winch.
Description: First Edition. | New York, NY : HarperVia, [2020]
Identifiers: LCCN 2020000143 (print) | LCCN 2020000144 (ebook) | ISBN 9780063003460 (hardcover) | ISBN 9780063003477 (trade paperback) | ISBN 9780063003484 (ebook)
Classification: LCC PR9619.4.W59 Y54 2020 (print) | LCC PR9619.4.W59 (ebook) | DDC 823/.92—dc23
LC record available at https://lccn.loc.gov/2020000143
LC ebook record available at https://lccn.loc.gov/2020000144

20 21 22 23 24   LSC   10 9 8 7 6 5 4 3 2 1

For my family

"In the absence of justice, what is sovereignty but organized robbery?"
Saint Augustine

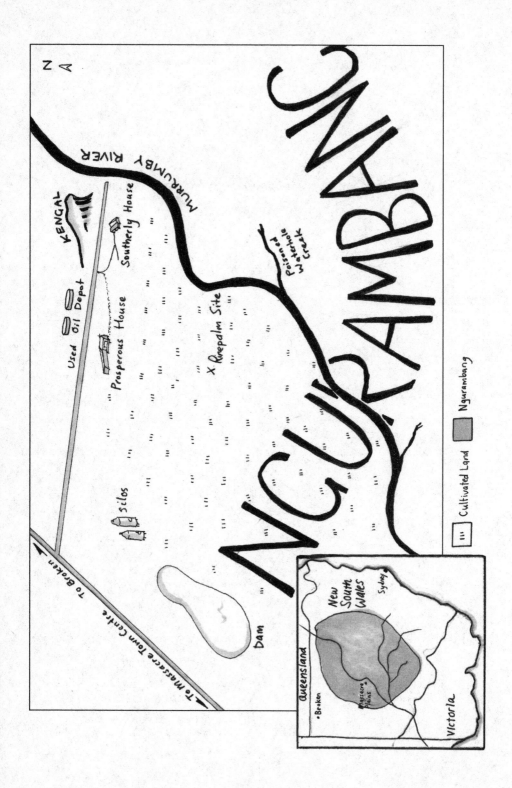

ONE

I was born on *Ngurambang*—can you hear it?—*Ngu–ram–bang*. If you say it right it hits the back of your mouth and you should taste blood in your words. Every person around should learn the word for *country* in the old language, the first language—because that is the way to all time, to time travel! You can go all the way back.

My daddy was Buddy Gondiwindi, and he died a young man by the hands of a bygone disease. My mother was Augustine, and she died an old woman by the grip of, well, it was an Old World disease too.

Yet nothing ever really dies, instead it all goes beneath your feet, beside you, part of you. Look there—grass on the side of the road, tree bending in the wind, fish in the river, fish on your plate, fish feeding you. Nothing is ever gone. Soon, when I change, I won't be dead. I always memorized John 11:26—*Whoever lives and believes in me shall never die*—yet life rushed through and past me as it will for each person.

Before I believed everything they taught me, I thought when all were dead that all were gone, and so as a young fella I tried to find my place in this short life. I only wanted to decide for myself how I'd live it, but that was a big ask in a country that had a plan for me, already mapped in my veins since before I was born.

The one thing I thought I could control was my own head. It seemed the most sensible thing to do was to learn to read well. So in a country where we weren't really allowed to be, I decided to *be*. To get water from the stones, you see?

After I met my beautiful wife—although beauty was the least of her, strong and fearless was the most of her—well, she taught me lots of things. Big thing, best thing she taught me was to learn to write the words too, taught me I wasn't just a second-rate man raised on white flour and Christianity. It was my wife, Elsie, who bought me the first dictionary. I think she knew she was planting a seed, germinating something inside me when she did that. What a companion the dictionary is—there are stories in that book that'll knock your boots off. To this day it remains my prized possession, and I wouldn't trade it for all the tea in China.

The dictionary from Elsie is why I'm writing it down—it was my introduction to the idea of recording, written just like the Reverend once wrote the births and baptisms at the Mission, like the station manager wrote rations at the Station, and just like the ma'ams and masters wrote our good behavior at the Boys' Home—a list of words any fool can look up and be told the meaning. A dictionary, even if this language isn't mine alone, even if it's something we grow into and then, living long enough, shrink away from. I am writing because the spirits are urging me to remember, and because the town needs to know that I remember, they need to know now more than ever before.

To begin—but there are too many beginnings for us Gondi-windi—that's what we were bestowed and cursed with by the same shifty magic—an eternal *Once upon a time*. The story goes that the church brought time to us, and the church, if you let it, will take it away. I'm writing about the other time, though, deep time. This is a big, big story. The big stuff goes forever, time ropes and loops and is never straight, that's the real story of time.

The problem now facing my own *Once upon a time* is that Doctor Shah from the High Street Surgery has recently given me a filthy bill of health—cancer of the pancreas—which is me done and dusted.

So, because they say it is urgent, because I've got the church time against me, I'm taking pen to paper to pass on everything that was ever remembered.

All the words I found on the wind.

TWO

By the river is where Albert Gondiwindi had wandered up to Prosperous as a little boy, wonder face, bare skinned, from the canvas shelter
of Tent Town to the tin of the Mission, along with his mother, and
his little sister inside her. Albert would remember how they walked,
or marched; there were police officers on horses to show them the way
past the red river, stained by tea tree and other things. Many years
later, on the day of his death, Albert wondered once again how it must
have been for the old people out by Murrumby when it flowed—a
time when the air was as clean as the time before the words *clean* and
dirty had ever been imagined. The river would've been clear twenty
feet down, and the earth hummed its own reverent tune, day in and
day out until one day. *How quickly things change*, he thought. In his
final hours, Albert sat looking the same way all the remaining Gondiwindi would soon gather and look. Ahead of him on the foldout table
was the almost-finished dictionary, beyond the table all the world. He
suddenly felt a great wind blow from the Murrumby and instinctively
slapped his hand atop the pile, protecting the words. In the distance
he could have sworn he saw a gang of brolgas flying, further afield a
swarm of locusts, the sky change color; all while the papers flapped
against his will. He closed his eyes, wondered if he was about to go

elsewhere, and then, as if encouraged by the wind, urged by the ancestors, took his hand away, and arced looking to the heavens to see the
pages swirl and blow and eventually disappear in the air.

She hung up the phone. Poppy Albert was dead. So far away from the
place where boys learned to kill rabbits and girls learned to live with
the grief. Far away where people were born guilty but couldn't admit it.
Where whole years vanished from her. Days spent working thankless
jobs or burrowed under a blanket, shunning whole seasons. The decade
had aged her like a coin, all the shine gone. In that place on the other
side of the world, she woke before the phone rang. Made coffee and a
tumbler of aspirin. It wasn't only in the mornings that she, August, was
trapped between two states—sleep and coming to, yet especially that
morning, on the cusp of being younger and older. She was about to exit
the infinite stretch of her twenties and had nothing to show.

   At the answering of the phone and the breaking of the news, she
felt something dark and three-dimensional fall out of her body, something as solid as a self. She'd become *less* suddenly. She knew she'd
felt that exact same way before, though she didn't feel tears coming
the way they burn the face and blur the eyes. Her face instead was
cold to the touch, her heart rate lowered, her eyes dry, and her arms,
chicken-skinned and thin as kindling, began to start a fire. She took
the newspaper from the mail tray, took the crate of wood and knelt
in the corner of the common kitchen. She spread the newspaper out,
smoothing the pages with the side of her fist and held the hatchet and
the cypress in each hand. Printed in the newspaper was a small photograph of a rhino. Above the picture it read in big ink block letters:
GONE FOREVER—BLACK RHINO EXTINCT. An animal *zip! Gone!*

She could taste what she imagined was rhino skin, a dry warm thickness, muscle and dirt. She hadn't told anyone about everything she couldn't bring herself to remember and not about the things she could taste and smell instead, things that one shouldn't be able to taste and smell.

Once, with a stack of textbooks on her lap—and knowledge of August's hunger—a friend of hers studying social work at night school, and having not known what it was to experience a terrible inheritance, asked her simply about her school life. August had gone along with the line of enquiry, told her how she only knew she was poor at lunchtime. Told her when she lived with her grandparents it was always good food, always leftovers from the night before. She'd been the only student to use the microwaves in the teachers' lounge. *Before that?* Before that she tried not to tell her that the lunches her mother packed were humiliating, instead she said they were just kooky. *Kooky?* August wound an invisible turbine at her ear. Her friend had nodded, had understood and closed her eyes in accordance with her training—a serene indication to go on. August had closed her eyes too and briefly let herself remember.

One day a jam sandwich, cut crusts, next day something the kids would make fun of—a tin of Christmas ginger bread in July, Easter buns in October. Sometimes a bread roll smeared with something incomplete, like ketchup. And a few times I remember opening the lunchbox and there just being imitation play food, a little plastic lamb chop, plastic-cast apple with no stem. It was my mother's sense of humor.

August hadn't seen the humor when she was a girl, but she had laughed about it then. They both laughed until something broke in August, and she *did* cry, the last time—but she pretended they were laughter tears. Afterward they went to the pub. August didn't tell her any more, not how she was baptized by the sun, and not that as far, far

7

away as she went from her country, from her home, she still couldn't remove the scent and taste of dirt and diesel and flesh and muddied water from that grey hemisphere of her mind. How the worst thing that could ever happen had already happened. Time's up.

The rhino in the news reminded August that she'd never been to the zoo, never seen a rhino in real life—it might as well have been a dinosaur. The paper listed other recent extinctions. And just like that she thought, *zip! Gone!* Poppy: Albert Gondiwindi was extinct. No more Albert Gondiwindi roamed the earth, and no more black rhino either. With an armful of sticks she fed the iron stove, close enough to redden her face in the eager first flames. Poppy Albert used to say that the land needed to burn more, a wild and contained fire, a contradiction of nature. He was talking about a different land though, not the one August had known for over a decade—in the grasslands forever wet, foreign forests of elm, ash, sycamore, hazel, and in the white willows that dipped into quiet canals. Where smaller birds in secondary colors flocked together and fires never licked. Where the sky fit into the reflection of a stone well, full with rainwater. Where low morning clouds played sleight of hand, and day never quite arrived before night.

She knew that she had once known the beloved land where the sun slapped the barren earth with an open palm and knew too that she would return for the funeral. Go back full with shame for having left, catch the disappointment in their turned mouths, go back and try to find all the things that she couldn't find so many thousands of kilometers away.

August found a replacement for her dishwashing shifts, packed the one bag she owned and, before boarding, switched off her phone forever. During the flight she watched the GPS on the headrest screen, the numbers rising and steadying, the plane skittering over the cartoon sea. At the other end, having reached a certain altitude, crossed the time lines, descended into new coordinates, she'd hoped it would be enough to erase the voyage. Erase the facts of the matter, erase the burial rites to be recited, erase all the erasures of them, and that fractured family they once were. Just as they'd been for a century: godless and government-housed and spread all over the place, and then August wondered if there was enough remembering to erase. During the flight she dreamed of Poppy Albert. He was featureless in the dream, but she knew it was him. They'd arrived in the middle of the conversation, she didn't know how they'd arrived there—in the field—he was telling her that there was a lot to remembering the past, to having stories, to knowing your history, your childhood, but there is something to forgetting it too. At the beginning of the dream, but as if at the end of a long conversation, he'd taken her hand and said that *There exists a sort of torture of memory if you let it come, if you invite the past to huddle beside you, comforting like a leech.* He was telling her more—that a footprint in history has a thousand repercussions, that there are a thousand battles being fought every day because people couldn't forget something that happened before they were born. *There are few worse things than memory, yet few things better*, he'd said. *Be careful.*

THREE

yarran tree, spearwood tree, or hickory acacia—*yarrany* The dictionary is not just words—there are little stories in those pages too. After years with the second great book, I figured out the best way to read it. First time, I went in like reading the Bible, front to back. *Aa* words first—there you find *Aaron*, and him in the Book of Exodus, brother of Moses, founder of Jewish priesthood. *Aardvark*—that animal with a tube nose that eats the ants of Africa. There are abbreviations too, like *AA, Alcoholics Anonymous*—where people go to heal from the bottle. That punched me in the guts. My mummy, she said, "The Aborigine is a pity, my son." She said everyone was always insulted by her no matter what she did, so she let herself do the most insulting thing she could think of—take the poison they brought with them and go to town.

You could keep reading the dictionary that way—front to back, straight as a dart—or you can get to *aardvark* and then skip to *Africa*, then skip to *continent*, then skip to *nations*, then skip to *colonialism*, then skip over to *empire*, then skip back to *apartheid* in the A section— that happened in South Africa. Another story.

When I was on the letter W in the *Oxford English Dictionary, wiray* would be in that section, it means "no." *Wiray* wasn't there though, but I thought I'd make it there. *Wheat* was there, but when I skipped ahead not our word for wheat—not *yura*. So I thought I'd make my own list of words. We don't have a Z word in our alphabet, I reckon, so I thought I'd start backward, a nod to the backward whitefella world I grew up in, start at Y—*yarrany*. So that is the once upon a time for you. Say it—*yarrany*, it is our word for spearwood tree: and from it I once made a spear in order to kill a man.

FOUR

The plane stopped on the runway and August disembarked into the heat wall, thirty-seven degrees—bathwater temperature. She was born into this, but she wasn't accustomed to it anymore. Here, she remembered, summer wasn't a season, it was an Eternity. Inside the terminal she overdrew her account when hiring the Budget sedan and drove seven hours west of the coast, along the City Highway, the Hinterland Highway, and finally the Broken Highway to arrive on the outskirts of Massacre Plains. Broken Highway slices right through the sand-budding grain fields, seas of sheep newly shorn, and oak scrub that had begun to grow in abundance into the drier clay earth. The biggest difference between before and now was not only the wearier livestock and thirstier crops, the extraordinary heat that had settled inland, but also that the distinct point between weather and desperation was tipping.

Rough Road Ahead traffic signs cautioned August's arrival in the Plains. She caught the first signs of visual heat that radiated from the split bitumen and the sparse foreboding landscape beyond the road. That far inland everything was browner, bone drier.

The town of Massacre Plains was home to roughly two thousand locals and their children and children's children. Half a town of wives tended counters and half a town of husbands were suicidal with farm debt, and most sons and daughters, seduced by a living wage, signed up as army cadets. All navigated boredom until the annual race days. Some made do on unemployment benefits and some had jobs though few had careers.

Murrumby River divided the people in town. Epithets were procured off supermarket shelves: Chocolate Milk were the old Mission Gondiwindi north of town, south of town in Vegemite Valley was where the blackfellas in the government housing lived, pegged after the salty sandwich spread, dark as molasses. In the center of town was where the middle class lived, according to a census like theirs, and were dubbed the Minties: named after the white, sticky candy sold in individual paper wrappers. The Minties's houses had doorbells and locked gates. Only in Vegemite Valley were the doors left wide open on the houses. Love and fighting traveled freely inside and out onto the streets. Through some doors pitiless diocesan priests used to visit, those entrances that led to broken homes, where shame-filled single mothers brought up silent boys who became angry later in life.

August didn't know and hadn't remembered everything dealt to the people of Vegemite Valley. Her memory had been good enough to bury the bad thoughts, although reliable enough that the good were sometimes suppressed too.

Out on the old Mission at Prosperous a copse of gum trees had remembered everything for two centuries. August didn't know all that the trees had seen. She didn't remember the whirly-whirlies throwing dust about the paddocks, those small harmless tornadoes, that as a child were an almost permanent fixture. Most farmhouses in Massacre Plains were on the grid and buzzed endlessly; others further out, like Southerly and Prosperous, would come alive with the spit and start of the generator. She remembered the constant chug of electricity. And she remembered—or wanted to remember—the cool of the river Murrumby. Poppy used to call the Murrumby River the *Big Water*, and it had once flowed through the country, from state to state, south to north. August's memory of the river was faint since the water had ceased flowing since she was a girl, and not just because of the Dam Built but because of the Rain Gone. And some say because enough people cry water in this whole region, Murrumby thinks she's not needed at all.

August stopped for supplies before the turn-off, wanted not to buy cigarettes but knew she would. The outside of the convenience store was wrapped in green netting, like an art installation, she thought. On the pavement, more green mesh was for sale; huge rolls leaned against each other, just as bundles of fabric do, or she imagined, people starboard on a sinking ship. Beside the bolts of green were crates of plastic rip-ties that she recognized as those that policemen used to carry on weekend nights.

She fumbled with the mesh hanging over the shop doors as she exited and came face-to-face with another customer, keys in hand, entering the store. He was an elderly man, and he stumbled back, startled, as August drew the screen aside.

"Sorry," she offered, and put her hand out toward him, suspended in the air. He steadied himself without her help and studied her face briefly.

"Now, you must be a Gondiwindi girl," he said, saccharine as butterscotch.

August gave a short nod, clutching the bag of groceries to her chest, dipping her chin into the crumple of foodstuffs.

"I know a Gondiwindi face when I see one." He gave a small smile as if it were a compliment. "Pass on our condolences from the church."

"I will. Thank you . . ." she hadn't known what mark of respect to bestow upon someone she didn't know; she settled with, "Sir, thanks sir."

August turned before he grabbed at the air like an afterthought were floating away. "God bless," he added. August got a distinctly awful feeling of pins and needles and could taste the smell of his acetone skin. She walked away without another word. Locals who didn't pay her any attention carried bundles for their own shopfronts. A couple of men crouched at their utes by the gas pumps, fixing mesh cut-offs onto their engine vents. August took in the clear, blue sky—the locusts were yet to arrive.

Inside the rental she could see the center of town nestled on the horizon. There, a lot of things had come to pass since she'd left. August had missed all the births, deaths, and marriages of nearly everyone. Enough time had turned to almost forget the town, though she'd kept a keen interest in the place that swallowed her sister up. She'd rung Nana and Poppy mostly once a month, checked the missing-persons database, and sent letters to her mother—bereft of replies. She read the online council bulletins that promised progress that never arrived—the fast train line that they managed without, the rural university that was almost built, the delayed library expansion. Even as August turned her back on the place, she still wanted it to own her. After some time, people seemed to get used to the sisters gone, and as much as August searched for the news of Jedda's safe return, she'd hoped for a renewed plea for hers. Neither came.

From the convenience store she drove two kilometers down the ridge to the last turn-off, another two to Prosperous Farm. The rented sedan pulled up beside the twin tin letterboxes, disturbing a flock of pink-grey galahs. She noted that only the yellow box trees had grown higher and broader along the vast shoulder where the mobile library once threw up gravel. Their street had been too far out of town to be visited by the ice-cream truck, but twice a month the library bus arrived, with its shelves slanting up from the floor, its magazine racks secured with long strips of elastic. August peered through the peppermint trees, crawled the car past the roses that divided at the fork of the property where the entrance split into a dirt drive to Prosperous House which was set twenty meters back from the road, and the other divide, a hundred-meter-long concrete slope up to Southerly House. Southerly House was and had always been freshly painted and flanked by a small fruit grove. Beyond the entrance and the houses, a vast field, five hundred acres of ripe wheat, spread out to the brow of trees that always remembered, those gums that gathered at the river.

The Gondiwindi had lived at different points along the Murrumby for forever. And during the last century and a half—ten kilometers north of town at Prosperous, below the 300-meter-high rock of Kengal. At any spot on the property, whenever one of the Gondiwindi in the field took pause and looked north, they saw the ashen granite of Kengal unchanged in the changing sky.

To her right the converted church of Prosperous was ramshackle now. Only a small congregation would have fit where no more than thirty pews had once measured out the entire ground floor. Its single-story extensions had been built like splayed wooden puppet legs from the body of Prosperous. The dozen original scattering huts that dotted the property, where children once slept, were collapsed and worn to mounds of firewood.

Bottlebrush combs of red and orange hung defiant in the still, hot afternoon. Banksia blooms weighed down their branches, leaked sap into the kitchen garden below the veranda. The once-orderly rows of vegetables had turned rogue. Tomatoes sun-dried before picking. Willie wagtails quivered their feathers between the fatigued jasmine and weeping lilly pilly. Prosperous pine boards had been shocked and split in the heat and the paint shaved by time. Dust coated the windows, tiles slid from where they'd meant to be. Everything was yellow-green, sick with hot perfume. It was hard for her to see where Prosperous House began and the scrappy garden ended. August wandered the property, pausing only to listen more closely to the familiar soundtrack playing, encasing the world, in cicada friction and bird whip.

She looked out to the tin shed perched above the tractors in the heart of the field, five acres distant. Looked out to the roof of the sheep barn, the metal tops of the single-ton silos, the arms of the remaining trees that made a natural path to walk through. She knew that at a glance or in a stranger's gaze, one wouldn't notice everything here. Not the way she and her sister had known it once, not the secret hiding spots or the things to covet or eat if you knew where to search. Not all the bones of things she could still see. She scanned for Jedda. Jedda missing forever.

She gave the Prosperous grounds another lap and watched for snakes, for the shadow things appearing in the daylight, and having scoured the place, finally *cooeed* into the back veranda. A curled-up kelpie lifted its head from one of the paired cane chairs and howled a little in reply, then rested its nose into its paws as if it were work-shy. She bent and gave the dog an assuring pat between the ears. She took her bag from the car and back on the veranda, opened and let the flyscreen door slap behind her for the first time in over a decade. The screen hit the frame and continued to bounce as she dropped the keys on the wooden sideboard that was crude and dust stuck and overdue for stain. She pushed open the door to the big room, filled with cardboard boxes and tea chests, looked through the downstairs rooms and the bathroom. Outside the kelpie walked beside her past the empty workers' annex. She peeked in the smaller garden shed, and, as she called out finally for Nana, meekly, she heard a voice bellow back, "Jedda?"

"It's me, Nan, August." She'd spotted her rounding the citrus trees, cradling a basket of pegs. "I'm sorry about Pop, Nana."

August noticed her nana wince, and regretted offering the standard commiseration. Everything was quietened in both of their minds as Elsie instinctively pulled August toward her by her arms, like a hand-reeled catch, and kissed the ear. She placed her hand at her granddaughter's cheek and looked at her as if to make certain she wasn't the lost sibling. She ran her arthritic fingers into the creases of her collarbone, quickly down the length of her arms, before August pulled her body away from being measured. Elsie, like Prosperous, like August, looked different now too, aged, as if gone to seed.

August was reminded of when Jedda disappeared for too long, how the family had drawn inside, their sadness like a still life. But that, she'd known, was because she had only been a child and her nana and poppy had reason not to lose themselves to despair. Now, though, there were no little children around to be frightened of the great grief that possesses a person. But Elsie hadn't reached hopelessness, the magnitude of her husband's death had not yet bent her completely.

Instead, in those first days after Albert's death, Elsie felt that he had still been there, napping in another room of the house, working in the garden, or cycling out on the road to keep his knees from aging. Elsie's thoughts zeroed in on her granddaughter—it had been such a long time since she'd seen her. She found it difficult to look at August and to not look at her, because Elsie could see how sick she'd made herself, how she'd kept herself in a boy-child's body all this time.

Elsie gestured for August to follow her into Prosperous and August took her outstretched hand as they walked inside. Inside, her Nana rested the peg basket on the dining table and sat on the day bed. She looked confused, but was lucid, when August stood closer to her.

"Cuppa, Nan?"

Elsie nodded and steadied herself upright, leading August and leaning on her by the waist, thumbing at her wet eyes. August didn't know if it was disappointment or sorrow she was feeling, and Elsie wasn't sure either.

"Milk and sugar?"

Together they prepared the tea. Elsie moved easily around the kitchen, her trouble was beyond the wrist, not the rest. August watched her Nana take the cooking pot and place it on the counter and then waited almost fearfully as she stared into it for a beat or two. "Can I help, Nana?"

"You may." She said after that uncertain pause where she'd been thinking of meat and two veg for dinner, "Get me the beans from the fridge, and you fix the potatoes."

The beans were passed along with a paring knife and, in the cupboard under the sink potatoes, were found where they'd always been. Elsie took a straight-backed chair into the kitchen, sat and topped the heads off string beans, and from a distance she tried to hold August with a silent gaze, pursed her lips at what she'd become, willing her to speak. And why should Elsie speak? After all, she thought, she'd been here waiting during all the years August was too young to run away and then during all the years she was old and capable enough to visit but didn't. Elsie thought again that August's lack of appetite had spoiled her once-beauty, and August, having sensed herself scrutinized, turned her body away from her nana and looked out the back door where the dog snoozed.

"What's the kelpie's name?"

"Spike. Your pop bought her for me last month. She's a good old girl."

August felt anxious to ask things, but didn't want to intrude right away. After some time she couldn't help it.

"Is Mum coming?"

"Reckons she'll get day release, but don't count your eggs."

"Is she okay?"

"Not since forever, girl."

"Will everyone come here? For the funeral and stuff?"

"Yes, love. Get the butter ready."

August opened the fridge and took the butter to the sink and returned to peeling the potatoes.

Elsie sighed aloud. "City folk are taking the house, Augie."

"What's that?" she asked, not sure she'd heard her properly.

"Council reckons there's nothing to do about it. We said no but town hall meeting few months ago said there isn't one way around it." She lifted herself from the chair and walked back to the day bed, exhausted with all the surfacing sad things. "It's not our land they say, not even this little house. It's Crown or something. Use the sage from the garden, dear."

August came back into the kitchen with a fistful of herbs. "How?"

"I don't know, August. They just told us to wait and see—" Elsie corrected herself, "what they told *me*."

"I'll stay with you if you like? Should I stay, Nana?"

"Don't ask silly questions," she said as her eyes dropped closed, topping the head off the conversation.

August took her pack and groceries into the attic bedroom. Now an office. Albert's papers and books were spread out on the glass top of a wicker desk. His chessboard sat without rank, a dish beside was filled with the wooden pieces. August remembered him teaching her, scolding her if she touched a piece and changed her mind. *"Uh-uh—you've touched it, you've got to move it."* Over the desk there was a missing shard from the stained-glass window, a petal from the Lutheran rose. It was a small window, the length of an arm. For a second August wondered what God would think of her now. What Poppy would think of her up or down there with God? Quickly she knew they were questions without answers, they were roads without destinations. Religion had left her and that house a long time ago. August thought about how people would descend on the house soon, how everyone she knew before would be there. She took in the room. She thought to herself—*I* know this place, but it had bunk beds before; it was *we* back then. In her mind ten-year-old Jedda is backlit, running from the attic room, down the stairs, leaping off the veranda and through the fields before the cutting. The tractors approached November as if the year were a song, harvest the chorus. Afterward those sisters would run through the field again, the wheat cut to fine stumps, the boar-haired field of their childhood.

FIVE

Yellow-tailed black cockatoo—*bilirr Bil-irr* is rolled at the end, the most musical part of any word is the *"rr"*—I can't think of any words in Australia like that, but if I was in Scotland then I could, they don't speak with flat tongues there. *Bilirr*—it's a trilled sound with the tongue vibrating close to the teeth. The *bilirr* is a magnificent bird, strong, eagle-wise. Black as a fire pit, the yellow feathers in the tail visible in flight. I saw the yellow-tailed black cockatoo all my life. All the Gondiwindi loved *bilirr*. Before Prosperous Farm, my mummy was living in Tent Town four miles downstream, where she birthed me there on the flat warm sand, below the caw of *bilirr*.

After Tent Town was flattened and the Mission turned into the Station, and me and all the other kids were taken away, I remember walking out onto the landing of the Boys' Home, standing under the sign that used to hang outside—Think White. Act White. Be White. I was looking at the blue sky and down again. When I looked down into the valley, I saw a woman walk toward me, and she walked right through the stock wire fencing that ringed the entire home.

I walked down on the grass to her and said, "Good day."

The spirit woman was empty-handed and showed me her hands, she looked like my mummy a little, and she said, *"Wanga-dyung."*

"What's that mean?"

She said, "It means lost, but not lost always."

I said okay, and she told me to practice it. I recorded it in my mind as my first-ever time travel because the sky, when I turned back to enter the home not ten paces, was grey and hung low. The woman was gone, just a *bilirr* remained on the fence. I knew it could have never been cloudless just a few seconds before, and at that moment I realized I'd gone, not the world.

yet, if, then, when, at the time—*yandu* The first time I heard *yandu*, it was run on with a jumble of others, it was like spotting the meat in a soup of words, and lifting it out to look at it. My ancestors were coming to the Boys' Home every day by then. A mob of them, old and young too, even little kids would arrive by the outhouse, any place— by my pillow when it was time for bed or even when it was time to make the bed in the morning. They'd look at me and wave, call me out to the river. The river would just appear wherever we were. Then we'd walk about and talk about this and that, and those ancestors were speaking English to me as well, so they could translate everything too. In the night there'd be a fire made, sometimes corroboree, and a big feed of kangaroo tail cooked on the hot coals or eels from the river cooked on the hot coals too. So it was around the campfire that I learned that word *yandu*—everyone was telling stories about this animal and that animal and this fella over here and that woman there, there were plenty of jokes and lots of laughter. My great-great-great-grandfather was there, and he'd do lots of the talking. I started to hear the music of the sentences, the pause, the *d* sounds bumping in his mouth. Most of the time around the fire with everyone else there I couldn't get a word in edgeways, but when I did, when I could find that word *yandu*, I waited for the first pause in his storytelling, and when it came I said, "*Yandu*," and he said, "When what?" "*Yandu*," I said again, wanting him to tell me the meaning—and he just put his arm around me, laughing and patting me. He said, "*Yandu*, son, is the glue of your stories." I remember that.

yield, bend the feet, tread, as in walking, also long, tall—*baayanha*
Yield itself is a funny word—yield in English is the reaping, the things that man can take from the land, the thing he's waited for and gets to claim. A wheat yield. In my language it's the things you give to, the movement, the space between things. It's also the action made by Baiame, because sorrow, old age, and pain bend and yield. The bodies of the ones that had passed were buried with every joint bent, even if the bones had to be broken. I think it was a bend in humiliation, just like we bend at our knees and bow our heads. Bend, yield—*baayanha*.

younger sister—*minhi* I went mustering when the droughts hit again and again and the skeleton weed took two years of crops and there was no work on any station for us. I loved mustering, being high there in the saddle, wearing the ten-gallon Stetson, relying on my stockhorse, leading the herd to water. They were fine years and I made friends for the first time in my life. There was so much I wanted to be talking about with people. I asked a roving man from our neck of the woods about his family, how his family were my relatives. He turned away threading the stirrups against his horse, sick and tired of my chitchat. I learnt that a lot of men on the farm and out in the bush like to focus on an animal or an engine to hide their faces before they tell their truths. "The family trees of people like us are just bushes now, aren't they?" he said. "Someone has been trimming them good." I wouldn't ever forget these words because they sounded like sad poems. And I guess that's a true thing, because all the years I've lived I've lost so many parts of the people that make me up. My mummy, my daddy, my cousins, and my younger sister, my *minhi*. When I was little and in the Boys' Home, I never forgot our people on the river. It seemed every night the moon came to the dormitory window to remind me of my family. I'd think of my *minhi* across the country in the Girls' Home, and my urine would run like quicksilver over the hessian cots, onto the stone floors to wake my schoolmates. I was just three years old after all. I never forgot her. She was just a baby, Mary was, when we were both taken away. That's a sad story with a happy ending because we found each other again. She is different from me, we don't hug each other and be affectionate like I'd want to be. But we got to be brother and sister again, which is special. I got to be the older brother again, and she got to be my *minhi*.

Six

August and Elsie couldn't bring themselves to eat in the end, and
Elsie, avoiding her marriage bed another night, had fallen asleep on
the couch. August walked into the field and could see that the windows of the workers' annex were darkened. She thought about Saturday when they'd gather together, imagined the lights on again. After
Jedda disappeared, no workers came and stayed and the annex doors
had been closed since, lights dimmed. Elsie and Albert had also let
the preaching and karate room in the front of the house turn quiet.
All the photos of Jedda were taken down and wrapped in muslin and
put away. And just like that the home became just a house; they never
really talked about Jedda Gondiwindi again. In the beginning people
had shaken their heads in the street, and mothers wept, and at afternoon tea the few people that came by wondered aloud how something
so bad could happen. How puzzling it was—that she could disappear without a trace. There were murmurs and tears, but no one had
answers. After that, childhood wasn't so carefree; it was risky. Kids
got picked up from school, parent volunteers crossed names off lists
and manned the bus stops, few were allowed to walk home alone,
and playing on the street was mostly forbidden. In spring no one sold
purple bunches of Paterson's curse to tourists by the side of the road.

Though, the thing about a small town in a place like Massacre Plains is they love their own. Or if they don't love them, they at best stick by them; defend them against the outside world of troublemaking out-of-towners, tourists, big money. But the Gondiwindi weren't their own. They never double-checked if they saw a Gondiwindi walking home alone. The newsreader said Jedda's name and flashed the school portrait on the screen only twice over a pressure-cooked week, and Jedda, like the kids who went missing, the brown-skinned children like her, became a mystery manufactured to forget about.

But the Gondiwindi (and the Coes, Gibsons, Grants, and every other family like them) couldn't forget. Almost every woman's hair in the family then took a journey into silver and, by the next year, all August's aunts looked old and grey on the tops of their heads. All the religion and the festivity of a full house became mute rooms, faded to white noise. That noise of the mind where all the questions restaged and all suspicion rehearsed. Over the once-comatose valley of town, their minds rattled with every combination. August, just nine years old—her heart stretched like bubblegum string until it snapped. And it stayed snapped.

Once August had run away from Massacre Plains and made something resembling a life, when someone would ask her if she had siblings, she'd tell them she had a sister but never said she was missing. August would furnish a space in the universe where she imagined she could have been; at twenty Jedda was at a faraway university, at thirty she was expecting her first child in the city. Or sometimes she'd just say she was dead. Life or death have finality, limbo doesn't; no one wants to hear about someone lost. Someone that just went and disappeared altogether.

In the field now her skin prickled, that big organ remembering everything that happened before. She thought about what her nana mentioned—of losing the house, of all the Gondiwindi leaving here forever, and even though the bad memories were beginning to seep back into her skin, it still didn't seem right to her to be forced off that place. Not, she thought, if they go all the way back to the banks of the river and further, like her poppy had always said. The air changed, a breeze pulled at the trees and August looked up from that dark field where stars were hidden. The possibility of rain was a simple smell, a good taste. She slipped off her shoes and within seconds the dirt that stretched out around her was covered in fresh scars from the sudden, heavy rain. It was a single burst. A thermal updraft but not enough to break the hard topsoil. August thought about what her poppy used to say, that rainfall after a dry spell is the perfect condition for good wheat yields and also, the perfect condition for locust outbreaks. Simply put, he'd say, *sometimes there isn't a silver lining at all.*

In the walls of her former bedroom she smoked out the louvre window, fingering the packet of cigarettes. Her mouth ached for something more, wanted some unknown balm, not a kiss, or a meal, or a drink, but something long denied. Since she was a girl the ache had scratched further inside her, for something complete to rest at her tongue, her throat. The feeling that nothing was ever properly said, that she'd existed in a foreign land of herself. How she saw home through the eyes of everyone else but her. The feeling had begun before Jedda vanished.

She stubbed the cigarette out, looked at the block of telly rehomed in the corner of the room. On the same telly, that was once downstairs, the newsreader had initially encouraged people to search their properties, dams, silos, and abandoned wells. Some people searched with dogs. August had wandered down to the flats of the Poisoned Waterhole Creek and ate roots and tubers for the first weeks without a sister. She'd taken slices of stringybark gum and let the paper melt on her tongue. Sucked at the bulrush reeds. She'd been compelled to eat the earth, become immune to it so it didn't hurt, eat up the whole place where Jedda was lost. *Forever?* If she could eat the entire earth, be of the earth, she thought she too wouldn't disappear that way. A month later when Jedda was still missing, Albert baptized August himself in the field under the hot cracked sun while she cried. Everyone was gathered and talking about the *sanctity of childhood, the kids* they kept saying, and then her poppy poured water over her head and recited the absolution of the dead:

"Suffer the little children to come unto me, for theirs is the kingdom of heaven. For unto Thee are due all glory, honor, and worship, with the Father and the Holy Spirit, now, and ever, and unto ages of ages. Amen."

He told August that it was to protect her, and she, feeling all the weight of blood rushing to her head in his hands, saw the world as she always felt it was—turned, upside down.

SEVEN

war—*nadhadirrambanhi* There was a big one here, that's how the town got its name in the end. The war lasted one hundred years. Everyone was fighting that war, even the Ghan cameleers and train-track fettlers were there and fighting alongside the Gondiwindi. It all started when the Gondiwindi were sick of the settlers taking over their land, digging up their tubers, ruining the grazing work they'd done forever. The Gondiwindi were farmers see, farmers and fishermen, and they cultivated the land here long before, they stayed even through the rare winters. They'd keep warm by turning their possum-skin cloaks inside out and rubbing the fat of the pelican on their skin.

So when the Gondiwindi were fed up, and hungry because their kangaroo wasn't coming in their hunting ground anymore and because their lore said that even during change, the land still owned them. That they could use the land how they needed—they got into the cattle then. They rounded them up with their mutts and dingoes and chased the heifers until they became tired, until it became a hunt and they'd spear them. Must've been frightened, those cows, so it was a good thing they never ate the meat—would've been tough as a chop from the Boys' Home. They ate the fat, and the liver and the marrow. The settlers got mighty angry that the wild Gondiwindi didn't respect their new fences. Then came retaliation. Thousands died, even the Gondiwindi babies too. Well, the river ran with blood then, and the dirt turned forever from yellow to pink. Massacre Plains had been born and the Gondiwindi, looking down the eye of a gun's barrel, were scared.

water—*galing, guugu, ngadyang* The Reverend wrote it in his journals as *culleen*—he was listening that fella, listening as close as he could. All my life I've been near the water, and we come from the water too, us people. First we were born from quartz crystal—that's hard water, we are kin of the platypus, that's the animal of the water, and then, my wife Elsie and I made Missy and Jolene and Nicki, born on the banks of the water, the Big Water—Murrumby.

a large waterhole, a watercourse downhill—*nguluman* There's one near the property, just there at the corner of the wheatfield, a little shoot off the Murrumby. The waterhole never fills all the way any-more. If the river ever gets going, it's only running a little, and the whole thing is never deep enough to fill the wetland and then trickle into the waterhole. They call that one Poisoned Waterhole Creek.

wattle flower, acacia tree—*yulumbang* The ancestors told me about all the plants and trees and how to use them. They told me that the plants were pregnant with seeds, that the plants were our mothers and so I was only to use them for the Gondiwindi, not for selling, just for living. Remember that, wherever you go and touch the trees and plants, they are sacred. The *yulumbang* is a great plant for lots of things, the green seeds can be roasted in their pods on the fire, then you eat them like you eat peas. If you roast them and make a paste, it

tastes like peanut butter. The light-colored gum from the *yulumbang*
can be sucked like a lollipop, but not the dark-colored gum—that one
is too bitter. The gum is called *mawa*.

weak, hungry, depressed—*ngarran* You should never say this word
too loud because it'll catch you hard. When you say the thing, sometimes you become the thing. August, when she arrived to live with
us, would scream and weep, and yell out "I'm hungry," but she was
ngarran, she was all those things. I knew she had *ngarran* from this
life and the past too. We'd say, *Close the voice, because it's telling you
wrong.* Anyone can say that, *I'm not ngarran*, because I'm in control—I
can make it small and put it into the palm of my hand. I don't think
it always works, but it gives the spirit a chance to rest. In the end,
ngarran is part of life—we can't make it disappear, it doesn't vanish
overnight, but we can tell it to shush in the meantime.

well/to make well, to make good—*maranirra* If it takes a village to
raise a child, it takes a village to drop one. Mistakes were made and I
want to make *maranirra* now. We should all make *maranirra*.

wheat—*yura* My entire life has been *galing* and *yura*. Even in the
Boys' Home we used to have to bless our meals, mostly served with
johnnycakes, or dense bread. We'd recite, "Blessed by God who is our
bread, may all the world be clothed and fed." I quite liked saying that
aloud. Many people know the wheat firsthand, not just in this country. Every person knows bread one way or another. The Gondiwindi
had their own flours, and they were meant especially for the body of
the Gondiwindi. We have always worked in the wheatfields too, my
daddy did, and his daddy too, and if the world ever stopped turning,

it'd be the last grain on earth, I reckon. Prosperous acres were fertile for the most part and although us mob lived on rich land—we never became rich.

where is your country?—*dhaganhu ngurambang?* The question is not really about a place on the map. When our people say *Where is your country*, they are asking something deeper. *Who is your family? Who are you related to? Are we related?* There's a story I read about someone who wanted to build a map that was the scale 1:1 so that the map covered all the oceans and all the mountains and land at its true size. That made the girls laugh when I told them—imagine walking underneath and holding the thing above your head in the dark? That's a little what a map does, takes the light out so you can't see. The map isn't the thing, this country is made of impossible distances, places you can only reach by time travel. By speaking our language, by singing the mountains into existence.

wooden dugout, or bark container or dish—*guluman* Elsie and me—we celebrated our marriage anniversary when the grandkids were little. Mary babysat. We took the Greyhound bus like they did in American blues songs. We went all the way to Alice Springs and then to Uluru—right in the middle of the country. We met some proper blackfellas out there, and there were women that were making their own *guluman* there too, and we bought one to bring home. It made me want to do things like that back at Prosperous. The *guluman* we brought back reminded me what the ancestors showed me and said, that our family had our own, used to carry fish to waterholes. Our people used to farm fish too! And after that trip, the *guluman* was a reminder of a bigger story of our people—how far we'd come that we could revisit ourselves, be proud of our culture again.

world, all over the world, everyplace—*bangal-ngaara-ngaara* Once, the ghosts came when I was meant to be doing chores, and away we went to shake a leg. I had never been to a dance in my life, I must have been about thirteen years old. All my family was at the corroboree and there they showed me the dance of the crow. We all danced and while we were dancing we flew into the sky, doing things that humans can't do. We went *bangal-ngaara-ngaara* and the ancestor, my great-great-great-nanny was there, and she was teaching me about dying. We were flying and she said, "No one ever dies." I said, "I'm sure they do because my daddy died." She took her claw then and ripped a feather off my wing and she said, "This is not you. If I rip all the feathers off you, it is not you." "What is me?" I said, and she said, "You is only electricity and electricity cannot die. You go somewhere else, but your feather is not you." We went to a thousand and one places in our dance, and she showed me that dust to dust is just where we are resting—in the ground some places, in the water other places, burnt in ashes other places—she just said, "They now soil, they now water, they now lightning." Afterward we flew back to the fire. All my ancestors danced through night, and we ate quandong fruit by the fire. It was sweet and I stayed awake a long time after dessert. But then it was time for bed and they took me back to the Boys' Home. When I lay in bed that night I was very scared that I was going to die, that they showed me dying for a reason. But I didn't die that night. I think they just wanted to tell me things, but not always in the way I thought. I realized I was just learning. It didn't need to be in a special order, they just had me learn what I needed for all the days, not just the one I feared.

Eight

August's compulsion to eat began before she came to live at her nana and poppy's. At her parents' home there wasn't much edible to a child, only devon meat if they were lucky, white-bread loaves gone too fast, fruit that was too old and destined to be thrown away, and food bank goods that needed to be worked into something else. Jedda and August both used to snack on uncooked sticks of spaghetti, dipping the ends into the sugarbag. Chewing them to a paste. Every now and then, though, once every few months, cheese would appear. A large block of cheddar wrapped in thin aluminum foil and soft blue cardboard. August would wait it out until her parents had settled in front of the TV and slip herself along the floor to the fridge. She'd jimmy the electrical plug first from the wall, slide around to the door, gently pop the seal open without the fear of the light coming on. Then she would bite hunks and hunks of cheese until it had gone and she was on the verge of tears from the ecstasy of it all.

When August's parents found the fridge bare they'd scream, bang things, slam doors. Her father, who had a hard face, would take off his leather belt and loop it, make a fish mouth with a fist at each end and *whack!* the leather strips together. Though he never hit her. He'd just scare the girls. They'd rinse her mouth with black soap and water and say, "Where'd you bloody come from! Were you born in the gutter?" She'd known she wasn't, but knew they weren't really asking her that. She knew where she'd been born, the birth certificate was protected in a plastic sleeve beneath the bottom bed of their bunks. She knew it was April Fools' Day in Massacre Maternity Ward when August Gondiwindi was born (feet first, Nana later told her). Parents: Jolene Gondiwindi, unemployed. Mark Shawn, unemployed. Siblings: Jedda, twelve months.

Their family had moved from Massacre Plains five hours south to Sunshine for those first years, into the tumbledown, long rows of fibro cottages where some of her father's family lived too. They had visitors all the time. August remembered always trying to hear what they said. Everything was strange to Jedda and August at home, not just the food and the disorder of days; it felt like life was muffled by some great secret. They just went along with it and made do, would hold out their hands and ask visitors for twenty cents or a piece of gum if they really wanted the girls to go away. They'd collect their loot and run into the small yard; make tents from dishcloths; play dance teacher, Jedda the instructor, August the novice. Inside the house, when August held her tongue out, she could taste cigarette smoke and flyspray in the rooms. She wanted to taste everything, even then, even the acrid air.

And how they came to leave Sunshine and arrive back in Prosperous House was the confluence of all the shambles of their childhood. How they had to be reminded a million times by the teacher to have their parents bring them to school on time, or to sign this and that, or to pick them up because the school guardian couldn't wait at the gates for no one all afternoon. Mostly their parents were more like playmates, their mother usually. Jolene would snuggle with them when she was high and play with them when she was drunk, run around the house below the wet walls that gave them asthma and the mold that grew like a grotty birthmark in the folds of wallpaper and across the ceilings.

When the sisters were playing like that everything was perfect.

Sooner or later their mum would leave the room. Then they could hear nothing but the Rolling Stones through the house until Jolene would forget to feed them dinner and they'd go and rouse her. Then it took a long time because their mum was always doing everything from scratch in that state and last minute and halfway through she'd forget and fall asleep. So Jedda and August would finish cooking while she slept, they'd make their favorite beans on toast, and when she woke they'd have washed their plates, brushed their teeth, and they would be tucked in; Jedda tucked August first and then herself. Hours later Jolene would come in and kiss their foreheads, unravel the hair from across faces. August pretended to be asleep. She loved her the most she ever would at exactly that moment. They were never mean and bad parents, just distracted, too young and too silly, rookies, she used to think.

Then, one winter an unusual fog cold engulfed the suburb, and it snowed for the first time in decades. Every tiled rooftop was frozen white except for theirs. The police noticed this when they drove by that bitter morning. Inside their house they found ninety-five marijuana plants beyond the manhole, kept vibrant by long fluorescent warming lights. When the police came to the door they knocked loud enough that the girls shook. And their parents were handcuffed and marched off to holding and then gaol, all before breakfast. The following day the house was in the newspaper and the social worker drove them to the emergency foster house. They shook there for days until their nana and poppy drove down and didn't leave until the girls were safe. While Elsie and Albert were gone, spiderwebs strung out into corners, snakes explored inside the empty house, and the whirly-whirly arrived to warn children away. But the duet that left returned as a quartet, singing "Wheels on the Bus" and playing "I Spy" all the way back to Prosperous. From the age of eight and Jedda nine, they lived with their grandparents, Albert and Elsie, back in Massacre's Prosperous House—the Mission church turned farm workers' quarters, that had an old coat of lemon paint and an extension built for shearers. Five hundred acres of not being able to shake the past, of where everything had gone wrong, over and over. They'd been returned to their birthplace, and it seemed as if their lives had become best-case scenarios.

August thought nothing could change as much as it did as when she was eight years old.

She was wrong.

NINE

worship, bend low—*dulbi-nya* I reckon Aboriginal people loved the Lord that the Reverend brought so much because they needed him the most in their lives. I think we always thought that there just *had* to be something better. Worship came easy, so this news about a fella Jesus from the desert on the other side of the world who had all the instructions for heavenly ascent—well, that was alright with us. Problem is they didn't let the Aborigine straddle the world he knew best—no more language or hunting or ceremonies. No more of our lore, only their law was forced. We were meant to be saved but we were still in bondage. We worshipped though, we bent low, *dulbi-nya*. We'd done it before in front of the giving honeybee, the generous possum, the loving sun, the plentiful waters—our lives were filled up with *dulbi-nya* long, long before.

underneath the earth—*ngunhadar-guwur* What's down there? Why those mining mob want to rip it all out and then it all belongs to them? I think all those shiny things *ngunhadar-guwur* shouldn't belong to anyone, only our mother. I think that currency should return, make a balm from the wound. It's strange isn't it? That word, *fortunes*. I think we don't have that word at all.

understand—*gulbarra* Our whole lives are spent doing that, trying to understand and be understood. When you're between young and old though, that is the time for deep thinking. The thing I came to understand is that the world didn't just begin when I was born. It's a certain moment in life when we realize that—when we can see that divisions were made when we were just some milt in a fish in the chain of life and death. I'm leaving a complicated world soon, a world up in arms, and I see so much fighting. *Love thy neighbor* that's a commandment from the Bible, *bilingalgirridyu ngaghigu madhugu*—that's our commandment, it translates to: *I will care for my enemy.* They both mean *gulbarra.*

teacher—*yalmambildhaany* At the Boys' Home is where I got my education, so they tell me that's what it was. I learnt to write and read there, but not like I know it now—learning the Queen's English came later. Back then we only wrote little maxims in learning cursive on our boards: *I love to sit in the sun. God made the sun.* Our *yalmambildhaany* name was Ma'am Sally-Anna Mathews, and she had the disposition of someone to match such a beautiful name. Ma'am Mathews had the iodine and boiled candy in her purse for all our punishments from the manager, for whom there would be no dew nor rain, except through him. She would even hug us! What a thing it was for us children without parents around to be hugged. I think my sister Mary never got a hug at the Girls' Home because in a warm embrace she froze. I'm sorry for my sister that she didn't have one little hope like Ma'am Mathews—a good-natured, but wrongly instructed nonetheless, *yalmambildhaany.*

time, a long time ago—*nguwanda* It's not always a good thing, looking all the way back. *Nguwanda* was a time of peace, they tell me. In other people's stories *nguwanda* was peaceful too, they've been told. Things change for good in many ways, so looking back to *nguwanda* is important—but it's just for understanding, not to stop moving forward, not to return completely.

to return—*birrabuwuwanha* I wasn't a very good father. I was distracted or I was working out on the field. When the Station was eventually closed down and the property went out to ballot for a Homestead Farm Lease, Bernard Falstaff, good man, let the Gondiwindi stay on in the sheds and work the field and run the cattle in exchange for a sort of ownership of Prosperous. Word got to me that they were looking for a manager for the seasonal workers. I rode out to Prosperous for the first time since I was taken away. The ancestors were with me and talking to me when I rode out there. They said I was going *birrabuwuwanha* and some were worried, and some were happy. I spoke to old man Falstaff, who was a science man who later taught me to play chess and was not keen on farming. He asked if I was married yet, I told him I wasn't but I hoped to be one day. He hired me to oversee the workers and to manage the old church. Not five years later I met Elsie and there we settled into our own corner. Even if I wasn't an attentive daddy, I think the girls had a good life where we lived. Mr. Falstaff let me plant the trees and treat that corner as our very own. So that's how we got to come home, to stay on country, thanks to Mr. Falstaff we all got *birrabuwuwanha*. How the ancestors loved it there too, we didn't even have to go out into the secret bush, we could stay right there and they'd show me everything I needed to find.

saltbush—*bulaguy, miranggul* There's the old-man saltbush, cottony saltbush, creeping saltbush, thorny saltbush, and the ruby saltbush.

They are good bush food: the leaves of old-man can be used to flavor meat and the ruby saltbush stems and leaves can be boiled and eaten like vegetables; the berries are big and red and sweet. The ancestors used all of the saltbush in different ways. The plant also takes the salt out of the soil, it can heal the ground while growing. That's something.

sap of trees—*dhalbu* The *dhalbu* of the bloodwood tree saved some of the Gondiwindi. When we were being gathered up to be taken away and taught the Bible and be trained as laborers and domestic servants, my great-aunties were frightened and ran. Tried to hide their light-skinned babies in the bush. Some did get away and were never seen again. And some couldn't leave in time and disguised their babies as full-blood by painting them dark with the *dhalbu*. Some of them were later captured. They wander around the river that appears when I travel with the ancestors, blood and sap soaked, hiding in plain sight now but still frightened.

say, speak, tell—*yarra* I asked Doctor Shah to *yarra*—tell me all the bad news. He obliged. "No worries," I said to him when he offered the place in Broken hospice. "I'll be leaving the world the same way I came—out by the river." He didn't much argue with me, just a few minutes, I think because he may have had to, but that fella has known me a long time, so we settled it like men and shook hands and he let me go on my way. Elsie's been crying since we got back to Prosperous, so I took her beautiful face in my hands softly and I said, "Aren't you glad you met a fine bloke like me?" She nodded, even if she was crying and laughing at the nerve of me. "I would've died happy the day I met you, Elsie, and now we have all this other time together. Aren't we lucky?" I said. And then we kissed and hugged and kissed and hugged until she came around to the fact that we're still alive now and still in each other's arms. When she was peaceful again, I came outside to finish my work.

scale a fish—*ginhirmarra* The ancestors taught me all the things I wasn't taught at the Boys' Home: they taught me men's business; they taught me where to find food, the names and uses of all the plants and animals. My favorite was eating the freshwater eel and the Murrumby cod. You can put the eel or fish—*guya*—whole, just as it is on the hot coals and break into the skin when it's done. You can put it on as it is, or you can scale and gut it with a sharp knife first. You take the back of the knife and scrape the scales toward the head, wash it, and then leave the head on. From under the tail to the top of the stomach, cut along and then remove the insides, wash it again. The skin will just come away when its cooked. If you eat the fish, it's important to know how to treat it after it's died for you.

scars or marks, little holes left by smallpox—*gulgang-gulgang* Lots of the ancestors who visited me had this on their bodies, not everyone, but plenty did. "What's that?" I said, when I was little and hadn't yet learnt not to ask someone about something different on their face or body. One of my great-aunts said it was *gulgang-gulgang*. Then she drew a picture with the end of a stick from the fire. She drew it up in the sky above her talking, and all the stars beholden to help her draw out her story. She told me sickness came in the wind, with the shepherds and in the wool of their sheep, and it was a cold time then. "Every day and every night was chilly cold even with the sun out. Everyone was going through the shivers. They couldn't speak about it either because their mouths were filled with blisters even though they hadn't been eating hot things straight from the fire. And some of them couldn't see because the blisters grew in their eyes too. The smallpox were all over the feet and the hands and the face, but not much everywhere else—so it was hard to walk or touch things, or eat. Impossible to see. Well everyone got sick then, and many people died," she said. "Forever?" I asked. And she said, "Never forever, but it was still not the right time to go for so many babies, nannies, and poppies, the weak ones. The old people, old people with mouths filled still with things they needed to teach." "That's sad," I said, and Great-Aunty said, "You'll tell them I told you and then they'll never do things like that again." I asked her, "Who do I tell?" and she said, "Just tell the truth and someone will hear it eventually." I guess this is what I'm doing, finally.

TEN

To Dr. George Cross,
The British Society of Ethnography

From Reverend Ferdinand Greenleaf, 2nd August 1915

I

I felt the great desire to address you, so late in the hour and—as is suddenly apparent—at the late hour of my life. The last time we spoke was many years ago now, in the Banquet Hall of the World's Fair mirage in that compelling city of Chicago. I think on the evening with a golden warmth hung around it, though I had still been a confused man of the cloth, and of the Empire. We spoke of your wife, and I send my best wishes to her and your family at this turbulent time. I feel compelled to clarify why I refused to bring the measurements of my residents to the New South Wales exhibit, refused to catalog the minutiae of my brothers' lives for all to see there against the ebb of Lake Michigan. In looking back, indeed, they are my brothers—we are bound by what we have undergone together all these years. Of course I mentioned none of this at the time, but no man would in those circumstances. Yes—*no man* would tell all the things I've come to know. Perhaps *to tell all* might be the sure way to ruin the great work we've accomplished here. But we live, Dr. Cross, in different times now. I admit to striking out some pages in my journal, and at times not having transcribed all events—anodyne nonsense at any rate? Yet I remember all the events more palpable than anything before or after. Only today I thought on it again and wondered briefly if it should be noted before handing over my living body. Perhaps.

In leaving this world it is my hope it came to something, salvation in some small part, and that the work remaining to do and undo will prosper on and save those wretches from themselves, even if my doubts have remained stronger than hopes.

You may be my last hope, Dr. Cross. I seem to be drawn to expunge the past to you. Alas, the state of affairs awakens truths in the spirit long denied. After many years I have recognized that in times of stress tongues either fold or flap, and having a crisis of the latter I hope you can find forgiveness for such blasphemous indulgence. Perhaps I have reached a place of understanding where I feel I must jeopardize everything so that I might be heard. And so, I have no choice but to write of the things that I have witnessed and known to have occurred on these dark plains since my arrival. Dr. Cross, I hope these words might reach someone in your influence who may rectify this situation. Calamity befalls the congregation of Massacre Plains and, furthermore, the decent Natives whom I have lived amongst. You are my last sane chorus.

Before I was detained I tried to assemble my personal possessions. In doing so I unearthed the Mission's early records and also my

childhood Bible, which was the only thing I came to Australia with
besides my father and mother on *The Skjold*, the final ship to the
Colony. *The Skjold* rode the seas that had little kindness. Aboard
in addition was master carpenter Mr. Huber, and master miller
Mr. Schmitt. I remember them both more clearly than my parents
or myself—I think perhaps because of how many had died on the
journey to the New Land, and because it was always Mr. Huber
and Mr. Schmitt who fashioned the coffins, lowering the Earth's
furniture into the sea. On reflection, I suppose those boxes must have
been the least masterful thing they ever made.

Concealed inside my child's Bible was a newspaper cutting
that had survived the many years lived there in the dust bowl of
the interior, clipped from *The Gazette* on the day of my thirteenth
birthday in 1851. There in plain English was the news that physicist
Jean Bernard Léon Foucault released his Pendulum from the roof
of the Panthéon in Paris, France—proving that the Earth rotated. I
have to hark back to my earliest hopes to wonder why I'd kept the one
birthday clipping of the many my father saved for me, but I know the
reason—how I too had always wanted to prove something. That the
Heavens rotated, that they could rotate and light upon any man. Even
a man here.

From the ever-flowing Murrumby River of this country, I had
for nearly thirty-four years labored to ameliorate the condition of the
Native tribes. *Here*, a peculiar place: searing-hot days, cool nights,
cattle runs, and more cattle than the eye can grasp, and filled with
the flora and fauna one would have classified only by the imagination.
Other curiosities too, though unimaginable, that comprise of
deeds too dark to remark. I'm noting all this in the recent past,
since by force of hand, Prosperous Mission has been taken by the

Government. I have done my best by The Book—all deeds will stand alone for judgment, eventually.

A month prior the only good news came from my Bishop via the Postmaster-General—a fob watch in recognition for my services. It was silver and heavy in the hand before confiscation, no matter it would have not brought pride noting the years coming after all that has happened. Perhaps I regret having built Prosperous Mission— where I had hoped to labor long in bestowing the benefits of the Glorious Gospel of the Blessed God upon those to whom we owe so much, but for whom we have done so little. What irony there is in the namesake itself, for my ambitions for the Mission's prosperity was to be all my faults.

Unsavory as this opinion is, and for reasons I cannot quite understand, there is no other place I would rather be. The night before removal I had a dream that I was trying to build something, though with faulty hands that no matter my pleading would not do as instructed. The task seemed to carry on to no end. The dream was finally ratified when I awoke to the sound of the townsmen gathered again outside my hut. I believe it was weapons they dragged across the outer walls. They'd departed, but I feared I may myself hang from the peppercorn tree for who I am, what I had done there—and now I fear I may hang abounded by wire. Because of the weight of time upon me I have decided not to be a man sent to the gallows of the secret bush or these internment fences without having said *all* the things I need to. To tell how wrongs became accepted as rights. I realize now that no matter what ruin befalls me, this is my pledge: I will tell that unhandsome truth, even if it will amount to last words. The circumstances of the times demand it.

ELEVEN

At first when August and Jedda had arrived at Prosperous they were distracted by the chaotic comings and goings at the house: on Mondays and Tuesdays, mothers' groups; on Wednesday afternoons, karate instruction classes; on Thursdays, needlework; on Fridays, Bible study; on Saturdays, field and garden work; and on Sundays, a free day. Church in the morning for Elsie and Albert and the girls, and then before lunch, Elsie would prepare afternoon tea in case anyone dropped around, which they nearly always did. Strangers sometimes, old people, whom Albert used to take on long walks around the property. Elsie would make a large pineapple turnover cake, lamingtons with coconut she shaved herself, or scones with cream that she beat in the chilled metal bowl before her hands turned permanently stiff. Elsie was the captain of the house and Albert the storyteller, but it was the food that they lived for, the food that they shared with every person who stayed or worked in and around the house—food was the center.

Elsie had tried to get August to eat normal, but something animal would come over her, even if she knew deep down they would be fed *Every. Single. Meal.* So, Elsie taught Jedda and August how to cook her way, cook more than just the toast, pasta, and potatoes they knew how. In near-perfect condition on the sideboard, Elsie had the twenty-seven volumes of *Cooking the World*. On weekends and nights, she'd usher the girls up on stools by the kitchen basin like they were giving confession. Sleeves rolled up high, no need for aprons, their nana said, because "We'll be exact, see?" though nothing was ever measured, just a roundabouts pinch, handful, shake, dollop; there was no need for an egg timer either. Then they'd shave this and that, then chop with their thumbs tucked in. August remembered that the best jobs were mashing with butter or stirring with cocoa because of licking the bowl. Volume One through to Volume Five was called *Home Cooking*, which her nana used the most, but it seemed to her like a bit of everything from everywhere else: shepherd's pie, fettuccine, vol-au-vents with asparagus cream, satay chicken skewers, feta and spinach triangles and—one of their favorites—curried sausages with rice. Curried sausages with rice made them weak at the knees. That was until Jedda and August snuck into the sheep shed on the other side of Southerly and saw tens of lambs being castrated, baby hooves hanging from the beams of the shed, blood down their legs, mewing for their ma's. Then the girls, the first in their family, never wanted to eat animals again. Volume Six to Volume Ten was Italian and Spanish food, Volume Eleven to Volume Sixteen was French and South American, Volume Seventeen to Twenty-Two was African and Asian Cuisine, and Volume Twenty-Three to Twenty-Seven was *Desserts of the World*. If they were studious and helpful and polite, then Jedda and August were allowed two scoops of vanilla ice cream from the tub. Served with tinned peaches and raspberry sauce just like the picture from Volume Twenty-Six, page fifteen.

Elsie also taught them how to greet people at the front of Prosperous and escort them into the big room for highlighting passages in the

King James. In the same room Aunt Missy would come and teach karate, which Jedda and August were allowed to join in on. They weren't
very good students—August would daydream and Jedda would be
swinging her arms and legs too loose for karate, and that'd turn into a
dance and she'd be out the door. Shaking up the hallway, a tune in her
head. She never could stay still; she was always dancing how she liked,
moving to music no one else could hear.

At their nana and poppy's place they got lots of hair washing and
their grandparents talked to them, watched over their homework.
But then they couldn't protect them from everything—not the bull
ants, or the rock snakes, or the sun without sunscreen, or a sore
tooth if they didn't remember to brush twice a day. Just like they
couldn't protect them from Mrs. Maine, the schoolteacher, who
clipped August upside the head when the answers weren't forthcoming, or Ashlie from Jedda's grade who was mean and nasty and
spat on her shoes for no reason at all. Not from their feelings when
their parents could never come back. When they were sat down and
told that brief yarn, that their daddy was needed in heaven and their
mummy was busy getting better, but couldn't yet get out of the shut
place.

It was true, everything changed when August was eight years old.
But it all changed more at nine.

When she was nine the whole world flipped inside out.

After nine she could see all the bones of things, the photo-
negatives, all the roots of the plants, inside of the sky and all the black
holes and burning stars. After nine she could see the little pulleys and
gears inside people's brains, see their skeletons and veins and blood and
hearts and the whole of the town's air coursing in their lungs. It was
too late to tell anyone. How she was scared to leave, even more scared

to stay. Because of the things she saw, those things that changed her tongue. Those things that were dead and done.

August woke late in the morning with the taste of mercury in her mouth. With her eyes still closed the smells wafted through the open window—the great early heating of the first Edible Things from outside. The oil in the gums, warm *karrajong* fruit splitting, the hot flesh-baring seeds, banksia flowers heavy with sugar—the syrup seeping off stuck stamens, and stigmas and ovaries. On the branch there was a tipping point, just as there seemed to be in the town. Days were getting hotter. Other wafts from inside the house—Dettol and hot steam rising from the staircase—soap and pine and castor. Dettol had been the familiar aid for every weekend lost to cleaning. Through sleep-blurred eyes August saw the room. The room and all the noisy years of a childhood that had slid through fingers. Out of bed she began to dress, with her footfalls the floorboards labored. *Everything breaks away from its joints*, she thought, *windows, walls, floors*. She imagined how the house was slap-sticked together back in the old days, with glue and hessian and then putty and plasterboard, all the while the Gondiwindi inside.

She imagined running her fingers into the heavy grooves of wet floorboards, running up the stairs on all fours like when they were kids. As much as she felt at home in the couple of days she'd been back, she understood, after all the time that had passed, that she was now a visitor there. There was an entire world that she only *used* to know. All she wanted was to be taken back to before she was nine years old, to that time before she woke one morning and noticed the strange skin luggage she carried around. Before she knew her body and all the pain and joy and thirst and hunger and fatigue and sweat and blood and shit and the things it could taste.

She held the handrail down the freshly mopped stairs and crossed the clean floor to the kitchen. She made coffee and tiptoed past Elsie asleep again on the couch and into the garden. She noticed the sky, blue and spotless after the previous night's flash downpour, as if the clouds had fled, ashamed of having made the farmers leap from beds in the night, into the anxious expanse, crossing their fingers for more.

Her nana still slept on, even after the sun rose bright and quick and heated the house. August took another coffee outside and spotted Eddie coming down the hill from Southerly House, limping through the peach heath, sweat-slicked shoulders, shoulders that had grown, August thought, an entire dimension of their own.

Her chest tightened and when he was close enough he called out, "Stranger."

August chuckled, she couldn't think of anything to say. There wasn't anything to say, there was no more childhood, no more Jedda, no more Poppy Albert, only the haunt of the past. Eddie looked at August with his blue eyes and leaned in for a hug.

August wasn't used to him, so the hug she braced for was more awkward than lifeless. It had been such a long time since she had been squeezed so easily, so familiarly, that through the feeling of fish hooks in her guts and the sudden smell of blood, she smiled.

"August Gondiwindi," he said to her eyes, "as I live and breathe."

"In the flesh," she said, avoiding eye contact, "pretty jet-lagged though."

Eddie Falstaff, heir of Southerly House, old friend, her first *real* kiss. Eddie had stood out in Massacre more than a Gondiwindi even. He had always been tall and protected in a frame like that. He was born at a short-lived time of abundance when children in Massacre enjoyed a period of fortuitous rainfall and plenty. For two good years people snapped ripe black plums from branches, stained teeth under mulberry trees; they took hunks of food into wide mouths. Mosquito-bitten legs ran year-round evenings under the stars, whipped through the lush wheat and barley and canola. August remembered when it was drier and Eddie Falstaff was ten, almost eleven, and how he'd told all his schoolmates that in his basement at home they had a golden cannon. *This big!*—as he arranged three of his friends, side-by-side, their arms outstretched. He'd forgotten about the lie until his eleventh birthday party when, after the birthday cake and chaff-bag race, the boys complained enthusiastically as one to his mother. "When do we get to see the golden cannon?" Eddie's mother had cocked her head and mouthed the words *"golden cannon?"* at Eddie before going in the house and leaving him to explain his way out of it. Eddie told August all about it after, but she'd already known since she'd been hiding in the bushes watching. August hadn't been invited to the birthday party because it would make other people uncomfortable, Eddie's mum had told him, and he'd relayed to her. Louise Hong from the Hong's Chinese Restaurant couldn't go so neither could August. Eddie thought his mother was talking about girl-germs, but August knew it was something else.

Eddie Falstaff didn't need to lie about the contents of his home—even during the drought, he was almost the richest kid in all of Massacre Plains, second to the Gadden kids whose family ran the local garage. The Gaddens that worked with all the best Holden and Ford lap cars every Grand Prix, when a hundred thousand bomber-jacketed blow-ins descended on Massacre. Barracking from the bleachers. It was the highlight event of every calendar year, and effectively, during those thin seasons, kept the region the barely oiled machine it was. Eddie's family owned the grain of Prosperous Farm, a thousand head of cattle, and also the pharmacy in town, before it burned down.

"How's your folks?" August asked, leaning into the veranda column.

"Ah, what are you gunna do . . . they're old. Mum's in Broken hospital."

"She alright?"

"Cancer."

August looked up at Southerly, imagined Mrs. Falstaff during her perennial spring-clean, holding the straw broom aloft, clearing cobwebs from fascias. "I'm sorry," she said.

"Sorry about your pop too, aye."

"Thanks, Eddie."

"I gotta bring down some of his books I borrowed and whatnot . . ."

"Books?"

He glanced at the wheatfield. "Well, your old pop must've rubbed off on me."

August was surprised, raised her eyebrows.

"He was out here writing that book, wasn't he?" Eddie gestured toward the never-dismantled folding chairs.

"A book?"

He held his hands apart in front of his face. "Big thing."

"What's in it?"

"Dunno. He was writing it while watching them survey."

"Them?"

"Rinepalm—strip mining." He rubbed his fingers together to sign money.

"Nana and Poppy never told me."

"S'pose there isn't anything we can do is why. They're a tin mine company, real boss—they've been looking everywhere but they've settled here. Whole town's rolled out the red carpet for them. See there!" He pointed out into the field where August saw only the rust-spotted tops of wheat stalks.

"Can't see nothing," she said.

"Look along my finger. Here." He drew her in with his free hand to see what he saw. And then she saw it, maybe half a kilometer out—three metal domes that looked to her like the heads of pins.

"What is it?"

"Drill sites—measuring or something, they reckon . . ." he dropped his arm, flinching. "They'll be here soon, you can ask them all about it. Seen them lot at Kengal too?"

"Who?"

"Protesters," he smiled, and widened his eyes. "They've been trying to get in here for months!"

A car pulled into the shingle driveway of Prosperous. August couldn't make out the people in the front and turned back to Eddie, but he'd already stepped off the deck.

"See ya soon, Augie," he said, going up the ridge, back to Southerly through the still-rising light.

"Yeah, I'll come see you soon," she called to his back and he raised a hand in agreement as he went.

Out of the car stepped the heavy frame of Great-Aunt Mary. Au-

gust noticed right away that her face had taken on sadness year by
year, her mouth turned down like the gob of a Murrumby cod. With
her was Aunt Missy. August thought she looked less spry and even
more grey in the head than she'd been before. She was still tall, but
everyone was—everyone still had their height.

"*AUG-UST!*" they yelped in unison.

August had always felt strange around Great-Aunt Mary, not just
because she was so blunt that the sharp things she said hurt, not just
because a stare could rock a boat right out of its mooring, but because
she didn't know about the bad in her own son, and August felt she had
to be sad for her, that her boy was gone.

Great-Aunt Mary and Aunt Missy dashed silently to the house,
heads bowed, as though they'd realized by closing the car doors, with
those final *thud thuds*, that Poppy Albert was dead, and the sole reason
August had returned.

"How are you, darl?" Mary asked.

Under the awnings Aunt Mary briefly took August's neck into
her arms, and August held her tentatively at the waist like they were
slow-dancing.

"Niece," Aunt Missy said, before taking her turn to slow-dance
August, too. August fell into the hug. "You are teeny-weeny in my
arms!" she said and leaned out, interrupting their choreography, holding August by the elbows, shaking her a little as if her body might
change back like a Magic 8-Ball reading.

"Els up?" Aunt Mary asked, as she entered through the opened
back door.

"Asleep on the couch."

"Good flight?" Aunt Missy said, letting her go and measuring her
up and down with eyes instead.

"Still tired, but it was okay."

"How many hours was it?" Missy asked, wide-eyed.

"Lost count." August smiled, and Missy poked her playfully.

They followed each other inside. Elsie was asleep on the couch still, the sheet twisted at her feet. Aunt Mary stood in the kitchen and held coffee mugs in the air and nodded at August like a response.

"Black, no sugar—thanks," she whispered, and gently took the stairs to the attic room for cigarettes. Also, she thought, she wanted to find *that book.*

The book, August recited in her mind and turned to address the room. "*Big thing,*" Eddie had said. She rifled through the papers on the desk. What exactly she was looking for in the book, she couldn't be sure. She felt, though, that Poppy had known something, had something to tell her. August felt that it was only he who had understood why she'd left without a word, yet he who wouldn't have himself left without a goodbye. She felt that her poppy had been the only one, unspoken as it was, who knew why she'd never stayed.

The book was second to food when August was little, then the book took the lead. Her books, though, were different from Poppy's. The mobile library had been stocked with yellowed romance paperbacks, dog-eared murder mysteries, and well-loved children's books. Staff always located a book for her—first, all those possibilities, all those happy endings; afterward, the perfect order of series, the succession of worlds for a while, until she'd needed more or grew out of others. They recommended *Goosebumps, The Baby-Sitters Club*, to Roald Dahl, Judy Blume, C.S. Lewis, Tolkien, Austen, Dickens, Faulkner. But in every mobile-library book, she could never find herself or her sister. Never a girl like August and Jedda Gondiwindi, not ever. She'd been reading nineteenth-century books, characters in which good and evil are clear, the books where time is evenly distributed throughout a life, and then the books where the characters could be both, times changed. In the pages she sometimes found those characters that lived in her childhood too, in the town where a person's life fits and flits and ends. She loved her books, the pages filled with company when she was all alone, having those few movable possessions that were often lost, waterlogged, or never returned yet had a way of replacing themselves. She was her grandfather's granddaughter, August thought, looking around the room at the comforting stacks of bound spines.

Albert's desk seemed littered with stuff—electricity bills, water rates, books on birds and beekeeping, childhood encyclopedias, pamphlets from the national grain board, notices from the local grain stores, charts for aerial spraying, Bibles, dictionaries. But there was an order to the chaos—Post-it notes were on everything, appearing to be illegible scribbles though they were his own careful script, all in her poppy's handwriting. One read *S116 of the constitution—consent to destroy* and was underlined several times—yet it sat beside a pile of books with no indication which one was relevant. August felt suddenly dizzy and placed her palms on the glass top and rolled her neck. The desk shifted easily with her slight weight. She inspected the other furniture more closely: the lightweight single bunk, the chipboard closet, and thought of downstairs too; the furniture could all be moved with a small heave, nothing was rooted to the floor in this Packawayable Forgettable House.

"*Cuppa!*"

The mug of coffee sat alone. The Aunties were out on the deck and

Elsie was awake and with them. August took a plastic kitchen chair out to join the women.

"Feeling better, Nana?" she asked as she approached.

Elsie hummed and lip-smiled and nodded all at once.

"So what've you been up to in *sunny* England?" Aunt Mary smirked, sitting her coffee cup beside her.

"Washing dishes, mostly."

"Is it ever sunny there?" Aunt Missy asked, as she swatted a locust from the side of her head.

August looked into her coffee cup and shook her head. She reasoned that of course the sun shone there, but it had felt like a long winter. Each year she'd lived in England the locals had talked about the arrival of winter as if it were a baffling thing, though she had always been ready for the relief of cold, as if her entire life she'd willed that frost on the rooftop. August honestly didn't remember the sun in England; instead she remembered the things she couldn't place in Massacre, those low clouds from the late morning until the early evening. The trees turning bare, ice on the windows. The narrow lanes, the stone buildings, and fancy old things that they didn't have back home.

"Joey will be here Saturday," Aunt Missy said, folding August into the familiar while looking down at her phone.

"How is he?" she asked.

"Deadly, aye." Aunt Missy shifted her chair to sit closer to August while Aunt Mary descended the steps to the vegetable garden. Aunt Missy propped her phone out between them. "He made an app, had this idea in juvie. They let him study computers and stuff. True god." She flicked her fingers gracefully on the screen, trying to find what August's cousin had made. "It's so good, it's called *Get 'Em*. It's this game where you fight the colonizers—you can pick your weapons and which country you want to fight for and everything." August looked alongside into her aunt's hand as colors blipped from the screen and the phone became a smooth stone in her palm. "Fuck—battery's dead," she said, dumping the phone into the mouth of her handbag, staring out away from the house. Then Aunt Missy let out a big sigh as if, August thought, suddenly her body remembered to breathe. "Dad had a good life," Aunt Missy added to the breath as she crossed her arms and patted the tops of her elbows, "And a hard life, too."

Aunt Mary was pulling up the slender stems of the potato bed at the edge of the garden. August imagined Jedda, *believed* for a moment she saw her and herself in the same spot with her bare eyes; they were burying chook eggs in the garden in order to grow eggplants, the way they had before their childhood seemed rigged. And then *poof!* She and Jedda disappeared.

Her aunt called out to the three of them on the veranda with her head and shoulders dipping in the work, "This all needs to go, Els. Get it all out and into crates before—"

"Before what?" August interrupted, surprising herself.

Aunt Mary tossed a stem onto the dirt behind her and straightened her back, hands eased on her hips. "Before the move, darl," she said.

"So it's official—Nana has to leave the house?"

"Yep."

"I don't understand why. It's because of the mining company, right? But just out in the field, isn't it?" August threw a single nod to where Eddie had pointed.

"You know what they're mining, Aug?" Aunt Mary's eyes were wide and her chin drawn to her chest like she had a story for her. "T-I-N—tin. You know what that looks like?" She was laughing, shaking her head, "This whole thing . . ." she stretched her arms out beside her, fingers spread wide, and then turned on the spot, shuffling her feet in a circle, "is gone."

"How big?"

"Two kilometers."

"They can't."

"They can."

"Southerly?"

"Gone."

"They own the land?"

"Nup."

"Why?"

"Crown lease, ninety-nine years."

"When?"

"When Eddie's granddaddy got back from the war, I think."

"What war?"

"First one."

"What about the wheat?"

"How much you think they make a ton?"

"Don't know."

"Diddly squat."

"What's a tin mine look like?"

"Big hole."

"Is it bad?"

"'Member *Wizard of Oz*?"

"Yeah."

"'Member Tin Man?"

"Yeah."

"Well there's a reason he doesn't have a heart, darl."

"What's that mean?"

"That tin don't love anyone or anything back."

August took a sip of coffee and looked at Elsie listening to them. August felt that her nana was young and old at once, but masking that, that she was full to the brim with the type of sad that makes the face look otherworldly, as if returned from the River Styx. Elsie looked at August square, choked for a moment, and put her hand to her mouth, blinking with the drought in her eyes. Successfully swallowing back tears. Aunt Missy rested her hand on her mother's lap and winked at August, "Let's see if they can get us to leave first." She flashed a cheeky grin just for her niece.

"Do you know where you'll go, Nana?" August asked.

"Not yet, honey."

August felt for words, but they all seemed clumsy. August wanted to take her nana's hand in her own and kiss it, tell her that she wouldn't let her lose the house, that she could make everything better. But that wasn't true. August couldn't say anything of consequence, she knew she hadn't paid her dues; hadn't lived through the house buckling in the years, or been in the streets where she'd double-take, swore she could have spotted Jedda, or stayed in a town where she second-guessed even a smile. August hadn't given the time of day to the sorrow they'd meant to be united by. She could taste the guilt then, it came from her throat, thick and wet and as black and dirty as diesel, welling up around the tongue. She looked around for the smell and the taste, but there wasn't an engine turning in sight.

"I need a toothbrush and stuff." She stood and gripped the back of the chair. "Do you want anything from town?"

"No thanks, Augie," Elsie said, as August lifted the chair, and with her free arm lightly held Aunt Missy and waved to Aunt Mary. "See you on Saturday," she said, and her aunts *yes darl'd* in unison and let her leave, each bending into the dirt and the handbag as she turned.

TWELVE

Reverend Ferdinand Greenleaf's letter to Dr. George Cross,
2nd August 1915, continued

II

I was once a simple clergyman and almost thirty-five years ago,
in 1880, I opened Prosperous Lutheran Mission for the Native
inhabitants of that particular cattle town, and its surrounds.

Officially our Mission will now come under the authority of
the Aborigines Protection Board, where I believe it will be run
as a Station, and no doubt run in order that the child of God
become useful and where the teachings of the Bible, Mathematics,
and English instruction might be put aside for other economic
practicalities, as is the case at Stations and Reserves I know of in the
district. On learning of the impending change, I might have left the
Mission then, having done little to unburden the Natives for whom
I have come to care deeply. I might have returned to a small cottage
and lived the rest of my days on an acre of peace, though with scant
peace of mind. Alas, it seems the past is not dead and I am being made
to suffer for this war that Britain has declared against the place of my

birth—a situation I had no say in. Yet it is not my fellow countrymen of German and Prussian descent that suffer this war at a distance the most. It is, as I will detail in this letter, the Natives—*mere children!*—who have been forced into servitude because the Government wishes them to fill the gulf in the industrial labor force. I challenge you to scrutinize what I will detail on these pages and not agree.

As I mentioned previously, my family arrived on *The Skjold* from Sachsen, Prussia, in October 1841. My Father was to join the vinedressers with his abundant knowledge of tilling the earth and producing table wine. My mother, in the role of homemaker and with the backbone of an immigrant, another set of working hands. We rode on the bullock wagon on that first journey through the inland to the south, my mother and father leading me toward our destiny. On that voyage I saw vividly—through young eyes perhaps—the Natives in a state of nature among the verdure and plenty of the land. It made a quaint impression on my mind. When we finally reached our new home, there was already an established community of good people who spoke our language. The townspeople were made up of those who had escaped religious persecution from Prussia and Germany and were willing, and able, to begin new lives in this great country, a country that promised opportunity and safety to the dispossessed.

In our new homeland we were assigned fifty acres and Father worked the land of the rocks, cut the trees, and dug up the stumps until the ground was flat and workable. Having no dray, his work was laborious, and yet he was full of faith that our small family would increase, and that this country would be his beloved and final home. Mother conducted her own business in town on Wednesday afternoons, when the wives brought their homemade butter, cheese, and honeycomb to sell. In that way the week was measured twice by nourishment, from Sunday morning mass until the produce market, and I, I was preoccupied always by my study of the Bible.

We settled very amicably into the town's life. My early years consisted of learning English at school and speaking it at home with my parents; only on special occasions, with vinedressers and their families gathering for particular meals or prayer, did we employ the language of my homeland, or ever discuss the politics of a place that all agreed remained in the past. Perhaps fifteen good families were known to my own. All were very fluent in the English language, and their interests at all times were to be enfranchised in the fine country where we'd settled—where we had pledged beneath Britain's flag and with full hearts, the laws under Queen Victoria. As a further show of respect, my parents soon made the arrangements to anglicize our name—our passage had been inscribed on the ship's logbooks as we had been known: *Grünblatt*, and on the 1st day of June 1844, we had officially and henceforth sworn ourselves as the *Greenleaf* family. I say all of this particular information because it is the truth, and because one must be reminded of this given the circumstances we are now facing.

By the time I had grown and was ready to pay heed to the Word and face the world beyond, I had become a religious man. Owing to the vastness of Australia, and as with most young apprentices of God, I had been traveling from Station to Station in the wilds of the interior. Myself alone covering great distances of thousands of miles, scattering the incorruptible seed of the Word amongst the White settlers, when, unexpectedly, I came into contact with the Blacks of Massacre Plains. There I found them in a condition most shocking to behold. I visited their camps and entered their wretched bark and

bough *gunyahs* where they slept in cramped and vulgar conditions. I
went from place to place, a spread of shambles a mile deep and wide,
and each time I met with the same wretchedness and woe. In some
instances, on making a first visit to a camp, the children ran away
from me, terrified at my presence, whilst their mothers—some of
them, alas! only children themselves—cowered in their little dens
like so many wild beasts, doubtless afraid of my ghostliness. Such
helplessness, such woe, caused by Christian White men! Yet this
situation, I soon learned from good authority and from personal
observation, was but an index to a ponderous volume of inequity
existing throughout the interior. I believe it was then, having seen
those depths of desperate subsistence, that I felt sincerely compelled
to help the Aborigine of the camps. I was as sure of this as I had been
of the Holy Spirit, my calling guided there by St. Jude himself.

The camps I speak of were run along the outskirts of the town,
where nothing, I suspect, in the shape of a township, could have been
more unprepossessing to a stranger than the province of Massacre
Plains. The town of low-biding hills covered in gray volcanic
boulders, sparse of vegetation except for the great white trees that
appeared muscular from the hundreds of miles surrounding, marked
purely for pastoral endeavors. In drawing comparison from the wet
southern Colony it had given me the impression of sheer and onerous
squatting country. What great difference I had witnessed from the
bustling towns of the south; there hills and mountains were lush
and many, and a crop took to the sun and frequent rain with the
knowledge there would be continued good weather. Yet in Massacre
Plains only a small number of houses had been established; two hotels
and three stores, each bathed in the dry heat and endless clear skies.
On strong recommendation I made my way to the most aristocratic of

the two hotels, where a room had been engaged for me by the resident police sergeant, which was all that could be desired in being clean and comfortable.

I subsequently reported myself to the indisposed Bishop of the Uniting Church, whom I soon judged to be a gentleman in the true sense of the word. My first duty was one connected with my functions as a clergyman, when I was called away to visit a dying lad. After which, with a Native police guide, I rode two and a half miles down the Murrumby River to a Station where I was engaged to hold service. On returning to my accommodation, I told the lady of the house what I had heard and what I had seen earlier in the day. She replied, "Reverend Greenleaf, I have often thought what a sin it must be for Christian ministers to pass through these parts and never to speak a word to the poor Blacks. I can assure you that of all the clergymen who have called here, you are the first who seems to care anything about them. If some earnest and kindhearted minister would only take the matter up, something might be done to induce the Government to take steps to alleviate their condition."

A long conversation followed, in which this lady, a resident of Massacre Plains for twenty years, drew a picture most sad to contemplate. The conversation sent me to my room filled to overflowing with the wants and woes of these unhappy people.

I threw myself upon my knees, and wept before God, and said: "O Lord, show me Thy way, teach me Thy path, tell me what to do for these perishing Aborigines." The answer did not come freely, though I knew that if I followed the right and just path I would be instructed. I rose from my knees calmly resigned to the Divine will; but not even then for a moment thinking it was my duty to become a Missionary. If I had known then what great burden would befall me, would later exhaust me, then I think I wouldn't have rested on my knees that night at all. If I had known the dark deeds, and if I had heeded the words of the apostle John when he said: "Men love darkness rather than light because their deeds are evil." And if I had realized that in the vertical sun of the interior, in all its dazzling light, that none shone from the Great Sun of Righteousness; instead, hidden within the blinding light were beliefs opposed to the principles of justice. Rife here are the darkest deeds ever performed by man upon his fellow man, which *makes countless thousands mourn.* That vile inhumanity practiced by the white-skinned Christian on his dark-skinned brother in order to obtain land and residence, for "peaceful acquisition"—that includes capture, chains, long marches, whipping, death on the roadside, or, if surviving all these—the far more terrible fate—being sold like brutes of the field as unpaid labor to the highest bidder.

How could it be that Australia, professedly the new home of liberty and *light*, had become a theater of oppression and cruelty? A land not only blessed by the Great God, with cloudless skies, and widespread prosperity and happiness to those who have been privileged to make it their own. And moreover a land that professes to reflect the noble institutions of Great Britain, those Godly and philanthropic fabrics, which are not only England's glory and boast but the envy of all the world beside—is shrouded in dark deeds? That a land so circumstanced and blessed by Divine Providence, had become the nursing mother of injustice. That deeds of infamy should be encouraged. What I have seen constitutes the foulest blot to rest upon the emblem of Australia's fame. *If* I had known, I would not have knelt that evening. I would not have called out, *O Lord!*

THIRTEEN

scattered all about in confusion—*dandan* The ancestors never come when the whirly-whirly is about. The whirly-whirly is called the dust devil by some people because it scatters everything about in confusion. We call them *dandan*—they are bad spirits, tunneling across the whole world, throwing up coal dust, sand, dirt, water, and snow. I saw them on two occasions during my life. The first time was as a boy, when we took the train to the big city to perform in the sesquicentenary Flower Show for all the gathering crowds. Our performance was called "The Development of Australia" and I was playing Half-Caste Boy Number Two and the other boys played the characters of Full-Blood Boy One, Two, Quadroon Boy One, Two, Octoroon Boy One, Two, and the big boys played Priest and Schoolmaster, one boy played Governor too. We had to act like gentry, the octoroon boys the most, the full-blood boys not at all. We ended up winning second prize. First prize went to the re-enactment of the landing of the *Endeavour* ship. At the end of the day a big whirly-whirly came through the back of the stage and the Koori actors had to be pushed up there by their guardians, that's how scared they all looked. Even the adults. I asked Tommy—Octoroon Boy Number One—why everyone was scared and he didn't have a clue, so I made certain to ask next time I visited my ancestors.

They told me, "That's a bad spirit, and if you get close to him he'll catch you. Never come and see us if you ever see the whirly-whirly man is around and making *dandan*." I didn't see another whirly-whirly for years. Yet I felt all that confusion all my life. I think we all have. Many years later the *dandan* arrived at Prosperous and stayed a long, long time, and after that I didn't time travel again.

searching, looking around—*ngaa-bun-gaa-nha* When I turned fifteen and was too old for the Boys' Home, I was a ward of the state still, working the local properties. At nineteen I was issued my dog tag. With it I could travel in a certain distance to work for meat and salt on the field or out mustering. I moved around far and wide looking for work, but I was looking mostly, *ngaa-bun-gaa-nha* for home.

sea—*murriyan* We never went to the sea. All my adult life it seemed it was only the White families that went on holidays to the sea. Even with my ancestors we didn't go to the beach; we did travel high above the seas, but I never felt the surf crash on my legs like I've seen on the TV. I'm going to leave the world having never gone to the sea, and that's okay by me. There are plenty things I haven't done, and it didn't make my life any worse. I have never taken an aeroplane trip, I've never gone to another country overseas, not like August. I've never lain under the house or climbed on the roof of Prosperous, or seen an opera in real life or learnt to play a musical instrument. I can't complain about this life—I'm a time traveler, after all. If I could have changed things, though, I would have. I would have been a boy with a sister and a mummy and maybe a daddy even, and we would have taken trips to the *murriyan*. As far as I time travel, I never have come across my own mummy and daddy.

shadow, evil—*nguru* You can't say much against the family—people
get worried and threatened if you turn on the group. I reckon it's because the group can't afford to lose anyone else after everything that's
happened. So I never told Mary what we thought of Jimmy. Elsie
ignored her intuition, and so we took in my sister Mary and always
with her, little Jimmy too. I was blinded by wanting family more than
goodness. What was wrong about Jimmy, I can't quite put my finger
on. He didn't throw tantrums or things about, instead he harbored
secrets and nursed great contempt for people wherever he went. He
did grow up into a cunning sort of lad, always the right thing to say,
always the right turn of phrase. I don't know where he got all those
things from because my sister had been nothing but good and hard-
working. There was honor in how she lived and worked, putting food
on the table is sometimes as loving as a person can manage, but love it
is nonetheless. Well, we didn't know, but he had a whirly-whirly inside
him all along, the *nguru* and *ngarran* too.

sing—*babirra* There's nothing to it, they said, just open up your
mouth and your body follows. Well, it's not that easy is it, not on the
ear for anyone hanging around? Good thing about living at the foot of
a field is you can walk enough paces and be pretty sure no one's going
to hear you. Whenever I've cried in my life it's always come when I
start singing. I could never hold a tune but that isn't the reason we try
something, not perfection. Perfection is just someone's little opinion
at the end of the day, and there isn't much that man makes that is perfect anyway. There's a saying I've heard that *wounds can only be healed
by the one who inflicts the wound*. I'd bet whoever first said that hadn't
had a good sing. Singing is a balm for the singer, and if the singer can
hold pitch then it's a balm for the listener too. Any song will do, the

field doesn't mind either way. Sometimes I'll sing the worship songs when I'm lost, a little line will get into my head, "Oh Jesus, show me the way . . . we go down to the river to pray . . ." I'll be singing low or loud and kicking in the dirt, and the tears will just come when they are ready. Sometimes I'll hear a chorus on the radio and it'll be stuck in my head for weeks, and I'll take it out to the field. Then the ghosts, the ancestors taught me songs too, and I'll be sounding like something you've never heard before, low notes that start at the feet and the high ones that treble in the chest and make my heart tremble. *Babirra* is good, it's food you can't see but fills you up anyway.

soil, earth, dirt—*manhang* In the kitchen garden we grew hardy vegetables—potatoes, carrots, cassava, the cuttings we got from the Chinese merchant who'd come through Massacre and take orders, from mob around town mostly. Over the years that Prosperous had existed, our people had gone without many things, but not us when Elsie and I lived here—we put everything into the soil, good manure, and turning, weeding it every day to grow our food. In the days when I was born there was less men around to work after the war, so the women worked just as hard. They used to grow corn in the summer rainfall, high stalks with husks the color of butter. But they stopped getting that summer rain. I think the town looked to Jesus instead, when he said in John 7:37, *If anyone thirsts, let him come to me and drink.* If they believed, if they had faith in the end of a drought, then *Out of his heart will flow rivers of living water.* But the water didn't come back.

In the science books at the library in town is where I eventually read about the soil. Terrible plants grow around here too, foreign weeds. The worst was originally grown by a lady, Mrs. Paterson, under the Hume Weir. In her innocent-looking cottage garden she planted a pretty purple flower and it soon spread like a certain death for grazing animals across the entire continent. That evil purple plant's name is Paterson's curse, and there's no way around that bugger. There were others, there still are—capeweed, skeleton weed, wild radish, wild turnip, rye grass, wild oats, and now that cotton too—they all suck the good and the water from the already-dry ground. Nowadays something always in the way. Back then too, when soil had gone to acid and lime had to be shipped out and sent over the mountains to put some life back into this place. Over and over that cycle never ended—taking the good out of the soil and trying to put it back with chemicals. I read that inside the soil there are the same number of microbes as there are stars in the universe, and how if you farmed the soil you took the chance of rain away with the nutrients. Well, that blew my mind—just because we don't know something, doesn't mean we will always find out the answer. But I found it out. Once you find a piece of something you know about, afterward you end up getting given more and more pieces of the puzzle everywhere you go. One thing comes and then the world tells you to look out for all the other missing information. *Manhang*—that's where the body goes eventually, and everything else from the *manhang* to the stars is eternally alive with our spirits.

FOURTEEN

It was ten minutes' drive along the highway into town. August slowed momentarily at the only rest area; it was unoccupied, but her eyes flicked there out of habit. *We had looked there for Jedda—a shoe, a scrap of dress, a scruff of hair.* Nothing was found, not the jelly sandals Jedda was wearing that day, not her school uniform either. August was distracted by the side of the road as she drove, distracted by roadkill and the shreds of tire treads scattered there, by the knot in her guts. She thought, in a panic, to pull over suddenly, to sort through the wallaby bones and black rubber for something. Imagined kicking through the rubbish and finding a girl's pelvis simply overlooked. She didn't pull over though. *I'm not mad*, she told herself. *That's a crazy-person thing to do*, and then she wondered what difference it would make anyway, the discovery of Jedda, her in bones, bones no longer pecked by crows. There wouldn't be any comfort for everything they'd lost.

In her mouth she tasted the sulphur sickness of the passing world outside the window, her thoughts jumped to her books back in England—the ones she loved, that would calm her in this state: Khayyam, Yeats, Plath, Borges, Rumi. She'd traced the words of the poet Tagore, when he wrote that *Every child is born with the message that God is not yet discouraged of man.* "But what does it mean," she asked aloud to the road, "when a child is taken away?" She knew it was man that was to blame. She knew she was to blame. She couldn't quiet her mind. "Happy thoughts," she said aloud, and all the bad memories jumbled together instead without chronological order. *Think happy thoughts,* she willed like sparking a flare from a dark ship.

Locusts' bodies splattered against the windshield. She saw them as myth animals, X-ray prawn appendages, dragonfly wings, edible to humans and toads.

Locusts? They never used to come this far south. After the dam they did though. *Yes, they did then,* she answered herself. The dam couldn't stop the river completely, it just controlled it. Nothing could completely stop the river. The river bends time, what happened at the river goes on for us forever. *Forever?*

August and Jedda would trace their journey, their girlish fingers against the thick glass of the TV screen, down the east of the country, heading toward Massacre. They used to draw crayon pictures of the cane toads following the locusts. The toads were slower, never quite catching up. The locusts would arrive, and eat and leave, and the toads would come after. Those toads had looked around with baffled, rumbling stomachs and gobbled up the native mice and the blue-tongued lizards instead. August remembered that. Remembered how they had to coax the dogs up inside, the working dogs who loved nothing more than catching toads and inadvertently poisoning their own rumbling stomachs. The country, after all, was an experiment of survival of the fittest, of the unraveling. Darwin was even the name of a town in the north. *Think happy thoughts.*

Flame trees were turning in the hot wind as she passed High

Street and ventured instead down to Vegemite Valley where no kids
were playing on the streets. August passed Aunt Mary's house, where
she had brought up her son, and where her door remained open for the
priest always. She drove at a crawl, looked into the open wounds of the
cousins and second cousins and wayward schoolmates' homes that she
recognized. She saw no one. She passed a house decorated with wind
chimes and hanging plants that had a LOCK THE GATES sign perched
ahead of the drawn front-window curtain. She pulled up at the curb
to make out the small print that ran at the bottom of the sign: FUCK
OFF RINEPALM. She had the unnerving feeling of being watched and
glanced over at the neighboring house and, indeed, a shadow of a person, someone she vaguely recognized from school, was standing at the
window. The man's face was stony. Suddenly he was joined by another
man at the window and she watched as they watched her.

   She didn't feel like the angry teenager who ran away, the one people noticed, but a sad shell of a woman, looked through. Like her
mother. She locked the door, began to turn the car around, intim-
idated but unafraid, and ventured back into High Street where only
people she didn't recognize at all congregated. She wanted to keep
driving past the new coffee shop seating, spilled under huge umbrel-
las onto the footpath, past the pram babies and toddlers and their
parents, the shops that had filled in where space used to be. Wanted
to drive past the department store and its extended window displays that had spread an entire block. Neither the coffee shop nor
the department store was wrapped in green mesh. August drove past
the original cream sandstone buildings where old signage was still
painted above the new pharmacy. Next to it was the real estate agency
and a FOR SALE sign hung in its window. Above the real estate agency,
a ghost sign was painted in a font from an earlier era: FARM & STATION

SUPPLIES: WE STOCK—IRON. LIME. CEMENT. BARBED WIRE. FENCING. IRON GATES. ETC. The new shops and the old rubbed shoulders, as if hope and despair played a fouled hand on the same table.

She wanted to keep driving, but couldn't. Couldn't see her mother in perpetual detention. She mulled it over. *What if she didn't recognize me, was happy without me, was a disappointment, had never got better, but worse?* She turned the ignition off opposite the green median strip that split High Street into east and west. That hadn't changed, the divide had always been there, but she'd never noticed it before: in the center was the sole statue of Massacre. A soldier in metal regalia, draped in ammunition and slouch-hatted, leaned against his gun. The butt steeped in a tussock of watered grass that was a brilliant green, nothing like the pale green that spread in the rest of Massacre. A council gardener, at that very moment, lowered his hedge trimmers to the base of the weapon and snipped in ceremony around the edge of bronze.

There was something graceful about the council worker, everything respectful about his manner around the statue—it was something in his likeness to the soldier, muscular and youthful, that caught August's attention. The bronze statue was puffed at the chest, certain in his stare into the northern middle distance. She knew that for some young people anything is something to look forward to.

She spotted a roller door being pulled against the shopfront and dashed from the car to catch the pharmacy before it closed for lunch. She took the cheapest toothbrush and scanned the ceilings for fire stains. There wasn't a lick of black smoke anywhere, the entire ceiling was tiled in light boxes, the walls fresh with paint and the shelves stocked full with medicines and snack food. Last time Eddie and Joey were there too, but only Joey had been caught when the place was alight. She rubbed the thought out as she paid and took the pharmacy bag in her fist.

Around the corner she looked for a weatherboard house painted black, red, yellow on the suburban street. It was still there. Aside from out at Prosperous, the Aboriginal Medical Centre and Land Council chambers was where August had spent most of her childhood—doing after-school painting in the garage with the other kids, getting cavities filled and teeth pulled or a doctor's note for being too sad to go to school. They all gathered there for gossip, all the Aboriginal residents of the Plains, the Gibsons, Coes, and Grants from the Valley. Each of the families came together there in refuge, standing around the barbecue, laying almost-burnt sausages diagonally onto slices of white bread lined with sauce. They played Aussie Rules football, and everyone jumped high into the air to mark the ball, cheer, kick, tumble. She wondered if someone there knew about the mining on the farm, or knew about what was happening to them—the Gondis at the old Mish. Maybe someone was there to tell her what a good man her grandfather was, "What a respectable man, an honorable man," they used to say. She peered through the dimmed windows. Empty. Every last piece of furniture in there was gone, gutted from the walls to the floors. Packawayable Place. As she adjusted her eyes she could see herself, but a different person—as a child on the street in the window's reflection, as if her younger self were catching a glimpse of a person that she would one day become. The girl looked disappointed because, August thought, it was too late, she'd already become the thing. *Think happy thoughts.*

"August?"

In the windows' reflection she made out Alena Dimitri's full mane of curls. She'd been neither friend nor enemy, just another student at the high school. Alena rushed toward her as quickly as she could wobble, thrusting her hand and ring finger at August and telling her she'd just married James, the Gadden boy. "Just last weekend!" she beamed. "Haven't seen you in ages!"

It was true, they hadn't seen each other since August walked out of the school between classes in the middle of term. After that Alena and most of the other eighth-graders swapped rumors about what had happened to August Gondiwindi. The unlikeliest scenario was more or less accepted as truth—that she'd run away to join a circus, freak that she was. Alena looked at her now with a little leftover pity, and a certain anxiety as if the tragedy of a Gondiwindi might be a contagious thing.

"How are you?" August asked, taking her offered hand and dropping it. Looking at the full stomach between them, she imagined the baby, saw the curved spine, an X-ray innocently bobbing in fluid.

Alena rubbed her bump, cradled it like a watermelon. "Hanging in there—and you, you're back?"

"Visiting," August said, looking at Alena's face instead.

"What a relief! This town's a dump."

"More than before?"

"This place has been scrubbed off any tourist detours, that's for sure."

"So you're Mrs. Gadden, aye?—they still do flashy racecars?" August said, looking pointedly at her ring, smiling.

"Do you know what makes money in this town now? Nothing except once a year when they export the sheep. That's it, races don't make anything. Everyone's hanging for the mine."

"You know about the mine?" August stopped smiling.

"I know it's out your way, isn't it?"

"On the farm, yeah."

"Something crazy, want to know something crazy? I was just thinking about you yesterday!"

"Really?"

"Got time for a coffee?" she threw her thumb to the wide cafe.

"I can't, sorry," August said. "Jet lag." Then, showing some remnants of manners, she asked, "What've you been up to?"

"Just teaching until maternity leave. I'm assistant teacher at the public school—six-year-olds, mostly—first grade," she smoothed the fabric of her dress over the watermelon again. "That's when I was thinking of you, at school yesterday."

"Yeah?"

"Yeah, we got sent these activity packs, different ones for different grades. They're from the mining company."

"What's in them?"

"Oh, just kiddie stuff, really, but you know—I saw the site proposal. Hubby is happy for the contract work that's gonna come in—but yeah, heaps of greenies are chucking a tantrum."

"What's it got to do with the school, though?"

"I don't know, primary-school propaganda. The kids get to build little cardboard things and pretend to put them in the ground and then there's these multiple-choice questions: *What is great about having a mine? A. Jobs. B. Jobs. C. Jobs?*"

She threw her head back laughing then, her mass of curls lifted away from the conversation.

"You really want to see them? I can drop them off—you staying with your grandparents?"

"Yeah. I mean, Poppy died."

"I heard," her face scrunching into distaste, "I'm sorry." She sighed as if for the two of them.

August could feel jet lag *had* buckled down on her. "I should go—I need to help Nana." She raised her hand and held up the pharmacy bag, as if it were proof.

"She okay?"

"She's okay," she nodded, and lowered the bag.

"I'll drop the stuff off Monday?"

"No worries."

She hugged August's shoulders briefly and pecked her cheek.

Before August walked back to the rental she took another look into the empty windows of the Aboriginal Medical Centre; she breathed against the glass, a hot breath that made no steam in the dry air. As she stepped onto the street a twin-cab ute drove past too closely, too slowly. Below its tinted windows in discreet silver letters the words RINEPALM MINING stretched along the length of the white, shining body as it sailed toward the town's end.

On return she daydreamed that the week after she wouldn't fly back to London, she wouldn't take the train to Guildford, not the taxi back to the White Horse in Shere, not carry her backpack up the iron stairs out the back of the English pub and sleep, wake, repeat. Not finger those dog-eared books of faraway poets until her next shift, not drown her hands in scalding soapy water and work off stuck gravy and Yorkshire pudding from plates. Not back to the scent of stale ale and starched aprons. That's what she imagined she wouldn't do.

Pulling into Prosperous and since shown, she could see the three drill sites in the field, and the roofs of high Rinepalm utes parked alongside. Inside, the sound of things being moved came from the old preaching room. August walked to the doorway and found Elsie in there taking a lid off a tea chest.

"I'm back, Nan."

Her nana looked animated in her long-sleeved black cotton dress that brushed at her bare ankles. She looked up at August. "Ed came looking for you."

"I'll see him later. Can I help?"

"Mmm-hmm."

Elsie knelt on the carpet and August did the same, a pile of cloth cut into squares lay between them. Elsie took a framed photo of Albert and sat it in the center of the cloth, then wrapped it like a baby swaddle. They'd never had photos in rounded frames, not like the antique oval ones of someone else's ancestors that August had seen in England. Years before, Elsie had run the mothers' groups in that same room, where the girls chatted and practiced the fold and pin of cloth nappies. The girls who came for free frozen meals and whose reluctances were only stoked seeing the walls hung with idols. Then they'd be in the kitchen, Elsie and her audience of new mums, their faded prams hustled together on the veranda, there Elsie would show them how to stew sugarless apples or mash up salt-free vegetables for baby. *Bub never needs salt or sugar, okay, girls,* her nana would say. *Salt and sugar are no good for bub.*

Elsie leaned over the tea chest and placed the wrapped photo of Poppy into it. August picked up another picture; it was of a group of people dressed in knee-length shorts and elbow-length shirts standing outside a bus. Both her nana and poppy were there, though they stood apart. She knew it was the Freedom Ride trip. The photo in its large frame always rested against the wall in the living room, ornaments arranged around it as if it were the centerpiece of the house.

"Should I wrap this too?"

"Yes, please."

"What was it like?"

Nana momentarily regarded the photo in August's clutch before returning her attention back on her own. "Bumpy."

"No, really?"

Elsie squeezed her eyes together as if trying to remember or push it away. Finally she said, "We had hope that people would become happy."

"What do you mean?"

"We were young and hopeful, I guess."

"And now?"

She looked at the photograph and cloth she was working on and pressed her lips together. "I think people need to make a different thing that makes them happy."

"Is that where you and Poppy met?"

"That day," Elsie smiled, letting herself remember. "And I left the same day, too."

"When did you meet back up?"

Nana kept wrapping and chatting, "I was meant to travel the whole country, that was the plan. But then I met Alb, and love threw a spanner in the works."

"Did you ever regret it? Coming out here to the farm from the city?"

"Never, not with kids coming along as quick as they did."

August just nodded as Elsie heaved herself up and headed into the living room, returning with a wide *coolamon* in her hands. She picked up a square of muslin for it.

"I always loved that. Did Poppy make that one or is it an artifact?"

"This? No, Poppy didn't make this one."

"Where'd it come from?" August asked.

"Your pop and I went away, we took a Greyhound bus trip for our anniversary when you were little, we went right to the exact middle of Australia—the local women made them." Elsie held it up at August and smiled. "What a thing to see—all that red earth and all those flowers. It was special to us. When we came home he went and made his own *coolamons* too—he called them *gulumans*."

August touched the lip of the *coolamon*, the thin rough red wood sloped into a long bowl, dark ochre and white were painted in intricate, blending patterns down the length of its base. Elsie covered it completely in the cloth. "You won't keep it out?"

"I think I'll have to pack the entire house up soon. Anyway it's not important anymore, these *things*. It's his story—it goes with him now."

"Are there any artifacts? From the Gondiwindi?"

"I don't think so. There was a war here against the local people. In that war the biggest victim was the culture, you know? All this stuff—" she lifted the wrapped *coolamon* out in front of her "—well, culture has no armies, does it?" she said.

August bit the inside of her mouth and began to wrap the next frame.

Elsie put her hand at August's ear. "Don't be sad for his life, August. He had a very happy life. We aren't victims in this story anymore—do you see that?"

They wrapped some more in the easy silence. Poppy the storyteller, not Nana.

A timer alarm buzzed from the kitchen and Elsie placed the lid atop the tea chest. She stood up and leaned against the door entrance, turned back to August.

"Please don't be a victim, Augie. It's an easy road, that one. I never let Alb walk it. The land, the earth is the victim now—that needs an army, I reckon. She's the one in real trouble."

"Nana?" August stepped out after her. "Why can't you stop the mine? Why can't people protest it? Isn't that what you want? That's what you meant—you had hope before?"

"I don't think so, Aug," she said, entering the kitchen. "Too many people want this to happen, everyone at that town hall meeting was for the mine. Everyone, darlin', even Ed."

"Southerly Eddie?" August asked, as she followed her nana into the kitchen.

She nodded. "It's progress, isn't it?"

Elsie washed her hands in the sink, then drew a bowl of cold water as August rested against the wall.

"We did that," Elsie continued. "We protested in the street, for our rights and against the wars overseas. We protested with flowers, protested to save the river being dammed, peaceful protests." She looked out the back window. "We carried flowers in the street. Afterward we threw the flowers on the side of the road when they all bent in the heat." She took a tray from the freezer and bent the plastic mold over the bowl until the ice cubes fell in.

"It's too late I think, Aug. We're just a few small people, anyway." She drained a saucepan of steaming eggs and placed them in the ice water.

August shifted to the sink with Elsie, "I don't think it's right, I think something needs to be done. It doesn't make sense to me."

Elsie touched the pads of her fingertips atop the eggs, reading the temperature like a ouija board. "You can't ask hungry folks to go on a hunger strike, bub. But . . ." Elsie hovered above her eggs and then pushed her thumb into a sphere, cracking the shell.

"You mean because the town needs jobs?"

"That too. Forget it, Augie, it's a done thing now."

She placed the first shelled egg on a paper towel.

"You said but? But what?"

"But?" she asked back to August and answered vaguely. "Well, food isn't just the things you can eat. That's all. You should take a walk. Have you gone down to the river since you're back or what?"

"I'll take a walk, yeah," August said, absentmindedly crushing the discarded eggshells on the sideboard.

August took her nana's elbow and hugged her tight; she'd felt breathless, like she'd shed a skin. As if she had something she needed to say, finally, but then couldn't find it.

With her hands in the water Elsie hummed the beginning of a tune.

"I'll see Eddie," August said. She looked back to her nana who was shelling eggs easily in the bowl of ice water. She didn't look up.

FIFTEEN

Reverend Ferdinand Greenleaf's letter to Dr. George Cross,
2nd August 1915, continued

III

It had become clear to me, in the granary of the Motherland, that
the first countrymen may have sown wheat but reaped thorns. I was
in many ways still a babe when we arrived in Australia. A small and
unworldly child. As time progressed, many of the kind residents of
our town, our town that was expanding with vineyards and less sour
white wine each year, revealed to me our heritage and how it was that
we ended up on the other side of the world. That they themselves were
persecuted and exiled and sought refuge in this country, and now to
suffer this great harassment because we came from that same place has
me questioning the reason of man to no end. I must tell you here and
appeal to your sensibilities—I am shoulder to shoulder with my fellow
citizens under the British flag and am no threat to the State. Yet, what
has occurred toward people that I know also to stand shoulder to
shoulder with Britain, and to be simple and good-natured in their lives
here, is most deplorable and must be aired.

After numerous subsequent visits through the grasslands to
Massacre Plains, I took it upon myself to write to the Colonial
Secretary. The letter was sent in May 1879 upon the subject, and,
after waiting two months, I received a kind reply signifying his
interest in my proposal to erect a House of Mercy, and requesting
certain items of information, which, according to my memory, I
supplied. It was six months after this reply, in searching for a suitable
site for a Mission, that I found a portion of the river at a dogleg rapid
below a large rock peak, large enough to get one's bearings from each
corner of the property's five hundred acres. The land had recently
been revoked from lease and I had hoped that I should thus escape
any unpleasantness with the resident squatter, but when word filtered
through the district that I would establish the Mission it was not well
received. I had come upon the sentiment while lodging at the less
aristocratic hotel in Massacre Plains, as my preferred accommodation
was closed upon arrival.

I had ridden the horse to the rear of the premises, where several
rough-looking men had gathered. I dismounted to enquire after
the manager. There was a strange manner to these men, and I soon
ascertained that they were, more or less, under the influence of
liquor as they hurriedly cleared away bottles and pannikins from
the back table. It was clear I had interrupted their recreation, but
on saying, "Well, men, I see what you have been doing, now don't
be dishonest, make a clean breast of it," they seemed to regain their
wits. I explained who I was and what I wanted. They directed me
to the front of the hotel and the manager received me kindly, at the
same time apologizing for the disorderly state of domestic affairs. On
signifying my wish to remain overnight, he said I had better go on
and bed down at the woolshed some three miles distant. But on my

complaining of fatigue, he agreed I could stay, saying he expected every patron to provide his own blankets. Having assured him I could do that, the horse was turned out and I turned in to my room.

To my surprise over the course of the evening, three of the young men came to me and said they had recently been making asses of themselves, and would I give them the abstainer's pledge. I should only be too happy to do so, I replied. The result was that six took the pledge, some for a year, and some for half that, but all with the understanding that it was not to commence until twelve o'clock at night, so that they might finish the supply they had on hand. I made myself as comfortable as circumstances would allow, my greatest discomfort being the sounds of revelry from the adjoining room, for as soon as my address had finished they hurried away to drain their bottles, which I think they managed to do. As I was departing the next morning and having not complained of the noise, the manager said that he had heard from other fellows in the region that I was a stuck-up parson and he was glad to find I was not so. Little did I know, those same men taking abstinence would later become the greatest cause of distress on our very lives at the Mission.

That day, on passing the local Police Depot on my route north, I found several unfortunate Natives chained like so many dogs to each other around the neck. They had no space to even turn their shoulders from each steel fixture. A bolt attached them to the main chain, with only a few links between each. The main chain ran along and was secured to a tree. As though that were not sufficient to prevent their escape, some of the poor beings were shackled by the ankles, and in such a condition of squalor that they had obviously sat there hour after hour, and perhaps day after day. They were awaiting the arrival of the Police Magistrate, and thence to be tried, or so the young constable told me. On my asking why they were without complete clothing—just a rag covering their modesty, and in their own mess, and, furthermore, chained!—he simply told me that it was "necessary." I had no business remaining there and no authority to intervene, so I proceeded north once again along an established wagon track, with little to engage my attention except for the birdsong and the appearance of a few weary kangaroos. Occasionally I passed a wool team with its inevitable Native girl or woman attached. On making brief acquaintance with several of the drivers, I asked why they had females with them. Some replied boastfully that they preferred their docility compared to the male workers, while others did not blush on admitting that they had them for immoral purposes.

The land I prevailed upon ran along the most bountiful area of the Murrumby River where around the banks hundreds of solid acacia pines were growing, fit for construction. The only requirement the Government made of my endeavor was that the Mission be at a sufficient distance from the town to minimize contact with White society. This requirement I met and over the years made further provisions to separate us as much as I could from the township. In the end this was for the betterment of my residents themselves. Only on the occasion of Queen Victoria's birthday commemoration each year did I encourage all the residents to visit the town for the blanket distribution. I encouraged them to return immediately and not to engage with the political discussions over Corroboree. It is common knowledge that the neighboring Natives like to gather during blanket distribution, each May, to persuade each other to demand autonomy. Although I know a marked diminution in number of the race gather

there and each year there are reports that death has been busy. They
say that soon, the miserable doling of blankets for the ancient lords of
the soil will no longer be required. They say with their decrease that
the Natives must soon wholly disappear from the face of the Earth.
It is written in the local express that soon the Aborigine will be as
rare on the banks of the Murrumby as in the streets of Sydney. On
the contrary I had still seen a number of, seemingly free, male and
female Blacks carrying rocks into the river, which I later learned were
for constructing fish traps. The Blacks of this area who seemed still
in relation with the land were perhaps the finest I had seen, very tall,
lean, and nimble.

My friend Pastor Otto Baumann, who had his own small Mission
of a hundred souls set up some two hundred miles south and four
hundred miles inland by an artisanal lake, had disposed himself,
sharing my ambition that Prosperous Mission would be complete
within the season. In God's grace, with my small wages from my
traveling work as clergyman, Baumann and I were able to begin work
in real earnest, cutting down trees and preparing timber for building.
In about a month, two huts—the first I had hoped for a married
Black couple as occupants and the other for myself—were drawing
near completion, and so it was the correct time to search for our
householders.

With Baumann, we discovered a little camp of women and
children south of the river and persuaded them to go along with
us. The women did treat me with great suspicion, and I reasoned
that they had not met well with White men before. They seemed to
understand none of my language and I, as to be expected, understood
none of theirs. This became a great frustration to me, and although
Baumann tried some of the few words he had mastered from his

region, none volunteered to speak the same language back to him, and we left without the women and children in our care. Baumann suggested that I learn some of the Blacks of Massacre Plains language. That I should integrate them into sermons if I were to truly have them converted to the Bible. Over the years I have tried. In those early days, Baumann and myself then gave in to building the huts of the Mission once more and erected a schoolhouse for proposed lessons. After only two months Baumann was obliged to return to his own Mission, so it was left to myself to set to work on sowing the grain I had acquired for a reasonable sum.

It was impressed on me the importance of sustaining a source of consistent supply at the Mission, so of the five hundred acres at my disposal, I set aside fifty close to the riverbank for the experiment of planting a crop. I planted a kitchen garden, the soil dug like ashes. Orchids, lilies, and mosses flourished among the strange grain crop that had been growing in some patches here and there by the river. Later, when I enquired, the Natives referred to the grass as *gulaa* and motioned to their mouths as if it were edible. The straw of the Natives' grain I threshed and buried in pits, and threw in with it everything that I thought would rot and turn to manure. I dug the lot in with the grass, and having removed the fallen timber to burn it from the ground, I dug in the ashes with it. I then hoed it up, never exceeding more than seven or perhaps eight rods a day. I had merely scratched over ground, but properly done this, I think, was almost equal to plowing. Then I let it lie as long as I could, exposed to air and sun, and, just before I sowed my seed, turned it all up afresh. Once I had reaped the wheat I hoed it again, and harrowed it fine, then sowed it with turnip seed, which mellowed it and prepared it for the next year. By this process it seemed the silt took on a good color after the once-over each following year. In that way it was not like my father's vineyard—which had been horribly dry, and had needed thrice doing. I was able to oblige a local settler to loan me two Blackfellows he had in his possession to assist me. Quite freely they got to work building, fencing, gardening, clearing, and assisting me with the new crop. The workers were able to communicate some of their greetings, and I dutifully noted them in my journal and endeavored thereafter to greet them in their own language—which seemed to please them deeply. In the evenings after my work at the Mission or when traveling the Plains, I read my passages by the bark resin light and after retiring thought on all that I had witnessed and thanked God that I had the piece of land in order to build a home of safety for the poor waifs and strays.

SIXTEEN

songlines—*yarang gudhi-dhuray* Means song having line and *birrang-dhuray-gudhi* means journey having song. These lines are our early map-making. They measure our places, our impossible distances, and they are passed down through story songs and dances. The lines are there, but sometimes the *gudhi* is lost. The Gondiwindi lost the *gudhi*, only now it's coming back to us again.

star constellation the Southern Cross—*gibirrgan* Sometimes only the women would come and collect me and we'd go and sit by the fire at the riverbank. They taught me how to count up to a thousand by counting the stars. First we'd start at the less bright ones, I'd count along my toes, count with each joint in my legs, then the brighter, those I'd count with arms, elbows, fingers, then the brightest with my face, *tap tap tap* on my nose, eyes, chin, and ear all night. The brightest stars were *gibirrgan*—the constellation of the Southern Cross, which features on this country's flag—it is made of five bright stars almost in a cross shape. The women told me the story of *gibirrgan* once, and they'd begin the story with "When the world was young": Nguwanda—a great leader of a tribe who had no sons but four beautiful daughters—was getting very old. He'd be leaving soon so he gathered his daughters together and told them he'd be going because he was at the end of his time, but he didn't want to leave the daughters without protection because they had no brother to look after them. He said, "I want you to come live with me in the sky and I've talked to a clever and magic man and he is willing to help you all come live in the sky with me." When their father died they went to see the clever magic man, who was sitting by a fire braiding a long silver rope, plucked from the wiry silver hairs in his beard. When the daughters found out the only way to reach their father was to climb the rope to the sky, they became even more scared. Eventually the silver-bearded man convinced them it would be safe, and they reached the top of the rope and stayed with their father, who was the brightest star—Centaurus. The Seven Sisters are there too. The Greeks call them Pleiades and we call them Mulayndynang.

suicide—*balubuningidyilinya* We ran the karate here and the mothers' group that turned into cooking classes; those young ones found something they cared for and that they were good at and could improve at. We tried to do something to keep the young ones busy. All the *balubuningidyilinya* is the old pain coming through. It breaks my heart.

rabbit, a wild—*wadha-gung* The problem was the rabbits, before myxomatosis got them. They were brought over by a grazier who thought he'd breed them for target practice on his station. He started with twelve pairs, and some rabbiters made a good living, but within a couple of years there were thirteen million of the buggers eating the seedlings and the crops and the native plants meant for the kangaroos, the bilbies, and wallabies. Then they brought in the foxes to get the rabbits but instead they went for the native animals. They built the rabbit-proof fence from one end of the country to the other to keep the rabbits out of the "granary of the Motherland." Too bloody late they'd built that fence.

raven, native—*waagan, wandyu* If you know Massacre Plains then I would bet you know the *waagan* or the *wandyu*. Everywhere you walk in this town or in the bush, you can be sure that he's watching you—waiting for you to become food, maybe. On the farms when the ewes are giving birth you have to keep a close watch and get the lambs off the paddock. The raven will eat them as soon as they're birthed otherwise. There's a story I got told about Wahn the *waagan* when I was time traveling way, way back then and how he liked to watch the pelican gangs. He sat outside a gang one day and waited and watched. After a while, an old pelican wandered out to ask Wahn what he was doing. Wahn said he was hungry, so the pelican went and talked to the elders of the group and they allowed Wahn to come and sit by their fire, and offered him a bit of food they had. After a while it was time for the pelicans to go and get more food for their babies nesting in the trees. Wahn wanted to eat the eggs of the pelican, but he found they were hatched already, so he put a spell on the tree and sent the branches high into the sky. The young cried out for food and when the pelicans came to feed them they had to climb the trees but couldn't reach their little pelicans. From then on the pelicans keep their babies low and always keep their distance from Wahn—as do all the other birds. Well, I love the *waagan* and I think he got bad press in that story. The *waagan* has a crafty reputation but that doesn't mean he's evil. He doesn't have many bird friends and he likes to be alone most of the time, but they are a faithful bunch. When they mate, they hold each other's beaks like they are having a long kiss, and when they are courting each other they interlock their feet midair. See, the raven he has his mate for life, and I think that's a good thing—how *waagan* keeps his family together. That's important.

respect—*yindyamarra* I think I've come to realize that with some things, you cannot receive them unless you give them too. Unless you've even got the opportunity to give and receive. Only equals can share respect, otherwise it's a game of masters and slaves—someone always has the upper hand when they are demanding respect. But *yindyamarra* is another thing too, it's a way of life—a life of kindness, gentleness, and respect at once. That seems like a good thing to share, our *yindyamarra*.

rib—*dharrar* In the Book of Genesis 2:18–22 it says that woman was made from man's rib. Elsie said, "That's a load of bullshit." I laughed. In the end though, I came home to the Bible because it was my friend when I was a boy. Just the goodness in there, and the stories. I think I take the words where I want them to go. My ancestors' stories and the Bible too. Anytime we argued in our marriage, she'd scream and point to her side, "I'm not your *dharrar*! You want a *dharrar*, get to the butcher!" It's a good insult that one, I hope we taught the girls that— not to be anyone's rib.

river—*bila* Now you know where the word *billabong* comes from. From us. Everything comes back to the *bila*—all life, and with it all time. Our songlines originate there, our lives fed from there, and it's where our spirits dwell in the end. Even the Reverend was drawn to the river, there he recited Isaiah 44:3, *For I will pour water on the* *thirsty land, and streams on the dry ground; I will pour my Spirit upon your offspring, and my blessing on your descendants.* Can't imagine how it hurts not to see that water come anymore.

queen bee, bee—*darribun, ngaraang* The *ngaraang* is in danger now, whole colonies are dying and the queen bee *darribun* is left, like on a chessboard, without any pawns, with all the worker *ngaraang* dying off. The bee puts off leaving the hive until later in their lives, when they are adults, because with less flowers it means collecting pollen is hard work for the bee, and many die of exhaustion before they make honey—*warrul*—and never return to the home. If the pesticides from the farms stress the hive or the bees while they are out foraging in a big sweep, they can die. This triggers a very fast, too-early maturation of the next generation of bees, and they leave the hive too early, before they're ready, and a whole colony collapses. The Gondiwindi have been like that, scattered children without the thing that nourishes them, without a compass to get back home.

quiet place with many pretty flowers—*girra-wiiny* Keep your eyes peeled for wildflowers on country, like wild flax and yellow wattle bloom, and the orchids and lilies—that's edible, they're called *dirramaay*. They aren't just for food and medicine, but their stems and leaves can be used for weaving baskets too. The flowers also tell us when other things are happening—like when the *ngawang*, the happy wanderer plant, flowers in purple then we know it's a time when the fat *guya* can be caught in the rivers and the lakes.

pair, two—*bula* I was buried by scripture, but buoyed by hope, and so when we got our second spring, having two little daughters again in Jedda and August, we opened up Prosperous for all the people. The *bula* and I would go for long walks up to Kengal Rock. I'd explain how the old people walked up there through those same pastures, used their stone axe before White men brought their own metal axe, where lovers met and they left marks on the trees, or long round scars where they would chop into the bark of the tree, gently break it away, and have a long, rounded dish for carrying baby. Or if the wood was strong enough, for digging roots and tubers of the plants. I'd lead them to the river to see where the old people fished and the rocks arranged on the bare river flat where irrigation was first made, and where the old people had fish traps. That's what the old people ate—fish from Murrumby, mussels from Murrumby, crayfish and *yingaa* too. And they ate kangaroo grass from the plains—they ground up the seed and made their own bread and cake in the oven of the earth. They made bread and cake long before the wise Egyptians did. *Bula* would look up at me at those times, eyes wide, all the wonder in the world bustling in their minds. They are my fondest memories, showing *bula* what great people they come from long ago.

parent, to be like the parent—*buwubarra* Elsie and I got to *buwubarra* to those sweet *bula*.

SEVENTEEN

August walked along the driveway and up to Southerly. Around the perimeter of Southerly House was a bandage of green grass. There were no native plants in the Falstaff garden, only hedges, tulips, half-century-old rose bushes, and the fruit grove. The house was painted pumpkin with a grey trim, but it used to change every few years: Dulux blue gum, Dulux crème, Dulux terracotta. August had paid very close attention to the Falstaff house. She was always hiding in the bushes or trying to get in the door one way or another.

There had been bigger differences from Prosperous than little—but the little had been on the outer walls—the gable ends had ornate patterns, the woodwork carved with intricate grooves, trim was polished, there were two fountains, solar garden lights, and a two-toned, diamond-shaped pebble path that ran to their veranda, and they had a yellow hose rolled neatly on a special hose-holder by the house. They'd always had a Welcome brush mat at their front door that looked as if it had never been used. There was no mat anymore; Southerly was different, that bandage of grass had grown out but Eddie hadn't bothered to attend to it. The whipper snipper was for sale now. It lay on the altar of the ute's flatbed like a crucifix. There was no point cutting grass when it'd be rubble soon. Eddie saw August approaching and wrapped his arms around his chest, pausing for her. He'd paused his whole life for her.

"Saw ya nan—she seems alright?"

August walked up to the foot of Southerly. "Think that's how she copes, keeping busy."

"How'd you cope . . ." he stretched his arms aside his body, that had filled out since he was a teenager, "for the last ten years?" He looked at her watching him pull a collared shirt on and his face blushed, his face that August noticed was a fully grown man's and no longer a boy's.

August heard a pulse in her ear, looked away, and sat on the step. "With what?"

"Everything . . . you know . . ." Eddie trailed off, sat beside her. "Did you ever hear from your mum?"

She hadn't, and had stopped trying years before. She figured her mother was ashamed, and buried by it, that she'd crossed a line between sad and mad.

"Nah." She reached into her pocket, lit a cigarette.

Eddie nudged her, "Go on." And she passed him the packet and a sleeve of matches.

He lit his cigarette and stole a look at her thighs, bare below her shorts.

"You eat much?" He could see it.

Her pulse became a thump in her ears, her tone defensive. "Yeah."

"You look different."

"How am I different?" She knew she was, but didn't know how. She couldn't remember what she was to anyone before. It felt as if she'd arrived at the person she was in the last decade without a choice. As if she resembled nothing so much as the face and name she was before. It was as if she couldn't remember herself the way she was supposed to be.

"You're still yourself, I didn't mean it in a bad way. You just look changed."

"So do you," August said, but didn't say aloud that she thought it was an improvement.

"You got a Pommy bloke, I guess?"

"No." There was something stuck between them. The old times that neither of them wanted to be aired. All the unsayable things.

He went on, "Of all the places, I can't believe you went to England!" Eddie undid his bootlaces, kicked them off.

"Why?" she said, thinking as she had thought as a kid, and still at eighteen, that England was where kids were born pure, with tea time and school head teachers, and long socks and boiled sweets and miniature sailboat races along icy rivers. Childhoods like in the old books she'd read.

"I dunno, because it's not your heritage. 'Cos Australia's still pink."

"What's that mean—Australia is pink?"

"On the world map—pink, isn't it? You're a British subject even if you're a Gondi!"

He laughed then, but August couldn't laugh. They'd joked like that when they were kids, but she'd grown out of it. Seeing August's stone face made Eddie wish he hadn't said the thing. He began to button his shirt to the throat, trying to hide the provocation in flannel.

"Sorry, it's just a joke," he offered.

"Why did you stay here then?" August dragged on the cigarette.

"For the view, and who else is gunna do it? No bastard."

She blew smoke into the hot air, away from the conversation.

"So you got a fella, or what?"

"What do you care?"

"I care," he said, and looked to find her eyes—her eyes that met his. They scanned each other's faces for a moment. Eddie leaned into the small curl of August's lip as if it suggested an invitation.

And they kissed, just like that. Just enough that their lips were touching, that their faces were magnified and momentarily blocked the sunlight, a tiny truce.

She turned away, stubbed the cigarette, and stood, "I gotta go," she began to make her way to Prosperous, "and help Nan."

"Alright?" he said, confused, but she was too far away to hear.

"Can I help?"

Elsie sat a pot of onions ahead of August. They cooked all afternoon and the heat brought in the wafts of the drying wheat. Elsie let August make the sticky white rice, and only chimed in to spill a dash of coconut milk into the murky bubbling water. She then had August cube the hard carrots and black radish and pick the coriander and green onions. Elsie took over stirring and added the brown sugar, aniseed and ginger and specially ordered red paste, and fish sauce. She dropped the pieces of chicken into the sauce. Her nana was glowing when she was cooking. Then she shook the little orange-and-black tin above the pot and the entire house reeked of Keen's curry powder.

The smell of the kitchen reminded August of the kids at school holding their noses as she sat down to eat her hot lunch, the students gawking back from their cut-crusted, soccer-ball ham sandwiches, their packets of Smith's salt and vinegar, their frozen juice poppers. There were other kids that got the same gawks: Jody, who spent the lunch hour begging other kids for "a bite" or for "ten cents for a sausage roll"; Luke, whose mum worked at the local motel and who always had hotel butter pats and a single roll of bread, and would sit in the schoolyard preparing his sandwich. There was also August's friend Louise, who ate cold noodles with chopsticks from a clear plastic bowl. If she wondered about division at school, they were divided only by being *poor* and *more poor*. Valley, or Mission farm, or suburb poor. There is something to food, August thought, no longer ever hungry but forever hungry—it made them different or the same.

Eddie had been at a different school. Had he been thinking about her since school, she wondered. Had he really wanted her heart, all broken too early, with its missing bits already? Or just wanted to kiss her because he was sorry, because he knew Jedda and Poppy too, because everything was beginning again or finally ending? She didn't know. She cared, but tried not to. Not then, not with everything else she needed to care about.

Later Aunt Missy arrived and Aunt Mary, Aunt Betty, and Aunt Nora too, who'd grown up with Poppy and then without Poppy, at and then away from the Station. Elsie wiped her hands, set the wooden spoon on the sink, and retrieved the linen. She handed August the stack of laundered sheets and sent her out to make up the annex beds while she and the Aunties continued cooking.

The annex doors had bolt locks without bolts on the outside; inside every surface was thick with dust. August, having worked most areas of the pub, even the bed-and-breakfast rooms, knew where to start, and opened up the windows first, leaving the doors ajar. Outside she shook the pillows, brought them in and concealed the yellow of them in patterned cases. She flipped the sagged mattresses and tucked the stiff sheets over them, tucking in the thoughts of how many had rested there before. She swept the floor, hung the wool blankets outside on the line and beat them with the worn broom until they shed all the flakes of skin and dust. Bringing the blankets in one by one, she laid them edge to edge on top of the sheets, turning the linen down to make an inviting triangle over each blanket. In the shaded area around Prosperous, she cut stems of native orchid. She didn't spot Eddie working in the field. She placed the flowers in water tumblers on each of the four side tables.

One side table had a shallow concealed drawer with a little groove at the top. August jiggled the drawer unstuck. A Holy Bible lay inside. She took it out and sat on the made bed. *This is a book*, her poppy had said the first time he placed one in her hands, speaking with fortified sureness. *I want you to read it as if every sentence inside is a lie and, if you find anything true, I want you to write it down.*

She hadn't known if it was a trick or a challenge, but he'd assured her she'd get a dollar coin every time she was right. It had been therapy in his mind, for Jedda being missing. She remembered how she'd filled half an exercise book over summer holidays, and was looking forward to a good amount of candy-buying money at the end. He'd rewarded her with two dollars for the trouble. August had looked through the pages of quotes she'd written and found the two marked "Yes" by her poppy, with a circle around the words. She could only now remember the first. It was Proverbs, *Death and life are in the power of the tongue.*

August took the Bible out of the annex and dropped it into the wheelie bin beside the house. It was never the book she was searching for.

Elsie's energy level had changed since August arrived. She'd charge on keeping busy like a train getting up a hill, and then would slow and become silent again, coasting down the decline. After the Aunties retired in the annex beds, neither Elsie nor August ate the curry;

they instead took turns making tea for each other. In the evening they cooked some more, a stew and a vegetable lasagna. All the dishes were cooled and Tupperware-sealed, placed into the fridge for the farewell.

August poured two glasses of wine she'd picked up from town, downed one quickly over the sink and then filled it up to a polite level. Elsie was ironing lengths of white tablecloths along the dining table. The iron steamed while she massaged her hands, waiting for the pain in her knuckles to pass. August placed and then nodded at the wineglass. "I can do the ironing for you," she offered gently, not wanting her nana to feel she couldn't very well do it herself.

Elsie took the glass with one sore hand and flicked the cord from the outlet with the other. "Did you eat anything today?"

August wanted to ask her the same thing, but they just let the question hang there. The sad, shrinking women.

"Should we sit outside?" August said instead, and pushed the glass door along its track.

They settled on the twin outdoor chairs, the cane bones cushioned with fleece throws. Spike padded up the deck and dropped onto Elsie's feet.

"Was Poppy writing a book? Eddie told me that he was."

"No, he was writing things down on paper—a sort of dictionary—he was trying to remember the words. He'd been writing it for a month or more."

"Can I see it?"

"I can't for the life of me think where it is, Augie. Have a look in his office, I'd like to see that too."

They sipped their wine. "I'll look again," August said.

"*Yingaa*, that was one of the words I saw him writing on those pages."

"*Yingaa?*"

"It means yabby, the bush lobster, you know . . ." Elsie sipped and added enthusiastically, "Our first date was eating yabbies."

"You and Pop?"

"He brought me out here," Elsie held her glass ahead of her into the dark. "It was the first time I visited Prosperous. He walked me out to the dam and told me all about *yingaa*. City girl I was then, I didn't know anything about yabbies, never had 'em before! I told him that and he ran back to the house and I followed him. Inside," Elsie shifted to turn to the kitchen, "he starts riffling through the garbage bin there," she laughed. "When Alb looked up at me I must've looked so shocked! I was thinking, *What's this man doing in the bin?* Then he held two chop bones up triumphant and we went back out to the dam with a line off of the clothesline. He tied up a bone at each end and dropped them in the water, and there we walked around the outside slowly dragging our bait. When the water flinched twice and he showed me how to ease my line out of the dam, lo and behold—well, that was my first feast of *yingaa*." Her nana shook her head and sipped again, smiling at August. "He was writing about that!"

"What a catch," August said, and the two women laughed.

"Why did you come back for Pop?"

Elsie thought for just a moment. "I think I noticed that your pop and I could do good things together. That our love could bounce off the world and I was that age, I guess. I was open to him and I knew straight away that he loved me, that he wouldn't put me down."

"Put you down?"

"That we were both Koori, that we would lift each other because we both knew we needed it."

Their goodness made August feel sad, thinking about her own

mother, how so much went wrong for her. "Why'd all the bad stuff happen to Mum, when you two were good together?"

Her nana shook her head. She didn't have an answer, and while she struggled for one, the lights in the workers' annex flicked off. They both looked over to the windows gone dark, the Aunties had turned in. "Who else is coming tomorrow?" August asked, taking cue that her nana didn't want to answer a hopeless question. Or couldn't.

"Just the family—mob from here and there. Uncle Fred should arrive, I think, all the way from the cane fields up north. You remember him?"

"Not really. Just his arm, and that he bought banana ice creams for us once."

Elsie drummed her fingers on her glass. "I used to think he was the most miserable man on earth, but I like him now. He's your pop's older cousin."

"What happened to his arm, anyway?" August asked, bold with wine.

"He came back from serving in the war. He wasn't injured there, but they said some shrapnel or something hit him. So he had all this pain in his arm when he got back, nerve damage or something. Doctors couldn't work it out; he traveled all over the country seeing specialists. No one could work it out and paracetamol didn't change a thing. He decided he wanted the doctors to take it off; he even worked with a bad arm slashing sugar cane to save up to pay for it himself. Not one doctor would do it though, 'cos of his functioning hand on the end of his arm. So, one day he got the idea to cut the thing off himself . . ." Elsie was shaking her head, her face dimmed once more. "You can't always see a thing that hurts. He bought an axe and a hatch's spring or what have you, started a fire in a tin pail, cut the hand off with his

115

homemade guillotine, singed the arteries, and then threw his hand in the fire so it couldn't be reattached."

August gasped and almost yelled, her face contorted in horror. "What the *hell*?"

Elsie continued, nonchalant. "So they took the rest of the arm off for him and now he is such a happy fella. Goes to show . . ."

"Show what?"

"The things people will do for pain relief." She rubbed her knuckles against her knee.

"Don't chop your hands off, Nan!"

She looked at August shocked, and they both started laughing again. When they'd laughed enough to stir the owls, Elsie said, "You've always had a good nature, girl—you know you can talk to me about anything, okay."

It was a statement; she'd just wanted August to know. "I know," August said, reassured and reassuring at once. August knew her nana wasn't her guardian anymore, that she could be her confidante, but August still didn't know how to say the things. The field was buzzing, a sort of beating rhythm. The locusts had settled into their meal for the night. There was a crescent moon and no light fell onto the old field.

"To Alb," Elsie said, raising her almost full wineglass to the darkness.

"To Pop," August said, holding her hand high, and the sliver of silver moon bent through the empty glass.

Eighteen

Reverend Ferdinand Greenleaf's letter to Dr. George Cross,
2nd August 1915, continued

IV

As the crops began to grow, I would visit the Blacks' camp and offer wheat seeds and the knotted carrots from the kitchen garden. In this way I began to build on the trust we would need to occupy the Mission. It was after many of my humble visits that the Natives in the territory, hearing that a home was properly prepared for them, began to arrive in groups of twos and tens at Prosperous Mission, our House of Mercy, for protection and food. The Lord blessed us during the following year's harvest with the first of many births at the Mission. A small, beautiful half-caste girl was born in December 1881 and I noted her birth in my logbook—she was conferred with good health and a Christian name—Mercy.

The accommodation was small, and our means were slender, but seeing so many unfortunate women and children in a state of hunger and nakedness touched my deepest sympathies, and I was compelled to admit them, even if I had hoped initially for married couples only. People of the town warned me that the Natives would never sleep in the places I planned to build for them, but when the second and third huts were completed I had the satisfaction of seeing the Natives happy in possession of their own dwelling. Quite a township sprang up in the lonely bush, with my own home, the schoolhouse (which also served as a church), fifteen two-room cottages for married couples, a dormitory befitting fifty girls and single women, another for the same number of boys and single men, a storeroom, three outbuildings, and last but not least, a teacher's cottage, for after the second year I was compelled to give up the duties of teacher and secured the valuable services of my learned friend from the south, Hans Keller, to fill that responsible post. In so doing I was free to assist the male residents erect fences for the Mission property to secure our crops and grass from surrounding stock. I witnessed them over the years climbing the few remaining gum trees and crossing the often fast-flowing waters of the river with such certain ease and immense grace, and I was glad to see them set to work keenly and under my clear instruction.

We had no regular or certain income except my donations for clergy work, so we were frequently reduced to the deepest poverty. In my frequent absence I appointed Keller to be at hand as Manager.

At times we were without either mutton or flour, to say nothing of the necessities of life. But although our work during the first many months was very hard, and our privations continued to be many, these trials did not affect us nearly as much as did the cruel conduct from those around us, people who were professedly Christian. Over the years I've come to understand they had one desire—and that was to deal with the Natives in their own way. In different ways these mean-spirited people sought to break up the Mission and to scatter the Blacks that had grown, in almost two years, in excess of ninety souls, including forty students on the roll and thirty in regular attendance.

On one occasion, in the third year of our Mission, while absent due to presiding over a wedding, an individual who passed for a gentleman sent a case of gin to the women's camp. At a small camp, only a mile from the Mission square, the "gentleman" had proceeded to make them all drunk, and invited his fellows. Keller informed me the scene that followed was pure evil—debauchery by the single and married men of the town against the hapless women and girls. On another occasion, again while I was away, the keeper of the less aristocratic hotel where I had once taken accommodation supplied the camp with drink again. He called in the White men whom I believe to be the same men I gave rights of abstinence to, and, as Keller again informed me, the scene was much the same. That following morning I returned to the camp and witnessed old women and quite young girls helplessly intoxicated. One poor creature, with a half-caste babe upon her bosom, staggered toward me. "What have you been doing, Daisy?" I said. "I have been drinking, *gudyi*." "Who gave you the drink?" "Mr. Murray," referring to the publican I had crossed paths with. Daisy was very upset and begged for my protection. She said she did not want to take the drink but they had forced her, and then forced her still further performing their sordid deeds, before leaving. Daisy was bruised and swollen about the face and a tooth had been knocked from her mouth. I decided it was best to send Daisy, whom I guessed to be about fifteen, out for service and so she was placed with what I believed to be a good Christian family in the north. Her family were quite distressed at this, but I vindicated that the families were known to me on strong recommendation and that she would return for visits.

I also obtained a firearm for the premises from Baumann, who showed me how to pack the gunpowder and to aim confidently. I endeavored only in the neediest circumstances to leave the Mission for formal duties as clergyman.

I did not want to leave my Mission, but at times we had no choice as far as funds were concerned. On each of my returning journeys I went around to every resident to let them know I had returned, reassuring those I had promised indeed to save. Some months later, one evening I was awoken to the girls running to my hut for protection, as wicked White men had broken into their dormitory. I dashed to the girls' quarters and shooed the two brutes away and was compelled to mount my horse and pursue the offenders. I rode four miles, not sure what it was I could or would do. Though I was unable to apprehend them in the end, I think it was clear to the residents that I was loyal in my avowal to protect them.

After many months of peace another unfortunate incident occurred, when in broad daylight a young settler from a neighboring Station deliberately rode into the Mission square. After tearing off the stirrup iron from his saddle and brandishing it over his head, he swore that he would kill the first man, Black or White, who ventured near him. After keeping us in a state of terror for half an hour, the settler threatened to break up the Mission, saying that if I did not abandon it I should have to stand the revolt by the town's men. They want to be a law unto themselves. I understood that the carnal interests of these men was why they wanted the Blacks to return to lives of disorder in the open camps. They would not tolerate someone who sought to bring "peace and goodwill" to the poor Black man, for it was common knowledge that the monstrous traffic of the Natives' bodies and souls had been routine before I arrived.

And so, after writing yet again requesting police intervention, which was to never eventuate, we took all safeguarding measures upon ourselves. I made certain that the residents did not wander away from the Mission any longer. I was sure to keep the girls busy with a female teacher sent from Sydney, who filled their days: schooling of most importance, and at times the rudimentary details of cooking, cleaning, and sewing as with most institutions. At close of day we made certain the children slept in the dormitories throughout the night. With the help of the male Mission residents, we reinforced our fences, and above the main house we engraved a pledge of our unity. With the chisel and by scorching each character it read:

BY GRACE ALONE

THROUGH FAITH ALONE

ON THE BASIS OF THE SCRIPTURE ALONE

I stood back to inspect it after hanging the beam and was very pleased indeed. For in my deepest heart, that trembled with fear, so accustomed to circumspection, I hoped it would protect us in the storm that I anticipated was brewing.

NINETEEN

play—*girinya* When we were boys at the Home we played cricket, handball, marbles, leapfrog, and spear games. We made the spears with bulrush reeds or maybal sticks that we'd run against stones to sharpen and tie little stones with string that we'd unravel from our blankets. One boy would act out the kangaroo and the other boy would do the throwing. We'd hide our toy spears under the stairs out the back where we lined up with our hands on our hearts to sing "God Save the Queen." Nothing is ever terrible all the time, even during the worst time. When you're a kid you always find a way to play, *girinya*.

platypus—*biladurang* There's a story about *biladurang* and how that platypus came to be only in this country—but it starts with a little duck called Gaygar. Once, long ago, Gaygar disobeyed her elders, disrespected the values of her family and she left the safe lake and began to swim into the creek away from her family into waters that ducks weren't supposed to go. There she was captured by a water rat called Bigun and he kept her up at a creek for a whole season. When she escaped back to the lake, all the ducks had their babies, and Gaygar had hers too. When her family saw Gaygar's young they shook their heads and told Gaygar she had to leave, otherwise bad things would happen to her family if she stayed. So Gaygar took her strange babies down through the water system, through the rivers and catchments. She finally found a spot where her young were happy. But it was too cold for Gaygar, since she didn't have fur like her children. When Gaygar passed away, her babies stayed in the cool rivers, all webbed feet, billed, and covered in fur. *Biladurang.*

plover bird—*didadida* I learnt this word at the Boys' Home. *Didadida!* We'd scream it and run, swing the switches in the air to scare them back. Most people would agree the plover is the worst bird to ever live, worse than any vulture or magpie. Every Australian would know that, I'd bet. They'll swoop at your face if you come near their nests, but even if you run away from the nest they'll chase you on and on. The thing is, when I became a parent myself I thought about the *didadida* again and how they are just protecting their young. The *didadida*—it even sounds like a name the young chicks would give to their comforting parents.

policeman, policewoman—*gandyan, gandyi* I've met nice ones and I've met rotten ones. Problem with coming across a rotten *gandyan* is that they are armed, not just with guns—tasers these days, too. Pocket electrocution that is. When I was a kid, everyone said, "Now wave at the policeman." I think when people put a cross on their wall, or pin a thing to their lapel, or a band on their arm—they are really saying, "Don't shoot *me*." We'd wave at them the same way. I even taught the girls and the grandkids that, "Look there, wave to the police car!" Of course it was different when I was alone and saw a *gandyan*—then I would become real invisible.

old man—*dyirribang* I was born in the middle of peace and war, right between the thought before the acts and the shadows that came after. When the soldiers who survived returned home the first time, they got given our land under lease, called Soldier Settler Allotments. *Dyirribang* Falstaff, that fella made a mistake, he got that land on the Homestead Lease on the vacated Station and failed to pay off the freehold. Failed to make the payments to make it his under Australian law forever. The Falstaffs never got to own the land, and the Gondiwindi never did too after that—the government owned it, ninety-nine years, enough time to tuck a mistake in the bedding of the next generation. Eddie will get to know the same feeling—being without a place or paddock to call home. That's how the mine just slid right in here, slithered up like a snake—worse than a snake—ready to make a million, a billion, or more for a couple of greedy mates.

magpie—*garru, wibigang, dyirigang* *Garru* is a messenger bird. They can be vicious like the plover, but the ancestors said they brought spiritual messages, that the *garru* love to talk if you can make friends with them. So I tried that, and now they come down here into the garden when they aren't nesting, and I'll say *garru nguyaguya milang mudyi*— magpie, my beautiful friend—and he'll be calm and gentle. He told me about his ancestor, the first magpie, and about how important it is to protect his babies from the goanna, that's why he is the way he is, and I told him how I understood completely.

mailman, messenger (with a message stick)—*dharrang-dharrang* Julie at the local library—a wise and kind woman—unearthed pieces of my puzzle in the library catalog that I wouldn't have found otherwise, she gave them to me like a message stick from long ago. Those things she showed me helped me compile my dictionary, helped me put together the picture properly. Julie was my *dharrang-dharrang*.

marks or tracks, impressions of passing objects—*murru* This is the tracks the snakes, the goanna, the birds, and us make as we crisscross the world. We all leave *murru* behind, so leave a gentle one.

TWENTY

For days the heat slammed the inland, and the residents of Massacre gossiped about the mine and how bad it would be for the environment and others bit back that they needed jobs. Though all sides of the arguing agreed they were owed something more. When the previous evening, like a virus, the true rumor that Rinepalm Mining had set an open day at the town hall filtered into the Valley, and back streets, the men and women, though on the edge of heatstroke, leaped from their houses and headed into town. Late in the evening when people were tired and quenching thirsts, and anticipating the new jobs they would have, they drunkenly sang along with the jukeboxes, some brawled onto footpaths, and eventually all returned into the night.

First thing on Saturday morning, while Elsie and August were outside arranging rows of chairs two deep around the fire pit, a woman from Broken Crematorium arrived. She stood beside Prosperous House, in her hands a wooden case no bigger than a jewelry box. August looked at the woman and her chest caved then and her neck became heavy with the coming of a sad feeling. Elsie arranged another chair, wrung her sore hands, and walked with her head high to greet the woman and sign the paperwork. Aunt Missy descended the veranda stairs and caught her mother around the waist with one arm. August couldn't bear to watch;

she fixed the last of the chairs and headed through the field toward the riverbank. Her nana had urged her to go, but she hadn't got around to it. More, she didn't want to see that the water was no longer there at all. She dragged her fingers through the overripe kernels of wheat that dropped easily to the dirt. Around the mining company drill sites, the wheat was slashed and the short stalks looked etched into the land. Further out the wheat had been flattened about the size of Prosperous House, pipes rose up secured with bolts, a single capped pipe stood in the center of the sculpture, barbed fence secured the whole thing, and from each length of linked wire *Danger* signs hung. August couldn't get close to the tall pipes that had appeared as pinheads from a distance, the ground around each entry below was worn with work-boot prints and a scramble of metal bits. August wondered what it was that was a danger; she imagined gas compressed under the pipes, flammable dinosaur bones and coal stones, all the element codes of a periodic table rising. She imagined falling into the tin pit, *all this gone*, free-falling a kilometer below.

She cut through the remaining acres that led down to the Murrumby. The ground between the wheat rows was cracked dry and she spotted something shimmering off the sun, a shard poking out from the dirt. She reached down to pick up what she realized was a piece of quartz. She held the crystal and glanced back to Prosperous; it wasn't so far away, not as far away as she could see in the memory that burst into her head like an unwelcome guest.

For Easter, Aunt Nicki had gifted the girls two large eggs wrapped in colored foil. August ate hers immediately, easily, but Jedda didn't want to; she kept hers still wrapped for the first week or so, nestled in the chest freezer. Then she took a lick, another day a little rabbit bite. The rationing went on for months. August became obsessed with her egg lying there and would lift the freezer lid and check on it almost every day.

Then one day she'd had enough. They were coming in from the fields, trying to trip each other up. August could see them from where she'd stopped at that moment. "*Race!*" August had screamed when Jedda was bending down, placing a piece of quartz in her bucket. August could hear her running, the treasures rattling in her plastic bucket a way behind her. In the sprint she'd hatched a plan and put on her best actress voice as Jedda neared behind her at the veranda steps.

"Snake, snake!" August yelled.

"Where? Where?" and Jedda halted, tiptoed to come closer to the back decking.

"It slid right over my foot, I swear, right under the steps there," August pointed, paused, and as planned, Jedda had crouched down to look. "I reckon it put poison or something on my foot, I'm washing it," August added, taking the stairs slowly. "You know I heard we are getting brown snakes down this way now, they migrate and stuff—did you know that, Jedda?"

And then as soon as August had entered the back door she slid the glass across quick and snipped the lock shut. When Jedda heard the snip of the lock she looked up.

August cackled and ran over to the freezer, taking out Jedda's prized Easter egg. She could hear Jedda threatening through the glass door.

"Don't you dare touch it! I'll punch your face in!"

But she unfilmed the top of the hardly eaten egg and started to bite it.

"August, I'll kill you, I promise I'll kill you."

August couldn't help herself. She took hunk after hunk into her mouth, the frozen chocolate cracking against the tongue, difficult to swallow.

Jedda became enraged, screamed all the swearwords that if their nana and poppy had been home would have got her a smack. Jedda began to thump her whole little body against the glass. August laughed and ate as fast as she could. Then Jedda ran along the deck and launched herself against the door. She hit her nose and lip and August saw blood smeared on her face, a blur on the glass. August tried to reason, *okay okay*, and shoved the last small piece of egg back into the freezer. She readied herself at the back door, ready to flip the lock and run for cover. But Jedda had found a huge rock from the garden bed and had heaved it as high as she could, as if all her new fury was in that action alone. Jedda dumped that rock into the sliding door, the rock that must've been as heavy as herself. The glass door shattered, shimmered splinters over the linoleum. They got in trouble, both equally, had to clean dishes to no end. Until there was an end.

August swallowed the memory, tossed the quartz back into the wheat stalks, and walked to the edge of the riverbank where the water level dropped down, way down to bare sand at the bottom. The roots of white-box gums dangled out to nothing through the sides of the bank. They'd started to stop growing leaves when August had left this place and no koalas would climb the trunks for food anymore. There wouldn't be anywhere for the platypus to swim.

She walked north along the Murrumby, where the water would have once flowed. She saw mussel middens and cicada shells discarded along the riverbed. Large boulders strung in lines across the base of the river, once stacked for catching fish. She walked through a soft trough of sand, where orange wanderer butterflies flocked; they rose up, startled as she passed them. The static of the bush grew louder, a hummed pitch, a constant, unseen excitement from insects in the trees, like sonic waves in space or from submarines that only ene- mies and whales and dolphins could hear, she thought. Through the black cypress pine Kengal Rock loomed, swept up one side like a wave forming, and sloping long out the other side to a plateau. The air be- came cooler as she walked toward what was once upstream. Further up, the pine trees had kept their cover; birds called out, *Wahn* the crow cawed, kookaburras bounded from branch to branch laughing late in the morning. A slow goanna ambled down the base of a squiggly gum. He looked wide and fed, *No good for eating like that*, her poppy used to say, *Got to catch them before they have a feed, otherwise they taste like dead flesh*. August could hear his storytelling clear in her mind. The goanna passed her as if he knew that she knew, but they'd never eaten goanna anyway.

This is what she remembers. Her and Jedda finding the secret bush, looking for that place no one else could see. Children could be brave then. They could run to the end of Massacre and not be chased by farmers or ferals, they could climb, and knew how, Jedda knew. Bro- ken bones were the building blocks for a kid's life in the bush. August had always been a little uneasy in the bush though—she felt as if she were always winded, holding her breath anticipating disaster. But she could bear it, with Jedda, and together they'd found an oasis in the scrub.

Little rivulets twitched, wanting to lengthen in the redder sand. She kept walking, and through the canopy saw purple and blue tents pitched atop Kengal's flat granite peak. Beside the tents she could make out a few people standing up there. One of them waved down at her—a big slow swing of an arm. August raised her arm back to whoever it was, a kneejerk reaction, and then turned back the way she'd come. As she began to walk she heard a *cooeee* and looked back, and the arm waved again, beckoning her up to join them. There were enough people to help set up, August thought, so she followed the river further and climbed through the Used Oil Depot fence and up the ridge.

After a short trek a young woman about the same age as August eased toward her, shifting her weight to balance herself down the steep decline.

"How's it going?" the woman said, smiling, swatting flies from her face. Before August could answer, she added, "Want some tea?" August shrugged, followed her up, turning to look down at Prosperous. From there she could see the back of the house, though the Aunties wouldn't see her there. She remembered Jedda and her climbing through the she-oak trees to Kengal, watching for falcons' nests, waiting for falcons. Their poppy pointing out Bogong Range in the distance, but they never could really spot it themselves.

The woman had two long braids down each side of her chest, and she wore cargo shorts that rode to the top of her thighs; long candy-stripe stockings ringed her legs and led under her shorts. Between her breasts fell a twist of leather strings and metal necklace chains and a pair of army-patterned binoculars.

"What are you guys doing here?" August asked when she saw a whole collection of people and their tents, hidden from view at Prosperous.

"I'm Mandy," the stranger offered, "and all these guys are water protectors, here to stop the mine."

August laughed at her sincerity. "You seen how much water there is in Murrumby?"

Mandy didn't laugh; instead she continued talking as if she'd lived more years than she had. "This rock, Kengal, is actually a volcanic filtration system for the river. It's a natural spring filter and it's four hundred million years old. In fact, it still filters the water underground—*half a kilometer* underground." She searched August's face, offended, looking for *her to what?* August wondered. "You must know that, though."

"No," August said, "but what do you do then, to protect the water?"

"What do you mean?"

"I mean—how do you *protect* the water?"

"We just make the mine stop."

"But how?"

"Direct action."

"What's that?"

"Blockadia. Chain ourselves to the machines—but we'll have loads more people soon. Our networks will arrive."

"Networks?"

"Earth custodians."

"You?"

"And them." She gestured to her camp. "We spend all year on the lookout for projects to target and then when we need them our supporters arrive and join in. Normally I'm a custodian of the old-growth forests, but then we heard this mine was going through—so, yep." She nodded, then, and hooked her thumbs into her cargo-belt loops.

"Whose mob are you?" August asked, accepting tea from another woman with a nod, and taking a sip.

"What do you mean?"

"I mean, are you Koori or what?"

"No, I just care."

"That's nice."

"You think I'm not allowed?"

"I didn't say that, I said it's nice—it's nice that you give a shit." August looked away, trying to spot Eddie around Southerly.

"I saw you arrive the other day."

"You saw me?" August asked.

"Sorry," Mandy laughed, and held the strung binoculars up from around her neck, "there's not much to look at!"

August made a point of ignoring the binoculars and looked around their camp. They had gas stoves, dozens of milk crates stuffed with things scattered between tents, sun chairs, lines strung with laundry. There were about ten of them, playing cards inside the makeshift kitchen, two large white plastic drums were marked drinking water and cooking water, onions and bananas hung from tarpaulin stakes, more milk crates.

"You know this is private property?" August said finally.

"You mean the *oil depot*?"

"Yeah."

"They can kiss my arse to be honest. There shouldn't even be a fucking oil depot on a, you know, a sacred site." She scratched the side of her neck elaborately and stared at August.

"Who told you it's a sacred site?" August knew Poppy had a story for Kengal, but he'd had a story for everywhere.

"I found a heritage study from the eighties. It's all mapped if you want to see."

"I believe you," she said, and threw the remainder of the tea into the rocks alongside her and handed Mandy the cup.

"Listen, if you want to come and hang out, we're here all the time." Mandy put her hands together as if in prayer.

"Maybe." August felt like she'd been made small by this woman. She started back down the ridge and Mandy walked beside her along the vague path.

August didn't know how to respond, didn't want to walk with the woman, and paused for a beat, hinted, "Bye, then." She took a step and added, "There's a funeral today, so maybe don't look down at our house, okay?"

"Of course, it's not like we're spying on you or anything, it's just that I noticed you." She cocked her head in front of August to make her look. August froze in the weirdness of the situation. Mandy reached out, tucked a band of August's hair behind the ear. Her stomach tightened and her hips ached suddenly. "You have such beautiful eyes," she said, willing August to stare back into hers.

August's breathing stopped for a second. Two maybe. And then Mandy just walked up the ridge again.

August made her way down, feeling sick and thrilled at the same time. "Mandy," she said as she walked down the ridge, and through the fence, down the shoulder of Upper Massacre Road to the entrance of Prosperous, past the rows of peppermint trees, the cars parked disorderly by the house. *Mandy*, the strange woman on the rock.

August removed her dirt-covered shoes at the back door. The house and yard were a flurry of people chopping firewood, rearranging the demountable furniture, and chatting about the scorched grass that grew like spider veins. The Aunties were laying dinner plates on top of the tables, wherever a chair could be squeezed in for a table setting. Children were running around, babies tumbling on laps and into arms, wriggling between conversations. People yelled out "Augie" and August waved, didn't want to talk, and quickly entered the kitchen just as old Aunt Betty scolded Aunt Missy: "Why aren't you wearing the hat I got you for Christmas?"

"Don't really wear hats all the time, Aunty."

"Well, I'll have it back then if you're not going to wear it!"

Aunt Missy turned from Aunt Betty, busy with a tray of curried-egg sandwiches, "Here we go," Aunt Missy whispered to August under her breath. "Jesus, save me."

August smirked, shuffled through the commotion, past Elsie explaining to Uncle Fred about the Heritage Society offering to come and remove the stained-glass window, ". . . piece by piece for us. An expert, they said, as if it's the only thing worth keeping out here." Uncle Fred shook his head and rubbed his good arm on the back of his neck in astonishment.

August weaved out the other side of them and went to the attic to change. As she closed the door she heard Aunt Missy and Aunt Betty laughing. She thought about how every family has its own special language. Its own weird sense of humor that's stuck in the past. The Gondiwindi sense of humor, she knew, was bickering until laughter. She whipped off her shorts and t-shirt, took the black slip from the pile and put it on. She pulled on the black blouse and long skirt and wrapped a clean pair of black espadrille laces around her ankles. On the back of the door a mirror hung from waxed twine and a thick nail. August stared into it, tucked and untucked hair behind her ear, the clump that Mandy had touched. She put on mascara and drew tinted lip balm over her mouth. She didn't look at herself for long, she hadn't ever. Since the age of nine maybe, on account of her lazy eye. And on account of not liking what she saw. She thought that she probably hadn't looked into her own eyes, or anyone else's, or even a camera shutter, for longer than *one Mississippi, two Mississippi, three Mississippi.* Whenever she had her photograph taken she would turn her face to the side at the last moment, and was used to people yelling, "August, you ruined it!"

There would be no photographs taken today. She strung the long strap of the small velvet purse across her body, put the packet of cigarettes into the pouch, and pulled a handful of tissues from the box on the desk and shoved them in too. She'd never been to a funeral before. The family never had one for Jedda—she could still be alive, after all.

Back downstairs, August looked at the collection of wine bottles sitting in a bath of almost melted ice water in the sink; ordinarily, feeling this way she'd pour her prescription, but instead she poured a glass of water and stood at the counter drinking it. When it was almost done she threw the remainder into the sink. Jedda used to do the same, their mother too. August had seen Nana do it the previous night before they'd gone to bed and asked her why they all did that, threw the last bit away? "Well," Nana had thought for a moment, "I think we did it because when the house ran on tank water there used to be sediment at the bottom of the glass, so you never drank the last bit." They had inherited the habit.

August lit a cigarette outside. "Get those darts away from the house, womba!" an uncle yelled from his perch in front of the cricket match playing on the TV. She held her breath and ran out beyond the garden.

The sun was high and nothing cast a shadow. A white plastic marquee without walls was suspended over the foldout tables filled with food and protected by gauze fly covers. A stack of plastic plates and cutlery sat at the end of the table, and a clutch of cold beer bottles perspired in the heat. Archie Roach was trying to be heard from the old speakers of the portable CD player. A barbecue plate was being cleaned with steel wool, the tossed water hissed and steam rose from the burnt parts. People gathered close to the house in twos and threes, shared awkward somber conversation. The fire pit waited in the distance near the first row of wheat. Now and then an unavoidable chuckle broke through the yard. Poppy had lived through and out the other side of adulthood and there were plenty of stories to share. Aunt Missy was telling Eddie about the time when she was little and her dad used to take her fishing for eels before school. "Slippery suckers. Your grandad had a twelve-foot tinnie for the river but it never got much use except by my dad. We took it out when there was any flooding of the dam. I remember it was early that morning, breakfast would come after the work he used to tell us girls, even if it was a Saturday."

"Mum too?" August asked.

Eddie smiled at August, and turned again to hear Missy continue the story.

"Yeah, your mum was there, Aunty Nicki too," Missy said, and put her arm around August's shoulders. "That morning all we needed to do was collect the bloodworms from the riverbank. We took the shovel deep in the sand, dug it fast so the worms didn't know what was going on, dumped it into a sieve, and let the sand run out leaving the worms wriggling in the strainer. You know how to worm, Eddie?"

Eddie slowly shook his head, laughing.

"Bloody young ones!" Aunt Missy said, nudging another aunty beside her. "So we had a bucket of worms and put our kit in the tinnie and pushed off the bank. Tied our hooks, cast our lines and soon Jolene's line was pulling real hard, Dad was screaming *You have to be quick, Jolene!* She couldn't do it, so Dad took over and pulled this giant eel into the tinny! We were huddled at the keel screaming, the eel thrashing on the hull. Dad grabbed his knife and went to cut the line free then the eel's big mouth grabbed the bloody knife off him and cut Dad's hand! We screamed more, there was blood everywhere and an eel with a sharp bloody fishing knife in its mouth!"

A small crowd of family members had leaned in to listen to Missy's story, their faces elated. "So Dad grabbed the worming shovel. *Close your eyes girls!* he yelled. We didn't though; we were screaming but still looking!"

"What happened?" August asked.

"He necked the head clean off! Back home he strung what was left and skinned it and then Mum took over, and we ate eel cake for the best part of two weeks."

"*Burramarramarra*—you got to be real fast with those eels!"

"What's that, Uncle?" Missy asked Uncle Fred.

"Jump hand do—make the hands jump!" Fred waved his good hand and arm to catch the imaginary eel. "They *are* slippery bastards."

"*Burramarramarra* that's for sure!" Aunt Missy said and laughed. The small gathering all chuckled; it was a good story. Poppy had been the family's unifying thread. August looked at them laughing, gathered together, and doubted she'd ever see any of them again.

August approached the food and drinks table. Under the plastic sheath of a loaf of supermarket bread, several flies were trapped, eagerly crawling over the crust. She opened the mouth of the bread bag and they flew out. Looking up from the table she spotted her cousin Joey.

Last time August saw Joey he was borrowing an elastic necktie from the region's worst lawyer, following a line of boys like him into the stone building, and then he never emerged from the courthouse. Four years' juvenile detention, one of which, when he turned seventeen, spent in the adult prison in Penn Town. He'd been lucky—all their cousins had been tried as adults, is what everyone had said. She'd been there on the night in question and had skipped school to be there for the half-morning trial, the gossip and styrofoam cups of tea shared on the court steps. After the trial she returned to Prosperous, and that same day wrote a note for Nana and Poppy, then ran away with her birth certificate. She'd hitched on a road-train truck along Broken Highway to the other end of the country. Got a job pruning on the vineyards, picking fruit, sleeping in a tent, then saved and got a plane and a job here and there and finally outside of London. And that's all she'd ever done: temp work and running. Nothing to show.

Joe's facial hair was long and sparse as if he'd persisted in growing it wherever it could. The hair wired like a small finger off the end of his chin and each half-corner of his upper lip.

"August!" he yelled when he saw her see him. He rushed from the plastic chair. He was wearing a proper suit and tie. He took August's neck into the crook of his elbow.

"Long time no see!"

"Forever." It felt so good, she thought, to see Joe.

"Come check out my car." He led her with the torch of his held-out light beer. "It's a Mazda MX-5, Aug. Bought it because—if you haven't heard—I'm a businessman now." He stood back and opened his suit jacket slightly, chin to the sky.

"Where'd you steal it from?"

He ignored her snark; he had too much to say.

"Mum show you the app I made? Raking in thousands, cousin. Five figures."

"High roller!" she smiled sideways at him.

"Aug, true god, in juvie I got like, the equivalent of three university degrees! Nothing to do there but read. I read about Mabo. That dude, what a smart fella. Anyway, Pop used to visit. We'd smuggle stuff to each other, smuggling ideas. I was in his ear for years—I said, *Pop! You got to claim the land as ours, Native Title!* Pop asked how much native vegetation I reckoned was on the farm. I thought fifty-fifty. *Try again*, he said. I'm like, I don't bloody know. He says it's five percent! Alright, alright, so we scrapped that idea. But then I got free lessons on computers there—well, for the small price of public safety. I just wanted to get out and make some money, you know? I was ready for it . . . Pop gave me the idea for the first game—you seen it?" He took a sharp breath and then let it out. "So, how are you?" He took a swig of his light beer then added, "Fuck, it's hot!" and pulled out his phone. But he caught something about her that made him tuck the phone back into his jacket pocket.

"You alright? You're a bit different, Aug."

"Haven't seen you since we were teenagers! You look bloody different, too!"

"Nah, I mean sad. You seem real sad."

"Pop."

"Ow, we're singing him, we're celebrating and carrying him today—don't be sad, cuz."

"Maybe I just feel weird, I don't know. Stuff changes. I feel as if I'm just floating through life or something. Like my whole life I haven't really been me."

August unclasped her purse, took out another cigarette, tapped the filter on his bonnet and lit it. She felt on the edge of tears. She'd never heard Poppy talk politics before, but he'd been talking about Native Title with Joey; it was as if she'd missed out on a version of him.

"I reckon us blackfellas feel that way these days, but you have to move on. What'd Pop say last time I saw him? Chinese saying—oh yeah! It goes, *One fella makes a net, another fella stands and wishes. Make a bet who gets the fishes?* Gotta make a net, that's the whole point of life isn't it?" Joey cracked a wide smile of white teeth.

"Is it?" August managed a tiny smile back.

Joey had known some things when they were kids, known before the other kids did that adults lie, that they can be mean and bad. He knew before the girls that waving to police officers in the street didn't make a difference to your life or death, and he'd known that Prosperous was really special before August ever realized, too. He heard something in the world the way she smelled and tasted it.

"You know much about the mine?" August asked.

"Motherfuckers, yes." He stepped back and pointed his beer up toward Kengal. "And those fucking hippies on a *sacred site*. Watch out, aye, they got nits those dirty buggers."

He lowered his voice, but continued talking just as fast. "This is the deal a-right—Falstaff's strapped for cash, they *ring* a coal-seam gas company and invite them! So they come survey, no good for CSG, but giddy-up, a fucking mecca of tin under here. So then the Falstaffs are like, 'Er, nah, we don't want to lose the house.' About six months later the company have dug up some technicality saying it's *government land* anyway, and they won't even get a part of the pie. Well they'll probs get just the value of Southerly House, good for them I guess. I mean the whole mine and Falstaffs discovering the ninety-nine-year lease could have happened anyway, but they kind of dug themselves an early grave. It's depressing, isn't it? Knowing this place is soon going to be a big pit." Joe stopped yapping and pointed his beer. "Look, Rosie's here."

His little sister was playing with her phone on the veranda steps.

"How old is she now?" August asked.

"Ten going on twenty-five, according to Mum. She's got a picture of Beyoncé in her wallet, prays to her like she's a saint. She's a good egg though, locked herself in her closet the other day after she read *Harry Potter* and found out she wasn't a real witch. She cracks me up." He nudged August, trying to rouse her to how he knew her before.

"Do you talk to Eddie?" August gestured to the field where she remembered Joe and he had spent every weekend and school holiday slashing rows for pocket money and then disappearing into the bush.

"I saw him before. We say hello when we bump into each other, small town but, you know . . ."

"What?"

"He got me locked up, didn't he? You ever heard from ya mum?"

"No, you?"

"What—*your* mum? Can't even remember her."

"Do you hear from your dad?"

"Good one. Nah." Joey spat on the ground behind him.

Aunty Nicki wandered out to the makeshift car park with two glasses of white wine. August thought she looked stunning, in red heels and a sleeveless black shift that stopped at her knees.

She leaned over and hugged Joe and August with her inner elbows, her hands occupied in the air.

"You two okay?"

Joe shifted next to her. "We're good, Aunty, telling Aug about Eddie's family and the mine."

Aunt Nicki passed August a glass of white wine.

"Thanks," she said. "Is it true? That they invited the mine here?"

Aunt Nicki rested against Joe's car.

"Mining—that's all everyone's talking about, isn't it!" She put her free hand on August's shoulder. "It's complicated, see. You know I work for the town council now?"

August shook her head as Joey started walking away, called to her, "Back in a sec, need another beer."

Aunt Nicki continued. "Well, that application came in a couple of years ago. There's about ten or so farms with CSG; now some of the farmers in Massacre don't like it, they're scared of the water table or the thing leaking, which it sometimes does, and then the family has to go stay in a hotel. Some like it because they get a bit of compensation, because this is a long drought; this isn't just crops dying, it's cattle too, and people need money. Now all that Eddie's family did was allow them to look, that's it. The other option is to lock up the gates, but they let them come. That's okay—that's polite, some people would say. Problem is, they've struck gold in a way. So, both houses are gone. That's it. Albert, he tried to get the council to survey, he thought there was cultural significance here, whether it's the scar trees or the house itself." Aunt Nicki looked at Prosperous. "But they don't have to unless the town council flags it. You get me?"

"So Nana *is* really going? When?"

"Well, next week. They'll all be gone next week. Nana'll be fine, she'll stay with Mary."

"Joe mentioned Native Title. That he talked with Pop about claiming the land."

"Couldn't ever happen—I'll tell you why—there's no artifacts. No water in Murrumby, no fish—and fishing would mean Nana, or whoever's living here, would have a cultural connection to the land to maintain, the . . . well, 'resources'—okay? Another thing, there's no language here. Our people's language is extinct, no one speaks it any more so they can tick that box on their government form that says "loss of cultural connection." You see?"

"Poppy taught us some."

"Heads, Shoulders, Knees, and Toes song? Yeah, he taught me that too. But I mean language that is connected to this place, this landscape."

"Nana told me last night Poppy was writing a dictionary."

Aunty Nicki shook her head before she answered. "Even if he was writing it, won't change anything. They grew up on the Mish, remember, and language wasn't allowed. Under Queen and Church here." Aunty pointed to the steeple, bent and rusted atop Prosperous. August wanted to stop her, correct her, tell her how she'd heard Poppy even when she was young, heard the way his tongue changed, heard words no one else seemed to know. But she didn't say anything.

"When are you going back to England?" her aunt asked, and licked her finger, smudged dust from her dress hem.

"Soon."

"How wonderful, living overseas. Bet you can't wait to go back." Aunt Nicki smiled and took August's hand then and they walked toward the gathering Gondiwindi who were descending from the veranda stairs in a slow, mournful swarm. "Come now, it's time to say goodbye."

TWENTY-ONE

Reverend Ferdinand Greenleaf's letter to Dr. George Cross,
2nd August 1915, continued

V

As the years passed, our numbers continued to fluctuate. Natives who had nowhere else to go came drifting in from neighboring rivers, some traveling hundreds of miles on foot avoiding capture to see our Mission for themselves. Although some men left of their own free will, many families stayed on and we made housing arrangements without fuss. In 1886 I sent a letter to the Department of Public Instruction signifying our continued need for materials and attaching a thorough list of the items we were in desperate need of—rations, sugar, tea, and figs of tobacco, and also boards, iron, doors, windows for the schoolhouse. Six months later the Department telegrammed to announce a visit to inspect our progress in order to approve funding. I immediately rounded up the children and for a week of days and evenings we practiced from the Bible until I had many quoting from it by heart. The Word of God was truly becoming a light to their feet and a lamp to their path! On the big day, and without a moment's shyness, little Mercy ran up to the inspectors and tugged at the sleeve of one of the gentlemen. She then quite confidently, and without encouragement, recited William Hickson's version of "God Save the Queen." Three hours later, at the close of the inspection, I was informed that all of the materials would be supplied as well as a skilled carpenter at our disposal. They had recognized the importance and the unmistakable success of the day school, and, furthermore, I think due to sweet Mercy, elected to raise it to the position of a public school, thereby securing to our institution all the benefits, they promised, enjoyed by every White school in the Colony. I was overfilled with joy and promise on that evening and I gave my thanks upon my knees for some hours.

And yet, the delivery of the much-needed items was delayed again and again. The season was very dry and the harvest did not wither for want of harvesters, but from the sheer violence of the sun. Our few head of sheep were dying of starvation. I prayed for help and direction, and—lo!—direction and help came!

An old Blackfellow came to my hut saying, "Plenty of fish down long river."

At first I took no notice, but as he kept repeating it, I said, "Alright, I will send a horseman tomorrow."

Upon saying this he became very warm. "You no send horse, you send big dray with me."

I was struck by the old man's confidence and thinking the Lord might provide, I approved a fishing expedition. The next morning, four men and the old Jacky led us to a section of the river that bottlenecked below Kengal. On reaching a short, steep slope to the river I had not before come across, three of the Blackfellows stripped from their clothes, bounded down the bank without a thought, and plunged into the waist-high water, and within moments began spearing the fish. Such a sight I had never before witnessed. The three spearmen kept old Jacky, another fellow Wowhely, and myself gathering up and bagging, and in the course of hours we had secured about six hundredweight. After thanking God we returned to the Mission and caused a general rejoicing throughout the settlement. The women immediately set aside two-thirds of the catch for drying and preserving.

As we were feasting that evening, Hans Keller and I heartily agreed that we had been blessed. I asked him whether he thought it correct, in such thin times, that we should allow the Natives to go about their old ways if we could sustain ourselves. With the assistance of his sated appetite, he saw little problem with it.

From that day forward I took to the capacities of the Blackfellows as a keen observer. They showed me the tubers at the river we could eat after roasting on the fire, and a type of native potato that the women pounded and produced from the vegetable a fine, fluffy cake. I learned more of their language and, over the years, listed 115 words of theirs that I have attached here—and in exchange, they took to my sermons with an equal fervor. Although not without difficulty in the language. I understood that the parts of my sermons that divided us were not the sentiments, but the words. That's what the Blackfellows told me when I explained God; they said *Baymee* to me, and furrowed their brows and nodded like we were talking in the seriousness that we were. And so, after much reflection and frustration, I prayed and asked the Lord—"Why am I only hidden with Christ in Paul? Why can they not be hidden in God with *Baymee*?" The answer I decided upon was that I should be flexible with words. That I should be open to translation, as it were.

So, in secret, I gathered with the men and gave sermons about *Him*, neither the Lord nor *Baymee*. I told the courageous stories and the enchantment of creation and they nodded and listened, enraptured in the tales. I never told Baumann, or Keller, or any Church or Government official who visited the Mission once I made this decision. At first, I thought that *Baymee* was their word for God, but deep down I think I knew it wasn't. I think I always knew we were praising their own God in the absence of mine. Because, where had the Lord Jesus been in those years?

We were dependent on only the land for our rations, and the materials from the Department of Public Instruction *never* surfaced, and I had still not yet built an official Prosperous Church. I had not yet installed the rose emblem of colored glass in its eastern facade. At least the river flowed on time, the sun rose and dipped each day; at least they could point their God out to me, *Baymee* they uttered. *Baymee* they said as the men pointed up to what they called Kengal— the great granite apparition that looms north of Prosperous Mission. I'd take their arm and point it just an inch or so higher, so that in my faith I could say we were pointing to the heavens, but their arms always dropped a little when I let go, and they would correct me at forty-five degrees, their fingers at the tip of Kengal—*Baymee* they'd confirm indisputably.

TWENTY-TWO

medicine man, priest, conjurer—*guradyi, gudyi, guraadyi* That's when the *gudyi* comes in from the church and tries to fix everything for the families. There was only one good white *gudyi* I've read of and that was Greenleaf, more or less. The medicine men of my ancestors showed me the plants most sacred to our people. The things Joey and the young ones need to know are all written here. There are no *guradyi* left, so our descendants must take the post. Claim that space where shame lived, where things were lost, where we were kept away from our culture.

mouth—*ngaan* Use the mouth now, say our words aloud—you're right sometimes when you just try. There are nasal sounds, the sounds you bring up to the back of your nose, like *"ny"*—which is made by *"n"* and a bit difficult, especially at the end of the words. *"ng"*—which normally comes at the end of English words—comes at the beginning of ours—and is made by *"n."* *"nh"* is not heard in English at all—it's like making a breath, sometimes in and sometimes out after an *"n"* sound. Then there are stop sounds—those you make close to your heart like *"dy,"* which sounds like *"j"* or *"t"* depending on the word, *"dh"* sounds like *"d"* or *"dy"* or *"dth,"* and then there is *"b," "g,"* and *"d"*—which sounds like English *"p," "k," "t."* There's also words that contain long vowels like *"uu," "ii"*—*"uu"* sounds like the *"oo"* in the word *book* and *"ii"* sounds like the *"ee"* in *feel*. The rest is just feeling the words.

mystery, sacred, secret—*ngayirr* The word *mystery* and the word *secret* mean the same thing in the old language, that is important to remember. I could think of a hundred reasons why I'm alive, why things have happened, why time measures our lives to a limit but that our mother is infinite. But the truth is that everything is just a question.

legs, to be long-legged—*buyu-wari* To be long-legged—that's the Gondiwindi! You know when you look at the shadow of yourself and the legs are long? That's what we have always looked like just standing there. I'm not certain it makes us great runners, but we have always been able to reach things in high places.

luck, providence—*mugarrmarra* Years ago the whirly-whirlies came to Prosperous—they stayed there for over thirty years. In the second week of the whirly-whirlies hanging about, I cycled out to Massacre Food Mart and I bought milk and a $1 Harbour Bridge scratchie. The prize was $10,000 instant cash. The lady behind the counter explained what it was to me, they were brand new, she said they had only been out for one month. Well, I never, ever scratched the card. I kept that scratchie with me all these years, the day the whirly-whirlies left it would have been void in any case. I reckon I was looking for some sort of sign in turmoil. Money seems like a good enough answer as any. I lost all the magic. I lost all the goodness. I even lost prayer, but I wasn't going to stop trying for my family. So I never reached for an easy fix. I just tried.

lust after, passionate—*ngurrunggarra* There's a story the ancestors told me about two lovers who, long ago, lived on either side of the Murrumby River. The Murrumby was a boundary between two territories, and both groups were friendly to each other, though both lived under strict tribal lore. The day came when one of the young men saw a beautiful young girl of the neighboring group. He fell in love with her immediately and decided to be her husband. Unfortunately, the girl had been promised a different fate. The two met in secret, though, and many meetings passed without anyone knowing about it. When they were discovered, the elders warned the young man not to *ngurrunggarra* the girl, otherwise he would suffer grave punishment. But they were so in love these two, they decided to elope, even if they'd be outsiders forever. They decided to meet at the river, and take off north to the bush. On the night they were to run away, they both waded into the Murrumby. When they reached the center of the river a rain of spears entered the water and wounded them both. The two sank into the water holding each other. And if there was water in the Murrumby, the frogs would still gather there today and sing two different tunes from either side of its banks, the young woman and the young man crying out to each other, mourning their lost love.

know yourself, be at peace with yourself—*gulba-ngi-dyili-nya* When I was younger and my body hadn't bent yet, strangers began to turn up at Prosperous. I'd look up from the field and see someone standing at the back door, many times it was a woman, older than me, clutching her handbag to herself, nervously walking beneath the peppermint trees and looking about. They were returning to make peace. I'd give them a cuppa, and if they felt like it, a walk around the property. They'd tell me how they tracked the place down, how they remembered being here. Some were old enough to remember my mother. They were freeing themselves from their lives of good grace or misery—either way, they needed to see where everything began for them. I would talk with them, would nod and acknowledge them. That's what the old, returning people wanted, someone there to receive them, believe them, help, in some way, to put the pieces together. *Gulba-ngi-dyili-nya* is important work, long work. Every person faces that crossroad, wondering whether or not to walk through the arch of peppermint trees.

koala—*barrandhang, gurabaan, naagun* After her bus trip and causing all sorts of trouble, Elsie drove down to Massacre Plains in a bronze Valiant. We courted at the Aborigines' dance. Then Elsie was tired from dancing and punch so I drove, even though I didn't have a license. We were driving along singing and yapping when a big BOOM sound came from under the car and we swerved a little. I pulled over and we looked behind us but couldn't see a thing. Elsie was worried, so I turned the car around and there on the road was a massive *barrandhang*—that's the name the ancestors had told me. Elsie, she was distressed and wanted to save the animal. She took a picnic blanket from the boot and we went to pick it up, but as she did, the *barrandhang*, in its shock from being hit I suppose, or filled up on eucalyptus, snuggled into Elsie and she was blissed out like she was holding a baby. I didn't like this at all, but we got into the car and I got to thinking about a place that rescued native animals, mostly joeys that were still alive in their mothers' pouches when the mothers had become roadkill. So I got my bearings and headed toward there. I glanced at Elsie a couple of times, and she was still holding the animal like a baby but I had to look back at the road to work out how to keep driving that car. After about an hour we found the place. It was well past midnight when I pulled the car up, but it didn't take a minute for the old farmer to come out with a shotgun. Oh, God! I had my hands in the air like in the films, and I got on my knees and yelled, "We hit a koala—help us please!" I look over at Elsie and she's stepped out of the car, the picnic blanket dropped away and the koala now hugging her bare around the neck. There wasn't anything maternal about the situation then, not with a half-conscious thing with claws that was just waking up to the scent of a strange woman. Me and that man with the shotgun could then see how big that animal was. He put the shotgun down immediately and I rose up on my feet. Elsie was still blissed out, but her voice trembled a little. "Alb," she said, "I think it's waking up." Well, the bloke moved real slow toward her, he said some calming words and told her he was going to take the koala. "Okay? I want you to let go and turn away fast when I say so." She nodded then, she knew she was in trouble. Just as the bloke came to grab the koala under the armpits, the thing latched its teeth into Elsie, and those claws too, ripping the back of her dress in one long drag away from her as he got the koala free. Well, there wasn't too much blood on Elsie, but that koala had woken up for sure—its arms and legs outstretched and braying loud! The man called out that he'd get the vet out in the morning. Elsie and I dropped in there a couple of days later. The *barrandhang* was fine. The farmer released it a few days later. We were happy to know it was okay and, well, Elsie never messed about with wild animals again.

jag-spear—*dhulu* I made a real *dhulu* myself as an older man. Not so long ago.

ill, to make ill—*duri-mambi-rra* I try and try to see my mother there on my time traveling, but I only see her walking in my memory, she's always defeated in my mind. I see her in the field, threshing, I see her sitting at the end of a bushel with a tin of tobacco. I can see her sitting under the tree when she was old and had already drunk her death, when the grog *duri-mambi-rra.*

incorrect, wrong—*wamang* I'm looking out on the backyard: the field, the crop, the dam in the distance to the right; the trees, the line, the river in the distance to the left; the kitchen garden here beside me. It all seems small and manageable. It's hard to imagine that something so big might swallow this place up soon. Hard to imagine problems coming home here again to roost. Don't know what it is about us that seems to rile the White man. The burden, the burden of their memory perhaps, or that we weren't extinguished with the lights of those empires after all. Some days everything seems *wamang* still.

TWENTY-THREE

Joe was with the Uncles, carrying branches of black cypress pine and gum to the fire pit. August noticed Eddie there with the men who were carrying dried lengths of geebung too. In his suit he seemed to have the confidence of a soldier off to battle, not unlike the town's statue. August thought about Poppy, trying to imagine him so young, thinking how she never knew him completely, only for some of his life, and wondered what it was like for him here in Massacre as a young man. Elsie was waiting at the fire. She was wearing a crepe navy blue dress, her hair looped into a low bun.

August stood with the women and girls who were bound together and heaving; sorrowful noises came from all the Aunties, even Aunt Mary was crying. The sun seemed to ease and August suddenly didn't feel sweltering hot anymore. A breeze felt as though it came off the water of the Murrumby, where it couldn't. She'd once heard Aunt Missy talking about the grief coming from *upriver*—or had it been from *underground*? She couldn't remember. Aunt Missy squeezed August's wrist. Missy was thinking about when her dad had taken her fishing, about when she was little he let her push her thumb into the soft soil and how he walked past her, dropping seeds into the earth, with the other hand she would cover them up. Aunt Mary was swaying by the fire. She was thinking about the first time she met her brother again at the Aboriginal Medical Centre Christmas lunch, how relatives had walked them to each other across the lawn, how they didn't know whether to hug or dance in the joy. She was thinking about when she buried her own son, how much she'd loved him, more than she knew she could, more than she was ever taught. And Aunt Nicki, who had let go of August's other hand, with eyes closed, asked the Lord, whom she never asked for anything, to end this chapter of their lives. Amen.

Nana took the black cypress-pine branches, the gum and geebung from the cousins and uncles and placed the ends into the fire. The men and boys stood back and waited. When the branches were smoking but not yet alight, everyone moved forward and Nana handed them out until she was empty-handed. August stood back from everything, just watching.

Once Nana took the jewelry box of ashes everyone went quiet, but music came from their feet when Nana spread the ashes into the fire. The flames rose and sank. She walked into the wheatfield, letting the grey gravel dust trail from the box alongside her. Nana dropped the box on the ground, threw her arms wide, and moved to those private songs of their marriage with her eyes closed shut. Elsie was thinking about Albert, thinking about his free spirit flying, whooshing into the air as he'd always said he could. Like an arrow through a heavy heart the long elegant body of the bird glided into a chorus of sobbing and landed out by the dam. Elsie opened her mouth and a deep noise came out, words she didn't remember that she'd gathered like years. August stared further out toward the dam as the ceremony continued and smoke rose, sweeping across the plains.

The whole world seemed to stop then: the cicadas went quiet, leaves stopped rustling, chairs didn't creak.

August couldn't taste or smell a thing. She spied the lone bird at the edge of the dam, dancing, as did her nana, who stopped moving when she noticed. It was as if the bird were coming toward the fire. Everyone else was looking too.

It was a brolga.

A few family members pointed in the direction of the dam where the red bonnet of the brolga rose and fell, and its white and blue-grey feathers opened and collapsed. At the edge of the water, with its stick-thin, sinewy legs and dipping knees, it danced. It flapped its wings, showing its black underside. When it bowed its head, August thought she could see its yellow eye. It had a trumpet call, its caw rising, rising. Then its beak dipped right down to the ground—and up, up its wings went, the long body of the bird rose, its legs cycling in the air before it fell again. As the brolga hit the ground, a wing, then the other, whooshed into the smoke blowing in the field. One leg up, and then the other leg joined so that the brolga was airborne for a moment, and then as its body, atoms, molecules joined the ground its head rose up with the billow of dust, rising. Over and over, the brolga repeated the dance. There was music. Everyone was still, watching—seeing suddenly not the freedom of the bird, but its belonging. She dropped to her knees and sobbed and wailed like she'd never done before. August saw something else in the bird, too. Her legs felt heavy and she fell where she stood, kept her eyes on the bird. *Jedda*, she thought, *Jedda*.

August could see her dancing, her narrow childish hips, her long limbs weaving in the air. She could see Jedda as she took his arm when he went to run his hand through August's hair. *Where was Jedda going with him? Who was he?* She tried to remember but couldn't. In this wakeful dream, this vivid echo, August peered over the bed, somehow controlling what she could see, and looked at the floor of their bedroom. Below the bunks their cassette tapes were strewn across the rug, she saw the Texta marker: Spice Girls, Hanson, TLC. She could see all their books and figurines and one cassette on the pillow of Jedda's bunk; it read *Letter to the Princess*. That wasn't a song, it was their secret recorded messages to Princess Diana of England. They used to record stories for her. *True stories?* August and Jedda were watching ballet dancers on the television when the news came on that Princess Diana had died. Why, she thought, was she seeing this now? Had she not gone to England for Jedda? she wondered, looking about their bedroom in her mind. Hadn't she flown to Buckingham Palace for her? Hadn't she done nothing all those years? Hadn't she just washed dishes, like when they were kids doing the chores at home? Hadn't she not eaten properly forever? Hadn't she wasted herself to stay a girl forever, *little girls forever?* The cement block of her memory, that smooth slab in her mind cracked, the grey wall crumbled then, and all she saw was Jedda dancing. The music to Jedda's dance. Chanting girls' voices: *Heads, shoulders, knees, and toes*, they sang that, *Balang gaanha bungang burra-mi, bungang burra-mi, bungang burra-mi . . .* she could see the little girls. August wanted to fall from the bunk bed and hug them, but as her head moved toward them, her neck dropped heavily like a body on drugs, a mind in the sea, and she was awake, in the field again. The brolga folded itself through the motions, *heads, shoulders, knees, toes . . .* poking into air . . . pecking into the earth. Again and again the body surged from the dust field, like future and past colliding.

Then the brolga's mates arrived from the west, a hundred sails flung into the sea of yellow-green. They followed the same motions, bicycling their own sinewy legs, but the first brolga danced the most: it stood forward in the pack, its wings spread out the widest. August could feel her face turn wet. A benediction blanketed the yard in all the words that weren't needed to be said. It was simply, painfully, the finality of a time. All along they'd wanted peace, or to be happy, and they are good things to want, especially for children, but they'd been drawn again and again into the past, where all pain lives. She wondered if everyone was haunted by being a kid. Haunted by the feeling of being unshielded. They weren't protected from everything, August remembered, not the words hurled by the other locals in town, not the slurred looks, not the school history books and those lies, not everyone around her whose spirits were shattered in a thousand pieces, and she remembered clearly now—how they weren't protected from everything at all, not even Uncle Jimmy Corvette who liked to climb into their beds when nobody seemed to notice.

She could hear gospel music playing around her when it wasn't. Under the eaves, down the veranda steps, and out into that old field ran the music, rustling dormant seeds from pods and pods from branches, and stuck-branches from trees. She looked back at the veranda of Prosperous and could see Nana and Poppy that night, dressed up for the fundraiser and waving goodbye to the girls. That was the year the gospel came to Prosperous and hadn't Jedda and August been over the moon? Nana and Poppy had bought a brand-new CD player to add music to the beginnings and ends of Bible study on Fridays. Poppy said it was *God's Will* and then he pressed the play button. Younger

Nana always agreed with God but smiled and winked at the girls about God's wishes all the time. They let the music run through every part of that house. They even opened up the windows and August had seen gospel leaking out of Prosperous like the smoke of something burned off the stove. Those wailing singing voices pitching camp on that farm.

No one knew what Jimmy Corvette was then—he was just babysitting that night, wasn't he? He said he'd brought a movie for them and did they want to watch it? It was on VHS. August didn't remember what the movie was called but she remembered it wasn't rated G or PG. The girls didn't like it, it was confusing, and Jedda and August squeezed each other's hand under the blanket when Uncle Jimmy kept running his fingers through their hair. August could feel popcorn shells caught between her teeth when he put his mouth on hers. Jedda looked away and then August looked away.

The next day at breakfast, around the cornflakes and coffee pot, Poppy held the newspaper aloft and announced to anyone listening that a statue of the Virgin Mary was crying blood in a country called the Philippines. August had thought that the Virgin Mary must have known what they were feeling then. August had wondered if she'd ever be able to cry again. She'd imagined when she did it would be of blood, too, but she didn't think she could squeeze a drop in any case. She'd been changed forever; she felt she were buried that day and all the days after, under a hundred babushka-doll casings, way beneath the wood and varnish. And she didn't ever want to listen to gospel music again.

Weeks later was the second time it happened, *wasn't it?* But Jedda led Uncle Jimmy Corvette away from August. Jedda saved her.

Her head seemed as if it could feel the rest of her body then, as if things were sinking in and her feeling was seeping out, like a sieve fallen into a bowl of cake batter. She sat on the sandy dirt, crying. All feeling crept over her body, everywhere, like waking up comatose nerves of the skin, the undead stirring. Her mouth, her throat, her nose—even her ears felt as if they were wet with tears. A word came into her mind, fully-formed, she knew what it meant—*burral-gang*—the brolga. She didn't know how she knew the word but she knew it. *Burral-gang.* The brolgas finished their dance. It was her, dancing. Jedda and her friends began to flee the paddock, spindly legs galloping south, away from all of them before taking full flight. August ran her fingers through the dirt, just scratching the surface. *Poppy*, she said out loud; *Jedda*, she said on the inside.

She closed her eyes, a dam had broken, broken their little hearts, hearts born as fragile as clay. With her hands flat on the dry dirt and her eyes blinded with tears, she felt as if she were back home, back on the land she belonged to. At the same time, she thought that this was the saddest place on earth.

Twenty-Four

Reverend Ferdinand Greenleaf's letter to Dr. George Cross,
2nd August 1915, continued

VI

Please forgive my lengthy digressions; I simply wish to illustrate everything in order for you and for whomever this may reach, to have a proper understanding of our Mission life.

There was order and grace to our lives at Prosperous Mission, the township built with the young men who had become fathers, and their children who were growing with the instruction of Godly ways, formal education, and most comfortingly, some of their own family members that had remained wild, unwilling to join our Mission, but who visited in peace and goodwill.

Although over these years I knew of and had witnessed the increase of the Native labor system occurring in the plains, and visitors were less frequent. As such—fewer young men lived at the Mission as they had been captured and compelled, I dare say with force, to touch the pen to assignment papers impossible for them to understand. Furthermore, they then became the Bond Service

Property of a fellow on a Station. And when they subsequently
ran away, which they most certainly did, a warrant was issued for
their arrest, the Police were set in motion. Then they were run
down or ferreted out, sometimes here at the Mission, taken to the
Police Depot and chained for weeks before being returned to these
monstrous Station men who waved in victory paper copies of the
Masters and Servants Act. Thus fracturing those beloved families I'd
worked so hard to keep intact.

In the sixth year of our Mission, we had a closeknit, and, in so far
as was possible, protected community of weavers, fishermen, children
of God, education, and good Providence—our crop of bearded wheat
yielded for two years straight. We had births, and, naturally, some of
the aging residents did die. I was surprised to learn that the Natives
had a great reverence for the dead, and I allowed them to conduct
their private ceremonies before we hammered together coffins, and
marked out a permanent cemetery under a copse of trees. It eased me
a great deal knowing that of those who passed at the Mission, all had
taken baptism beforehand, some at my assurance, yet with their total
acceptance, on their deathbeds.

At the turn of the seventh year of the Mission, a great disruption
seemed to take hold of the community of Massacre Plains. Social
issues were becoming increasingly hostile; the Government had
come down heavily on the immigrant goldminers, and the Worker
newsletter had printed three issues within the year, igniting division
between what were called the *silvertails* and the *hoi-polloi*. Though
both factions of society, mind you, were agreeable in their prejudice
against the Native.

One evening, a group of White men broke down the fences and
entered our reserve. Asleep in my hut, I awoke to the great chanting

of the horsemen calling out for enacting "vengeance" and suffering an "eye-for-an-eye." I immediately threw on my pantaloons and boots, retrieved the shotgun from its high place upon the shelf, and raced to the yard. The girls and women were screaming and running, first to the men's hut; but on seeing that the White men had barricaded it and set the men's quarters alight with their torches, they ran toward myself in a swarm. I let them pass, and the women and girls began to pour into my hut for safety. Into the yard, the Native men were leaping from the windows of their own quarters as the fire began to lick and flame. I demanded to know the business these intruders had; however intoxicated they were with spirits, they remained atop their horses, armed with whips and gripping their rifles with alarming certainty. The six of them, yelling over the top of one another, replied that our Blacks, "Niggers" as they referred to them, had speared their cattle, and I knew by their tense faces that I could not resort to reason or Scripture. That they were set on vengeful murder that evening. The Blackfellows meanwhile had scattered from their large hut to camouflage themselves within the bush.

I reached the White men who were still mounted on their horses and pointed my rifle at their beasts. I demanded they take their leave or I would fetch for the authorities. I admit, my hands were shaking and my nerves were unsettled. I felt immensely out of my depth. Keller, without a weapon, was gathering those frightened children who could not fit into my hut into the schoolhouse. I held the rifle at my shoulder, and tried as I might not to shake with it, when one of the White men, illuminated by the fire, galloped his horse around the center of the square and approached me at speed and, with his boot to my head, knocked me to the ground.

Throughout much of the rest of the ordeal I lay unconscious on

the dirt of our very own open square. When I awoke in the care of
Keller, the men's dormitory quarters were sending cinders into the
sky. A horse lay by the fire, dead with a spear through its chest. The
White horsemen had fled taking two women with them, much to the
distress of the female residents whose wails echoed beyond the acacia
pines.

Keller immediately informed me that a Blackfellow who tried
to stop the kidnap of the women had been lashed with a stockwhip
upon the neck and dragged from the pommel for numerous turns, on
his back and his front, before being shot. I remember even through
the smoke that the scent of blood was strong. I touched the top of my
head absent-mindedly, but the smell of blood was not my own. I came
from the dirt to assist the injured Blackfellow. I staggered toward the
shape on the ground and fell there on my knees and was sorrowed
to find it was Wowhely, a good and honorable man about half my
age, my friend. On seeing me approach he said he was frightened. A
pool of darkness had seeped over his chest and stained the hands of
his brothers and my own. I realized that I was only useful for giving
prayer. I said to him, "You needn't be scared because the Lord Jesus
is always near those who put their trust in Him, those, like you,
Wowhely, who are passing through the dark valley."

A song began to come from the mouths of the men then; it rose
up from Wowhely's lifeless, bloodied body and seemed to carry lit
into the night sky, a song that surely caused angels to cover their faces
and weep. The next day the Natives held their ceremony in private.
The following day we laid Wowhely's prepared and blessed body to
rest in the eternal home of the cemetery. The cemetery that had been
swelling in size, growing with the suffering that hung like a pall of
locusts over the plains.

TWENTY-FIVE

harrow, plough—*gungambirra* All you need to work the land well, it's all here. Even before the Reverend, who thought he was farming for the first time, we knew how to *gungambirra*.

hole used as a sleeping place—*nguram-birrang* With our girls we'd head south, down the Murrumby. After the dam was built we'd head north with the granddaughters. We'd camp high on the Darling River. Lots of other families would be there too, their cars rigged with kayaks and canoes, fishing rods, foldout chairs, four-person tents. They were the loveliest times, those trips away. Seeing something different, having an adventure, finding where the Murrumby ended, and the later years, where it had begun. I'd show the kids how the Gondiwindi slept in the early days, so I'd dig out the ground near the bank and light a couple of fires in the afternoon; while they were going I'd prepare our fire pit for the evening. Then I'd do some fishing upstream. When it was getting real cold and all the kids had bathed and got into their pajamas and it was time to cook dinner, I'd shovel out the coals from the other fires I'd made and feed them back into the main one. I'd lay a couple of beach towels down into the little *gulamon* shapes I'd made and then tell the kids to get to bed. Well, weren't they amazed!

A warm little ditch to lie in and tell jokes to each other by the fire until dinner and then bedtime. Joey would be propped on his elbows after the girls had fallen asleep, and me still awake in another, and we'd talk boys' talk until the fire went out and the Milky Way reeled like a film above us.

hollow tree set on fire, smoke coming from top—*dural* My ancestor, a great-great-great-uncle of mine, took me for a walk one day. "We're going for dinner," he told me. I must've been about eleven and was quite used to time travel by then. So my great-great-great-uncle, who said his name was Cooradoc, pointed to a dead tree, its branches had broken off and the entire trunk was grey. Uncle Cooradoc tapped his axe on the dead tree and a scurrying noise came back. Then Uncle made a fire with flint stones and the long grass, and cut into the tree to make a hollow. He handed the fire to me and said to hold it there in the dead tree. Faster than I'd seen a hungry goanna, Uncle scaled the tree. He told me to let go of the grass then, which was a good thing because my fingers were beginning to singe. So the fire blew up the hollow fast and the next thing I know, Uncle is climbing back down with a possum in his fist. "Dinnertime," he said, and smiled. "That," he said, pointing at the tree aflame, "is *dural*. And this?" he asked, holding the possum between us. "*Bugari*," I said.

Holy Spirit—*mudyigaali* One day I decided that I might kill a man. I was at the end of my thinking, and at the end of your thinking even the unthinkable becomes an option. Well, I rested on my knees like I had when I was a boy. I prayed and asked and tried to find an answer from the *mudyigaali* but none came. I went down to the riverbank and screamed to the spirits too, but they wouldn't come, this was still the time of the whirly-whirly. The next morning, I dragged August outside. I didn't hurt her, I just needed to do something. Earlier, when the morning star was still visible, I'd boiled water in the steel saucepan. I'd let it cool in the moonlight, I'd sat a quartz crystal in there even. In the morning, I'd forgotten, and Elsie's friends had turned up for morning tea. Well, I was quite desperately sure on the thing I thought I might do. So I took August out by the back of the shearers' sheds and baptized her, or what I thought was baptism. I said, "Sorry, Augie, it's to protect you, darling." And I poured the water from the saucepan onto her hair. Poor thing, she cried, children do that when the world gets loud and confusing. Well, I gave her a hug and sent her on her way and bought her something later that day from the paper shop. It was a little case with miniature books inside by Beatrix Potter. After that I planned the murder I was going to do. I couldn't square that away with anyone though, not Elsie, not the ancestors, not the *mudyigaali* itself— it was something in that part of my soul that belonged only to me.

horses, place of wild horses—*yarramalang* When I was mustering, we'd saddle up at sunrise, have tea and johnnycakes, and take off and work until sunset. Some of the stations were more than ten thousand square clicks in size. That sort of country reminds you why people think of this land as wide and blue with endless yonder. I've seen it with my own eyes! The only change in routine was colt breaking or heading back to Massacre's smaller farms for shearing season. I didn't use a stockwhip myself, I had a kindred spirit in a pair of kelpie mutts. Those dogs would sleep with me in the swag even—three heads poking out the end each morning. Me reading them a passage or two before the day of work they had to do. They worked just as long as us jackaroos, those dogs. Once we were moving a few thousand head of sheep north and we had to cross some wild country. Well, there was a beautiful green valley that opened up as we went north. The bloke I was working with was keen to follow it a way lower to cool off. I gave in but warned him just a quick dip and then we'd have to go. We started down the valley and there we saw them, about twenty wild *yarraman*, which meant we wouldn't be cooling off after all, not with the dogs and the chaos that would have scattered the herd. Isn't anything more beautiful in the world I reckon than a pack of wild animals. That's what those places are called, *yarraman* heaven—*yarramalang*.

TWENTY-SIX

She only knew that someone had hooked under her arms, lifted her into the air, and up to the attic room where dust played with the sunbeams so it all felt like a dream. Eventually when the daylight set itself aside, August stopped crying. Eddie brought in wine and they got drunk and she talked and laughed with a loud abandon, then returned into the field. Uncle Eric took out his clapping sticks and whacked them while relatives sang and danced and green wood cracked and sparked from the night air and the earth being welded together. She slept all day Sunday, and no one came up the stairs to disturb her except for Nana. Elsie brought breakfast at midday and dinner at midnight and she kissed August's head like her mother used to do and she told her she loved her and to rest.

August lay there awake after Nana had gone to bed late on Sunday night. She struggled up and showered and got back into bed naked. August ran her hand over her arm under the blankets. Closed her eyes, cupped her breasts, and found the place of relief between her legs. She rose her hips and tried to feel better, whole, relieved, not shameful. When she was younger, when she had finally grown tiny handfuls of breasts, she thought of Eddie. *Please* she whispered to no one in the dark. But it didn't work, it wasn't what she needed.

Instead she tucked herself, like Jedda used to do, wrapped her arms across the topography of blankets and cried out for her mummy.

When August got up Monday morning she found her clothes had been folded, the desk papers had been stacked in neat piles. She rifled again through Poppy's desk and still couldn't find more than a few sentences in his handwriting. She opened the attic wardrobe that shuddered in the movement, Jedda's empty wire and wooden coathangers clanged together, below them there were three large boxes. August took them out one at a time and emptied the contents on the bed. The boxes were full of Jedda's and her childhood things. The cassette tape was there, *Letter to the Princess*. She found the other cassettes with music recorded off the radio, but not the tape recorder they had. An American-flag-patterned photo frame with a black-and-white instant photo-booth picture of Jedda and her and their mum, folded in half so that two of the pictures fit. They must have been in kindergarten, five years old. She found her own Cabbage Patch doll and lifted her dress to see if her memory was right, that they had operated on the doll. A line of cotton stitches ran down the doll's belly. August smiled. Inside the second box she lifted out the white fur body of Mother Goose. Once, out of nowhere, their mother had given the girls the toy. She had cupped their chins in each hand, and she said, "For my baby swans," and Jedda had whispered "cygnets" as her mum left the room. "What's that mean?" August had asked her. "It's the name for baby swans," Jedda had said, and fished a book from her schoolbag and showed August a list entitled "Animal Groups and Their Young." She pointed out the picture of the swan babies to August. Jedda let her play with the toy while she read aloud the names of all the animals and their young.

The book felt magical in August's hands and she wondered then how she could know all those things from the two opened pages. Mother Goose's eyes never moved; she had a peach-and-blue patterned bonnet and a green patterned bow around her neck. The toy goose, the girls discovered, read along to the stories once they placed the cassette in its player under her velcro wing. Her orange hinged beak would open and close, lip-syncing the words of the story sheet.

She found two grey, worn Agro dolls and cartoon Saturday mornings began to replay in her mind. Mornings soft with cotton nightdresses, blankets dragged from the bunk beds to the living room, rubbing sleep from the warm, soft skin of their faces. Faces still round like when they were babies. They'd won the dolls. She and Jedda used to make parcels to send into *Agro's Cartoon Connection*, a morning television program hosted by a lady and a puppet named Agro. Every Saturday the lady would open packages from kids who'd made things and Agro would joke about his useless cloth arms. Inside the parcels were pieces of cross-stitching, Spirograph stencils, and drawings. She and Jedda used to beg Nana to post their creations. She caved in twice. On the second try they won two Agro dolls for their mouse maze that was made from toilet rolls taped together and painted perfectly. Jedda did the painting since she was the careful one. August had written the letter because that was the only job left.

Dear Agro, my sister and me made this mouse maze for you.
Lots of luv from Jedda and August.

The presenter did say, "Today's prize winner is a brother and sister from Massacre Plains," and at first Jedda and August said *awww* and August stamped her foot and Jedda karate-chopped her own leg— they were so angry that a brother and sister had won instead of them.

But then the presenter said their actual names and they jumped and screamed and their nighties flew up above their bellies. The commercial break came on and they ran into the field, past the vegies, out through the ankle-high wheat shoots and galloped and whooped like cowboys. *Yeeeeahh haaaa!* they screamed. August hadn't even cared that she'd discovered she had a boy's name. She wet her underwear she laughed so much.

Also in the box was a stack of school journals. She lifted them out and saw several tubes of Lip Smackers flavored lip balm at the base of the box—each of the lids was missing, the contents gone. On seeing the empty tubes she remembered how she used to eat them: watermelon, strawberry, lemonade wax flavors filled her mouth. Inside the journal with August's name on the cover, she'd written Monday and the date in the top right corner in shaky print, below it, *On the weekend our mum and dad took us camping in a brand-new caravan and we found wolves in the forest. The wolves were friendly so we spent the camping trip playing with them.* The teacher had corrected the spelling in red pen and added below the drawing that accompanied the unbelievable entry, *VERY interesting.* The book was crammed with writing, stories she'd wanted to tell. In another entry Jedda had begun, *It was a cover-up. Alice fell down the rabbit hole and she* did *land in Australia.* The story was unfinished and the teacher had just drawn a red question mark below it. The rest of the pages were blank.

August placed everything back in the boxes in no particular order, each item precious.

After she dressed and descended the stairs, she put the kettle on and found a tiny scrap of paper taped to the coffee tin: *Out for the day, love Nan.* The rental keys were on the sideboard, and in that moment August took them in her hand and imagined driving those six hours to the women's prison. In her mind her mother would be there, waiting, returned, dressed in her old jeans, ready to play with Jedda and August, ready to return to the sisters as if no time had passed. But it had. She dropped the keys.

August navigated around the kitchen easily, noticing how she had become used to the home again. She remembered where everything was, where all the items fit. She knew the best coffee cup to use for maximum coffee. She knew that the kitchen table rocked and the folded coaster needed to go under the leg for it to be stable. That the floorboards made it impossible to sneak. That the cold and the heat coming in had no insulation either way. It wasn't so bad, she thought, the Packawayable Home. It could be worse. If she peered under enough carpet of her memories in the last ten years, she knew it had been worse, much worse.

She looked into the annex outside but the rooms were all empty. In the shearing sheds August found a scramble of bike parts, rusted pastel low-liners and red and blue racers without wheels or handlebars. Under a sheet sewn from hessian bags, she found a newish, black mountain bike with flat tires. It had its own hand pump clipped into the middle frame and August got to work until the tires were hard, *But not too hard in the heat, 'cos the air'll expand*, Poppy said in her ear. August walked the bike past the peppermint trees to where Eddie was out talking with the postie. The postie drove off and Eddie walked to meet August, grinning. He rested his forearms against the handgrips of the mountain bike and straddled the front wheel. He admired August Gondiwindi, out at Prosperous Farm on a pushbike.

"Did you see Nana this morning?" she asked.

"Haven't. You feeling better, tiny dancer?"

"What does that mean?"

"You had the moves the other night!"

She didn't remember a thing. "Are you joking?"

"It's okay," he squeezed the brakes gently. "Everyone was dancing. I stayed with you a while and then your aunty put you to bed." He tried to look into her eyes. "You okay now?"

She wasn't okay, but she said she was. "I'm alright. It's a bit heavy, coming home."

"You going somewhere now?"

"Just to get online. Library." August wondered if she was going to confirm her flight or cancel it.

"I'd let you use ours, but it's disconnected already."

"No worries."

August looked out toward the field. She could see trucks way out. More trucks than before.

"What are they doing?"

Eddie let go of the bike, straightened up, and looked out to the field. "Getting ready."

"For what?"

"Stripping everything."

August rested on the bike seat.

"I talked to the hippies at Kengal the other day."

"What do they have to say for themselves?"

"Reckon they're going to chain themselves to machines."

The two of them looked up at Kengal. "You should stay," he said matter-of-fact.

"Aren't we all leaving?" she said over the whiff of sentiment.

He looked back at her and smiled. "Yep."

What a smile.

"Want to come to the library?"

"Me at the library?" he laughed. "Can't. I've got about a hundred years of machinery to move from the sheds."

"Did Poppy ever go out to the sheds? I mean, the last couple of months?"

"Nah. You still looking for that thing he was writing?"

"Yeah, but running out of places to look."

"Wanna help me in the sheds?" Eddie asked, laughing.

"Nope. Look at these hands." She showed him her palms as if they were useless for manual work.

He looked at her hands and grinned, gave her a low-five. "I'll see you later?"

"Alright." She put on a pair of sunglasses. "See ya!" she flung a pedal up and began to ride. From under the peppercorn trees she could make out the protesters standing outside their tents.

"Just print your name here," the librarian at the information desk pointed at a form. As August wrote her name she asked, "Are you related to Albert? Albert Gondiwindi?"

August nodded. "My grandfather."

"Lovely," she said, folding her hands on the high desk between them and smiled her cracked lipstick smooth. Her name tag was crooked; Linda handed her a two-page list of titles.

"Would you ask him to return those books tomorrow, end of the week at the very latest? Most were ordered in from the city branch. Otherwise he'll accrue a lot of fines."

They exchanged smiles and nods. She couldn't say the words that meant her poppy wouldn't be back.

Outside the library's entrance was a building directory in black and white. August's eye caught *Council Chambers Level 3*. She thought to pop in and say hello to her Aunt Nicki.

She took the elevator. The office was open plan and no one was manning the desk. Beyond a wall of glass on the right, the entire staff seemed to be sitting around a long conference table. A projector played graphs. Aunt Nicki must have seen August come in because she came out of the glass door quickly and jog-walked across the room to her.

"August."

"Hi, Aunty."

"What are you doing here?"

"Just thought I'd see how the other half live." She mock-nodded approvingly around the office.

Nicki laughed impatiently. "You know, I'm in a meeting now, but are you in town for long? Want to get lunch?"

"I can wait."

"Here, I've got a voucher for a free coffee at the cafe, take that and—" she power walked to her desk nearby, opened her purse, and took out a little card, "have a coffee, and if you are still in town at midday then come find me, okay?"

"Okay."

She hugged August and tapped her on the side of her arm. "See ya at twelve, my shout," Aunt Nicki said, and scooted back toward the glass wall. August turned to walk back to the elevator, where the doors were idling open, but something caught her eye. She looked back at Aunt Nicki's desk and swore that on it she saw her childhood cassette recorder—a vintage thing, rectangular, black, with a red button for recording letters to Princess Diana.

Then she reminded herself they must have manufactured fifty billion of the things when they were still being made. She stepped into the elevator and descended.

Outside there were crows watching her, while a sprinkler spat intermittently over the lawn between the footpath and the building. Crouching beside the bike padlock, she skimmed through Poppy's overdue list:

A Million Wild Acres by Eric Rolls
Blood on the Wattle by Bruce Elder
Cooper's Creek by Alan Moorehead
The Fatal Impact by Alan Moorehead
A History of Australia by C.M.H. Clark
The Story of the Australian Church by Edward Symonds

The list went on, there must have been at least forty titles on the subject of Australia alone. She'd seen the books around the house, in Poppy's office. She wanted to see them again, flick through the pages, try to find Poppy's words. Aunty Nicki wouldn't mind. She cycled straight home.

Nana still wasn't back when August returned. She lugged all the books and papers down to the living room, spread them and matched each title with the list, stacking subject piles across the floor. She took breaks for coffee, and padded around in her worn sleeping t-shirt, shorts, and sneakers. She arranged the Post-it notes on the tabletop. She found the gardening radio that only played short wave, and listened to songs she couldn't sing along to. She skimmed through all the library books until she'd assembled small towers, sorted into their categories: Christianity. Plants. Animals. Cosmology. War. Art History. Farming. She thought she understood then that Poppy was really up to something with these books—he was trying to explain something big.

Several times she stepped out on the veranda and searched for Eddie in the fields. She watched him leading huge machinery across the land, trampling the crop. The sky was wide, heat blurred at the edges.

August was back inside reading one of the library books, *On Animism*, when Eddie came and asked for a quick glass of water.

"They already turned your pipes off?" August asked, side-eyeing Eddie, filling the glass.

"Wanted to see you."

He drank the glass fast and passed it back for a refill. Eddie licked his lips and side-eyed August back.

He looked down at the books and papers between gulps. "What's all this?"

"Poppy's stash of overdue library books."

He sat the glass down, wiped his hands on his t-shirt, and grabbed the book from the counter. He turned it in his hands. "What's animism?"

"When you believe that the earth—and all living things—are alive with ancestors, with spirits."

"Is that what you believe?"

She looked at the book. "I think so."

"Why'd your pop have it, you reckon?"

She smiled widely, "I think he was trying to save the farm."

"How would he have done that, you think?"

"Dunno, reckon he was trying to explain how the land is special?" Eddie raised his eyebrows for August to go on. "I just remember how much he loved, *truly* loved, the land, the property. You remember?"

"Yeah, I remember," he said and placed the glass in the sink.

"Hey," August said, "have you got a cassette thing—to play cassettes?"

"Not bloody likely."

"Come on, you must—you guys always had everything!"

"I'll check after a few more hours of work, yeah?"

"Thanks," she said.

She passed him at the sliding door.

"No worries, mate," he said.

They were friends again after all those years.

Late in the afternoon August walked with Spike around the vegetable patch, picked the shriveled beans that grew through the chicken wire, put her hand under the skirts of strawberries that lapped up the last hours of sunlight. The fruit was hot-sweet. She imagined smiling, serene Poppy in a floppy sunhat, wearing a blue singlet, leaning into the vegetable patch and dusting soil from beetroots. Him carrying a plastic bucket up and down rows of struggling plants, distributing small blessings of water. She never saw him sad on the land. She missed him. At that moment August regretted having been gone so long.

She walked further, let the sound enter her ears—the way the locusts twitched, the warble from birds that seemed to come from a hundred directions at once, the slow build of a draft passing through thousands of bearded stalks. Spike wanted to run—he dipped his back, edged his paws to August, slapped them into the dirt, and gazed at her with his mouth open, barking, tongue out, eager for her to join in. She looked at him for a moment and he threw his paws again, dipped the spine. They ran down to the dam for Spike to drink at the edge and then back, alone and not alone at the same time. So many people ran beside her in her mind. Not only Jedda.

August truly felt like herself there on the land. Her people's land. Her people with her on the land. The dog ran off into the bush and August wandered over to the one-ton silos and opened the hatch, no grain fell out. She looked inside the opening, the grain covered less than a foot of the base; it looked wet and lumpy in places and clung to streaks of rust on the steel walls. She and Jedda used to pretend they were bubblegum machines, the nitrate fixers and the lupin pulses their candy.

When Jedda first disappeared August used to daydream about all the ways she herself would end up dying in Massacre Plains, a recital played in her head: *Hang myself, choke on diesel fumes, drown in the manure pumps, suffocate in the hay bales, sink into the wheat seeds, get sucked into a thresher, tumble down an abandoned well, fall in a mining shaft, a horse hoof to the head, trampled by a cow, crushed by a tractor without a roller bar, crushed by a tractor with a roller bar, a grain bin without a harness, an aerial sprayer falling from the sky, killer water disease, killer viral disease, dying of thirst, dying of infection, a gun to the heart, a gun to the head, drowning in the dam, burned in a wildfire, snapped by a venomous snake, swallowing poisonous berries, deadly spider bites, a swarm of wasps, a murder of crows, buried in a silo.*

Years after Jedda was gone, August had read about pilot whales in the newspaper. She'd read how if one of those mammals were sick, and beached itself, then the rest of the family would do the same thing. That the pod couldn't exist with one of their own gone, and so they went too. It was natural, August thought a long time too late, that it was normal to want to go as well. That in the face of loss, only losing oneself seems like an answer. August was about to unlatch the main door of the second silo when Eddie pulled up on a 50cc dirt bike beside her. His arrival brought her back to the living.

"Girl's bike?"

"Yep," he said, and revved it weakly. "You want a double?"

"Where?"

"Just a turn."

August climbed on. They drove right out to the end of the crop—five hundred acres distant. They swerved through hardened tractor-tire marks in the once-muddy groves. She watched their shadows as they passed the dam. They were separate, two bodies. They looped past the farthest fence, down past the sheep sheds. Near the river flocks of cockatoo screeched and beat their wings and flew for cover in the gums. Eddie stopped the bike at the stables. "Where's Mister Ed?" August asked, but knew the answer. No one had mentioned him since she'd arrived. "He was old" was all Eddie said. The girls had begged Eddie's mum to name the white horse Mister Ed, after the old TV-show horse that could talk. She relented to the two barefoot girls who saw him arrive by trailer and ran along up to the stables to see. He'd been dusty white, he'd smelled of dry grass, of turned earth.

August drove the dirt bike on the way back, proud she remembered how to do the thing she'd almost forgotten. Eddie wrapped his arms around her, leaned into her back. She felt exhilarated, alive, rushing through daylight. She looked to the side again at their shadows—together they looked like a sphinx.

She pulled up at the driveway, her hands slick with sweat. She dismounted the bike and held one handlebar until Eddie took the weight.

August stood with her hands on her hips. "Remember how summer used to be the beginning of everything, how the world got so much bigger every year at the same time, that there was no end and beginning and we forgot we even had to return to school?"

"Sort of," he said, and rolled his eyes.

August heard the collective bleats from the sheep shed.

"What are you doing with the rams and the ewes?"

"Stock and station agent will be out tomorrow. They're off to auction."

August scrunched her face, "Hope they don't have to go too far?"

Before Eddie could answer they both turned to the sound from the driveway and watched the car pull into Prosperous.

"Leave you to it," Eddie said, and waved to the car and pushed the motorbike away.

August approached the driveway and stopped under a mallee, reached her hands to the branch above her head, let her body drop. She swung gently from the tree watching her nana exit the car carrying a flat cardboard box. August hung there and looked above the peppermint tree arch to Kengal; she could make out a few silhouettes. She closed her eyes, imagining strange Mandy leaning into her face, kissing the lids of each of her eyes that she thought were beautiful.

"You look just like you did as a little girl," Nana called out warmly.

"I feel like a little girl." August smiled and released herself from the branch and padded toward the car to help. "Where've you been?"

"Looking at old-lady homes."

"I thought you were staying with Aunty?" August looked to Aunt Mary climbing out of the driver's seat, and back to Nana.

"I'd have a cot in the sunroom and no privacy. I love you," she turned and touched Aunty on the arm, "but no thank you."

"Are they paying?" August nodded toward the Rinepalm trucks in the field.

"No, I won't get a cent. We've saved next to nothing over the years. Enough of this talk—it bores me, August. Go back to your tree." She chuckled to herself a little then and they carried the box inside. August followed. She badly wanted to listen to Jedda and her tapes to Princess Diana. "Have you seen the old tape player, Nan?"

"Albert was using it for his book. Don't know, darling."

"Okey-dokey. I'm starting to feel like the book has just disappeared from the face of the earth." She swung her arms from behind her to in front of her. She wasn't bored, exactly, but moving her arms like that, she felt like a teenager, like she was part of a home again, standing there with her family, doing nothing in particular. Nana and Aunt Mary ignored her, instead they began sorting dishes of food from the chest freezer. August looked through the sliding glass door to the dam.

The brolga was back. *Burral-gang*, she whispered, and went outside. Spike followed her and they crouched together under the banksias in the setting sun. August watched Jedda dance again. She looked back to the house. Her nana stood in the doorway braced against the frame, smiling and wide-eyed at August.

Twenty-Seven

Reverend Ferdinand Greenleaf's letter to Dr. George Cross,
2nd August 1915, continued

VII

The family of Wowhely bequeathed his fishing spear to me. It was a sight to behold, notched and smoothed, the entire length in Yarrany tree wood and six darts protruding at the end—its workmanship was evident. It was grander than mahogany furniture, in that its veneration began before the tree was even cut. Fearful of it being stolen and burned by the White men returning and razing my hut in my sleep, which they might have done with ease, I sent it with Baumann on his next visit to the city to deliver up to the museum, which I know he would have dutifully done.

Throughout the past decades, bullets and spears had traveled between the Natives and the Whites. The old gunyahs were razed. Other camps of free Blacks were also razed and word reached us that in other parts, the west of the land, blood ran even thicker. Many events occurred, and in each incident, those men responsible for causing us such distress were never brought to justice; understandably, there was retaliation, much to the detriment of my nerves.

I myself lost my naivety a long time ago. I have witnessed the cruelest acts that man can inflict upon his fellow man with clear vision and sound mind. It seemed every White man was cut from the same cloth, born disgruntled by the Natives. During the trips I made for service and enquiry, I continued to come face to face with brutality. Sometimes I passed the thin remains of my fellow man, cracked and discarded like the mussel shells I'd seen by the riverbank. In 1891 for instance, I saw two Native boys running along a track twenty miles from our residence, both boys' bodies were sheened with fear. I stopped them and asked them to explain themselves. The two boys explained in English that they had been in the employ of a local Station master, the eldest being fourteen, and both had run away after being flogged. The eldest boy turned to have me see his back. An inch-deep slice was evident, blood congealed and the white of inner skin wept as if it were fresh. I dismounted the horse and as we were conversing, the Station owner in question arrived on the stallion; he didn't regard my presence, even when I demanded he address me, but instead drove the boys back with the stockwhip those twenty miles. I regret not taking pursuit, as I learned that the elder boy was later lashed to a fence in a crucifixion pose and then flogged until he fainted. The second boy was treated in the same manner, and after one lash wore out, the settler began to attach another when the boy, in his agony, screamed out, "Oh, master, if you want to kill me cut my throat, but don't cut me to pieces." The brute, unmoved, continued flogging until the second lash had worn out. News of this horrible deed reached our town and the inhumane monster was brought in. He admitted to flogging the first as much as he had the second boy because "they could bear it," adding that he had "lost his temper." The magistrate inflicted a fine of £5 for flogging the younger boy and £1 for the one who could bear it.

Around the same time of the year, with my own eyes, I'd happened upon a Native woman owing to another settler being debauched, violated viciously, out in the open upon the ground seventy miles north. I was ordered away by firearm by a fellow brute keeping watch, no doubt intent on having his turn. I needn't tell anymore; it is all a horror. I reported the incident to His Excellency the Governor, but nothing came before the Courts.

The few cases I came to hear of that were brought before magistrates I made an effort to attend in the viewing stalls. All cases of this nature were indulged in by the judges turning their heads or at most imposing the cost of a paltry fine. In Australia where so much is said to overseas officials, written in the bulletins of the humane treatment of our Aborigines, the conduct of the settler and local magistrate are not enquired into. It demands strict enquiry, it has for so many years, yet I had and remain resigned to a ceaseless state of bewilderment, anger, and fear. I do hope someone of influence, as yourself, dear Dr. Cross, might read these words and be willing, surely abler than myself, to do something?

I will continue . . .

By 1892 we had incurred a great interest from the Aborigines Protection Board once more in our activities at the Mission. They once again sent out observers and once again we made provisions to welcome them, our hopes desperately pinned on securing a regular income. What great surprise then greeted us that the Board was interested in the wonderful craftsmanship of our residents. A contract was delivered by hand from America, a request for items to display at the World's Fair, a celebration of Columbus and his great social achievement for humanity, to be staged the following year. All colonies of the world were participating, and they'd made direct interest in exhibiting the Aborigine. The Colonial Secretary refused to have a Native leave for Chicago, but they wanted evidence of the progress of Darwin and someone to present the evolution of our Aborigine. This story you know firsthand, Dr. Cross.

My passage would be paid and I was to be engaged at £90 per annum for the duration of the Mission activities and my part in it. There was no question in not accepting such a firm commitment to our cause, and so with great enthusiasm, we set about instructing the residents on how to make the display pieces. Captain Everill sought to procure illustrations by the Native children and self-portraits of the Aboriginal race of the Colony, statistics connected with the initiatives of the Protection Board, together with any collections of weapons of war. Dr. Cross, you requested all available information connected with the physical development of the Aborigines from the leading districts of the Colony. In the letter it stated the need for "plaster casts of the skull of three Aborigines." On my writing back to ask on what grounds, you responded it was "for collections of ethnology" and expanded to make clear the casts were to be used to "prove cognitive development of savages." You must remember I made clear in my reply that I would only have my residents participate in the submission of crafts and weaponry, and not the scientific details you were after. It was gracious of you to relent in the end.

Within two months we had thirty fine pieces of cross-stitching, lace, and needlework patches with Psalms and domestic invocations, each measuring a square foot. Mary stitched one of the finest that was trimmed with neat yellow rosebuds, it read *Cleanliness is next to Godliness*. We were supplied with fine varnished wood, glass, and small nails in order that they were framed.

During this time we continued to instruct the children to ask

God to bless them and preserve the Empire in its unity. We taught them to love, honor, and respect the country in which they lived, and moreover the flag that waved over them. At that time, in 1893, 150 residents remained. The depression of 1890 was felt there on our little Mission and for many years hardship reigned beyond comparison. Some of the residents took to supplementing school lessons and assisted the remaining seventeen children in my absence.

Keller and the other residents carried on the managing duties during my expedition. My absence totaled 143 days where a second-class cabin on the SS *Margot* was provided for me. The ship had fine iron balustrades throughout and a salon. On disembarking in New York City I took the Great Northern Railway by passenger locomotive to the City of Chicago and was put up in a clean boarding house for my assigned three days of the Exposition. There, I spoke with you and others of the excellent progress made by our Mission residents and within New South Wales, but said nothing of all the woe. The Exposition, I admit, was quite remarkable, and I was glad to be informed months later that hundreds of thousands of spectators had viewed the Australian display. I conversed with many interested people and petitioned some interest into supporting our endeavors from keen philanthropists, and promptly wrote to Keller to express my brimming hope that our House of Mercy would prosper once again. It was, in looking back, but a blinding hope in me to ignore what I had seen and hope for what I had not. Perhaps, like the thousands of visitors tossing coins at the feet of the human zoo, I too had been tricked by the rush to progress, and by the pillars of gold and copper, and dazzling light of the White City.

So it was with no small measure of relief finally to return to Massacre Plains and our home, where I dutifully set to work making repairs and storing rations for our residents, purchased with the promised wage.

As a new century began, it was plain that challenges would still beset us. In 1908 Prosperous Mission nearly halved in numbers to only ninety-five residents after a terrible bout of consumption that was made worse with the flooding of the Murrumby. The Natives who were in the habit of frequenting the Mission to stay a night or two and converse with relatives had mostly disappeared.

And the children had grown up. Little Mercy, one of the first children our Mission welcomed, was in love and I had the great and honorable joy of presiding over her union to another resident, a dear and clever fellow named Solomon, whose father had been decorated with a brass plate many years before by explorers. Its inscription read "King Billy of the Badlands." Solomon carried it in a dillybag at all times.

In 1909 dear Mercy gave birth to a healthy daughter, whom she gave a lovely Lutheran name, Augustine. The celebration of the event was quickly muted as that same month the Protection Board sought to impose tighter restrictions on the Mission and ordered that all but the full-blood Natives should be handed over for employment, scattered like numbers.

Well, we locked the gates. The mothers cried out and I wouldn't allow the division. The full-bloods and the half-castes saw no division in each other, and I complained at length on this matter to the Constable who came to enforce the law by delivering me a petition. "After all I have done for the Board," I said, aghast at this draconian decision-making. He merely shrugged. I felt I were eating my words and they were inedible.

TWENTY-EIGHT

house, dwelling place—*bimbal, ganya* When we arrived to make Prosperous our home once again, before the whirly-whirly arrived and stayed, the ancestors would walk with me for hours down along the riverbank. I listened and looked carefully. And they tried to show me things while I was working the field, they'd run alongside the stump-jump plough, pointing things out, but I was busy a lot of the time. Once they showed me the houses that used to be in Massacre Plains, how they were round, made from the red stringybark—*gundhay*. How the wood was easy to handle, how the roofs were reinforced with clay moldings and gum branches. We had a home, they tried to show me. A real *bimbal*.

husk, of seeds—*galgan* All life comes from the seed—*yurbay*. When you harvest you make sure you keep your husks safe. There are companies like the mining company trying to own the seeds. This is a scary thing to me, people trying to put a price on the farmers' seeds. In Mexico, in India, everywhere crops are grown—even in this very country there's a monopoly of bad guys trying to own the seeds. Can you imagine! Owning the center of life, one company!

hunt—*barra-winya* The women would collect berries while the men hunted for kangaroo in the mornings. After they had dealt with the catch, they'd take some fat of the animal and go hunting again for the sugarbag. First they'd find the honeybee on the purple flowers. Gently they'd catch one and with a hair from the hunter's head, slid through the animal fat, would entwine the hair around the end of the bee. They'd let go of the honeybee—*ngarru*—and follow him, as he became heavy and stressed. The first place he'd want to go like that would be home, and so the hunters would follow and were always led to the sugarbag hidden in the tree.

gaol, shut place—*ngunba-ngidyala* When your own daughter and then your grandson get put in gaol it must make the family look like trouble, I'm sure. But it isn't so simple. Both Jolene and Joey made mistakes but the punishments outweighed the crimes. As much as the government wants to convince the population otherwise, it is an old thinking—locking us up as a solution. I think in this country there are divisions that run further than the songlines. The closed place, the shut place—the *ngunba-ngidyala*—is first built in the mind, and then it spreads.

geebung—*bumbadula* This is a magic tree. The wood of the stem of a young tree is shaved and mixed with breastmilk for use as eyewash to treat conjunctivitis in babies. The unripe fruit are also used to treat burns, scratches, and rashes and the ripe flesh around the seeds is eaten straight from the tree. The ancestors even used the *bumbadula* to make dye to color baskets. The older, hard fruits are roasted and cracked, and the nut inside is eaten. Doesn't that one sound magic to you?

granddaughter—*garingun* My poor, darling *garingun*, there is no love stronger. It's there forever. I'm so sorry for her. I'm so sorry. My biggest regret is that I let her down. That will be the heaviest thing I carry with me for all time.

grey shrike thrush—*yurung* The *yurung* is a warning bird. When he calls, bad news is coming. Small and grey. He tilts his head high when he has news, his throat drops, his sharp beak points to where the news needs delivering. The call, you've probably heard too, it goes *coo, coo, coo, coo* followed by a trilling and then a final, rising *cooee*. Hold fast to your affairs then. The *yurung*, no matter how cute, gentle, and delicate looking he is, only brings darkness. He visited me often.

fish—*guya* The old Reverend in his notes, he wrote down *cooyah*—but the word comes from further back in the mouth, *guya*.

fishing—*ngalamarra* If the water comes back to Murrumby, and the fish too, the best way to catch a fish is with patience. *Ngalamarra*—there's two types, saltwater and freshwater, running water and still. There's still saltwater too—in the estuaries on beaches, but I only know freshwater. Only still freshwater now, but the river! The songlines of our ancestors follow water like markers on a highway. Many fish are endangered now, don't take the perch, don't take the grayling, no freshwater cod from up north, no gudgeon, no jollytail. Never buy fish from the food mart, or the restaurant, or Nemo's fish and chip shop in town. You want to eat it? You catch it! Everyone should learn four things—how to *ngalamarra*, how to love someone boundlessly, how to grow your own vegetables, and how to read. The patience for *ngalamarra*, respect for loving, the soil for gardening, and a dictionary for reading.

flour made from millet seed—*buwu-nung, dargin* When the millet plant is late flowering and the seed heads have turned golden brown, then you can cut the heads off and save the mature seeds for planting again—these are the swollen ones and will come away easiest from the cluster. The rest of the seed head needs to dry in the sun for a few days, and then the seeds should fall away easily. Next grind the seed as fine as you like. You can grind them rough for porridge or into *bawu-nung* for making bread. This is our harvest, since forever.

flower, a kind of flower—*bagabin, narranarrandyirang* The banksia flower is my favorite, not just because it's large and proud looking like the hibiscus, but because it reminds me of something bigger. See, the banksia is a tough-looking flower but it still protects itself with sharp, jagged leaves, sturdy wood and roots. Its nectar feeds the bees, the birds, and us people. When the flower finishes its cycle its pods burst open and seeds are released, and the cone will fall from the branch. Now the cone has two uses, one it can start a fire very well and keep it going like a piece of coal; the other thing it can be used for is to filter water, it'll run right through it.

forbid to tell a thing—*walan-buwu-ya-rra* This word literally translates to "strong-law speaking" and the ancestors told me that it is as serious as scripture. There were things they showed and told me that I was forbidden to tell to the wrong person. Some things are unspoken, and you carry them up until the end. That's *walan-buwu-ya-rra*.

earth oven—*gulambula* The ancestors showed me how they cooked in the *gulambula*: first they dug a pit about a meter long and half a meter deep, making sure to get any clay out of the earth as they went. Then they filled the pit with firewood and then with the clay they collected, they rolled it into lumps and placed them on top of the fire-wood, as the wood burned the clay would dry and become very hot. After a couple of hours, the clay lumps were then taken out with sticks used like a pair of tongs and placed to the side, then the pit was swept out and lined with green leaves, some laid down the green grasses or green wood too, not dried. Quickly, a possum wrapped in paperbark was laid, covered by more green vegetation and finally the clay lumps were returned on top. All this was covered with the earth to make a nice, tight seal. When it was ready, they dug up the *gulambula* and then we ate the steamed dinner. Then we talked about the little things that are big things.

edible milky yam—*murnong, bading* In the old times, if you didn't catch anything hunting or now if you are a vegetarian, this one is a good meat replacement. The *murnong* has the yellow, firework-shaped flower, and the tubers that grow under the ground you dig like car-rots, and just the same way, you can eat them raw or cooked in the *gulambula*. They taste a bit sweet and a bit like coconut; *murnong* is very good food.

emu feet—*nguruwinydyinang-garang* Biyaami, or Baiame, has such feet—sometimes in my dreams I float around with useless hands and feet. Hands that won't do the things I tell them to while I'm sleep-ing, and feet that won't run fast enough to escape the bad guys. They might as well be flippers in sand then. Think about how impossible it is that a goanna looks like he does, and then look at your lover and wonder how they look the way they do. Now imagine the lizard in a rage, and then imagine your lover really angry. I reckon that it's not so hard to imagine the blending of human and animal. We all come from the same soil. Well, Biyaami had emu feet, I don't know why, they are as good a feet as any. I asked my ancestors and they said, "Little one, what does it matter? Some things just are."

TWENTY-NINE

August spent the morning packing Prosperous's shaving cabinet, medicine cupboard, and linen press into boxes. She scoured the attic again for Albert's manuscript though came up empty.

Before lunch she went to see Eddie. August felt light and excited; she thought about the books Poppy had put together and a little lamp of hope began to burn in her guts. She was thinking about the conversation she'd had with Eddie the day before, about summer, the world getting bigger. She wanted to talk to Eddie about how everything didn't have to end. How she could stay, how they could save Prosperous and the farm, she thought, as she walked up the hill toward perfect Southerly House. She heard a rumble, and in the field she could see Rinepalm trucks entering the southern cattle road, a crane arm bent over a cab, another piled high with what looked like fences and scaffolding, supplies for a more elaborate set-up.

The door was open, but the flywire door was shut.

"*Oi*," she sang, and let herself in. No wooden surface had been polished in a while, walls were stripped of the landscape paintings, the molded ceilings were the high home of spiders now.

She walked through the house and found Eddie in the back room.

He was wearing jeans, kneeling beside a cardboard removal box.

"Oi," he said, glancing at August and taking a swig from a beer bottle.

"You on the booze already?"

"Going down like nails. You want one?"

"Why not." August took her shoes off and walked them back up the hall to the front door. She came back and Eddie passed her an opened beer then put his phone in the top of the tall speaker. Pearl Jam was playing halfway through *Ten*.

"Remember this?" Eddie said, and raised his beer to tap against her own.

She felt fifteen again. "I feel like your parents are going to come home and I'll have to sneak out the back door."

"Good old days," he said, and stood, stretching out his back. "You could have left your shoes on, it'll be rubble soon."

She held the beer against her chest, took a breath through a smile, looked around the empty space.

"You want some help?"

"Lunch first?"

"I'm fine."

He assembled a box quickly, taped its base, and threw it at August.

"How much am I getting paid?"

"My eternal gratitude."

"Everything I ever wanted," she said, sitting at the foot of the bookshelf, swigging at the bottle.

After a few minutes of silent packing Eddie asked, "You know that book you were reading about the spirits in everything?"

"Animism," she said, hands deep in the box.

"Do you reckon your pop went to the land then or to heaven?"

"You mean, do I believe in the afterlife?"

"That," Eddie said, and took the last mouthful of his beer.

"I think he'll go somewhere, but I don't think there's a heaven." August took another gulp and added, "Pearl Jam *and* talking about the afterlife—I really do feel like a teenager again."

He stood and continued packing from the back of the room, removing spines from wallpaper-lined bookshelves. He shook his head. "It's silly. Doesn't change anything whatever we believe."

"Believe?"

"It doesn't change the fact you end up dead, does it? I hate religion."

August rolled her eyes in his direction. She didn't think Eddie was stupid, but felt like he'd just never stopped saying the stupid things they'd said when they were young. "You hate religion—that's original. What about all the churches and paintings and poetry?"

"What about all the wars?"

"I'm having déjà vu. I think I've had this conversation a hundred times *and* I still think humans would have warred and slaughtered each other with or without religion."

"Over land?" he turned and looked at her with a gravity, but also a question. He moved back to the bookshelf. "Or race wars?"

"Yeah, and even if we all had the same skin tone, it'd be language, and then even if we spoke the same language, it'd be eye shape, nose length, people with thick hair . . ."

She sat down her empty bottle, got off the couch and stood beside him, lifting a handful of books to pack. "How's your mum doing, really?"

He put another handful of books into the box. "She's okay, I think she's about done with life, though. She always hated the country."

"Australia?"

"Farm life."

She looked again around their huge, now-empty home. It was big, as she always thought it was and even seeing it again with adult eyes.

"Couldn't have been that bad," August said, but guessed it was.

When Eddie was thirteen years old and August was eleven, a black book was swiped from a massage therapist in Broken and lists of names were smuggled around the region. After that loads of parents got divorced. They'd watched Eddie's mum beat Eddie's dad with a fresh strip of willow branch as he left the property, but not for the last time.

"You know they reunited in a way again, when Mum got sick. I guess that happens when . . ."

He looked tired with trying to work out his feelings, bowed his head into the box. "I reckon I liked your pop more than my old man."

"Pop?"

"Yeah."

"I reckon he was likeable, that's for sure. I know I liked him more than anyone else." He paused before he spoke again, quieter, gentler. "You really thought your mum would turn up?"

August sat back on the couch, exhausted, she knew maternal empathy hadn't been sealed by the umbilical-cord clip. Enough time as an adult made her know this, but she was confused about what the whole trip meant, what Poppy's death was supposed to mean. What Jedda missing meant. They'd waited for a death certificate for her, as families just like August's do. Or waited for an end to a life in gaol. So many people gone and dead—she thought more loss would make the family close, a whole thing again.

"*I* turned up."

He dumped more books and sat beside August, looked at the almost bare bookshelves. "I was hoping you would. Do you know where she is even? Your mum?"

"Last news from Nana was that she was trying to get day release. I don't think she can leave anymore."

"Why?"

"I don't know. I think for some people you always find your way home. Gaol becomes like home. Reckon Kooris know how to stay locked up."

Eddie pulled at a frayed part of his jeans.

"But," August added, "I reckon we're meant to stretch our wings, move around, it feels so natural to travel. I think Mum just couldn't see herself out of a cage. Maybe she stopped waking up and thinking of somewhere else."

He lay his arm across the back of her neck, grabbed her shoulder, and pulled her into his chest. She let her head rest there. She realized she was desperate to be touched.

"Families are tricky, Aug. My dad disappeared forever then just shows up for Mum's finale."

He ran one hand hard along the top of his thigh as if he were somehow cold in the high thirties.

"I'm sorry."

She looked at him playfully, wanted to forget the muddied water, the diesel, the dirt, the flesh that she was beginning to taste and smell again, wanted to wash it out of her mouth. "Let's have another drink!"

"Ah, you haven't changed after all!"

She hadn't, she thought. She still needed to be numb. Her drink of choice was always oblivion. She couldn't bear to feel so much and they each drank another beer hastily. They wanted the same thing that they both didn't want to admit.

August walked to the stereo and skipped the song on his phone. "Better Man" flooded through the speakers. The sun was high and streamed through the skylight, a column of white light fell against the way ahead of her. Eddie's shadow came behind her, his arm reached around her waist and slid the volume up. August sculled the beer while he stood close, not touching her. She stood her bottle atop the speaker and turned into him.

Avoiding his eyes, she looked at his lips as he mouthed the lyric *waiting*.

August reached her face up and kissed him hard on the mouth. He pulled her so their hips pressed against each other. His mouth was soft, the short stubble on his face brushed around her lips and didn't hurt.

He picked her up, their teeth bumped. Her toes barely off the floor, he carried her blindly down the hallway and together they fell onto his bed.

They were on their sides, facing each other. He held her around the middle, tight and kind at the same time and mirrored everything she did, and she mirrored everything he did. His hand on her waist, her hand on his waist. Her hand smoothing up his back, his hand smoothing up hers. His lips on her neck, behind her ear and her lips on his neck, behind his ear. It tasted like salt. His breath turned into a groan. His hand on the small of her back, her hand on the small of his and with one hand he unclasped her bra, then unbuttoned her blouse.

A metronome ticked faster through their kissing that was full of wet hot breath and needing. It all felt synchronized, as natural as swimming.

She tugged at his waistband and he stood up flinging each of his cap boots against the wall. Quickly, he dropped his underwear and jeans and kicked them across the floorboards. He stood naked, unashamed, fine hair ringed his nipples, a line spread from his penis almost to his navel. He smiled like a question; she returned the smile like an answer.

From the end of the bed he crawled slowly above August as she eased her neck into the pillows and closed her eyes. He kissed down to a cup between her abdomen and hip. "This," he said, and licked the skin.

She looked down.

The muscles across his back shifted with the movement of his arms. There was a line of tanned skin at the back of his neck. He unbuttoned the top of her jeans, slipped his fingers between the denim and her like testing the heat of bathwater, as if he feared it was too hot. He kissed her and she flexed her hips away to stop his hand from going any lower, guiding him to stay high. As soon as his fingers touched her clitoris, pins and needles started from the bottom of her feet, the palms of her hands, filling out the rest of her body. Like she was being dipped into the stars, like sherbet and Pop Rocks on the inside of her skin. Her legs and arms became heavy, the same way grief felt, and for a moment she wondered whether she was actually feeling sad, and not pleasured.

He kept one hand wedged in against her and took the side of her neck with the other, his mouth on hers was wetter and hotter. Then he rested his face into the side of her neck for a moment. Further down his tongue circled each of her breasts and down again the length of her arm until he reached the hand. He turned his head, opened his mouth, and bit into the inner skin of her forearm, softly first and then his eyes looked up at hers as if asking if it was okay, waiting for that little nod from her. August nodded. He bit harder and harder, then stopped and sucked at the skin. Kissed it better. He pushed off the mattress with his lower body and sat at the end of the bed with bent knees, his chest was upright. Above her his fingers worked at the zipper of her jeans.

He looked at her face. "I want you, August Gondiwindi."

"*Wait*," she whispered.

He stood off the mattress and pulled under her knees to draw her to the edge of the bed and buried his face into the parting of her jean buttons. He kept moving and kissing the curve in her. Kissing what curve he could find.

"*Wait.*" She wanted to be drunk. She wanted not to feel it all, not to become something else, let go, transform. Not to fall into the act where Eddie's body was just another, blended into the memories and desires and smells of others.

"For what?" he looked up from her bare torso. "Another ten years? All I've wanted—is to do this to you." He grunted then. He looked back at her face, she nodded, relinquished.

She groaned and lifted her arm and inspected the bite mark. It was faint and didn't break the skin. A clearing opened in her mind, in it a memory lodged clear of Jedda and her fighting.

August had screamed out to their nana, she felt the yelp at her throat then, "Jedda bit me!" And Elsie appeared in her mind, she was there in the room telling Jedda off for playing savage, then took August's wrist and inspected the bite mark on her arm. She could see the front-tooth gap in the skin, the gap that Jedda didn't have, but that August did. Elsie told the girls to get to the bathroom and there she squeezed a full tube of toothpaste onto the bowl of the sink. Elsie told Jedda to help August put the paste into the tube and told them both, a punishment for August, a lesson for Jedda that, "It's impossible to unsay the things you shouldn't."

August wanted to keep collapsing into the sheets, but her mind was tracking. She gently pushed Eddie's head from her, shifted in the bed, and began to tell him that story.

"*Shh*," he said, and tried to lean her back, kissing her neck, coaxing her to come with him.

"I don't want it," she said, the words dropping from her mouth like heavy rocks into calm water.

He pushed off the bed swiftly and stood. His penis, in a spread of fine brown hair, was full and quivered above his thigh. "What *do* you want?" He looked as confused as August was.

She didn't know what she wanted. But somewhere she knew she didn't want the blindness of fucking. Of feeling. Perhaps, she thought, she was too used to feeling the ache of never being satisfied.

"Yesterday, you said stay. But the tin mine?"

"Stay in the continent, yeah! Move to the city with me!"

"And what if Jedda came back here? What if she came home and no one was here?"

"Is this a joke?"

"And just forget about Prosperous? Because I don't know who I am without this place." August said the thing before she knew it was true. "Because some people have nowhere else to go back to ever. Just the idea of Prosperous here, when I was away, was a comfort. It's a place I could always come back to. All that childhood stuff, stuff your parents keep for you, stuff from when you were a kid—there's nothing of that for me."

He was yelling now, "But you *never* came back."

"If I wanted to though, I could've," and she too yelled. "I'm back *now*!"

"That's part of being an adult, August, you make your own place to come back to. You think I want to be in my childhood home forever?" He slapped his arms against the bed. "Fucking hell, August! You want the truth?"

"Truth." She parroted the word. She pulled the sheet over her chest, not knowing at all if he had the answer. Then she whispered, "Why are you angry?"

"The truth! The truth is that I wanted to run away, too. Why did *you* get to leave? Why did everyone else get to move on but me?" He threw his arms into the air and slapped them back down on the mattress, paced back and forth near the foot of the bed, and punched the wall. Flakes of plasterboard split into the warm air.

He looked at her then, and spoke through his teeth. "You want to know the *truth*? *I* wanted to sell the property. *I* wanted to get paid finally. A fucking wage from this constant slog that gave me *nothing*. I used to work the field and look over at Prosperous every fucking day, waiting for you to come back. You want the truth? Prosperous is a dwelling! They fucking surveyed the property—it's not even a house! It was a slave yard, August, where all your grannies and poppies learned to be servants and fence builders and if my fucking grandad hadn't let the Gondis live at that *dwelling*, you'd all be homeless drunks like the Vegemite Valley lot. *We* saved you! You want that truth? I'll show you the fucking truth."

He ran out of the room and August threw the covers back to find her bra and get the hell out of there.

He stormed back in before she could leave, yet he was slower, sure now and still naked, and emptied a box of books onto the floor. He snatched a pile of envelopes without addresses on them. "I've been packing this whole house, haven't I? *Reliable Eddie!* You want to know what I found? I found this before your pop died! I didn't even have the guts to show him! Here! I'll read it to you!"

He jumped on the bed, standing over her feet. Their legs were touching, their bodies separate. His face was flush with adrenaline; she cowered into the pillows. He pulled out the first small card from the envelope. "Thank you for your contribution to the Falstaff Collection. The Museum Australia. *Submission:* Message stick, elaborately carved with kangaroos, emus, snakes. Number, 1. Dated: 500 years. Axe heads, approximate number 10; Anvil stones, 5. Dated: 400 years."

His legs were shaking, his hands and voice too.

He ripped out the next card, "*Submission:* Wooden club, elaborately carved with tribal incisions. Number, 2. Dated: circa, 5,000 years. Shield, engraved with pattern, Number, 1, 70cm × 11cm. Dated: 3,000 years."

He ripped out another. They were both trembling now. The taste was nausea.

"You want to hit me?" he screamed. "This is where all your culture is! Under fucking glass! The *dates*! My fuckhead father donated the last one! In 1980—just before we were born! *Submission:* Wooden shovel, intricately carved with brolgas, used for digging earth mounds. Number, 1. Dated 7,000 years. Milling grinding stones, approximate number, 35; Anvil stones, 7; Fire stones, 30. Evidence of agricultural activity dated: circa, 10,000 years."

When he'd read the last card he ripped the quilt away from the mattress and slapped the envelopes onto the bed, and walked, inconsolable, out of the room. August pulled the sheet off her body and grabbed her clothes, dressed, and ran. They both knew everything had been said.

She hurried through Southerly's English garden to the other side of the low fence. The dirt was hot, unbearable to walk on with bare feet, but she wanted to feel it, feel the boil of the ground, flinch over the protruding gum roots. She wanted the bull ants to stun her. They fled up the roots instead.

She took a good look at Prosperous from the dirt driveway. It was a relic, not a house. Above it, she imagined she'd spot birds of prey, but no birds at all circled in the white-hot zenith. Only on the roof gutter a lone shrike, cloaked in sun, its head cocked, watched.

Thirty

eternity, things to come—*girr* Did you remember that the "rr" is trilled? It sounds like disappointment when you say it *girr*. And this might disappoint you, but I can't tell you what the things to come are, what happens tomorrow, just as nobody can tell me.

day after tomorrow—*nganha-gunhung-guwala* The last weeks of my life have been spent sitting out here at Prosperous. I can look up and see all the work I've done in the years. Repairing the roof, installing sealed windows into new frames, the guttering, fixing loose floorboards, painting the outside. I haven't done much work on the thing the last few years. Eddie lends me the tools I need and holds the ladder. And the rest of the time I've spent at the library. I will miss the library when I can't visit there anymore. I'm going soon, I'm going *nganha-gunhung-guwala*. I'm trying not to dwell on it too much and trying to finish these words during the hours I have each day. Maybe I won't finish everything I meant to, but maybe someone else will tomorrow, next day, someday. Remember Matthew 6:34, *Therefore do not worry about tomorrow, for tomorrow will worry about itself. Each day has enough trouble of its own.*

dead man—*gudin* After they'd drained the dam, and searched the property three times, after I'd made my spear and sat with my evidence for long enough, I left the house in the night, and pushed the car out the driveway and halfway up the street before turning on the ignition. I drove to the boardinghouse flats he lived in. I crept up the side of the building and looked in the window. He was watching telly, feet up and drinking a beer like he didn't have a worry in the world. I leaned my spear outside his front door; I put my boot between the screen and knocked. "Who's there?" he said. "Me," I said. He cracked open the door and I shoved my boot inside, grabbed him by the throat and with the other hand brought the tip of the spear to his chin. "Walkabout time," I said. I walked him to the car, put him in the driver's seat, and told him to drive out to the back of the satellites. I held the spear low against his side: "Drive steady or you'll be in trouble." We didn't pass another car at that small hour. When we arrived, I told him to walk out nice and easy for a talk. Under the light of the satellites, I asked him flat: "Where is Jedda? You tell me and I won't hurt you too much." He put his head in his hands, swore he didn't know, but I knew then. Only a guilty man hides his face. I took a couple of paces back and raised the spear. "The further I go back the further this thing is going to go through you, Jimmy," I warned. Well, just like that he took off and I threw my spear, got him in the back of the thigh. He staggered a little and I took chase, but the bastard held the thing there and ran into the night. So I knew then. I knew everything had fallen apart.

THIRTY-ONE

*Reverend Ferdinand Greenleaf's letter to Dr. George Cross,
2nd August 1915, continued*

VIII

For a number of years I have been in fear for my life, as if a likely
denouement to the recent events. Two months prior I was ordered
to report to the Police Station of Massacre Plains. There I was
questioned for some hours, interrogated about my ancestors, my
Bible, and my loyalty. The Mission was raided many times, our
rations halved again and again. The people of the township, who
never looked favorably on my work with the Natives, had, in recent
years and months, threatened myself to no end, and for what reason?
Each day I have searched Scripture and my heart and head trying to
understand.

From the beginning of the new century it seemed Australian
nationalism was growing, and every newspaper devoted great space
to explore the topic. Some people had an unwavering conviction that

Australia should be united under a common identity, founded on the pioneers, the geography, the flora and fauna—not the immigrant, nor the Native.

And the Aborigines Protection Board's eventual reaction was swift and unyielding. Seven boys, John, Michael, Bobby, Percival, Samuel, Graham, Richard, and three girls, Isabel, Sally, Kathleen— that on this date range between two years of age and seven years of age—were forcibly taken in the years 1908 to 1914 to the city, I believe, or taken to children's "homes" throughout the state to be trained for work, trained to be pliant. They were too young to be sent away—eleven years would have been sufficient! We were unable to find exact information of where the children went. Their parents cried every day. Many parents ran away, choosing to conceal their infants with them in the bush, though most were captured and divided.

You may think, dear Dr. Cross—what does this prove? I say, in sober truth, that a species of slavery *does* exist in this part of the King's dominions.

After these incidents a great agony settled in the Mission and in my heart. I feared we were all breaking apart when I received the first of the news on August 26, 1914, that there was trouble for my fellow countrymen: the descendants and immigrants from the Prussians and Germans of Broken were being harassed. Their houses razed, their German-language books burned. The newspaper brandished all the news we'd needed to understand:

BRITAIN DECLARES WAR ON GERMANY

It was not a fortnight after this that the Constable, the one who had shrugged his shoulders, ordered me to the Police Station. My hour had come round at last; Keller's also.

At the Police Station, they had us register on a yellow form our name, date and place of birth, address, trade or occupation, marital status, property, length of residence in Australia, nationality, and naturalization details.

We filled them out and the Constable laughed. "We don't like you, Greenleaf," he said. "And now we can do something about that."

I was ordered to report each day to the Police Station and they would decide, depending on my continuing, full cooperation with the Protection Board, whether they would send me to gaol or not, or worse. But what could be worse? Nothing could be worse than seeing those children too young transported away.

I had visited the Police Station and signed a registration form each day for nearly twelve months before my internment. I know the others have been sent to internment camps elsewhere. I acknowledge that they endured a terrible fate: their family bonds broken, businesses shut down, and livelihoods taken from them—but they haven't become the enemy to *two* crowds.

I retired to my hut during the days when I heard the wagon and vehicles arriving to take the children away. I kept pressing upon the residents that my hands were bound, that I could not do a thing against the Law. They ceased to address me fondly as *gudyi* and turned from me, as they should have, as I deserved, with a deep and wounding contempt.

THIRTY-TWO

carving on trees at graves—*muyalaang* The books say a civilization must meet four criteria: it must show house building, domestication of animals, agricultural activity, and reverence for the dead. Reverence for the dead, this is the carving on the trees, this is the ceremony, the care. The Gondiwindi didn't throw them in the earth and walk away. There was great mourning and care of the body, dance and ceremony, and a permanent place for those to rest. I have discovered, just recently, that the old people built a cemetery too, but I cannot find it. It seems when I ask the ancestors, they show me many places—too many unmarked gravesites all over this country—and they cry, and say they weren't responsible. But when the ancestors were in charge of their living and dead bodies they can find the spot, and we take flowers to those holy places. We have always been a civilization, us.

catch you, crush you, kill you, eat you—*dha-l-girri-dhu-nyal* We were having a barbecue at the house one Christmas night. It had been a hot, ragged sort of day. We had family over, a few were getting on the bottle. They weren't driving and they knew they could stay out in the shearers' annex, which we always kept neat and tidy. By 10 p.m. everyone had gone to sleep. During the night something woke me.

It wasn't the ancestors because the whirly-whirly was still out. It was a creak of the floorboards. I went out to the kitchen and looked up the staircase to the attic. Well my guts got punched because Jimmy Corvette was climbing the stairs. He saw me and came back down immediately, the stink of beer on his breath. He acted a fool then, like he was drunk. "I was gunna tickle the girls," he said, giggling. "Get out," I said. I told him he was a fool who couldn't handle his liquor. At the back door I grabbed him by the shirt. "Not back to the annex. Walk home," I growled into his face. And when I said *dha-l-girri-dhu-nyal*—he knew I meant it.

catch, take unawares—*girra-warra* Jimmy ran off with that spear in his leg and turned up in the hospital, infected. He wouldn't say I had done it, even on his deathbed. I signed the visitors' log, I walked in and asked him where Jedda was. It took me a long part of a day to get the words out of him. "I didn't mean to, it was an accident," he said. "Where is she?" I demanded. I won't forget his four-word response: "In the water, Uncle." I peeled his bandage back and spat into the wound. I told him when he got out of hospital I was going to torture him to death if he didn't take me to Jedda. I meant it. Visiting time was over at 8 p.m. Well, he died of sepsis through the night and I never found our darling all the rest of my days.

cold, be changed, be dead wanting cover—*baludhaay* When our loved ones are gone, and bent and lying out in their graves, the eternal home of the soil, they need to be kept warm, so we cover them. The old people they *baludhaay* their people, their loved ones. To keep them warm, and to help them in the next part of their journey—which was to change form. I just wanted, all this time, to wrap Jedda up safe and warm.

THIRTY-THREE

August walked below the shrike and didn't cry. On the veranda she spotted Aunt Missy and Elsie inside the house packing. She spun from the back door, facing the field to smooth her hair. She held the box in one hand, and with the other she ran her fingers along the faces of the buttons, to be certain they were all fastened.

With the blunt end of a butterknife, Aunt Missy was prying little rectangle gold and silver plaques from the bases of Poppy's fishing and vegetable garden trophies. On the table a corkboard was spread with white glue for the plaques. A box sat on the floor accepting the tens of plastic molds of miniature cups and chalices. Poppy had spent his retirement on the upkeep of the garden and fishing at Lake Broken and along the full end of the Murrumby, the other side of the dam, two hours south. He never displayed the trophies. Aunt Missy sorted them straight from the storage box.

"How are ya—you missed lunch?" Aunt Missy kissed her cheek and then narrowed her eyes, sniffed at the air around her. "*He-llo*," she said stirring. "Where've you been, niece?"

August put her hands on her hips, nodding at the trophies. Trying to ignore her but more trying not to tremble. "Can I help?"

Aunt Missy started cackling then.

Elsie looked out from the doorway of the big room. "What's so funny?"

"Nothing, Nana, Aunty just farted." August looked at Aunt Missy as if to say *shut up*. Her aunty smiled back at her as if to say *I won't*.

Aunt Missy lifted her chin to Elsie, "August thought it was a new perfume from town."

Elsie shook her head and ducked back into the big room, mumbling under her breath.

August took Aunt Missy's elbow gently, serious now. "Eddie's family had artifacts, from here. They donated them to a museum."

"What do you mean?"

"Papers, he's found submission papers or something." She paused and looked toward the end of the lounge room. "We shouldn't say anything to Nana. She's got enough going on."

Aunt Missy glanced behind her, then back to August. "You sure they're from the property?"

August nodded and shrugged. "It's weird."

Missy pinched her bottom lip, deep in thought, and broke from it, scrunched her face at August. "It's sad." She looked through the back sliding door, out to the trucks in the field. "Where is he?"

"At home."

"With his folks?"

"Alone."

"What did he show you exactly?"

"He's got documents, like lists of donated items. Spears and stuff."

Aunt Missy squeezed her bottom lip between her fingers again.

"I took these," August added, gesturing at the small box in her hands.

"Take it to the car, we'll go through it." Aunt Missy nudged the box and August toward the back door, picked up a trophy, and wandered toward the big room. As August went to the driveway she heard Aunt Missy call out to Elsie, "Early tea, Mum?"

Up at Southerly, Eddie's car was gone too. August fingered through the box, sat the envelopes to the side, flicked through small pocket-size leather books. Inside the books were larger envelopes and letters in thick yellowed parchment written in copperplate. She couldn't understand a word. Inside the small envelopes the cards were there, the ones Eddie had read. They were written in courier typeface, *The Historic Museum Australia* printed in the top center. Next to each item a call number like books at a library ran down the right-hand side.

Aunt Missy leaped off the veranda stairs and buffeted her handbag against her shoulder as she rushed to the car. She slumped into the driver's seat. "I told her we're picking up fish and chips, so remind me."

She turned on the ignition. "What's in there?" she nodded at the box.

"All that stuff."

"We need to drive out a bit to get phone reception."

They parked on the outskirts of town near the satellites, the afternoon light stretched onto the front windshield. August could see the shape of her aunt's head, the round curve visible through the white-grey hair thinning at her crown. It was as if time slapped August in the face, roused her from some long sleep. Aunt Missy opened her phone, August rested her head on her shoulder and watched the screen as she typed in "The Historic Museum Australia," tapped on "Archaeology Collections," then "Aboriginal." She scanned half a page and read aloud:

"There are roughly 17,000 collections, some consisting of only a single object, and largely the results of the pioneers of Australian archaeology; usually untrained, curious but dedicated people keen to understand Aboriginal prehistory and salvage material evidence of the past. The first artifact entered into the current Anthropology registration system was a fishing spear from the Murrumby River region, donated to the Museum in 1896 and held in the Falstaff Permanent Collection. Some of these collections —"

The phone turned black. "You *ever* charge your phone?" August asked.

"No," Missy said, dropping the phone into her lap. "Dad would have loved this . . . it would have meant so much to him." She looked in the rear-vision mirror and sighed, "Gawd."

"Sorry, Aunty."

"If we can find the Falstaff Collection, Augie, it means maybe we can stop the mine. We have to find it." With her fingers she cleared the tiny black streams of mascara from her cheeks.

"Library for the internet?" August asked.

"Good one," she said and pulled the car back onto the bitumen. "You know I looked for stuff, I looked for Gondiwindi stuff, *our* family name! For *Prosperous* info, our home. Lo and behold it was under Falstaff the whole time, aye?" Aunt Missy glanced at August as she drove. "When's your flight back to London?"

"Couple of days."

"You really going back to England, niece?"

August looked at her hands, picked at the dry dishwashing skin flaking off and then up at the road through the windshield. "No."

"Good. You're home now. That's good, darling."

There was a different woman manning the desk at the library.

Her name tag read: *Julie*. She let Aunt Missy charge her phone in the socket beside the computer terminal. Missy got back to the museum website, looked up the page they were on, and read aloud the end of the paragraph, *"Some of these collections are not well documented, but collectively they reflect the rich evidence of Aboriginal past as well as the pioneering effort to save and understand it."* In a new window she typed *Falstaff + artifact + Murrumby* while August approached the front desk.

"I just wanted to tell you I'll bring the books in soon that my grandfather borrowed. Another lady warned me yesterday about fines."

"No problem," Julie said. "I'll make a note of it. What's your grandfather's name?" Julie readied her hands at the keyboard.

"Albert Gondiwindi."

Instead of typing she dropped her hands and tilted her head in one motion. "Mr. Gondiwindi, I'm *so* sorry, I heard he passed."

August nodded, tapped the desk as if everything were cleared away.

"Can I help you with anything while you're here?" She glanced to Aunt Missy busy at the terminal. "Are you doing research too?"

"Yeah, maybe you can help." She thought about what they'd need. "Do you have any information about the Aboriginal Mission out at the Murrumby River from early last century?"

"Yes, I do. Would you like to see the archive your grandfather and I went through?"

August's heart skipped a little. "Yes, please," she said, feeling her face break into a smile.

"We don't have much, to be honest." She motioned for August to walk with her to the twin history shelves. It seemed to August that Julie knew exactly where to go. "This book," she reached up to a tattered and very thin blue hardcover without anything on the spine, "was the one your grandfather was most interested in, I'd say . . . with the research he was conducting."

"What exactly was he researching with you?" August took the book into her hands. The hardcover was woven and its title was embossed, ornate brown lettering: *The First Australians' Dictionary.*

"I think he was putting together a pre-colonial history of the local area, a family history. This one," she placed her index finger on the book August was holding while scanning the same shelf, ". . . and another were helpful for him but I can't see it."

She gently took the book back and opened it, showing August the title page. "It was compiled posthumously, but I believe the original author ran the Mission in the late nineteenth century. It might be small—" she turned each page carefully, there was a long introduction and then no more than twenty pages of words, listed like a dictionary, "but it is likely the only published record of the Mission." She closed the book and handed it to August. "Have a look at that. It can't leave the library, though."

"Thank you." August looked at the book and turned back to Julie. "Do you have anything on this man, the author?" She ran her finger along the name Ferdinand Greenleaf.

"Actually, there's just the one thing your grandfather ordered in. It's a PDF file—it can't be photocopied or printed, though." She looked behind her but there was nobody there. "I can email it to you though, would you like that?"

"Yes please," August added, as Julie took out a scrap of paper. "What is it?"

"It's a serialized letter, I think just a few pages." She handed August the paper and pen from her blouse pocket. "Write your email," she said with a little urgency, anxious to return to work.

"Thanks. What is a serialized letter?"

"It means it was once printed, in newspapers and such. And I'm so sorry for your grandfather's passing." She glanced at the central desk and the person waiting there to be served. "Let me know if there's anything else." She smiled sympathetically and returned to her post. August took the book to the computer terminal and pulled a padded chair up beside Aunt Missy.

"Look. Language book." She placed it gently on the corner of the booth tabletop and opened it. "Reverend Ferdinand Greenleaf," August read aloud.

"Are we in it?"

She scanned through the introduction. The type was small and difficult to read, "It mentions the Mission, it says Prosperous in the introduction." She read a small notice on the back page.

"It is my hope that these few words safely find you. I was sent to this island of punishment, privation, and misery. I am certain I will not survive, and so I appeal to you to think on what it means to be Australian, to be citizens of a young country with boundless skies, and to consider the treatment of our fellows, no matter from which land they have arrived, and no matter of their forefather, their tribe.
In truth,
F. Greenleaf."

"Google this fella, Aunty."

Missy typed but nothing came up so she returned to the Historic Museum Australia website.

August turned to her with a sigh. "I have to return the rental to the airport."

"Good," she said absently, looking at the bottom of the website and pulling up a street map. "Reckon we should drive it to the airport tomorrow. We can visit the museum, drop your rental off, and get the train back." A huge grin spread above her chin. The pair of them must have looked mad, the way they were smiling at each other in the silent library, holding back a *whoop*. "Abso-bloody-lutely!" August whispered, the two of them containing their giggles. Aunt Missy unplugged her phone and August rested the book at the library desk where Julie stood behind. She was on the phone but acknowledged August again, nodded and smiled.

August grabbed her aunt's arm. "Dinner?"

"Thanks, Bub," she said, and hooked her arm into August's as they walked, clutched together up High Street. August looked at the shop-front where a lovable Pixar character smiled from the sandwich board of Nemo's Fish and Chip Shop.

Aunt Missy turned to August holding her purse out pointedly. "Best barramundi in Australia!"

"Don't the kids get it, that they're *eating* Nemo, not having a play-date?"

Aunt Missy turned and whispered in August's ear, "Shut up." She was giggling as they joined the eager line of customers.

"Oops!" She held August on her outer arms, and moved her in the queue. "Hold our spot, cash only, back in a tick."

August stood in the heavy, greasy air while Aunt Missy ran to the ATM. Directly in front of August in the queue was a severely sun-burned man, probably around her own age, she thought. He was wearing a t-shirt roughly cut off where sleeves once were; it hung loosely on his strawberry-milk shoulders. A tattoo covered his entire shoulder—a huge constellation of the Southern Cross. He glanced back at August for a second before placing his order. August stared at his tattoo: those stars that led them astray at night, all the trouble Eddie and Joey and her had got into when they were teenagers, when they were bored out of their minds, when the silence became so deafening it burst their eardrums. August was daydreaming looking at his inked skin.

The man turned back again. "You like that?" he asked her, pointing to it, without waiting for an answer. "That's the Southern Cross, lady. That means you don't belong here."

She stood there dumbfounded, blank-faced. After a moment she wondered who he thought she was, or who exactly he thought *he* was.

Aunt Missy reappeared, though August decided not to tell her about the tattooed man—they were having too much of a nice time together.

"Three pieces of crumbed barramundi, large hot chips, large tabouli salad, please," Aunty said, and then looked at August. "You eating? Want a Chiko Roll?"

She thought about it, her mouth salivated and she nodded. She was, for the first time in a long time, ravenous.

Elsie, Missy, and August ate dinner on the rear veranda. They heard someone knock on the front door that was never used. Missy got up and yelled around the side of the house, *"Aroundthaback!"*

"Do you have to yell?" Elsie asked, speaking with a mouthful of food.

"Barramundi'll go cold if I walked around there dragging my fork."

A woman in a ranger's uniform appeared at the side of the house with a clipboard and a fake smile. Missy nudged August.

"Evening, ladies!" the stranger said, too enthusiastic. "Hope I'm not interrupting dinner?"

Nana stood up, wiping her mouth and fingers on the paper napkin. "No, no," she assured her.

"I'm Karen, just here from Rinepalm Mining head office to see how the transition is going for next week." She rested one foot on the veranda stoop, and propped a forearm on her knee like she was about to launch into a story.

"Almost packed," Nana said.

"Okay, well you just let us know if you need anything, anything at all."

She was staring at the sign above her nana, which had been there since August could remember. It read: *Best friends use the back door.*

"Oh, I love your sign," the lady said. "I'll remember for next time."

"But you're not our best friend, Karen," blurted Missy.

Elsie swiftly turned and whacked her shoulder with the back of her hand. "Missy!"

The lady laughed it off. "Anyway, I like that sign . . . ," she said confidently, Aunt Missy's insult rolling off her back as she walked away.

Missy jumped up and grabbed the plaque from the nail, held it out to her. "Why don't you take it?" she said, sweet as pie. "Go on," she insisted, holding it over the veranda rail.

August watched wide-eyed, popped a hot chip into her mouth like it was popcorn.

The woman hesitated. "Couldn't possibly," she said, waving it away and retreating to her SUV at the driveway mouth. "Goodnight, ladies," Karen added, waving the women away, too.

Missy cocked her arm and threw the thing in the dirt behind the woman, her voice raised to a yell. "'Cos *where the hell* are *we* gunna put it!?"

They heard the car drive off and Elsie shook her head and yelled at Missy. "I like that sign, don't give it away or bloody throw it!"

She whacked her daughter again with her napkin.

"Mum, it's a bit dirty, anyway. Everyone laughs at it. *Back door?*"

"Don't be ridiculous."

"It's junk."

"It's priceless."

"Mum, I got it from the Mother's Day stall at school for maybe twenty cents." Missy walked down and retrieved the sign, mock-dusting it off. "Where you going to put it anyway, no back doors in apartments."

"Shush now." Elsie said and snatched it from her. She was smiling out the corners of her mouth, she looked at it in her hands and then decided, "Albert hated it too." She giggled and tossed the thing over the veranda, back onto the dirt.

The three of them broke from a giggle to belly laughs. August felt there, felt effortlessly at home, felt as if a vibration were being shared between the three generations of women. Felt as if she might laugh that way, on Prosperous, after everything, after death and theft and secrets and lies and the muddied water, and the diesel and the blood— after all that—she felt as if she was home. Belonged.

Their eyes were glazed with laughter when August dropped her hand on Nana's. "I'm not leaving."

Nana caught her breath, smiling still. "Not running off again?"

"Nup," August promised. "Promise."

Nana dropped her other hand atop August's and squeezed it,

looked out into the field. "Good," she said, and looked back at her. "What about the car?"

"Taking a little trip tomorrow," Missy said.

"Where?" Elsie asked.

"Just returning Augie's car to the airport. We'll get the train back, Mum."

Elsie smiled. "Drive safe, then!" she addressed August sternly. "And get your money back on that ticket."

August nodded but doubted she'd be able to.

"You wanna come, Mum?" Missy asked.

"To the city?"

"To the *city*! You could visit some old friends."

"All my old friends are dead, girls. Now help me before you leave."

They cleared the dinner plates and began washing up. Another knock came on the front door.

Elsie shot Missy a dirty look. "Cops! Look what you've done—Rinepalm gubba's called the bullymen!"

August walked to the seized wood of the front door, and called out, "Who is it?"

"Alena."

"Go around the back."

"It's *my friend*, okay?" August explained as she grabbed her hoodie from the kitchen bench. "Back in a tick. Save me some dessert?"

"There's no dessert," Aunt Missy yelled, as August jumped off the veranda.

Eddie's car was still absent and Southerly windows stayed dim as the sun dropped.

Alena was holding a tray covered in foil and smiled when she saw August, gestured back to the road with her chin. "Hey, gotta run—hubby's in the car."

"No worries, what is this?" August said, and walked alongside Alena back to the road. "Lamingtons. Aussie food for ya!" She nudged August and passed her the tray. Alena's car was parked at the letterboxes, beyond the property line. She seemed jittery as they reached the peppermint trees. She wrapped her hand around August's forearm, dipping her head to peer through the trees onto the road.

She lowered her voice. "Listen, he won't let me give you the school stuff."

"Why?" August whispered back, noticing then how little Alena had changed since school, how she had flipped from giggly to cautious, and how she still looked much the same, in spite of being pregnant and the faint lines on her face.

"I don't know, he doesn't want any trouble with the mining people is all."

"Don't worry about it, Alena—it's not going to stop anything, you know?"

"I know, I just wanted to show you. Anyway, cake is alright instead?"

"Yeah, thanks heaps for this." August said, as they approached the Mercedes minivan. Through the back-seat window she could see a small child strapped in rolling a Matchbox car over his bare knee. James Gaddon, whom August recognized, was leaning out the driver's-side window. "How's it going?" he asked.

"Fine."

"You back in town for long?"

"Maybe," August said. "Maybe not."

"Keep the tray," Alena said, and kissed her on the cheek and walked to the passenger-side door.

James looked at August with an easy contempt. "I'd go with the latter one. You're a blow-in in this town anyway, so don't stick your nose in shit where it don't belong."

August saw Alena jump in the car and slap James across the arm. "Yessir," August said, and mock-saluted him. He started the car and she gave him the finger as they drove off.

She looked up at Kengal. She couldn't see anybody, but it appeared as if there were more tents up there: little angled tops, stegosaurus bones. She took the lamingtons inside.

"I got dessert!" August yelled to her nana and Aunt Missy washing dishes at the sink.

She ripped the foil off the wonky lamingtons crammed over the cling-wrapped tray. Chocolate sauce and coconut were smeared everywhere.

"Still edible," she said, and took a lamington and placed the rest on the kitchen bench. In the space left from where she'd taken the lamington, she saw the word *Pack* in purple. "Covert Alena!" August hooted, and slopped the entire tray of lamingtons onto the foil covering, then removed the cellophane.

"*Rinepalm Mining Activity Pack*," she read, and pulled it from the cellophane, waving it.

"What's that for?" Aunt Missy screwed her face up.

August looked at it. Realized it wasn't especially informative. "Alena wanted to be a smuggler for a day, I guess." She held it limply beside her and offered to dry the dishes.

"August, if you want to do your investigating, then go into the bedroom and look through all the mining papers I've got in the dresser.

You can have a read on the bed." Elsie winked at August. "You're a smart cookie. You always were, Augie."

Missy looked at her mum, "What about me, Mum?"

"You're the light relief, Missy," Elsie chuckled, as she stacked clean plates into the packing box.

August kicked her shoes off to go to her nana's room.

"No, Aug, read it in the car tomorrow. Stay, we've got to help pack and clean."

Aunt Missy and August worked in a frenzy, filling and taping boxes and scrawling the contents along the sides and top of the cardboard. Elsie was impressed. She handed August the mining portfolio, as if it were pocket money.

"Did you read it?"

"No," she said. "Lies in there, coming straight from the horse's arse."

Later, in the attic room, August read through it. The portfolio explained Rinepalm's plans, its pages had plenty of stock photos of employed people in identical shirts. There were old letters collected within the portfolio that her nana and poppy had received about the mine proposal. There was lots of talk and promise in the words but not much depth, August felt. She sat in the single bed and took a closer look at the activity pack.

It *was* weird. It was stranger than the mining portfolio for adults, but she couldn't put her finger on how. The graphics were as chaotic as a Happy Meal box. Crosswords featured words like emerald, diamond, ruby, iron, ore, silver, opal. A mole in a hard hat was the mascot. He wore a tiny orange waistcoat. There were drawings of industrial drills burrowing down into the layers of the earth, a cross-section view. In one of the layers the designers had drawn a skeleton of a stegosaurus. She counted on her fingers the other dinosaur names she could remember: brontosaurus, pterodactyl, triceratops, tyrannosaurus rex. That was all. She thought she should probably go back to school.

Inside the plastic sleeve there were glossy cardboard pieces perforated into sheets. She took the sheets aside and popped out each of the numbered pieces. She followed the instructions and made herself a little drilling rig. She placed it on the bedside table. Alena was right, it was pure propaganda—bite-size, child-size, colorful, cheery brainwashing.

She looked out through the missing shard of the Lutheran rose toward Southerly. It was dark there. Eddie had loaned Jedda and her one of his walkie-talkies when they were kids. They'd take it in turns to tell kid jokes: August remembered one of Eddie's, a kangaroo and a rabbit are doing a poo in the bush, the kangaroo asks the rabbit if he has problems with poo sticking to his fur. The rabbit says no, so the kangaroo wipes his bum with the rabbit. August smiled at the memory resurfacing as a shore exposed at low tide, she heard Jedda's laughter squeal in her mind. *Over and out*, he'd say. *Over and out*, they'd say.

After Elsie had gone to bed, Missy came up to the room with the shoebox from Southerly. They went through a few of the pieces sleepily.

"We could claim Native Title," Missy said, her face revisiting the idea.

"You reckon? Joey said—no it was Aunt Nicki, or both of them—that it'd be impossible."

"This is the missing piece, August, these are artifacts; we're not extinct with this. I reckon it'd stop the mine at least. Let me read the submissions to you."

August crossed her legs on the bed and leaned back into the wall.

Missy read the detailed descriptions of the artifacts aloud slowly, her voice rose a little at the end of each sentence like she was steadying, bracing against a tear. While her Aunt Missy read, August tucked her legs under the covers and lay her head on the pillow. She looked up at her aunt. It was just like getting a bedtime story. She felt so happy to have her sit so close and read to her.

Missy noticed August slipping into sleep and got up and tucked the blankets in, popped the lid on the shoebox. She said she'd lock the house up and for August to pick her up in the morning from her place in the Valley. She'd bring sleeping bags and stuff. August asked dreamily for a hug and Missy held her tight and then kissed August on the forehead.

When her aunt closed the bedroom door, August rolled onto her side away from the wall. She thought about the words Eddie had said: *slave yard.* It couldn't be true. The cardboard purple, green, and orange drilling rig cast a small shadow beside the bedside lamp. August reached out and switched off the light.

Open road, going somewhere, elsewhere—she loved that feeling. She knew that about herself. She knew she loved leaving more than a drink, more than sex, more than hunger, the books. The road didn't have a caved-in feeling or a hangover; it could have any wonder in the whole world. But she felt different then, without wanderlust. She felt the pull like magnets to Prosperous, and the road, even with her Aunt Missy, felt ominous, strange—she wanted to be home almost as soon as they'd left.

She had ached for that thing, that feeling to want something. To feel like she had a purpose. That she was part of something. While living in England, she took trips alone some summers. She spent her spare time looking for cheap train tickets, forums where people couldn't follow through on their plans. She'd gone to the harbor of Portsmouth, stood ahead the ache of its blue mouth, where the fleets had departed and caused it all. She wandered the streets of Bath and Oxford and London. Every place was interesting enough for a girl from Massacre Plains. Though she really saw little, the footpaths mostly, the churches, the supermarket aisles, the bakeries, the bookstores, the bars.

One place stuck. She'd planned to hitchhike to Edinburgh but only made it north of Middlesbrough. She spent a few days in the plains beyond, where she discovered Hadrian's Wall. The wall had been built by the Romans when they were brutal conquerors or bringers of civilization. She didn't know. Along the wall that crossed three rivers she found a small museum at Chesters Roman Fort, and with no other visitors that day, the curator had given her a tour. She'd shown August a Vindolanda writing tablet, one of a thousand. It was two miniature slices of wood pressed together by time and discovered in a dig only decades before. When the archaeologists had opened them they found hieroglyphics inside, yet just as soon as the tablets were opened, the writing disappeared in the elements. Finally after experimenting, the inscriptions were able to be photographed under special lighting. They were cursive Latin, and the curator had told her they were still being deciphered—almost two thousand years later. And then the curator picked up a piece of ceramic that had inscriptions scraped into the clay, made before it was set as stone. She'd translated it for August, that sad-looking young woman alone in the museum at wall's end. *"Read, and good luck to you."* "Who wrote it to who?" August asked, and the woman explained that at the time the pen was as important as the sword, that words were paramount, and that the message was made when the tile was still soft, and that it must have been a gesture from one stoneworker teaching another stoneworker to read. August had smiled, though she didn't take a photo. She'd never taken photos. Looking back, she didn't know why; it was as if everyone around her were taking the photos on her behalf in a way. She was just an observer on their vacations; she'd write a poem instead. Besides, she never did like her photo being taken.

The stone, like the North African redware, the bronze saucepan from Italy, the ivory from India, the pottery water containers, the glass bottle in the shape of a West African head, made in Germany, the curator said, or Egypt—it was all a picture, a sculpture—an incidental passage of time, there upon a shelf on the wall. A line of stones that over time had no sure beginning or end to its construction. It was evidence of the other, that it had once been a bustling sort of city in the middle of nowhere, where different cultures came together. There were Syrians, North Africans, Hungarians, Bulgarians, French, Spanish, German, all "serving" the Empire, a gaggle of languages.

She had walked to a higher point overlooking the rolling green hills, where ordered rows of fencing had twisted loose. She had thought about how everywhere in that place Romans had written the local people out of their history. She was trying to figure out how people valued a thing, what made something revered while other things were overlooked. Who decided what was out with the old, what had to have a replacement? What traditions stayed and what tools, household items, art, things, evidence of someone, languages, fell away. But when she tried to draw a vague line to the artifacts of Prosperous she was stumped—why the artifacts of Middlesbrough were important and not those from home.

August didn't tell Aunt Missy about the wall she'd seen when they stopped at the petrol station to pour the thermos coffee. August slugged the last of the water and dropped the plastic bottle into the bin.

She wandered idly back from the recycling station to her aunt, who was tapping her foot at the opened passenger door. "Quit ya dawdling—we haven't got much time to stop the mine!"

"Is that what we're doing?" August asked, jumping into the driver's seat and pulling at the seatbelt.

"I reckon we are."

They passed roadkill, but no wildlife bounced into the path of the rental. August asked about what Poppy was like at the end, about where he thought he was going.

"He worked in the garden right up until the end; he used to think retirement was for suckers. He always used to say, *You've got to keep busy.*"

"I mean the afterlife?"

"He said he wasn't going to be a star so don't bother craning your neck."

"Did he?"

Missy laughed. "Yeah."

"What else did he say?"

"He said religion is being afraid of death, that it was made to calm the philosophers down, or something. Ah! He did say something that I liked. He said none of us should be scared to go to sleep." Missy was silent for a bit and then said, "That's nice, isn't it?"

"Yep." August said. "What do you believe in?"

"Same as Dad. We go back to the earth and become other things in nature."

"Did he say anything about what happens next, at the end?"

Missy took a big breath, tried to erase the lifeless image from her mind.

"Those final stages went on for a couple of days. The soul and the mind are there, but the body can't do anything else to be with the mind—it's like he became split. The natural split. At that moment I didn't want it to end, I just wanted another day, then you want another hour, another minute. It's all precious in the end! It's like there are never enough details left. I wanted everything back. Fingerprints, photos, every story, nights that were longer. A right time to die? To be separated? There isn't, August. It hurts all the time, it hurts to lose someone, doesn't it?"

August was crying. "Yes," she said.

"In the hospital in the end the nurse said something nice to me, she said she was sending me *white light*."

"White light?"

"Think about it, Aug, it's beautiful—it's like the light breaking through the gums, the day reflected off the top of choppy water, all the sun's energy in that moment. That nurse, she wanted to send me electricity, you know?"

"Divine light," August said.

"Yeah, holy light from nature, that's beautiful."

"You think you'll go to heaven, Aunty?"

"Nah! I'll be back as a tree or something that doesn't move. I just want to chill out and not have to go hunting for food, you know?"

Later August stopped for Missy to take over the driving for the last three hundred kilometers. August returned to reading the cards aloud. "Wooden shovel, used for digging earth mounds."

"Can you believe it?" Missy said. "Our ancestors! Take my phone, check and see if there's that thing from the library lady."

August opened up her email on Missy's charged phone; there was an attachment from a council address. In the body of the email Julie had typed: *I hope all is well. I had a look at it again. It's Reverend Greenleaf's letter to the organizers of the World's Fair in Chicago. If you need anything else, I'm more than happy to help.*

"You want me to read the letter aloud?"

"Go on."

"It's old, Aunty, I'll get the accent all wrong."

"I'll bet fifty bucks you won't."

When August reached the end of the letter, Missy had to pull over. She walked out on the rest area holding her stomach like she was going to vomit. She was breathing deep, walking in little circles. *"Our people!"* she said, but in a different way. Hurled the words out of her body, like the backlash of an axe caught in the timber knot of their family tree.

August imagined the Reverend out in their field, in their home. She couldn't believe that he lived out there, that he *made* Prosperous. Imagined him trying to protect those ancestors at the same time as punishing them. August remembered reading John Milton in England; he wrote about justifying the ways of God to men. She couldn't remember the whole idea, but it seemed in the car then, as if they had all been wronged by people justifying the ways of God and not themselves, and that the Reverend had been wrong too. *Hadn't they all been godless and free and moral once?* She wondered.

"And what do you reckon happened after? After the government ran the Mission?"

"When it became a station?"

"Yeah," August confirmed, fearful of the answer.

Missy started the car. "Real bad stuff, worse stuff."

"He was kind, you think?"

"No. He was bad in a long pattern of bad. I reckon he just thought he was doing right."

"He regretted it."

"Yeah, but only when it happened to him too, aye. But there's stuff in that letter, evidence of us Gondiwindi you know? Native Title evidence."

August stared into the road ahead. "Yeah," she said.

The rest of the drive August asked Aunt Missy more about what Poppy had been like as a dad, what Jolene had been like as a sister, what Nana was like as a mum. She told August little snippets and they tried to laugh, as much as they could after reading the letter. They talked about stories of Elsie and the stories about August's mum as a girl and they wept easily about the stories of Albert and tried not to talk about Jedda. They stopped at roadsides for candy bars and chewing gum. They listened to pop songs on the radio. The air kept coming in thick until they crossed the mountains and the temperature dropped with the cool off the ocean.

When Missy saw the water, her spirits lifted again, and she tapped the GPS screen. "Only a hundred kilometers left to go!"

"We should've brought Joey along too," August said.

"Should of, you're right."

"Where is he?"

"Tramp Jungle, I don't know, nightclub opening in Broken. Tramp Jungle?"

"Sounds . . . fun."

"My handbag, Aug," she motioned for August to open it. "Forgot I brought my own music!"

They listened to Missy's burned CD of Tracy Chapman, and when "Talkin' 'Bout a Revolution" came on she wound down the window and sang her lungs out. The rushing air caught in the window and hurt August's ears. They listened to her *Greatest Hits* album on repeat until the words lost their meaning.

Eight hours after they'd set out from Massacre Plains they parked at the city beach. Missy bought a lamb souvlaki wrapped in warm pita, August ordered the falafel, sour yogurt dripped off both of their chins into the evening sand. The ocean was foreign to August. She'd wanted to know it, but not float like the bodies on the surface of the water. She imagined herself instead going deep down into the part of the ocean where no light gets in. Where the fish look like aliens, glow-in-the-dark, sharp milk teeth.

After they ate and the car park became deserted and dark, they brushed their teeth out the swung-open doors and spat onto the bitumen. They rolled back their seats and slid their legs into the hollows of sleeping bags and looked for stars that they couldn't find.

THIRTY-FOUR

Biyaami, spirit that ruled the Gondiwindi—*Biyaami, Baiame* When the world was young still, my ancestors told me, Biyaami came upon the earth and decided to make it a beautiful place to live, so he made the plateaus and the mountains, he made the deserts, and stretches of sand and seashores. He planted shrubs and flowers and trees and ferns in different places. Then he needed to make the waterways in order to feed the plants and trees he'd created. So he made the oceans, beaches, lakes, and rivers too. He blew on his creation and had a lovely breeze sweep across the land. He loved what he'd made so much that he decided to stay up in a cave on Kengal Rock with Mother Earth. In the meantime, Marmoo the evil spirit had been watching all Biyaami had created and was jealous. He decided to destroy everything that Biyaami had made, so he went into his own cave and made some little strange creatures. The creatures flew sometimes, crawled sometimes, wriggled sometimes, and had legs to get about, and of course wings too. Marmoo made millions and millions of the strange creatures and then released them into Biyaami's creation. The creatures left Marmoo's cave like a plague and ate and attacked all the beautiful plants. High on Kengal Rock Biyaami and Mother Nature saw the ugly brown patch that was growing larger and larger over the land. Biyaami started to fret while

Mother Nature thought quick on her feet and ran into their cave to make a creature with long strong legs and a lean body and a sharp beak and white feathers. "What's that?" Biyaami asked. "It's a bird," Mother Nature said. And she made many other ones, with different colors, and beaks, and shapes. "What does it do?" Biyaami asked. "Look!" Mother Nature said, and released the birds from the cave—there they soared down and ate all the insects. Before long the insects were under control and there was no more plague.

be anxious, longing for—*bunba-y-marra-nha* I spent all my days fishing. I wasn't wading out to get a good catch, I was always looking for Jedda. We never said to each other what we were doing, not when Elsie extended the garden, looking, not when she'd spend all her days walking through the bush, looking. We were filled with *bunba-y-marra-nha* only to wrap her and have to rest on *ngurambang*.

Biyaami's son—*Gurra-gala-gali* I asked the ancestors once if there was just one single belief in the world. I asked what about Gurra-gala-gali, and the story he died for Biyaami, how it sounded like the story of Jesus to me. My great-great-great-grandfather said, "This is not a toy, this belief we have." He said, "Are you experiencing me talking to you?" I said, "Yes." He told me that Biyaami is the creator, but we don't worship Him or His son. We worship the things He made, the earth. Of course, the ancestors showed me how true they were in the end. Gurra-gala-gali was just a son, a coincidence.

blood—*guwany, guwan, guwaan* There's two bloods running through me: where I come from and where I am. Some things I cannot understand and I am ashamed at what one of my family members has done. It severed a vein, that terrible thing. It is not part of me or our family anymore, my nephew. He has drained from who we are like the *guwany* leaving the body. In that case water is thicker than blood.

bogong moth—*buugang* The Gondiwindi used to travel south to feast on bogong moths from the mountains, the alpine mountains, when the country still had seasons. The ancestors took me on a long walk there once. It was in summer and the *buugang* had traveled from the north to the cool mountains to escape the heat. When we arrived there, we collected the *buugang* and all sat around fires. There were people from all over *ngurambang* there, about five hundred fires I must have seen! Everyone was there to cook and feast on *buugang*—which tasted a little like a pork chop, but more nutritious. After that I felt strong walking back to the Boys' Home.

book, paper—*garrandarang* My daughter Nicki is going to look after this dictionary. She'll take the *garrandarang* to the council, she said. She said she'd do something good with it, protect the resting places on the farm with it.

breast—*dhudhu* This is the female word for the chest. Now, this is the first word I ever remember my mummy saying to me. That might sound funny, but I only knew her as a small boy, until I was three years old. I knew her as a young man much later. It was the first word I ever heard because *dhudhu* is also used to say to infants, "Here, here, baby. Here, here, little one, come to the chest, lie against my heart."

brolga—*burral-gang* The ancestors came back quickly once the whirly-whirly left. They returned to talk with me just one last time. And then the brolga appeared. They told me that the *burral-gang*, it was Jedda, that she was safe. That she'll always be a brolga. They said they didn't need to come back anymore to see me. They said I was like an initiated man, that I had caught up on all the things I needed to know. My great-great-great-grandfather laughed again and put his arm around me. He said that he wished they could have taught me all these things from when I was a little boy. "No matter," he said. "You are resurrected, a man brought back from extinction! Jedda is resurrected too—*burral-gang*." He said that I would have big challenges ahead of me, but that all I had learnt would show me what to do.

burnt grass—*bimbayi* My ancestors took me out to show me how they used fire. The women arrived with their branches aflame and one patch at a time in a line about a few hundred yards from the riverbank, they burnt one tussock after another of the grass and then with a shovel they beat the fire out. Eventually they built a long firewall, then waited until there was the finest breeze which took fire onto all the wild grass that ran from the river. The fire spread easily and I could feel the heat radiating off the field. Then the fire reached the breakwall and stopped. They went around and beat any stray flames and then they sped up time for me, so I could see the changes. The ash receding into the earth, feeding the soil, and quickly the rain fell, the sky cleared, saplings popped up, then buds, then the stems grew longer until the buds broke and yellow blossoms covered the patch they'd burnt. They had grown long tubers, good for roasting and grinding into flour or boiling and adding water and beating into a sort of gruel. Everything was cooked twice and the excess flour they stored in their homes, or possum-skin bags in the earth mounds. The kangaroos came too and one was speared for a feed. Now, in those same places, wherever the Falstaffs' wheat and cattle haven't made home, the acacia trees have shot up in abundance. In some places they've shot up ten thousand to an acre where edible grasses once were.

THIRTY-FIVE

August and her aunt slept on and off until the sun rose, orange, red, pink over the ocean. The taste of salt filled the car. Seagulls swooped. Surfers in short-legged wetsuits hurried past the car toward the glassy water that peeled hollow off the beach and from the headland right into the yellow shore. They rolled the sleeping bags, locked the rental, and walked south along the bike path. All the houses were quiet. Big houses, mansions with moneyed cars parked outside. In the backyards August saw swimming pools fenced in glass, pools five meters from the edge of the ocean. After a kilometer or so people appeared with their leashed dogs, teenagers unstacked identical chairs outside coffee shops, and men and women began to run past them with rhythmic breath. At a small cove they rolled their tracksuit pants above their knees and waded into the lapping seawater silently. It was colder than Aunt Missy expected and she fled from the shoreline. They laughed and washed their feet by the bike path tap and on the return to the car, they both looked out to the wide sea.

"Mob here must've ate plenty of fish," Missy said, nodding to the calm expanse of water, the slope to the rock pools, perfect for netting.

August hummed in response. They returned to the car and a few blocks from the beach, bought veggie sausage rolls at the first Vietnamese bakery they spotted. They followed directions for twenty minutes on Missy's phone until they found the closest car park to the Historic Museum Australia. August took the handful of submission cards and slid them into her coat pocket.

A strong southerly wind blew through the grey, angular city. "They won't just give them back, will they?" August asked, as they crossed against the traffic lights.

"Let's see what's there first. Maybe they'll get us to fill out paperwork or something. I'm sure this happens all the time."

"Repatriation?" August had seen it in a newspaper; shrunken skulls returned to Indigenous people two hundred years later. Or they'd wanted them returned. She couldn't remember.

"Where they give your family's artifacts back?" she asked.

"Yep."

"Yeah, I'm sure with the evidence we've got—they won't just keep them."

They stood outside fifteen minutes before opening, and looked up at the building. It wasn't Buckingham Palace huge, but it was a decent size. Six tall squared sandstone pillars tapered into careful angles, and then held up a great triangle of sandstone. In the flat rock beneath the triangle the word "MUSEUM" sat lonesome. August figured when it was built they didn't know exactly which type of museum it would eventually be. The building was as grand to Australian buildings as Southerly House had been to Prosperous. It was spectacular.

"Looking at it won't make it smaller," Missy said, one arm bracing her cardigan and handbag against her body while the other swept broadly toward the building, the arm saying *let's go*.

August dug her hands into her pockets and together they crossed the park. They were the first people in line. Inside, the air was pleasant, neither too warm nor too cool. It smelled of paper. Missy smoothed her grey untamable mane so August did the same to her own thick hair. They purchased two adult tickets, and Missy checked her hand-bag and slid her telephone into August's parka pocket, patted the sides of her cardigan where there were no pockets. Missy took her hand and squeezed it hard, looked at her with excited nervousness. They walked single file through the metal detector doorframe.

The entrance was white and as wide as a petrol station. Arrows pointed in the direction they were supposed to follow. As they entered the first room, they craned and looked at the entire ceiling hung with gum tree cuttings, the sound of didgeridoo played from hidden speakers. They looked at tall carved and painted totem poles, bark canoes suspended over exhibit shelves, headdresses stitched with shells, and wide colorful dot paintings. They approached each item both searching for the title of "Falstaff Collection." August saw a piece of bark, smoothed and painted in a watery charcoal, then painted with a big fish that looked like a Murrumby cod, the colors were white and ochre. The section of the stomach was hatched, the fins were painted with the dominant spines only, as if the painting explained the way it moved. The parts of the fish that Poppy had taught them to eat were all painted white, and the bone structure was all exact. It was an X-ray of the fish, and reminded August of when Jedda had disappeared and how she began to see people and things the same way. Opposite there were tens of dillybags arranged horizontally, encased in glass. A massive scroll hung on the wall above, a painting on white parchment. It was of a blood-red crocodile with a snake body angled vertical to the sky and people seemed to be tumbling down the insides of the animal, some swimming toward the mouth, trying to escape. Six figures were painted on the outside of the animal, their hands near their faces as if telling the people trapped inside what to do. It made August tearful.

At the entrance to one room a sign read: *Warning to Aboriginal and Torres Strait visitors: This room contains images of deceased persons.* A group of schoolkids hustled past them into the room without glancing at the notice.

"Do you want to go in?" August whispered to her aunt.

They both leaned forward and took a tiny peek into the room. August saw a huge picture of Aboriginal men in a black-and-white photograph, with chains tied around their necks, staring into the unseen lens. They leaned out, upright.

"Nah," Missy answered, shaking off a little shiver. August thought about the Reverend for the umpteenth time, imagining him in a black-and-white image on their field. Was he good? she thought.

They returned to following the main arrows. There were touchscreens and plastercast caves to sit inside. August watched a video filmed in the 1960s of a group of women sitting cross-legged making a bark painting. These were *real* Aborigines—not like Aunty and her, she thought.

They walked so slowly, even when groups of schoolchildren bustled about them and hustled through the rooms saying *cool* and *weird* every few steps. "Weekday," August whispered to Aunty, but she didn't take any notice. Hanging across a wall was a beautifully stitched possum-skin cloak about two meters wide and tall. On the skin side it had been intricately painted with people dancing and birds' necks stretching upward, kangaroos whose bodies looked curved, as if they were still in the womb.

"Here, take a photo of that," Missy whispered. She stood beside it.

"Just get my hand, I'll tell you when the coast is clear . . . now."

August looked at the screen as she tapped the camera icon. Missy's raised fist was barely in the frame.

"It's okay?" August asked, and showed her the photo she'd taken.

"Yeah." She pushed August's hand down to hide the phone.

There were documents under glass cases. Large books, the first signatures of something, in calligraphy. August couldn't read a thing.

There was a painted map of where the rivers were from. Missy arranged August to stand right ahead of it while again she stood beside it. August raised the phone.

"Miss, no photos in here." The security guard held his hand out and stormed toward Aunty's phone in August's hands.

"This is a painting of *our country* and I'm her elder, so I'm giving her cultural permission to take a photo—okay, Mister?" Missy was rude without meaning to be and up until that point August'd thought she understood city museum manners.

"That's your warning, no photos," he repeated, and flexed his neck as if it were more threatening than his face.

"Sorry," August offered, and put the phone in her pocket as he continued his staring competition with Missy.

Right away Missy shuffled on, her gait was skittering, jagged. August watched her skip the display of clapping sticks. She strutted past other hip-high displays as if nothing could impress her. August caught up to her and they both looked into a low glass cabinet. There were nardoo stones sitting in the center of grinding plates. August guessed most people thought they were rocks until they read the descriptions. Missy jabbed her finger at the glass. "Can you see through this?" she asked August sternly.

"Yes," August said tentatively. "It's glass."

"Not that." She took a step back and now jabbed her finger at the air, pointing down. "This."

"No. It's wood," August said with a low chuckle, just polite enough for a museum.

"This is tokenism, man. Liberals trying to feel good."

"It's appreciation for art, Aunty." August could see she was getting serious.

"They should work out how many of us they murdered and have a museum of tanks of blood. There'd be signs that said *Bloodshed—1788 to Yesterday—Stay Tuned!* That's what a museum of "Indigenous Australia" should look like—that's the one the White people get to visit, and then, *okay*, we have our own museum . . ." her aunty's argument was losing steam. Not because she wasn't sincere, but because Poppy's voice had begun whispering in Missy's ear instead: *You tell 'em, my daughter! Tell 'em when the explorers came looking flash in their coats and drill trousers, and on their big tired horses, they had shiny cherrywood-handled guns and moleskin leather shoes and had already invented wheels, whips, and germ warfare.*

Daughter, do you hear me?

Daughter, will you tell them?

Missy tried to ignore her dad, tried to find the things they'd come for, but Albert kept talking in her ear as she tried to find her way out of the maze of displays.

Here, in Sydney, the coast was getting crowded with them folks from overseas and they all needed more land to grow food, because they were real hungry folk too.

Missy went to walk past a display of weapons, but her father compelled her to stop.

Look at the boomerang and the woomera, Missy! They shot and shattered our boomerang and our woomera! They didn't just take our land with guns and bullets; there were other ways just as lethal—look, Missy. Look harder!

Her dad, Albert, was pestering her now, he was seizing the opportunity now that she stood in front of all the evidence.

They gave us blankets, Missy—they took the land that way too—with smallpox-infected blankets! They put arsenic in the flour, Missy! They divided us and ruled! They thought that us "Stone Age" people needed to be exterminated come hell or high water.

Albert wasn't finished but Missy dismissed him—she was sick to the guts, sick in that place.

"Where's our fucking artifacts, I need some fresh air!" she said in a rush before storming down the remaining corridor, disappearing under an exit sign.

August thought to go after her, but didn't. Her Aunt Missy needed a moment, to take a breath.

August liked the museum and was relieved to have some time alone. There was something satisfying about losing someone at a music concert or an art gallery or a museum. She wasn't obliged to turn to whoever she was with every two minutes and come up with new responses. *Amazing. Beautiful.* They weren't the words for what she saw in the museum; the things she was looking at deserved words that, she thought, didn't exist.

She continued through the exhibit, slowly and gravely. August stood in front of a yellow painting. All she saw was yellow ochre, a pattern that pulsated, as if it were a Magic Eye stereogram poster, and something hidden might suddenly become visible if she blurred her vision. She wanted to cry, she felt as she had at school, dumb at everything, trying three times as hard to problem-solve, trying three times as hard to make friends. But some things she didn't know, because she was never taught. Everything hurt her head. It was as if she were walking through a cemetery, tombstones jutted. She'd realized then the purpose of their history class where they'd been mentioned like important footnotes, just like the purpose of the museum, how it felt like a nod—polite and reverent and doused in guilty wonder—of a time that had now passed. *Past or passed* she thought as she followed the arrow to the archaeology collections.

August looked carefully into each display for *Falstaff Collection* labels but found none. She looped back again, staring into cabinets of wooden implements, stone pieces, bits of flint. Nothing was from their part of the river. She walked out of the exhibit to the information desk in the lobby. She spied Aunt Missy outside the museum glass doors on the entrance steps.

"Hi," August said to the clerk at the information desk. She didn't know quite where to start; it felt as if she were looking in the wrong place for answers. She asked about the artifacts, and took the handful of submission cards from her coat pocket and placed them on the counter. The clerk regarded the cards and recited them over the telephone and then led her down the hall, through code-secured doors and into the offices hidden out the back. August was introduced to a curator's assistant and he introduced her to a researcher. The museum people located the artifacts on their database easily: they were *currently in the collections*, they said. They were helpful, kind even, and they handed August the forms she'd need to *book a viewing*.

August wanted to hand the papers back and to tell them everything, draw them close and whisper that their lives had turned out wrong, that she and her family were meant to be powerful, not broken, tell them that something bad happened before any of them was born.

Tell them that something was stolen from a place inland, from the five hundred acres where her people lived. She wanted to tell them that the world was all askew and she thought it was because of the artifacts, that she thought they should understand it was all so *urgent* now, that they knew truths now, to tell them that she wasn't extinct, that they didn't need the exhibition after all. *All the hidden pieces were being put back together*, she wanted to say.

But she didn't say any of those things. She thanked them, accepted the handshake, nodded as the door was held open for her, in and out of the climate-controlled space.

August exited the curated light and joined Aunt Missy outside. She wanted to go back to Massacre—the countryside had got into her skin again, so quickly, she thought.

"Can we go home now?" she asked.

"What did the museum people say?" Missy bit her fingernails.

"We have to fill out these forms. I've got everything." August rustled the forms beside her. "We can do it back home, yeah?"

"Can we go back inside? I really do want to see the artifacts," Aunt Missy said, sincere and contrite, with a softness in her face like a child.

"They're all packed away, Aunty—we have to apply with these papers to see them . . . but they said they normally have them on display all the time!" August didn't know why she lied to her. Would it be any consolation that more eyes flicked at them, that schoolchildren had said *cool* when they saw them? That they were labeled in a glass display or tagged and serial-numbered in a box on a shelf? She didn't think so.

"But it's going to take time! We don't have time!" Missy said, frustrated.

August choked, tried not to cry. "They said it's the only way."

"You sure you have all the things?" she pointed to the papers.

"I promise. To the airport?" August put her arm around her.

"Alright then," she said, deflated.

They dropped the rental off, ate McDonald's fries at Terminal 2.

"Botany Bay just down the road, August."

"From here?"

"Yeah, just behind the airport."

"Where the First Fleet came?"

"Yep." Aunty didn't say anything more, she was too sad and too tired for anything else.

They took a train from the airport to the city and then out to Broken. They must have looked like the most despondent Aboriginal women in the entire world. They had run out of things to hope for. They had a destination, but it looked bleak from seats 18C and 18D.

Missy turned to August after some time and lamented, "It wouldn't change a thing. The artifacts. People don't care."

"Yes they do, Aunty," August said gently. "Otherwise they wouldn't be in a museum."

"Nup. People need tin. People so scared of not having everything . . ." she let out a big breath, "that our people are gunna have nothing." She closed her eyes as if that settled it.

After a while it sounded as if she were sleeping. August felt for Aunt Missy's phone still in her pocket and took it out. In the search engine she typed *tin mine* and then clicked on *images*. Fourteen million entries popped up, the phone told her; six were displayed on the screen. August clicked on the first to enlarge it. It was a color photo: blue sky, green grass ringed around a wide, deep hole that had stony-looking levels going down from the top, like seats in an ancient amphitheater. She pressed the button at the top to lock the phone and put it back into her pocket.

August had always thought important events happened in every other country except for Australia. That the tremors of their small lives meant nothing. But at that moment, on a train going to the deep past and the place she knew best, she felt as if she'd awoken from a stony sleep to find herself standing on the edge of something larger than she'd ever been able to see before. After digesting all those schoolbook lies, after reading that Reverend's letter, after walking the aisles of the museum, she knew that her life wasn't like before. There was an expanse behind her; their lives meant something, their lives were huge. Thousands of years, she thought to herself. Slipped through the fingers of careless people. That's what homogenized Massacre thought, that they were a careless people. Anyone watching the TV that week must've thought it—that Jedda was just a little brown girl gone missing from a messy brown family. Other people didn't have lumps in their throat year in and out, century after century. They didn't know what it was like to be torn apart.

They pulled into the station at a minute past midnight and began walking on the safe side of the railway strip, past the empty benches. August carried the rucksack and had both nylon sleeping bags draped around her neck—she imagined them like the possum-skin cloaks she'd seen at the museum. She felt for a moment as if she were a queen arriving for a coronation that she couldn't live up to. Joey was standing on the platform, waiting.

"You both look shattered."

"Exhausted, yep," August said, thrust back into the moment.

Missy nodded, glad to see her son again, to be home again.

Joey was jittery, he rubbed his palms together. "So . . . I've been with Nana all day. It's a bit wild out there."

"What's wild out where?" Aunt Missy snapped.

"Well, a little circus. Just a word of warning for when I drop you off, Aug."

"Spit it out!" Aunty shouted.

"They started clearing the trees yesterday arvo, knocked one of the sheds down and now the protesters are all over Prosperous. Chained themselves to everything." He started laughing then through a wide, dramatic mouth and clapped his hands together.

"Oh my God" was all Missy said, over and over, as they sped along the highway until they arrived at the turnoff of the Upper Massacre Plains road. As they drove down it, they could see an orange haze coming from Prosperous that blurred the usual stars on the horizon. "Oh my God."

They drove on, it felt, in slow motion, finally steering through the arch of peppermint trees. And there they saw it all: the field ablaze, the silhouettes of people running, and a few police cars parked beside Southerly, misery lights flashing in the maw of the dark. Aunt Missy said a final, foreboding, "Oh my God" and the car turned right to Prosperous House. Lit by the field, standing on the veranda were Elsie and Aunt Mary who flagged them down as if Joey's Mazda were a rescue ship and they were stranded in a sweep of wild ocean.

Thirty-Six

*Reverend Ferdinand Greenleaf's letter to Dr. George Cross,
2nd August 1915, continued*

IX

Many more of the German and Prussian descendants' homes and businesses were razed by fire, and more posters hung about the town of Massacre Plains:

"INTERN THE LOT!"

"ANTI-GERMAN LEAGUE MEETING"

Before my departure a notice was nailed to the Mission Church, which read: "DO YOUR BIT. KILL A GERMAN."

I'm certain I will die here. What use is this petition then? I fear my truth will go unnoticed and my life will simply be reduced to the coat of arms of a distant land. What use is determining our value or morality under the colors of a single flag? As you, Dr. Cross, whom I believe to be of Irish stock? Be it Ireland's flag. Be it the British flag or German or Australian? What use is persecuting us upon the weight of inconsequential coordinates on the globe, of that trifling place of our birth?

I am a Lutheran minister, and I haven't thought to be anything else all my days. However, later in my clergy work my friend Baumann had condemned our Founder, the theologian Martin Luther, as a hatemonger. Baumann told me of the things Luther wrote in regard to the Jew. He informed me that Luther had gone so far as to compose a petition calling for the eradication of the Jewish race—"the cockroaches," as Luther, a man of Scripture, had referred to them.

"We *must* look forward," I had said in response. Yet the dishonor I felt was pointed. What woe filled my spirit—that I should have lived my life spreading the Word under the banner of Lutheranism, when its Founder held such misguided ideals. I sought verification, and after I'd read the document that Baumann gave to me I threw it against the threshing floor after not ten pages. What horror. I felt I was questioning all that I had knelt before. God above all? The law and the Church? Church above all men? The White man over the Black man? And all men above beasts? What have I done? Have I become the beast? I am despised as a beast and I fear hatred has reduced the so-called *civilized* man to a pack of murderous barbarians.

The words! What have we done by taking the words of our God and turning them on their heads for our own purposes? And I am of that number. What have I done, dear Dr. Cross, that I feel such guilt in replacing *Baymee* with the Lord? What right had I to erasure? What right did I have to say one belief begets another? What right does any person? *What has man done to man?*

I fear I am losing my faith completely, in the Church and in Humanity. *If* I had known the dark deeds, I question whether I would have asked to be shown back to the sea, and the unkind ocean, asking it to sweep me homeward. Though, I remained.

In closing, I beg for reason and for you to insert this letter—or its sentiment—in a rightful place. Although I deeply deplore that Great Britain has been compelled to declare war against Germany, the land of my father, I am a British subject and am willing to defend the honor of His Majesty King George V, of our beloved Australia. As a clergyman without chattels, I can only offer my body and life and this humble truth.

With sincerity,
Ferdinand Greenleaf

THIRTY-SEVEN

Aunt Missy ran up the steps and ushered Elsie into Prosperous. Joey wandered onto the veranda, held the rails, and looked out over the field as if he were watching the lit new year arrive over a town oval, exchanging fire over the theater of the trenches.

Up at Southerly there were two police officers outside their car; the other officers were running in the chaos further out. Eddie was there outside Southerly. August could see the orange light flickering off his outline. She turned from him and stared into the flames off the crop as she followed Joey onto the deck. From there she could make out firemen holding a hose that sprayed a huge stream of water from the dam, the water looked white in the dark field. She saw a policeman tackle a silhouette to the ground. There were maybe thirty people running about. August looked for Mandy, but she couldn't make out their faces. It reminded her of childhood, clutching sparklers in their little hands, running through the night air and innocent: everything in the past was backlit in her mind.

She stood close to Joey. He laughed; he looked strung out. She leaned in to look at his eyes, dilated as dinner plates.

"How was the nightclub?" August asked.

"Sick," he said, and she shook her head. They could see the protesters standing atop the machinery way out, those on the ground kept running from the cops. The knee-high flames were racing down the dry field quickly, west toward the feed sheds, about half a kilometer from Prosperous and the drill sites. The fire brigade would contain it there, August reckoned. It wouldn't reach the house.

Joey looked the way he had looked into a campfire when they were young. Elated.

"You never had a riot in gaol? Set your mattress on fire?" August asked.

"I never got involved, was pointless. At least this isn't pointless. It's cool. You ever been in a riot?"

"I went to an anti-war protest in London. But it was calm from the back of the crowd." She thought about it—they were just numbers, the gentle, shuffling bulge of dissent at the end of a line. She moved inside the house where Elsie was weepy, and Mary was rapidly explaining, filling Aunt Missy in on the details. August hugged her nana tight and rubbed her back.

"About four yesterday arvo the bulldozers started. They've got logs strapped across the front so they can clear a big sweep. I was here with Mum. Next thing, a bunch of protesters are out in the field, standing in front of the machines! Fucking mad!" She added just as fast, "You wouldn't get me out there in front of a bloody ten-ton truck."

"How'd the fire start?" August asked.

"We were about to leave and the kids, *kids* they are, locked up the gates and said, 'No one in, no one out.' I called the cops and Nicki."

"Why'd you call Aunt Nicki?" August asked.

"She deals with the mine, doesn't she? So, then the cops come. The kids out there start filming stuff and chanting 'Lock the gates. Lock the gates.' We locked the door and stayed inside waiting for the cops when this one dreadlocked fella threw a bottle of something on the field . . . We saw it! . . . Bugger lit it!"

August wasn't listening properly. She was putting pieces together in her mind. She stood up, interrupted Aunt Mary. "Has anyone here seen the book that Poppy was writing, the dictionary, since we've been packing?"

"No."

"Have you seen it *at all*?" August whined.

"No!" Aunt Mary yelled. "I'm telling a story!"

"Nana?"

"I don't know where it is. For God's sake, August, the garden is on fire and you're worried about a *book*?"

A policeman appeared and hesitated at the back door for a moment before he spoke. "All you lot need to get out now. Take your things, this place'll go up like a tinderbox if the wind changes."

The Aunties gathered the bags that Nana had prepared, everyone was yelling at each other with care as they left the steps of the veranda to the cars. August ran up to Eddie as he hosed the garden with tank water.

She could hear her aunts calling out "August!" behind her, but ignored them, heading for Eddie. "Hey?" August barked at him from a distance.

He watched her run toward him and bent the hose to stop the spray. "Aww, Aug, please forgive me?" He twisted forward a little toward the chaos as if in physical pain. "I didn't mean to say those things, I promise you."

August ignored it, she didn't need to go over what he'd said. She had a more pressing question on her mind. "The other night—after the memorial—who put me to bed? Which of my aunties came upstairs?"

"What?"

"*Which aunty?*"

"Don't know her name."

"Black dress?" August said, trying not to yell near the police.

"Red shoes," he said.

"Did you tell the local council about the artifacts?"

"I'd just found them. Day before your pop passed, Aug—I promise!"

August ran back down to Prosperous. Elsie and the Aunties were still pushing the bags into the boot and back seat. Joey was standing on the veranda watching the field. August grabbed his arm. "Where's Aunt Nicki now?"

"Home probably."

"Drive me there?"

"It's one a.m., idiot."

"Alright, time to clear out. All valuables are in my car," Aunt Mary directed.

Elsie pointed August to Joey's car. "August, you go with Joe—there's no space."

"I'll go with Joey," August said, looking at Joey for confirmation but he was looking back to the fire. "We'll leave soon, yeah?" August reached out to him, tugged on his sleeve. "We go together, yeah?"

"Yeah," he said vaguely, and turned to the women.

"You just both leave when the cops tell you to, leave soon, okay?" Aunt Missy warned, pointing at the two of them. "Joe! Snap out of it!" He nodded.

August gave Elsie a quick hug before Aunt Missy and Aunt Mary hustled her into the car. They cradled bags on their laps, while August helped heave the doors shut. When the car left, Joey said he'd take August to Aunt Missy's and to grab what she needed.

"And to visit Aunt Nicki on the way?" August asked as they walked back to the house.

"Alright, we can stop there—but tell me why?"

"I'll tell you in the car . . ." August climbed the stairs to get her belongings from the attic. She grabbed her passport, threw it in her duffel bag and dumped the box's contents into another filled to the brim with Jedda's and her childhood things. She heaved the box and duffel bag and stumbled, upright, down the stairs.

Joey stood in the kitchen and reached out to help with the box.

A sudden white light flashed and lit up the interior of the house like a camera flash and a boom shuddered through the field.

They ducked, August dropped the box.

August could feel scorching heat, her skin dried and felt as if every particle of moisture drew from her pores, eaten by the dry air. They heard the *pop, pop, pop* of tin, that sounded like ricocheted gunshots. They stayed on the lino floor of the kitchen. After a few seconds they braved the kitchen window. Silhouettes of tin sheets peeled into the sky from the shed, and then they heard the beams crashing into the cackling, sparking fire. They watched the quick disappearing act of the shed as it collapsed, spewing flames.

August grabbed the box and the contents and together they fled outside.

"I'm driving!" August yelled over the whining burn of tin and oil. "Get off the ecstasy, Joey."

"Eat a fucking hamburger!" he yelled back, entranced by the

now-raging fire and stumbling to the car with the keys outstretched ahead of him. August took them from him.

She drove steadily as Joe directed her to Aunt Nicki's place. She pulled up at the curb. It wasn't much for a council worker: a simple brick house, it couldn't have had more than two bedrooms. It was in the nice part of town, though, Minties area. August banged on the aluminum screen door; it shook in the frame. As she waited she turned to Joe in the car, he shook his head behind the wound-up window, lowered himself further into the seat. A light came on in the house, a head peeked through the curtain, then the rattle of a lock and chain.

Aunt Nicki popped her head through the gap in the door wearily.

"Aunty, have you seen the dictionary Poppy was writing?" August asked.

"What?"

"Did you bribe them with the dictionary? Did you say you'd make the Gondis claim Native Title if they didn't give *you* some money? Or have you just kept it?"

"Aug, it's the middle of the night!"

"I need to read what Poppy wrote please, Aunty. *Please.*"

Nicki narrowed her eyes, but her body had taken the blow. "I kept it to protect the family, my love."

"I promise you, Aunty, I'm so ruined—there's nothing to protect anymore." August said, holding her chest, sincere.

"It's in the council office. Tomorrow we get it, okay? Goodnight, niece."

She closed the door. Rattled the chain. Flicked off the light before August could tell her that Prosperous was aflame, that tomorrow wasn't good enough. She flung herself back into the Mazda.

"She's been hiding it. I need to see it, Joey." August said as she drove out of the street.

"What?"

She didn't know where to start.

"Poppy's book he was writing. It might save the farm. I gotta read it now."

"Where is it?"

"In the council office."

She slowed at a corner, turned, sped up again.

"I wanna see it now, sick of waiting forever!" August yelled, and in that moment she felt devastated by all the years she'd wasted. August pushed the gear into fourth. Joey tightened the strap of his seatbelt.

"I'm not doing anything illegal—I'm still on probation, cousin."

August accelerated into the main street heading toward the council offices. She reassured him, exalted, "Gondis are born on probation, Joey."

THIRTY-EIGHT

afraid to speak—*giya-rra-ya-rra* My wife was waist-deep at the local pool when I fell in love with her. She was a warrior that day, and every day after. That was the day we met, and there she was. She arrived out at Tent Town with a busload of university students from the city one day when we were still handsome and young. She was one of the university teachers there, and she said that they had come out to the countryside to talk to the Aborigine about human rights! Well! She was beautiful, and she was smart—so I listened right away. I myself was out there at Tent Town visiting some shearers who I was sent out to get for the week's work at Prosperous—that was a hot week—must've been summer if we were shearing. So those university students were telling us about equal rights and this and that and I was listening. She and the others asked us what were some of the things in Massacre that we thought were discriminatory? Well, it didn't take a minute for us to list this and that. "Look around," I told her. I mentioned the pub and the schools and the fact we were separated and the fact there was no land around for us and that the kids weren't allowed in the local swimming pool—not even in this heat, I said. Then her eyes widened and they all got so excited. "We're taking the kids for a swim then!" they said.

Lo and behold, about thirty kids were picked up and piled into the bus with all the university students and their cameraman too. Me, I was on the bus too, but I was just floating in there, floating after the woman I'd decided that I loved already. We arrived at the town swimming pool and those university students get the money out and hand it to each of the kids to go and buy their ticket. The kids smiled so big, never seen kids smiling like that before in my life, I reckon. We could smell the chlorine, see the pool through the turnstiles. We arrived at the ticket booth, and that was it, all over—"NO Aborigines," the pool attendant said, and pointed to the kids to look at the sign. I remember the kids just staring up at the painted letters like they'd been punched in the guts, like all the air and happy life got pushed out of them. Some of those kids started crying and I was mad at those university students. Why they had to come and shame the kids in front of everyone?

The students were arguing with the pool attendant, and then a big crowd of Massacre residents come gathering around saying, "Go home blackfellas, get, get out of town." The university people, Elsie there too, were still arguing with the pool attendant and I was standing back, saying "There, there" to the little ones, that I'd take them myself down the river when we got back to Tent Town.

Then the fight starts heading away from the pool attendant and it's all around the bus, see. There's a sort of play happening, a jostle for the stage and one of the university students was questioning a local lady wearing gloves in front of the cameraman, just beside me and the kids. The university student asked something like, "Ma'am, why do you not want the Aboriginal children of this town swimming in the pool?" "They're bad," she said, "they don't belong here, should go back to their huts!" she said. The university student asked her again, voice raised now, on the edge of a big argument, gesturing to the kids and me. "Don't they look like good kids to you that just want to go for a swim and cool off, just like the privileged White children?" she asked. "You don't think they are good children?" The woman couldn't even look at those kids, she just raised her voice above the din and said, "Yeah, a good one's a dead one."

Well, I hustled the crying kids into the bus then, I didn't want them hearing another thing. The fights continued outside and the camera kept rolling when there were conversations to film. Finally, persuaded by Elsie, and twisted by the arm seeing the video camera in their face, the kids were allowed to have a swim. Elsie jumped in too. I stood out and watched and dropped my hand into the pool and splashed a little. Elsie was laughing. Not an ounce of fear about her. She wasn't ever *giya-rra-ya-rra*. She dried off and got dressed and I talked to her until she and the students left the pool, and she said they were going to many places after Massacre. "Causing trouble?" I asked. "I hope so," she said, then winked at me and laughed.

She left after that, all the university students and the bus too. I said I'd stay on with the kids and we'd walk home later. Not a minute after the bus rolled out of the car park of the municipal pool did the attendant and his gang come and throw me and the kids out! Shame. They were happy enough though, those kids were. They dived in the clear cool water. It didn't matter to them how long it lasted. It was that it happened, I've reckoned. And me, I became more afraid because they didn't just despise me, but I realized when I was watching the children, hearing the things that children should never hear—that they despised our kids, too. Only part of me was happy, because Elsie happened to me, and I knew somehow that I'd be seeing her again soon.

Years later, even after those laws about the public pools and the cinema seating changed, I could still recognize that fear that people had toward us, that distrust they had of our kids, and since that day I saw Elsie at the *galing* I've been reminded time and again that people's attitudes don't change just because the law changes. I was afraid to speak for so long, for so much of my life, but I'm not anymore. I refuse to *giya-rra-ya-rra*!

alcohol, wine, strong drink—*widyali, girrigirri* One day you wake up and there's the dry of the drought at your door. Then the great flood, playing tricks on your mind, and then the drought arrives again, the summer lengthened a month every year until we find ourselves where we are now. Nothing so sad as the skeleton of a bullock or a heifer in a field, its skin draped over it like a bedsheet. What a drought does to the mind is a cruel thing, and many men from the farms around here have found the only solution is wrapping their lips around the barrel of a shotgun. Divorce is now commonplace in an area where it wouldn't have been thought of fifty years ago. There is a limit to *better or worse, thick and thin*—sometimes the thin gets to be completely out of sight. Sometimes it's the boys off the farms, lost in the cities, and there isn't even anyone left to fight with, a person is left wrestling themselves. That's when the *widyali*—poison in its own right, but balm in the mouth of poisoned spirits—looks like prayer. But tortured people and the drink is like throwing petrol into a fire—don't do anything except make it worse. Won't quench a drought, that *widyali*, won't mend your heart either, won't even let you forget about it, not for long. That poison is best given a wide berth—haven't seen anything good come from it and the drugs all my long life.

all together in one place—*ngumbaay-dyil* To be isolated is to be unable to act. That's what we were—isolated—from our family, from our language, from our cultural ways, and from our land. And then we were taken *ngumbaay-dyil*. But it wasn't really that we were together, it just looked humane, a face in a crowd. But we were brutalized, we turned on each other, we were isolated in our humiliation but we couldn't leave neither. We were like roos in the headlights, the old people, my old mummy, me and my sisters, even my daughters, growing up around sad ghosts on the Mission. Having their own struggles. We weren't really all together in one place, we weren't residents in those places, us kids on our cots, we were criminals by birth, inmates since we could walk. Together and isolated at once.

always be, exist—*ngiyawaygunhanha* A person exists beyond the living and the dead, in the planes of time where gods roam, when they know the seen and unseen at once. That is to be *ngiyawaygunhanha*.

THIRTY-NINE

August parked opposite the town council. Joey was yelling at her to get back into the car. She shut the driver's door behind her. He leaned his head out the passenger window. "If you're not back in five minutes I'm leaving, just like you and fucking Eddie left me at the pharmacy!" he jeered.

August got back into the car and shut the door. "I didn't leave you that night," she said, searching his face.

"Just joking, aye. Go on, do your crime, Gondi." He threw his hand toward the council building.

August rested her head against the seat, realizing how tired she was, but tried again. "We were just off our heads, Joe. I'm sorry Eddie told you to keep watch. We were just kids."

"I know that, still don't know what the hell we were doing there. Dumbasses." He looked out the passenger window, away from their talking.

After a minute of silence she asked him clearly, kindly, "What was it like?"

"Crap."

"I'm sorry."

"It's not your fault. I was a fucking troublemaker, I was."

"It was Eddie and my fault, it was us, not you." August took his hand. "I'm sorry, cousin."

"I forgive ya."

"Do you remember when Poppy put that sign outside Prosperous?" August asked.

"Back door?" She caught him grin a little in the High Street light.

"Nah, that was Nan. The other one."

"Nup."

"No Grog, No Cash, No Yarndi, No Good Times Here."

Joe let out a single *ha*. "I remember now."

"'Member family got pissed off—said he was typecasting us?"

"Nah. Did they?" He looked at August.

"Yeah," she said. "I heard them talking like that. I was lying near the front door when it used to be open; it had a screen with metal diamond shapes and I was lying there playing with my eyes. Like, looking at the diamond shapes and then adjusting my vision and looking out to the acacia trees and then back and forth."

"You always were a little weirdo," Joe chuckled quietly.

"I remember thinking that my eyes are special, I can make them do this wild blurring thing. I can see things how I want."

"And?"

"And then I could hear everyone arguing out on the back deck about this sign. Arguing that they weren't this and we weren't that. Defending ourselves in our own home."

"Mmm?" Joe said, waiting for August to get to the point.

"I just remember thinking we should all lie here and see how cool our eyes are. I was hoping they could see what I saw."

"What are you talking about?"

"Seeing two things at the same time. Here and there, close and far, now and before."

"Is this before Jed . . . ?"

"After," August said. "Poppy was so paranoid, wasn't he?"

"He was just protective."

"He was a *didadida*."

"I remember that word! What's that?" Joe asked.

"Plover bird, I think."

A minute of silence passed before Joey asked, "What'd Aunt Nicki do?"

"She has a dictionary that Poppy wrote, and she hid it and maybe used it to get money from Rinepalm, but probably not. There's something important in whatever Poppy wrote, though. I have to see it now." August said all this breezily, having calmed down.

"Where is it?"

She pointed up to the council building. "Third floor."

Joe got out of the car and closed the door behind him. August watched him through the windshield as he strode across the street.

She came to and jumped out after him. Pulled her hoodie over her head, and hissed to Joey, jogging to keep up, "How we gunna get to the third floor?"

She followed him around the back of the library. It was dark, no streetlights shone there. Joey dropped to the ground, fumbling in the raggedy grass.

He stood up with a dark mass in his hands.

"Smash it," he said, and August saw his wild grin in the darkness. He took a few steps away from the library window.

"Move back," he said.

August walked over to him and grabbed the rock. "I'll do it. Let me—I'm not on probation."

She stood there with the rock hiked on her shoulder, balancing it with both hands. She thought she was like Atlas then, holding the weight of their world. She hurled it at the window; it damaged the chook-wire-reinforced glass, but didn't shatter it. She went and retrieved the rock. Joey checked the side of the building and nodded that the street was clear. Then August realized she wasn't Atlas. She was Sisyphus. What good would it do to smash a window? Raid a council office? Look through an office of paper for a pile of paper? What was she thinking?

But August wasn't thinking, she was *feeling*. She felt strong and powerful enough not to throw the rock. She turned and dumped the boulder behind her. "Poppy liked the library," she said.

Joey broke into a loud, bellowing laugh, enunciating "Ah ah ha ha ah."

"Should we go back to Prosperous?" August asked.

"Let me throw it." He picked up the boulder.

She grabbed it from him, like she wanted to grab it from Jedda long ago. "We can't, Joe! We'll talk to your mum tomorrow. We'll get her to talk to Aunty. We can't smash the library."

"It's just a window."

"Yeah, I know, but Poppy *loved* this place. Wherever he is right now he's shaking his head at us."

He was still then, and quiet, as if Poppy had himself arrived and told him to quit disturbing the peace.

"We go back to Prosperous," August suggested.

He shrugged. "And after that?"

"We stop the mine." The words came out of her mouth as if they were the first sure things she'd ever said.

"Yeah. Let's go."

They walked back to the Mazda.

"Reckon we're too old for crime?" August asked.

"Nah, it's just we'd definitely *do the time*." He clapped his hands together, widemouthed and proud of the rhyme.

August turned and parked outside the driveway. From high up in their seats they inspected the field: the flames had been mostly doused but the fire still smoldered in places; a paddy wagon was being fed with a handful of protesters.

"We can stay in Prosperous." August angled the car toward the house.

"Yeah, it's fine now," Joey laughed. "Just a little grass back-burn, aye."

They brought doonas and pillows from the attic room, made a camp on the veranda, and fell into the down in their day clothes. They looked out to the now-contained fire.

"How was the city?" Joe asked, his face subtly lit, propped on his elbows.

August was propped on her elbows too, looking out. "Did your mum tell you why we went?"

"Nan said to return your hire car. You're staying?"

"Yeah," she said, and looked over to Southerly. The house lights were dark. "And . . ."

They faced each other, their heads on the pillows, but August couldn't make out Joe's face. She could only hear his slow, deep breathing in her direction.

"There's Gondiwindi artifacts in the city, at a museum. We went to see them."

"Yeah?" Joey was speaking in sleepy, slurred words already. "Hah?"
He was silent.

August closed her eyes and dreamed of drenched England. A market erected at the dawn stillness, in the center of the stone-bed street. Children skipping. Every ripe memory of an imagined childhood played like a reeling color film, plump shining vegetables, sick-sweet fruits.

"Check me, check me. Got it? Fe fi fo thumb, thumb. brrrrrrrrr, bddddddddd. This just in, the cat sat on the mat. Ready?"

August turned her head and saw a news reporter standing in front of a cameraman in the field, beside Joey's Mazda. The sun was a dull circle in a green smoky sky.

"I'm here in the rural drought-stricken community of Massacre Plains. Throughout the night, violence erupted on this former farming property where local police officers were forced to defuse a situation engineered by environmental protesters. Protesters have been arrested throughout the night, though, as you can see, around forty remain, in what is known as a 'lock-in.' Negotiations are forthcoming. Rinepalm Mining has federal approval for a two-kilometer, 300-meter-deep tin mine, a boon for the local economy with work to commence in the next few days. Amanda McMurray, reporting from Massacre Plains."

August watched the woman suddenly slouch her shoulders, the cameraman lower his camera, and jumped up. She grabbed Joe from the back of his hoodie and dragged him into Prosperous.

She slid the door across and locked it. Drew the never-used sheer curtains across and pulled the blind over the kitchen-sink window.

"News people are here. Cameras."

Joey got to his feet, he looked excited, fixed his hair with his fingers. "Really?"

"Come, look from upstairs," she said, and sprinted to the attic window.

Through the Lutheran rose they could see a few stray vehicles, one police car. Everything seemed calm for that moment. August looked out toward Southerly but couldn't see Eddie.

Joey followed her back down the stairs to the landline ringing, she picked it up and said nothing.

"Hello?" Nana asked.

"Nana?"

"You're there?" she said, shocked.

"Why'd you ring, Nana?"

"To see if my house was still there, I think."

"Everything is fine, no more fire. Joey and I are here. Don't come though, it's still a bit disordered."

"Are you both okay?"

"We're fine."

"Is Edward okay up there?"

"Everyone's fine, I promise. Just rest and I'll come see you soon, at Aunt Mary's?"

"Yes, darling, come here when you're ready."

Aunt Missy got on the phone. "August?" she said, and sounded as if she were moving with the phone to another room. "What's happening there?" she whispered.

"News people outside, there's a police car, some protesters are still out there. Why?"

"Well, I wanna come, I wanna protest too."

August held the receiver, nodded to Joey. "Your mum wants to come protest?" she smiled.

Joey nodded, sprinting on the spot, throwing punches into the air.

"Are we doing this?" August said to Aunt Missy.

She whispered, "Yes. I'm coming now. Shh." She hung up.

"What do we do now?" she asked Joey.

"Let's just rumble on the front line!"

"I thought you were on probation, that you hated the hippies?"

"I thought they'd be banging drums and shooing incense, not going sick."

"What are we gunna do about Aunty Nicki?" she asked Joey, by now jittery with excitement.

"We go talk to her after."

August stirred instant coffee into two mugs, flung the blind open, and looked out into the field. She thought how for so long she'd been living her life in a box of to-do, like a never-ending winter, her own long hibernation. She had lived her life as if it were full of potholes, tripwire, landmines, too scared to move properly. But she was here, she thought, and she cared about something and for her family for the first time in forever. She reckoned she wouldn't fall into quicksand on the edge of town.

Joey was lacing his sneakers. "They want to take land that wasn't theirs to take, land was given that wasn't theirs to give! The buck stops here, motherfucker."

August handed him the coffee cup. "Don't get crazy."

"Oh, I'm crazy for it."

"Don't hurt anyone?"

"Never, but I'm gunna go smash some stuff up . . ." Joe sluiced the coffee she'd made down the sink. "There's no fucking time for that."

The phone rang again, August picked it up.

"Hello?"

"You fucking Abos better get the fuck out of this town!"

The line dropped out. She didn't know who it was, though the caller sounded like a teenage girl.

"Who was it?"

"Prank call," she said. The insult stayed inside the phone receiver as she sat it back down. Nothing could touch her. Maybe the girl was frightened of the world she didn't even know properly, maybe no one ever told the girl on the phone about the great land and the great people who'd survived all this time.

They stood out on the deck with their hoodies tight over their faces and ignored the reporter when she kept calling out, "Excuse me? Excuse me?"

August looked up at Kengal but the camp appeared packed away; over at Southerly the windows were drawn and the door closed. The field hadn't burned completely; there were still hundreds of acres wanting harvest. When they were kids, she used to imagine what happened to the wheat after the trucks came to empty the grain from the silos. Bakers in every country pounding wheat heads, grinding, milling, adding yeast, salt, oil, sugar, fire. Breads rising all over the world from what was grown here.

"You wanna?" Joey asked.

"Should we wait for your mum?"

"She'll find us," Joey said, eyes glittering, his mouth certain as he turned to the horizon, staring out into the distance.

He took her hand and they descended the steps, trampled through the potato bed, and walked over the smoldering black field of Prosperous Farm to the protesters chained against the tractors lashed with clearing logs.

As they walked August thought that grief's stint was ending. She whispered to Jedda and to Poppy: *I am here.*

She looked for Mandy as they got closer to the three tractors parked near the drilling sites. A big banner hung from the forks of two tractors that said "RESIST." Mandy was chained around her waist against the drilling fence, her hair still in long braids, her arms above her head holding a white plastic barrel, her mouth open and drinking from the spout. August thought she looked brave, or careless, that Mandy had a way of moving her body that August remembered feeling, only as a child. Mandy passed the container on when she saw Joey and August, stretched her arms out beside her, like Aunt Missy had done at the museum.

"Fellow water protectors!" Mandy exclaimed as they neared.

Joey yelled back, correcting her, "No, we're the custodians of this land." He confidently turned to the five other people lashed against the wire fence, "And we're going to stop this motherfucking mine."

The handful who had heard Joey's proclamation cheered. He turned to August and she nodded, smiled, put her hand out to receive the chain from another protester.

"Welcome," the protester said.

"Welcome," she said back to him.

After a couple of hours of chanting and water breaks, Eddie came outside. He marched angrily across the burned field. "Hello?" he yelled, confused.

"Hello!" they yelled back in unison.

"What the *fuck* are you doing?"

Joey screamed at him, maybe the way he'd always wanted to. "Back off, Falstaff. It's *our* land."

"It's the fucking mining company's now, you dickheads."

Joey cut him off. "We are the company and the government. This is our minister, second female prime minister, in fact!" he said, and pointed to August. "I'm the president, we co-run this country, and these guys," he pointed around to a few sheepish faces, "are our Senate and board members."

Aunt Missy was walking through the blackened field. "Here comes your local MP right now. Vote well, son." Joe pointed to Aunt Missy, who was wearing a t-shirt that read *Treaty* across the front. She smiled wildly.

"Joining in, Eddie?"

He leaned in and they exchanged a small hug. "I don't think so, Missy."

"You could right all the wrongs!" she said, as if it wasn't such a difficult thing to do. She held out her hand to take a piece of chain. "It's not gunna fit around me!" Aunty started laughing, buckling her nervous body and rattling her bit of chain against the fence.

A cheery voice came over a loudspeaker from the couple of police cars. "You are on government property, time to clear off, folks. No charges if you leave now."

A protester helped padlock Aunt Missy to the fence and tied a bandana around her chin. "For pepper spray," the man said.

Mandy picked up her own bullhorn, aiming it back to the police, "We'll leave when Rinepalm do." There was a box taped to the mouthpiece and her voice came out in autotune.

"I'm not getting arrested, guys." Eddie threw his hands out as if giving up reason against insolent children. "I don't think it's a good idea, being out here. Sheep are scared shitless! They're bringing in soldiers, it's on the news. I'm outta here!" Eddie turned away, shook his head, and stormed back to Southerly. They didn't say anything.

A policewoman passed him on her way toward them with something in her hands. "A GoPro camera," Mandy said. "Cover your faces."

"What's it for?" August asked, hiding her face under the hoodie.

"They just try to fuck with your head, make us think they control the story, control the data—state control, you know?"

"What was the fire for?"

"Attention. Chaos."

"You guys could have burned my nana alive!" August was serious.

"We came through the night before and built a fire breakwall, just a magic trick."

August couldn't see her face, but she sounded genuine. She believed her. She watched as three police paddy wagons pulled up near Prosperous.

"There are more police than us," August said.

Mandy nodded out toward the dam, "More of us will arrive soon."

But the field beside the dam was empty. The policewoman walked down the row of them against the fence and then a hundred meters or so to film the others chained to the clearing tractors.

The protesters started chanting under their covered mouths, "Re-sist, re-sist, re-sist," over and over. Joey joined in. Mandy turned back to August, her face still concealed. "Keep your face covered and they can't have you. As soon as they have your identity they can do anything to you."

"What do you mean, *do anything*?"

"You can't make a move before someone's watching, but if you stay off grid, cover your face, they can't take you, your thoughts, the things you're really angry about."

August looked at her as she faced the police. "I'm nobody, anyway," she said.

Mandy turned to August. "You *are* somebody. But these days we can't do anything as somebody, we can only do something as nobody. The nobody of everybody."

August thought for a moment. "I don't get it."

"When something is important enough that it's personal to everyone," Mandy added.

"Our problems are never anyone else's, that's how it seems."

Mandy pulled the bandana down from over her mouth, and continued. "I agree that's how it's been. Look at it this way—when people travel overseas the first thing they do is learn a handful of words, learn the local language—*please* and *thank you* and *hello* and *goodbye*, maybe even *where is the supermarket?* People do it because it makes life easier but they also do it out of respect, don't you think?"

August nodded.

"And then we're all migrants here, even those first-fleet descendants; we forget we're all in someone else's country. And too often we don't have the vision, the respect, to bother learning the native language! To even learn to respect the culture where we live."

"Because it doesn't make life easier?" August asked.

"Because we have to learn it's personal—we learn that through looking after the land. That we'll all continue not really having a collective identity unless we take a long and hard look back and accept the past and try to save the land we live on . . . that's what I think." Mandy pulled the cloth back over her mouth.

To August it was true, this *was* personal. Further out she spotted Aunt Mary and her nana approaching. "My nana," she said, as Joey yelled, "Nana, come over here with us!"

As she drew near, Elsie put her hands on her hips, stern like. "What are you lot doing?" she demanded.

"Nan—we've got to do something. Don't you think?" Joey said.

Elsie shook her head. "It's a bit late, darlings."

"How long are you lot gunna stay out for?" Aunt Mary asked,

looking around at them all. *"Missy!"* she barked, noticing her against the fence, *"You're* too old for this!"

"Not that old!" Missy cried back.

Joey spoke up. "We can't do nothing!"

Elsie folded her arms across her chest. "We're just the world's quarry of choice and I don't see any way around that. But without protest, we wouldn't have our rights, none of us would have civil rights, the vote, decent working week." Elsie and Mary nodded to each other in agreement—they'd seen it all. Elsie bit her lip, calmly tapped her fingers and inspected all the riffraff before her, and then spoke again. "Well, I'll cut some oranges then if you're staying out, it'll be thirty-nine degrees by midday."

August reached out for her hand as she turned to leave. "We're going to save your home, Nana."

Elsie bent down to her in response and spoke softly, her face at her ear. "Home was Albert; seeing him come across the field, and *him seeing me.* No one sees me if I stay here, August."

August understood what her nana meant. She had lost a witness too, someone seeing her. She'd outgrown her big sister. But she'd also found the solace she felt in that moment, on the land, making it personal.

"We've gotta try, Nana," she said back to her gently.

Elsie stood upright. "Yes, you're right, you must try. I'll be waiting for you at the house, but I can't bail any of you out if you get arrested!" She chuckled a bit, "Joey, come and get the oranges," and walked unhurried across to Prosperous. Joey unshackled himself and ran the distance after her. Minutes later he ran back with a string bag of fruit quarters.

Elsie was right. The sun blazed down as if the field were going to catch alight again, and then the new digger reeled into Prosperous. And after it, two military-green humvees revved into the entrance-way. August rubbed her fingers against the velvet pile of the wheat stalks flattened beside her thighs.

"Hold fast!" Mandy yelled.

"Mum, please go back to Prosperous now?" Joey called from one end of the fence to the other. "I don't want you to get hurt. Please, Mum."

August looked over to Aunt Missy, where a protester was helping to unlock her. "I'll be here in spirit!" Aunt Missy said, and scuttled along the side of the burned field, around the vegetable garden, and up the stairs of Prosperous.

"Hold fast?" August asked nervously.

"Stay strong, don't let them break you." Mandy said.

First they water-hosed them; it didn't cool them down but tore their clothes and bit the skin showing. The hours passed and they still didn't move. Across the field by the dam a crowd drew closer. It was a bunch of the mob from the Valley. They assembled with the help of the protesters. Aunt Carol Gibson let herself be locked against the fence, a bike lock around her neck. They all G'day'd each other and got back to the task.

Aunty Betty yelled out to August from her hold, "Sacred ground, girl."

Mandy turned to August, "To riot is the voice of the unheard." She pulled out a small camera and filmed the police gathering ahead of them. The officers were wearing gloves and long sleeves; they were wearing boots, batons hung at their thighs, their faces shielded in Perspex.

A protester rushed past them dropping earplugs and goggles into their laps.

"Don't fight back," Mandy said. "They can't arrest us for sitting in."

"Okay," she said.

Hours later though, the protesters on the tractors threw back fist-size rocks toward the water cannons, and as time drew on, as the sun began to set, the police squirted tear gas that made stinging barbs in their eyes, noses, throats.

Spray bottles of water were shared, people were crying, trying still to yell "Re-sist!" until their voices were slowly silenced as the police made their final advance. Moved in on the inert of them, the peaceful, the passive. Some got carried away, others stayed lashed to the fence.

August had forever felt like she was a remaining thing of the past that she wanted to destroy, a face she wanted to scratch off, a body she wanted broken, her skin torn to shreds. She was feeling something close to that against the fence, hosed and chained. She was chained like the people, the Gondiwindi who came before her, but it was her choice then, she thought. It felt that everything was so close, that they could all feel the past, that it gnawed at their ankles. That it filtered into their voices as they screamed together "Re-sist!" into the dying light. She felt whole, fighting for something, screaming in the field rather than eating it, tasting it, running away.

The sky above the Murrumby had changed from blue to white-yellow to orange-pink to clear purple and, just before night fell, a Rinepalm bulldozer came through crushing the trees along the property, uprooting the dirt-stuck roots into the air. Then August heard Aunt Mary's voice break, her boat snapped loose from the anchor, and she wailed across the field. Aunt Nicki was standing beside her, the cassette recorder and a stack of pages in her hand.

FORTY

REVEREND FERDINAND GREENLEAF,
LUTHERAN MISSIONARY
28TH FEBRUARY 1838–1ST JANUARY 1916

There were many expressions of regret in the town of Massacre Plains yesterday morning.

The late Reverend Greenleaf born in Sachsen in 1838 was the only son of Norman Greenleaf, a landholder, and has been laid to rest. A religious gentleman who was a well-known and combative figure in the interior, his death comes after this newspaper recently, and controversially, republished his heartfelt and passionate letter to the British Society of Ethnography.

The letter was smuggled out via the renowned photographer Mr. Paul Dubotzki. His message stirred our readers' deepest sympathies and enraged the Anti-German League. It has been reported that Mr. Greenleaf, who was interned on Torrens Island before being transferred to Holsworthy Internment Camp, died of natural causes. The editors here at *The Australian Argus*, however, would like to think he might have died of a broken heart, such was his fierce commitment to justice for his friends the Aborigines. We will remember him as a British subject and a soothsayer of our turbulent age.

The deceased has no immediate kin.

The Australian Argus
2nd January 1916

FORTY-ONE

Nana had initially folded under the town pressure. "Maybe we give up a little for the betterment of everyone else," she said. A writer named Montaigne said the same thing, August told her, but he'd been wrong in giving a seed to receive a shoot of the plant—he wasn't thinking that people *are* the seeds.

But still they stayed on until the end, and further.

Until Aunt Nicki broke the truths to Aunt Mary, and confirmed all Nana's worst fears—that Jedda was gone. Never to return.

Until a digger felled the last peppercorn tree and white things tumbled from the dirt and roots, like sticks of quartz, like bones. A waterfall of yellowed bones.

That's what they saw, unshackling from the waist and running to the sounds of gasps and cries. The hundreds of bones from the earth. A digger's mouthful of bones, falling.

Almost immediately after that, historians declared the cemetery was culturally significant—they said the cemetery site, containing the bones of up to one hundred former Aboriginal Mission residents, had never been noted on the Prosperous area plan. The cemetery was found in the more productive area of the property, and the remains in the paddock had been mistakenly ploughed and cropped by the Falstaffs.

Aunt Nicki brought the cassette recorder out to Prosperous and handed over Albert's Native Title application. She hugged August. She swore she was just trying to protect the family from what was inside. "You must come to terms with what's in here, August," she said. Aunt Nicki cried then, and August thought that maybe she really was being sincere. Much later Aunt Nicki moved to the city and after August read Poppy's book, she thought that perhaps someone had hurt her when she was a little girl, too. Or maybe she was protecting Aunt Mary. No one really understood, not yet.

The tape Albert had made was his recital, his private sermon, going through a list of words, trying as he did to work out or remember how they were pronounced. It was special to the whole town, having that recording of his voice, him speaking the old language, kept safe. Digitized. Captured forever.

The smells, tastes, and burdens left August. She ate again too; she wasn't *ngarran* anymore. English changed their tongues, the formation of their minds, August thought—she'd drifted in and out of herself all that time. The language was the poem she had looked for, communicating what English failed to say. She'd come across the Pink Map and arrived. Her poppy used to say the words were paramount. That they were like icebergs floating, melting, that there were ocean depths to them that they couldn't have talked about.

Eddie left town and later August received an email from him. He had enrolled in the city university and his girlfriend was expecting a child. That's all he said. They both knew what everything had meant, that there was a truce in the distance they kept. He signed off—*We go right back.*

And then six months after the protest it rained for forty days and nights straight. The locusts disappeared. Some people said it was a miracle, others said it was global warming. August thought Poppy would have had her write it down in the exercise book. The farmers planted corn in the summer rain. Miracle or not, the rain filled Murrumby River for a while, before most of it was used to irrigate the crops. Joey reckons he saw a platypus in the water, kangaroos returned to drink from the bank, and more birds appeared.

Around the same time scientists wrangled permits and, with the anthropologists from the museum, they estimated the Gondiwindi milling techniques to be around eighteen thousand years old. They said it rewrote the history of world agriculture. They said the Gondiwindi also built large dams and then carried fish and yabbies in *gulumans* over large distances to stock the new waterholes. They said they domesticated animals; they said the Gondiwindi ticked the boxes to classify as a civilization. The evidence of their civilization, after so many years of farming, was difficult to find on the surface of the land. But they said it was embedded in the language of Albert's dictionary, that with the Reverend's list and all the words that Albert wrote, and other old people remembering the words too, that it would now be recognized as a resurrected language, brought back from extinction.

The evidence and all that heavy rain meant the mine was delayed and no one went back to dig any deeper. The land of Prosperous has begun to grow over itself, like the blanket covering the dead. They say the fate of Prosperous might linger in the courts for months or years more. The conservationists versus the mine, the Gondiwindi versus the mine—

other people would get sick of waiting, not them. The mining company proved they had obtained S116 of the constitution "consent to destroy" from the town council, but most of the shareholders had since backed out anyway. Yesterday, the case finally made the High Court. While they were waiting for the news to come on the television, Elsie was leaning into Aunt Missy's garden, picking yam daisies for dinner. She looked up at August standing at the back door and waved the yellow flowers in the air, and winked.

And August is still there in Massacre Plains, in the Valley with her nana and Aunt Missy and Aunt Mary too. All the family, all the Gondiwindi mob. All the women together, Joey too. She had run away looking for something, run her fingers through the reeds beside foreign rivers, down the spines of books, dipped into holy water in the European churches. She realized she'd fled there for Jedda, but that she had stayed there looking for those words that she'd understand, that would explain what it all meant.

Albert didn't tell them all the things he knew. He needed his family, his town to find out, to want to find out things for themselves. He wrote that in his dictionary—how he noticed the soil, then read about something else, and everything snowballed after that. How the things he needed to know opened up to him once he opened his eyes. Once *he* was seen.

When August was a little kid she couldn't rely on the certainty of even a day. She thinks now that that's why she needed to control things around her, the things she ate, the things she said. She tried to keep herself and her life small and manageable. Much like a poem. The condensing of the wide, unknowable past that runs right up behind them. She doesn't do that anymore. Her life isn't a poem; she knows it's a big, big story. Her people go all the way back to the riverbank, and further, after all—the river and what happened at the river was a time traveler, their story has no bounds in time. She and Joey learned it's the grandkids who inherit everything their ancestors did before. They carried the past with them, though they never knew. All the years that she had been adrift and tethered at once amounted to *something*, though. She'd rediscovered her family and who she truly was because of who they truly were.

August listened to the letters Jedda and she had composed to Princess Diana. They were funny—she thought they both sounded like sweet girls, giggling and taking turns to hog the recorder and to tell her how they were going to be princesses one day too. They turned into sad letters when they heard she died in the car accident. *"We are so sad today,"* they said. After all that time August had Jedda's words again, too. No one ever found Jedda in the water. But she wasn't lost like they'd always feared.

August couldn't sleep in the nights leading up to her mum's release. Missy drove Elsie and August to the Women's Correctional Facility to pick up their mother and daughter and sister. August and Jolene sat in the back seat on the way home, and August laid her head in her mother's lap for the first time since she was a girl. She dreamed of Jedda and herself in a cave of towels and bedsheets.

> *Knock knock.*
> *What's the secret code? August and Jedda asked.*
> *Burral-gang?*
> *Gaygar?*
> *Wahn the crow?*
> *They were giggling, and their mother too as she pulled the sheets open on their cubbyhouse.*

August felt her mother brush her fingers across the hair on her face and looked up. She'd been there, she had the secret code, she was there then with eyes alive with something buried. They farewelled Jedda together, all together.

August and Joey printed out the pages of their grandfather's dictionary for the local kids. They included some of the stories they remembered, the stories August's mother and their aunts remembered too, the ones that their Poppy hadn't got around to telling.

They wrote in the Foreword:

Maybe you are looking for a statue, or a bench by the banks of the Murrumby to honor the people who have lived by the river. Better, there is water returning, nudging what was dead. Better the burral-gang *congregate here often. Better these words and better we are still here and that we speak them.*

FORTY-TWO

artist—*bundadhaany* What a wonderful thing to make something.
I saw a painting in a book, it's called *Dluga Street*; it was painted by
a *bundadhaany* called Bernardo Bellotto. He was an Italian fella. He
painted the city of Warsaw, Poland—there were twenty-six of them,
in a style called *vedute*. He made those paintings, detailed lives of
the people and the city, and he passed away just a handful of years
before Australia was invaded. Almost two hundred years later the
Nazis bombed Warsaw, killing hundreds and thousands of people,
horrible annihilation. In this dark time almost the entire city of Warsaw was burned and destroyed. The people left were thinking about
moving the city somewhere else, rebuilding a new Warsaw. But then
they had all these paintings of the city, these great detailed things by
the *bundadhaany* Bernardo Bellotto, and they rebuilt the city from
paintings done generations before the city was bombed to bits. I want
the younger ones, the next little ones to read this book and for them
to look into the riverbed, to stare up into the tops of the gums, to look
and know and name the birds. To recognize that city that no one
seems to see anymore. I wouldn't be invisible anymore, none of us
would be.

ashamed, have shame—*giyal-dhuray* I'm done with this word. I'd leave it out completely but I can't. It's become part of the dictionary we think we should carry. We mustn't anymore. See, pain travels through our family tree like a songline. We've been singing our pain into a solid thing. The old ones, the young ones too, are ready to heal. We don't have to be *giyal-dhuray* anymore, we don't have to pass that down anymore.

ashes—*bunhaan* I want to spread everywhere I can over Prosperous, I want the body to float up to the leaves, I want to rest in the wheat-field, the last yield, before it's dug open.

Australia—*Ngurambang* That's my country, anyway. It spreads to al-most the size of England, from the mountains in the north, to the boundary of *Ngurambang* in the south. The water once flowed through the Murrumby from the southern rivers, filling the creeks, the la-goons, the lakes, and feeding everything in its wake. *Ngurambang* is my country; in my mind it will always be on the waterfront. Five hun-dred acres where the Gondiwindi lived, live. Australia—*Ngurambang!* Can you hear it now? Say it—*Ngu-ram-bang!*

THE DICTIONARY OF
ALBERT GONDIWINDI

A Work in Progress

yuyung – backward
yuwin – name, a word or sound
yuwarrbin – blossom of yellow box tree
yuwarr – aroma, perfume, odor, smell
yuwambanha – frighten away evil spirits by a hissing noise
yurung, walung, yubaa, galing – rain
yurrumbanhayalinya – care, take care of another's child
yurrumbamarra – bring up, rear
yurrubang – big and very tall
yuri – needlebush plant
yurbay – seed
yuran, barra-ma-li-nya – convalescent
yurali – blossom of eucalyptus
yungir – crier
yunggaay – mallee fowl
yumbanidyilinya – cry, to be sorry for making one cry
yumarradinya – cry while walking along
yulung, yuwumbawu – thistle, milk thistle
yulun – blackwattle tree
yulubirrngiin – rainbow
yulu – claws of animals or birds
yuliyiin, nanay – lean, thin
yugaway – sleeping place
yugaawirra – recline, like a dog
yirra – lengthen or become longer

yirin – fish, scales

yirimbang – holy

yirigarra – beam or glitter

yirbamanha – leave, to go bush

yirbamagi – to go to

yirayin, yirin – light

yiraydhuray, yirigaa – star, the morning star

yiray – sun

yirawulin – sunset

yirawari – cloud, thundercloud

yiran – long or far

yiramurrun – boy, a tallish boy

yiramugu – blunt, not sharp

yiramiilan – sunrise

yirambin – kangaroo teeth

yiramarang – youth (before having tooth knocked out)

yiramal – riverbank

yiradhu – day

yingulbaa – crayfish holes

yingilbang – ill, very ill

yingil giin – consumption

yingil – sick, ill

yingang – locust

yindyamangidyal – careful, respect, gentleness

yindaay – horse, stallion

yinaagang, migay – girl

yiing – happiness or joy

yidharra – hurt, injure

yibiryibir – brush

yibirmanha – paint, decorate

yibirmaldhaany – painter

yawarra-ndhu – be careful

yawanhayalinya – care for as a mother a child

yawandyilinya – care for oneself

yaryanbuwaliya – everywhere

yarrudhang – dream

yarrayanhanha – go about

yarrawulay – blossom of the yarra, river red gum

yarraman – horse
yarradunha – beat on the boomerang
yarngun – root of tree
yarany – beard
yaradha – fish gills
yara – large, great, high
yanygayanygarra – help
yanhanhadhu – goodbye
yanhambilanha – walk
yanhamanha – chase, pursue
yanhamambirra – let go
yangarra – grind seeds, to rub on a stone
yandhul, yaala – now, at the present
yandhayanbarra – eat for the sake of company
yandharra – eat together
yandangarang – false beard, a mask
yambuwan – everything or anything
yama-ndhu gulbarra? – do you understand?
yalul, durrur – always
yalmambirra – teach
yalara-nha – hiss like a snake
yalgu, yabung – drought
yaldurinya – confess
yalbilinya – learn
yalay – body part, the soft between ribs and hip
yagay! – pain, an exclamation of pain
yagar – edible lettuce-like plant
yadilinya – ready to go
yadhang – because, well
yadhandha – berrigan or emu bush
yaba – carpet snake or diamond python
yaanharra – spear, long fishing spear
yaambuldhaany, yaambulgali – liar, bullshit artist
yaala! – go that way! that way!
wuyung, buragurabang, wiibagang – currawong
wuyul – corkscrew spicule of grass
wuurrawin – through
wuurranngilanha – encompass, surround

wuurra – entrance, doorway, opening into
wuru, nan – neck
wurrumany – son
wurrugan – fastening or tie
wurrawurramarra – pain, feel little pain
wurraangalang – fuzzy box tree
wurraan – hair
wundayan – niece
wunaagany, waringinali – cousin
wumbay – last, the last
wumba – evening star
wululu – duck, pink-eared
wudhamugu – person without hearing, ears shut
wudha – ear
wubunginya – enter, dive, go under the water
wuba – hole, a burrow, rat, native
woomera – tool that throws the spear
wiyay – back, part of the back
wirrimbildanha – leave a portion of food
wirridirrrangdirrang – redback spider
wirrang, barrbay – brush-tailed rock wallaby
wirramarri – fish, large cod fish
wirralgan – oracle (magic stone)
wirradyil – flat piece of bark on which the dough is spread
wirimbirra, wurimbirra – care, preserve
wirgany – air, in the air
wirgaldhaany – carpenter
wiraydhu marramali – it is not possible
wiragala – eastern ringneck parrot
wir – air, sky, the heavens
winhanga-y-gunha-nha – remember
winhanga-dili-nya – feel, know oneself
winhanga-bili-nya – believe
winhanga-bilang, winhang-galang – clever, intelligent
winha-nga-rra – listen, hear, think
winha-nga-nha – know, think, remember
wingarra – be sitting down
wingambang – yolk of an egg

wilima – middle

wiinyugamin – bush fire

wiinybangayilinya – fire, make a fire for another

wiiny – fire, fuel, wood

wiiliin – lips

wiilban – cave

wiilba – branch, twig

wiilawiila – ornamental feathers for the head

wiila – crest of the cockatoo

wiibadhuray – tea trees or hop bushes

wigay – damper, bread, cake

widyunngga? – how?

widyunggiyan? – like what? like which?

widyungga – to arrive

widyarra – drink

widyali, girrigirri – alcohol, wine, strong drink

widyalang – child, not yet walking

widyagala – cockatoo, Major Mitchell

widhin – gap or opening, absent

wi-nhumi-nya – wait, sit down again

waylang – fruit, hard fruit

wayirawi – fancy idea, a dream

wayimaa – cockatoo

wayawayanga-nha – encompassing

wayamiilbuwawanha – look back

wayal – kangaroo skin

way! nyiila! ninggi! – look out! beware!

wawinha – fly, move the wings

wattleddhandha – camp, temporary

warunarrung – grandson

warrul – honey

warru – hornet or wasp

warriyan – brush wallaby, red-necked

warri – blackthorn

warralang, dhuwaa, wiinaa – eastern brown snake

warradagang, warrygandhuray – orange

warraal – echo

warraa-nha – scream or to shout

warr-bulang – game of handball

wargang – canoe, boat

wanya – shifting ground

wanhanha – throw

wanhangidyilinya – abandon oneself to despair

wanhamindyarra – care for no longer

wanhamidyarra – be careless

wanhabanha – leave behind, forsake

wanggaydyibangarra – make fire or heat

wanggaay – child, a little

wangadyang – ants, food ants

wangaay – meat, provisions

wangaa – lazy, idle

wanga-dhu-nha – I forget

wanga – cormorant, black

wanduwa – green wattle acacia

wandaang, dyirr, birig, guwindarr – ghost or spirit

wanda-ba-dyuray – fighting

wanbang – star constellation not identified

wambuwuny – kangaroo, grey

wambuwanybang – duck, also the name of constellation

wambunbunmarra – covetous, greedy

wambanybang – male of birds, drake

wamal – weapon

walwaay, waliwigang – young man

walunginya, maranginya – good, to be good

wali-wali – crooked, bent, askew

wali-nya – go alone

walgun – ignorant, confused

walgawalga – cormorant, black shag

walgar – clavicle, collarbone

walga – hawk, sparrow

walar – smooth

walang – hard, stone, money

walan – strong

wala-ma-nha-yali-nya – care until strong, raise a child

wagara – grey butcherbird

waga-dyi – dance

wadhi – stick, used to strike with
wadha-gung – rabbit, a wild
waaya-ma-rra – coiling like a snake
waawing – caverns where bunyip lie
waawii – bunyip
waangarra – cry like a crow
waalurr – earthquake
waalan-gun-ma-la – brave
waagan-waagan – barbs of a spear (like waagan's beak)
waagan-galang – crows, many crows (raven)
nurranurrabul, nurranurra – constantly, always
nundhugadiyara – mimic
nunba – close
nunay – bad
nunarmun – uncle
nulabang – many
nuganirra – beat regularly, the heart
nirin – edge
niigigal – kiss
niga – I do not know
nidbul – flax, native for making string
nhila – it, she, he
nguyaguya-mi-lang – beautiful
nguruwi, burrbiny, binbin – belly, abdomen
ngurumarra – close the eye, a sacred stone
nguru, ngurruwi, wubaa – bag, other marsupial pouch
nguru-murr, yurung, dhurany – clouds
ngurrunggarra – passionate
ngurru-wi-ga-rra – see, new or strange things, to wonder
ngurru-warra – claim as one's own
ngurru-mirgang – blue, as the sky
ngurrawang – nest of birds or possum
nguram-bula – bower bird, the spotted bower bird
nguram-birang, ngunhagan – friend
nguny – gift
ngunmal – fence, a fence
ngunhadar-guwur – underneath the earth
ngunha – elbow

ngumbur-ba-rra – howl, like the wind
ngumbaay-marrang – some
ngumbaay-guwal – another
ngumba-rrang – bug
ngumba-dal – union, unity
ngumba-ay – one, alone
ngulung-gayirr – ceremonial crown, brow band
ngulung – face, forehead
ngulumunggu – outside of a thing
ngulangganha – call out, cooee
ngulagambilanha – home, to be returning home
ngubaan – husband and wife
ngu-nha – give
ngu-ng-ga-nha – bring to give
ngu-mambi-la-nha – borrow
ngu-m-ba-ngi-la-nha – hands, hold up the
ngiyindidyu dharraay – I want please
ngiyambalganhanha – converse together
ngiriya-ga-rra – pass through
nginhi-guliya – all these places
ngindhuba nganhalbu – you or me
ngindhu gindaywaruwar – you are always laughing
ngiina-ngiina – lot, a lot, many
ngi-ngi – be
ngi-ngari-ma-giy – all day long
ngayi-ny – mind, the mind, thought
ngawum-bi-rra – show, to show
ngawar – bag, marsupial pouch of kangaroos and possums
ngawaal-ngawaal – faint, giddy
ngarruung – decayed
ngarruriyan – hawk, white hawk
ngarriman – manna from the bush
ngarri-ngarri-ba-l-guya-nha – panting for water, as a dog
ngarrarr-gi-dyili-nya – feel sorry, distress oneself
ngarrarr – worry
ngarranngarran – bluebells
ngarranga – after
ngarrang, nharrang – lizard, water dragon

ngarrang, bidyiwang, nharrang – eastern water dragon
ngarradharrinya – cry or weep
ngarradan – bat
ngarra-gaya-miil – star seen by the people
ngarin – morning
ngaray-wirr-gi – to sleep
ngaray-m-bang – sharp
ngara – charcoal cinders
nganundhi? – about who?
nganhundha – me, with me
nganhiyany, yangiirang – all about, all along
nganhi-gunhung-guwala – time, another time
nganhi-gu – belonging to that, distant in space and time
nganhayung galingabang bur – our children
nganhali – from there
nganhagu – belonging to that, for that
nganhabul – over there
nganha-yung – ourselves, our own
nganha-wal – up above, up there, high in the sky
nganha-ny-garri – here or there
nganha-nguwur – behind there
nganha-guliya-gu – belonging to all of those
ngandhi-guliya-gu – for those all
ngandhi? – who?
ngamuwila – desert pea
ngamurr – daughter
ngamung – breast
ngamu-gaang – girls without mothers
ngamu-dyaang – boys without mothers
ngambuny – lizard, big spotted
ngambar-gaa-nha – covet, to be covetous
ngambaa – curious, inquisitive
ngamba-rang, birrany-dyang – boy, a little boy
ngama-ngama-rra – feel about, feel for
ngaligin-gu – ours, yours and mine
ngalguwama – above
ngalgarra – light, to give light, to shine
ngalar – clean, clean

ngalan-y – crystal, white quartz
ngalan-y – flame of a fire
ngalan-bang, nyiil – peak of the mountain
ngalan-bami-rra – kindle
ngalamali – to fish
ngadi-galita-bul – time, a long time
ngadhuri-nya – care for, tend
ngadhu wanga-dyung – I am lost
ngadhu minya – I can explain
ngadhu mamalagirri – to visit
ngadhu – I, one person
ngadhi-galila – belonging to me
ngabun – mother's father
ngaagirridhunyal – I will see you
ngaa-nha – behold, see
ngaa-ngidyilinya – see oneself
ngaa-mubang – person without sight
ngaa-bun-gaa-nha – searching, looking around
nga-ngaa-nha – look after, to care for
narruway – mirage
narrundirra – kick
narru-buwan – bees' nest
narru – hammock, sling for carrying child
narriyar, wiwin – hot
narrbang – bag, a man or woman's dillybag
nanhi – cracks, in the ground
nanhaybirri – eager, be very eager
nanhamalguwany – lost, something lost
nandibang – brown snake, eastern
nanan – fast-running, quick
namunmanha – hand, hold the hand to the mouth
murun-gi-nya – live, to be alive
murun-dhu – I live, I breathe
murun – life, breath
murrung – grey box tree, eucalyptus
murrugarra – read
murrudinayilinya – contempt, treat with
murrudhadhun – duck, spoonbill

murrubir – heaven

murru, murruway, ngubuli, gawala, yabang – road, track, or path

murru, murrawaygu – carving on trees, weapons, implements

murrin, wiray – no, not

murrang, waa – mud

muriin – canoe, bark

murangarra – alive, to be alive

muraany – cockatoo, white

muny – ant lion

munun – big, much

munirganha – jealous, be jealous

munhilbungarra – dig

munhilbang – hollow tree

mungarr – kidneys

munga – fruit of kurrajong tree

mundu – covered, of a tree and its bark

mundhay, mirrung, dhurang – bark of trees

mumbal, nyimirr – blossoms

mumala – grandfather

muma – comet

muliyiin – finch, zebra

mulbirrang – parrot, eastern rosella

mulanguwal – part of something

mulaa – night or darkness

muguwar – silent, quiet

mugumnawa – in, internally

mugul – silly

mugugalurgarra – keep secret, conceal

mugilmugil – wild orange or wild pomegranate

mugilbang – wild lemon

mugii-nya – close the eyes

mugi – eaglehawk

muganha – find, pick up

mugang – grub, of trees

mudyi, maamungun – friend, countryman

mudyi – mates, friends

mudhamudhang – acacia tree

mudhaany – content

mubany – man and wife
modyigaang – elder
miyagan, wayadan – kindred, relations
mirrway – paint, colored clays
mirriwula, mirriyula – ghost dog
mirrirang – hail
mirrimirri – wicked, like a dog, thievish
mirri – dog
minyang-guwar? – what place, where?
minyali? – about what?
minya-nganha? – what is that?
minya – question (what?)
mimudya – mimosa acacia plant
mimagang – crested bellbird
miimi – sister
miilwarranha – open the eye
miilumarra – glance or wink the eye
miilgany – openly, face to face
miilbi – hole, a well
miilalmiilal – wakeful, awake
miil bulal – both eyes
miil – eye, also the stars
miidyum – wild tomato
migiimanha – flash of lightning
migii – lightning
midyungga-ga – I don't know when
midhang – alone, single, one
mibar – cocoon, butterfly inside
mayinyguwalgu ngunggirridyu – I will share with other people
mayinyguliya – human-like
mayiny – people
mayanggang – case and bag moths
maya, gulay – fishing net
mawa – sticky gum from trees
marrungbang – justice
marrung – caution, guard, cunning
marrun-gadha-li – sweet tasting
marrubil – fine and pleasant

marru-wa-nha – form or make
marranmarran – unripe, raw
marramurgang, dhan – fist or closed hand
marramarrang, nularri – haste, hurry
marraldirra – frighten
marragir, marragiyirr – naked, a widower
marragarra – hold fast
marrabinya – hands, stretch out the
marra-nung – channels made by receding waters
marra – hand
marbirra – frog
marayarrang – carving on trees, composed writing
marara – carved trees with designs
maranggaal – red gum tree
marang ngurung – goodnight
marang – well, good
marambang ngulung – beauty, handsome face
maram-bul – right, good, correct
maradhal – past, long-distant
manygan – parrot, blue bonnet
mangganha maganha – choke or drown
mangga – baby, chicken or pup
mangalanha – conquer, get the mastery of
mandur – quiet or undisturbed
mandu – besides, else
mandara, binda, maybal, marrady, babang – grass tree
mandaang guwu – thank you
mambuwarra – look
mambanha – cry, mourning
mamaybumarra – hold down, subdue
mama-dya, mambarra – native cherry tree
malungan – female, a young woman
maliyan, baga-daa, yibaay – eagle, wedge tail
maliyan – star, red bright southern star
maldhanha – get, provide
maldhaany – maker, person who makes
malbilinya – obedient
malangun – girl, a little

malang – could, should, would
maladyin – ill, infirm
maguwar – happy
magadala – red soil
magaadhang – clover, wild
madhubul-mugiiny – blind, all are blind
madhu – enemy
madharra – chew or suck
madhanmadhu – forest, the bush
mabinya – stop or wait
mabi, babila, mugiiny-mabi – eastern quoll, wild cat
maarung – circle
maamungun – countryman or friend
guyunganmadilin – myself
guyang – fire
guyal – dry
guyabadhambildhaany – fisherman
guwunggan – flood
guwiiny nganhala – it is over there
guwiiny gandamay – it is difficult
guwaywinya – wait for a short while, sit, stay
guwayuwa – briefly, for a short time
guwayu – time, indefinite time, later
guwarra – fetch, fetch back
guwariyan, garrang – cockatiel, quarrion
guwanguwan – bloody, much blood
guwang, guwaang – fog, rain, mist
guwandiyala, wandayali – echidna
guwan-ba-ga-ga-rra – bleed
guwala-nha – happen, come to pass
guwabigi – to rest
guwaali – wait for me
guuray – fat
guun, gurril – flint
Guudha – God
gurwarra – save, deliver from danger
gurwaldhaany – Savior, deliverer
gurulgan – bullfrog tadpole

gurudhaany – goanna

gurruwir – news, sad news

gurruulgaan – being that causes thunder

gurrugandyilinya – cover oneself

gurrugan-balang – cattle, bullock, cow

gurraggarang – frog, to indicate rain

gurra-galang – bitter medicine

gurra-gal-gam-bi-rra, guru-ga-ma-rra, gurra-gal-ga-rra – finish

gurra-ga-ya-rra – finish speaking

gurra-ga-dharra – finish eating, eat all

gurmiyug – cumbungi root

guriin – charcoal or black

guriban – curlew, bush stone-curlew bird

guray-mugu-mugu – in distress, suffering

guray-dyu-ngi-nya – long for, be in love

gurawiny – flowers, not buds

gurawan – fish spear

gurang, gurawung, guyang – bandicoot

gununga – hiding inside

gunhindyang – motherless

gunhinarrung – mother's mother

gunhimbang, gunhi, ngama, baba – mother

gunhari – belly, paunch of animal

gunhama, badyar – ant, black ant

gunhagunang – cough

gunhabunbinya – sit down

gunguwari – halo, a circle around the moon

gungun – bark, a piece of bark for a dish

gungarra – comb

gungalang, yanangaari guygalang – green tree frog

gundyung – black jay bird or white-winged chough

gundhaybiyan – blossom of stringybark tree

gundhay – red stringybark tree

gunaru, gudharang, guwiyarrang – wood duck

gunal – female of animals

gunaany – shallow

gunaagunaa – butterfly

gumbang – grave, a grave

gumbadha – metal
guluwin – far off, distant
gulur, ngay – but, however
gulun – burrow of wombat
gulumba, gulibaa – box tree, coolabah
gulu, galgu, dang – millet seed for flour
gulgarr – concave, tray or plate of bark
gulgang – head, top of the
gulgandara – before, both time and place
gulganagaba – bird, the jacky winter
gulgama – gully, valley
gulbirmarra – part, divide, separate
gulbir – few, not many
gulbi – mist or smoke in the air
gulbalanha – peace, be at peace, no fighting
gulamirra – seek in vain
gulamilanha – alone, to be alone
gulambali, birriyag – pelican bird
gulamarra – open
gulamalibu nunbabu – to open or close
gulabirra – refuse, reject
gulaay – crossing place, bridge
gulaa – anger
gugubarra – kookaburra
gugi – cup, of bark
guganha – crawl or creep
gugan – caterpillar, a yellow
gugabul – fish, Murray cod
gudyiin – ancient time
gudyi – basin, bucket
gudhingan – composer of songs
gudharang – duck, wood
gudha – baby or child
gudal – flat
gubir – macquarie perch, also called black bream
gubang – hickory tree
gubaldurinya – conquer, drive off the enemy
gubadhang – finch, diamond sparrow

gubaadurinya, durrudurrugarra, gubaymanha, gulbadurinya – follow
guba – cooba wattle acacia
giyira, giira – future, the womb
giyingdyung – marrow, from inside bones
giyindyarra – lick
giyarinya – frightened, be frightened
giyang – lungs
giyanda-dila-nh – escape
giyan – centipede
giyalang – belonging
giyal, guwiindha – shame, ashamed
giyal-giyal – cowardly, partly ashamed
giyal-gang – field mouse
giyaa-warra – frighten off, drive away
giya-rra – fear, be afraid
giwang wuurrranha – moon setting
giwang bagarra – moon rising
giwang – moon
giwaang-giwaang – mad fellow, fool
giwa-l-dhaany – cook, the person cooking
girri girrigirri – red
girran-girran – ill, poorly
girra-wiiny – quiet place with many pretty flowers
girra-ma-nha – feel hot, to be burned
girra-m-bi-ya-rra – scold, speak with anger
girra-girra – lively, be well, be alive
girarumarra – blow, as wind
giran-giran, manggaan – broad, spear shield
giralang bundinya – star, a shooting star
giraangang – foliage of trees, leaves
gingari – flint knives
gindyarra – lap or drink water like dogs
gindhaany, bugari – ringtail possum
gindaymanha – to play, to have fun
ginda-y-waruwar – laughing always
ginda-y-ga-la-nha – laugh at each other
ginda-y-awa-nha – smile, laugh
ginda-nha – laugh

ginan – kind, gracious
gimarra – milk
gilaa – galah
gila – so, then
giiny – heart
giimbir – fountain, spring, well
giilang – story
giigandul – wattle with silver flower
gigiy – eaten enough
gigirr – scent or smell
gidyirriga, badyariga – budgerigar
gidyang – hair of body, wool, fur
gidyagidyang – egret, little
gidya-wuruwin – afraid, very much, overcome with fear
gidya – broad-level wattle
gibirrgirrbaang – star constellation of Orion's Belt
gibirgin, malanygyang, dindima – star constellation the Seven Sisters (Pleiades)
gibir – man
gibayan – nephew
gibany, darran-dirang – revenge, avenger
giba – magic stone
gaymaan – kangaroo grass
gawuwal – lagoon, lake
gawuraa – feathers
gawunang, giwambang – moonlight
gawimarra – gather or pick up
gawaymbanha – welcome, tell to come
gawaan, gabaa – White men, strangers
garriwang – currawang tree
garrindubalunbil – beetle in wood
garril, wurung – boughs or branches on trees
garraywarra – look for, seek, find
garraygal – palm of the hand
garray – land, sand
garrawi – roe of fish
garrari – net
garranygarra – send

garrandarang – paper, book
garran – hook of any kind, fish hook
garrabari – corroboree, a special dance
garraba, marrin – body, human
garraayigal – hand, grasp
garraawan – light wood for making fish spears
garra – hold, catch, stop, take
gariya wanhamindya nganhanduyan – do not break a promise
gariwang – cold east wind
gariwag – leaf
garingali – dingo
garila – corella bird
garba – fork, fork of a tree
garay – sand
garal – wattle tress
garaan-dharra – eat forbidden food
gany, yingiyan – like, similar
ganhur, buringin, marri – kangaroo, red
ganha-nha, bunha-nha – burn
ganginmarra – lie, tell a lie
ganggang – gang-gang cockatoo
ganggaa – spider
gangarrimaa – ring or circle
gangan – hawk, fish hawk
gandyar – spirit being, he sees and knows everything
gandaru, gungarung, yambil – crane, blue, white-faced heron
ganda – bend of the leg under the knee
ganang – beeswax, wet
ganaa-ba-nha – ride on horse or any animal
gana-yi-rra – peppermint tree
gambang, dilaang, dirraybang, gumbal – brother
gambal, buragi, yungay, gamidha – bustard, native bush turkey
gamalang – raspberry, native
galiyang, birrgun – fork-tailed swift bird
galing-gaan – bowels
galindulin – eel
galin-gabangbur – children
galin-dhuliny, gibirrngaan – black snake, red-bellied

galin-balgan-balgang – dragonfly
galigal – knife
gali-ngin-banga – desert place without water
galguraa – friar bird, noisy
galgambula – oven, for cooking in the earth
galgaang – affliction, wherein is pity
galga – hungry, empty
galanygalany, galan galan – cicada, locust, its sound
galang – belonging to a group
galagang – wild onion
galabarra – halve, separate into two
galaabanha – noise, make a noise
gagalin, bidyin – fish, golden perch
gagaamanha – lead astray, seduce
gadyilbalungbil – burrowing black beetle
gadyilbalung – beetles generally
gadyal – hollow
gadyag – nasty, horrible
gadya! – get away!
gadi, dharang – snake
gadangul – lizard, small one
gabur-gabur – rotten or broken
gabuga – brain, eggs
gabudha – reeds and rushes
gabin-gidyal – beginning, a
gabargabar – green, color
gaban, barrang – white
gaban – foreign, strange, unknown
gaba-rra – fishing, dragnet
gaanha, dharal – shoulder
gaanha-barra gaanha-bu-nha – carry on the shoulder
gaalmaldhaany – composer, poet
gaagu-ma-rra – embrace
gaa-m-bila-nha – hold a thing
gaa-l-marra – compose, songs
gaa-darra – erase
gaa-ba-rra – carry on the back
ga-rra – be or being

dyirribang – an old man
dyiridyinbuny – diver bird
dyiramiil – charming, winning, eyes-up
dyinmay, gurray – fight or war, tribal
dyinidnug – duck, shoveler
dyindhuli – hunger
dyindharr – lean, barren, bare
dyinang, mundawi, dinhang – foot
dyilwirra – climb, a tree
dyigal – fins of fishes
dyibarra – speak
dyandyamba – medicine, from the core of tree fern
dyagula – lyrebird
dyagang – boys without fathers
dyabaraa – bulldog ants
dyaba – girls without fathers
dyaabiny – flying ant
duyan – fat, meat
duwambiyan – root of edible pink fingers
duruung-gar-gar – glowworm
durrur-buwulin – ever, always
durrumbin, giima – caterpillar
durru-l-ga-rra – hide
durru-l-ba-rra – burst
durrawiyung – duck, grey teal
durrawan – currawong, grey bird
durrany – cloud, long white
duri-mambi-rra – ill, make ill, cause to be ill
duri-duri-nya – ill, to be ill
dundumirinmirinmal – snail
dumiiny – death adder snake
dumi-rra – carry
dumbi – blush
dulu-dulu – logs of wood, big
dulbun-bun-ma-rra – bow, or to bend
dulbi-bal-ga-nha – hang down the head
duguny-bi-rra, dugu-winy-birra – be generous
dugu-wirra – catch

dugin – shade
duga-y-ili-nya – fetch for another
duga-nha – fetch water, draw up water
dubu – frog or toad
dubi – chrysalis, pupa butterfly grub
dirriwang – emu feathers
dirrinan – bulbine lily
dirrigdirrig – bee-eater, rainbow bird
dirrang-dirrang – red ochre
dirramaay – edible herb
dirra-dirra-wana – herb
dinggu – wild dog, dingo
dinbuwurin – lark, native
dinawan, gawumaran, nguruwiny – emu
dilga-nha, bunganha-ba-nha – comb the hair
dilan-dilan-garra – shake
dila-dila-bi-rra – cause confusion
dila-birra – scatter, sow
diikawu – emu bush, spotted
digu, mumbil, munbil – blackwood, black-timbered wattle tree
digimdhuna – fig or fig tree
digal – fishbone
dibiya – duck, whistling tree
dibang – nails or spikes
dhuruwurra – cast off, shedding
dhurri-rra – lay eggs, to be born
dhurri-nya, dhurrirra – born, to be born
dhurrgang, nguruwiya – owl, tawny frogmouth
dhurragarra – follow up, track, pursue
dhurany – news, or message
dhuragun, bunbun – bittern, native
dhungany – greenleek parakeet
dhundhu, ngiyaran, gunyig – black swan
dhundhal – close or near
dhumuny – bardi grubs, used for fishing
dhumba – brittle gum, eucalyptus
dhulubang – soul or spirit
dhulu-ga-rra – guilty, to be found convicted

dhulu-biny – level, even, flat

dhuliiny – goanna, sand monitor

dhulay – fish, the river gar fish

dhul – brown

dhugamang – lobster, white-clawed

dhugaaybul – very

dhubul – bore, underground water

dhubi – cicada larva, beetle

dhirril – sparrow hawk

dhirran-bang – noon, midday (sun in the zenith)

dhirraany, gandiyagulang – mountain

dhiraa-nha – rise like the dough

dhindha – ball, anything rounded

dhin – nut or berry

dhilbul – coot, purple swamphen

dharrang – message stick or letter

dharran – creek

dharrambay, gimang, dirru, galbu – kangaroo rat

dharra-barra – eat, cut with teeth

dharra – eaten, swallow, engulf, absorb

dhara – cast out, away

dhangaang, dhal, dharrabu – food

dhang – seeds, grains

dhandyuri, dhandyurigan – mussel shells or shellfish

dhandhaang – river catfish

dhamiyag, baaliyan – cumbungi, bulrush reeds

dhamaliiny, dharramaliyu, bulbul – bull roarer, whirler

dhalba-nha – bruised

dhalba – rain, the cloud burst

dhala-y-ba-rang – mad frenzy, anger, excitement, sudden

dhala-wa-la – forest country

dhala-rug – wattlebird

dhala-ba-rra – crack, burst, break

dhala-ba-nha – ruin, destroy

dhal-bi-rra – beat time on the boomerang, as the men do singing

dhaganhu ngurambang? – where is your country?

dhagamang – crayfish, whitish-blueish claws, not a yingaa

dhagal – cheek, jawbone

dhadhi? – belonging to what place?
dhabugarra – bury
dhabugany – buried
dhabudyang – old woman
dhabal – bone
dhaan yanha – come here
dhaalirr – kingfisher bird
dhaagunmaa – cemetery
dhaagun – land, earth, dirt, soil, grave
dha, -dya, -la, -ra – on, at, in, by
dha-l-mambi-rra – feed, a child or dog
dawin, bawa-l-ganha – hatchet
darruba-nha – leap over
darriyaldhuray – bedroom
dargin – across
danyga-ma-rra – compete, to vie in throwing
dani – wax, gum or honeycomb
dangarin – shell fish
dangar, dhandhaang – fresh water catfish
dangal – covering or shelter
dangaay – rainwater, oldwater
dang – roots, edible
dalungal – fine fella, excellent person
dalawang, gabu, gabudha – box tree, apple
dabu-ya-rra murun – life, give, bestow life
dabu-wan – leech, small one
daanha – knit, make a net
buyaa – law
buya-marra – beg
buwi-birra-ng – boomerang of bark, a toy
buwawabanhanha, gugabarra – boil
buwanha – grow
buwaa-bang – orderly, tame
buwa-garra – come
buwa-gany – edible root
buwa-ga-nhumi-nya – before, be before
buwa-dharra – fill the mouth
buurri – boree tree, weeping myall

bururr – hopbush
burrindin, gulridy – magpie-lark, peewee or mudlark bird
burrbang – ceremony of initiating to man
burral, darriyal – bed
burral – birthplace, the spot, the soil
burra-m-bin – eternal
burra-giin – beeswax, dry
burra-di-rra – cut down
burra-dhaany – ball, bouncing
burra-binya – leap, jump
burra-ban-ha-l-bi-rra – fire, light a
burguwiiny-mudil – blacksmith
burbi-rra – beat the time, and sing
burba-ng – circle, a round shape, heap
burany – parrot
buram-ba-bi-rra – share
buralang – black-faced cockatoo
buraandaan – heron, night heron
bura-mi-nga-nha – cause to be
bunyi-ng-ganha – breathe
bunyi-ng – breath
bunhiya – wild oak tree
bunhi-dyili-nya – beat
bungi-rra – swing
bundi-nya – fall
bundi-mambi-rra – let fall, cause to fall
bundhi, nalanala – club, thick knob on end, war weapon
bundharran – paddle
bundharraan – canoe oar
bundarra – freeze, feel very cold
bunda-nha – draw, a picture
bunda-ng – cicadas, butterfly
bunda-l-ga-nha – hanging, be suspended
bunbiya – grasshopper
bunba-nha – escape, run, moving away, fleeing
bunba-na-nha – run after
bunan, bundhu – dust, rising vapor
bunan – carried by the wind, dust storm

bun-ma-rra, ma-rra – make or do
bumbi – smoke
bumalgalabu wayburrbu – right or left
bumal-bumal – hammer, a stick
bumal – hammer, stone for bruising nuts
buma-ngidyili-nya – beat oneself
buma-l-gidyal – fight or battle
bum-bi-rra – blow, with mouth
bulun – egret, white crane
bulan-bulan – parrot, crimson rosella
bulaguy – saltbush
bula-bi-nya – couples, to be in couples
buguwiny, bugaru, gungil – grass
bugurr – climbing plants or vines
bugu-l – fishline
bugiyunbarrul – time, after sunset, twilight
buginybuginy, manygan – blue bonnet parrot
bugarr – carrion
bugarnan – bad smell
bugang – necklace or beads
budyabudya – moths and butterflies
budyaan, dyibiny, dibilany – bats, birds, general flying creatures
budulbudul – far off, high, the bluish air at a distance
budhi – corner
budharu – flying fox
budhar-ba-la-nha – kiss each other
budhanbang – duck, black
budhaanybudhaany – common sneezeweed, old man weed
budha – sandlewood
bubul, dula – backside, buttocks
bubu – air or breath
bubil – wing, feather
bubay-bunha-nha – lessen, get small
bubay – little, small
buba-dyang-marra, garrigaan, banhumiya – fingers of the hand
biyambul – all
biyal-gam-bi-rra – hang (transitive)
biyal-ga-nha – hang (intransitive)

biyaga – often, many times
birring, birrgan – chest of a man
birrinalay – blossom of white box tree
birri-birri-ma-rra – meet
birri – white box tree, eucalyptus
birranilinya – run away with
birrang-ga – high up
birrang – journey to another place
birrang – blue sky, the horizon
birran-dhi – from
birramal, yirrayirra – bush, the bush
birramal-gu yakha-y-aan – gone to the bush
birrabuwawanha – return, come back
birrabunya – cormorant, little pied
birrabirra, malu – lazy, tired
birrabang – outside, up, above, far
birra-nguwurr – behind
birra-nguwur – back, that which is behind
birra-bina-birra – move gently, whisper
birra – back, the back
birra – fatigued, tired
birinya – scar, make a
birgu – shrubs, thickets
birgili, birgilibang – scorched by fire
birdyulang – scar an old scar
birdany – blossom of ironbark tree
birbarra – bake
birbaldhaany – baker
biran, birrany – boy
biralbang – duck, musk
bir – birth mark
binydyi – stomach
binhaal – eldest, the
bindyi-l-duri-nya – cut into a tree to get possums out
binaal, wirra – broad, wide
bimirr – end, an end
bimbun, gumarr, mudha – tea tree or paperbark tree
bimbul – bimble box tree

bimbin – brown treecreeper, woodpecker
bimba-rra – fire, set the grass on fire
bilwai – oak tree, river she-oak
biluwaany – red-winged parrot
bilin-nya – go backward
bili-nga-ya – backward, going
bilbi, ngundawang, balbu – bilby
bilawir – hoe
bilawi – river she-oak tree
bilabang – billabong, the milky way
bila – river
biiyirr, magalang – back bone, spinal column
biilaa, ngany – bull oak tree, forest oak
bidyuri – pituri
bidya – male
bidhi, babir – big
bibidya – fish hawk, osprey
bayu, buyu – leg
bayirgany – leeches
baryugil – eastern blue tongue lizard
barru-wu-ma-nha – gallop, run fast
barru-dang – juice from a tree
barru – rabbit-like rat (probably bilby)
barrinang – blossom of wattle trees
barri-ngi-rra – leave, let it alone, never mind
barri-ma – musket, gun
barrbay, wirrang – rock wallaby
barray! – move quick, quick!
barrage – to fly
barradam-bang – star, a bright
barrabarray! – quick!
barra-y-ali-nya – rise again, resurrection
barra-wi-nya – camp, hunt
barra-wi-dyany – hunter
barra-manggari-rra – love
barra-dyal – flame robin bird
barra-barra-ma – handle, anything to hold
bargu-mugu – cripple, one limbed

baradhaany – red-necked wallaby

bangal-guwal-bang – belonging to another place

bangal – time, or place

banga-ny – broken

banga-nha – break into rain, begin to rain

banga-ma-rra – break

banga-l – fire sticks, friction

banga-di-ra – chop, cut, split

banga-bil-banga-bil – cutting instrument

banga-bi-lang – broken in pieces

bandya-bandya-birra – cause pain

bandu – march fly

bandhuwang – scrub or mallee trees matted together

bandhung – mallee tree and scrub

bambinya – swim

bambigi – to swim

baluwulinya – be pregnant

balunhuminya – die before another

balunha – die now

balun – dead

baluga – dark, fire has gone out

baludharra – feel cold, be cold

balubuwulin – dead altogether

balubunirra – murder, kill

balubalungin – almost dead

balubungabilanha – kill each other

balu-bunga-rra – extinguish

balmang – empty

balima – north

bali – baby, a very young baby

balgal – sound, noise

balgagang – barren, desolate

balgabalgar – leader, elder

balanggarang – bud, top bud of flower spray

balang – head

balandalabadin, gubudha – common reed

balan-dha – beginning, of time

baladhu nganhal – I am from

baladhu ngaabunganha – just looking
baladhu – I am
balabalanirra – beat a little, slap
balabalamanha – lift softly or slowly, move
balabala-ya-li-nya – whisper
bagurra – blossom of kurrajong tree
bagir-ngan – cousin or uncle
bagaaygang – shell, a small one
bagaay, galuwaa – lizard, shingleback
badyar, gunhama – black ant
badhawal, bargan, balgang – boomerang
badharra – bite
badhang, buwurr – cloak, possum skin
badha, yiramal – bank of the river
babimubang – fatherless
babildhaany – singer
babiin – father
babala – leatherhead, noisy friarbird
baaywang – big hill
baayi – footprint
baawan, gargalany – silver or bony perch fish
baalmanha – floating
baala – footstep
baaduman – red-spotted gum tree
baabin – nettle plant
baabaa, ngandir, nguramba – deep

AUTHOR'S NOTE

This novel contains the language of the Wiradjuri people. Before colonization there were two hundred and fifty distinct languages in Australia that subdivided into six hundred dialects. The Wiradjuri language is a Pama–Nyungan language of the Wiradhuric subgroup and has been reclaimed and preserved through the efforts of Dr. Uncle Stan Grant Snr AM and linguist Dr. John Rudder. The spelling and pronunciation that Uncle Stan and John compiled is within these pages. If there are any errors, they rest solely with my interpretation. Historical spelling of the Wiradjuri language in this book has been sourced from the records of H. Withers, a local landholder from Wagga Wagga (records: 1878); H. Baylis, a police magistrate from Wagga Wagga (records: 1887); J. Baylis, a surveyor landholder from the Riverina (records: 1880s–1927); and C. Richards, a linguist and scholar (records: 1902–1903). Further and updated study of the Wiradjuri language can be found in *The New Wiradjuri Dictionary* authored by Uncle Stan and John.

The experiences of the fictional Gondiwindi family reflect those experienced by all Indigenous people touched by violence, segregation, abuse, and the dehumanizing policies and practices of colonialism. As part of these separation policies, the government and churches banned and discouraged the use of the native tongue. They did this by forcibly removing children from their families, where they were taken into missions and institutions in order to expunge the Indigenous culture. This practice began in 1910 and continued until the 1970s.

Cultural knowledge, community history, customs, modes of thinking and belonging to the land are carried through languages. In the last two hundred years, Australia has suffered the largest and most rapid loss of languages known to history. Today, despite efforts of revitalization, Australia's languages are some of the most endangered in the world.

The depictions of violence and intergenerational trauma suffered by Indigenous people affected by separation policies has been documented in various publications including the 1997 *Bringing Them Home: Report of the National Inquiry into the Separation of Aboriginal and Torres Strait Islander Children from Their Families*. Depictions of mission life from the perspective of Reverend Greenleaf are derived from the writings of Reverend J. B. Gribble including *A Plea for Aborigines of New South Wales*. Gribble founded and ran the Christian Warangesda Aboriginal Mission in Darlington Point, New South Wales. Prosperous Mission, Station, and Home were inspired by Warangesda, which ran as an Aboriginal mission between 1880 and 1884; as Warangesda Aboriginal Station under the Aborigines Protection Association between 1884 and 1897; under government management by the Aborigines Protection Act between 1897 and 1925; under private management between 1925 and 2014.

The girls' and boys' homes mentioned are fictional, but have been drawn from the descriptions of the Aboriginal Girls' Training Home of Cootamundra and the Kinchela Aboriginal Boys' Training Home. In reality the children's experiences were much harsher in comparison to those depicted. Prior to the opening of the Aboriginal Girls' Training Home at Cootamundra, children from all over the state were sent to Warangesda. In *The Stolen Generations—the Removal of Aboriginal Children in NSW 1883 to 1969*, prepared for the New South Wales Ministry of Aboriginal Affairs, Professor Peter Read estimates that there were "300 girls placed at the Warangesda dormitory and subsequently in service before 1916." In Beverley Gulambali Elphick and Don Elphick's *The Camp of Mercy: An Historical and Biographical Record of the Warangesda Aboriginal Mission/Station, Darlington Point, New South Wales*, the authors write that "apart from the occasional child mentioned in the Minute Books of the Aborigines Protection and Welfare Boards and the enrolment registers for the Kinchela Aboriginal Boys' Training Home, no records now exist, if indeed any were ever kept, of the other children removed from Warangesda between 1909 and when the Camp of Mercy closed in 1925. A conservative estimate for this period would be 200, making an overall total of 500 children removed."

There were many births and marriages held at Warangesda; there were also many deaths at the mission site. As stated in Ray Cristison and Naomi Parry's *Conservation Management Plan Warangesda Aboriginal Mission and Station*, "The main cemetery containing the remains of up to two hundred former residents, remains part of a ploughed field."

The geography of the fictional town of Massacre Plains was drawn from towns in Wiradjuri country and also the Rock Nature Reserve—Kengal Aboriginal Place. The fictional Murrumby River of this novel was based on the tributaries of the Murray–Darling

Basin. The names of places, including Massacre and Poisoned Waterhole Creek, are indeed actual place-names in Australia and are a reminder of the atrocities inflicted upon Indigenous people during colonization.

Many of the native plants and cooking techniques can be explored further in Bruce Pascoe's *Dark Emu* and Eric Roll's *A Million Wild Acres*. Additionally, Yuval Noah Harari's *Sapiens: A Brief History of Humankind* also explores the history and sophistication of Indigenous Australians.

I encourage readers to explore personal histories from former mission, settlement, and station residents, collectively known as the Stolen Generation, including *Is That You Ruthie?* by Ruth Hegarty; *Up from the Mission: Selected Writings* by Noel Pearson; *Follow the Rabbit-Proof Fence* by Doris Pilkington Garimara; *If Everyone Cared* by Margaret Tucker; *Of Ashes and Rivers that Run to the Sea* by Marie Munkara, and the works of Jack Davis.

Further reading about Indigenous culture and history includes *Indigenous Australia for Dummies* by Professor Larissa Behrendt; John Harris's *One Blood: 200 Years of Aboriginal Encounter with Christianity: A Story of Hope*; and the works by historians Henry Reynolds, Peter Read, and Marcia Langton. Further study of Australia's languages can be found at www.firstlanguagesaustralia.org.au.

Australia is the only Commonwealth country to not have a treaty with its Indigenous populations.

Acknowledgments

My deepest respect to Elders past and present for their contribution to the survival and maintenance of the Wiradjuri language. Thank you to Dr. Uncle Stan Grant Snr and Dr. John Rudder for the first dictionary, and the final updates, and their unwavering work and vision. To Geoff Anderson and the Parkes Wiradjuri Language Group and Parkes Aboriginal Education and Consultative Group. To Bruce Pascoe for writing *Dark Emu* and for steering me in the right direction. Dr. Naomi Parry for her expertise and assistance with the history of New South Wales missionary life. To the Rolex Arts Initiative and Wole Soyinka for their support and patience. Charles Sturt University and Booranga Writers' Centre, Wagga Wagga, for having me stay and work on this novel countless times over the last decade.

Thank you to everyone at Penguin Random House Australia and at HarperVia in the US.

This book is for and with thanks to all Wiradjuri mob, and especially my family on both sides including dearest Nana, Mum, Dad, my aunts, uncles, cousins, nieces and nephews, Tania, Andrew, John, Arnaud, and my heart, Lila, for always keeping me afloat and utterly loved.

And to Poppy, in the eternal garden.
And my brother Billy Joe, forever, and ever.

Note from the Cover Designer

To me this book is all about the use of language to map a life, a story, a landscape. In particular, the maps and stories of the Aboriginal peoples of Australia. With its beautiful, descriptive translations of Wiradjuri words, it often reads like poetry.

A photograph or a literal illustration felt wrong for the cover. Instead, I thought about the journeys that the characters make. I thought about the landscape, the scorched earth. These marks seemed to represent that: the ploughed mud, the shape of wheat as it rises to the sun.

The design is also very much about the spaces between those marks. When I made it, I had just read the author's description of the Wiradjuri word *baayanha*—yield: "In my language it's the things you give to, the movement, the space between things." It's such a beautiful and evocative idea. I tried to get those marks as close as possible without touching. The cover is held together as much by the space around things as it is by the painted lines and text.

—Jon Gray / gray318